Hum Rise

The Disclosure Files™ - Book Two

Nancy J. Nelson

BROWN LEAF PRESS

Published by Brown Leaf Press. Los Angeles. CA

ISBN: 979-8-9919647-2-2 (Paperback)

ISBN: 979-8-9919647-3-9 (eBook)

Library of Congress Control Number: 2025922366

Cover Art by David Leahey

Interior Formatting by Atticus.io

First Edition 2025

Contents

Chapter One

Victoria Heywood, the newly-appointed Deputy Assistant Secretary for Office of Multispecies Relations—"OMR" for short—paused before walking out onto the stage. The room was packed; this was her first press conference, and media outlets had gone all out to ensure their representatives were in the room to learn firsthand about the extraterrestrials the government now claimed were visiting Earth.

It had only been a couple of months since Vicki first discovered that aliens were real and interacting with humanity. It had only been two weeks since she helped put a stop to the Partnership, a rogue corporate conglomerate that intended to use alien technology to rule over humanity. This was also when she learned she was capable of being ruthless.

Vicki stepped forward but didn't even reach the podium before the reporters began shouting out questions. Maybe her prepared remarks were unnecessary. Maybe she could simply respond to the questions for the entire forty-five minutes the press conference was scheduled to take. She hated making anything that resembled a speech. But then she glanced back at her staff and realized she'd have to do it. She sighed, then mounted the lectern and began to speak.

* * *

Jerry Smith watched from the sidelines as Vicki white-knuckled the podium. It wasn't because she was scared of public speaking, but because she knew that she sucked at it. It had been that way ever since their first day of training as new State Department hires a decade earlier. Vicki was a great diplomat, but she didn't have the media skills. He watched as she doggedly recited the comments he had helped prepare.

He knew he was lucky to be here—to be a part of the most historic and exciting event to ever happen. Even if only half of what Vicki told him was true, the country—and the planet—was going to experience an amazing transformation. Extraterrestrials! Flying saucers! Advanced alien technology! And as Vicki's deputy, he would have a front-row seat.

Now Jerry had a front-row seat as Vicki came to the end of her speech, then looked up at the audience and gave her first real smile.

* * *

"Victoria! Victoria!" The older man standing up in the second row was from the Associated Press.

"Go ahead," she nodded.

"Why are the aliens revealing themselves now? And why in the United States? Is it because the U.S. is the chosen country?"

Vicki had already prepared for this line of questioning.

"They're revealing themselves now because we humans have finally reached a level of technology that allows us to have meaningful conversations with them. And, no, the United States is not some mythical chosen land. The extraterrestrials are not only in the U.S., but all over the world—they just happened to come across the right group of people with the right skills in Los Angeles to get the word out. Besides, English is the most widely spoken language in the world, so it simplifies things for the ETs."

All true, but she didn't say anything about the upcoming vibrational shift. While that had been covered in the interviews between Jessica and Melly, it wasn't as exciting as real aliens: it could wait until humans learned about the Suede Nation—an Earth-native species living in the planet's interior.

Only one unbelievable thing at a time. ETs were enough for now.

She also didn't say anything about the Partnership and its plans to take control of humanity. That had also been covered in the *Melly Speaks* interviews. However, with the destruction of the Partnership's compound by a strangely localized earthquake, that was no longer on anyone's mind. It still wasn't public knowledge that Vicki had triggered it.

"But why *you*?" A young woman from the back of the room spoke in an aggressive tone of voice. She looked Instagram-ready and surprisingly young. Judging by the amount of grey hair in the rest of the audience, the other news organizations had sent their most senior representatives.

"As I've already said, the extraterrestrials came across the right group of people with the right skills. In my case, I think they decided they needed a diplomat."

The woman continued on. "But why did they use a novice video-maker rather than a professional media organization like one of us?" She motioned at the other reporters in the room. "Any of us could have done a better job than 'Jessica and the Bug.' "

Vicki stilled, anger flaring, her body rigid. She needed to squash this before it had a chance to spread. She took a breath before starting to speak.

"Melly," she said, steadily staring at the woman, "is not a bug. She is a high-ranking member of the Council of the Galactic Federation, and is from one of the mantis species. They are an ancient and powerful race. You can refer to her as Council Representative Melly, Representative Melly, or just plain Melly." Vicki then looked out at the rest of the audience. "This is your only notice: *Anyone* who refers to Melly as a bug will be thrown out of this room; both they *and* their entire news agency will be banned from subsequent press conferences. There will be no second chances."

The other media representatives looked embarrassed, as if they had been thinking about referring to Melly as a bug, too. Vicki didn't blame them. She had done the same thing—at least in private—before she got to know Melly better. But there wasn't time now to be understanding. Too much was at stake.

The young woman, however, pretended not to understand.

"But it's not as if it's an insult to call her a bug if that's what she is; I'm just saying what everyone else is thinking."

"Words matter," Vicki snapped, then nodded at the Diplomatic Security officers standing in the back. Two of them moved forward and took the woman by her arms. She looked shocked and began protesting, but they dragged her out without saying a word.

Vicki waited for the commotion to die down, then smiled at the room and asked, "Any more questions?"

* * *

That bitch!

Being forcefully escorted out of the building! Kicking her out as if she were some kind of criminal! Amanda had planned to use her access to the ET story—the story of the century!—to take her media career to the next level. Maybe even star in a movie about aliens landing on Earth. With her long hair, golden skin, and sultry pout, she had the looks. But that State Department flunky had ruined everything before she even got started.

It's not like she was new to the issue. Amanda had been one of the few media people allowed to attend the super-exclusive Family Day event at the Partnership's Los Angeles compound—the one that had been destroyed—a few months earlier. She had seen the tech, had seen the devices. This was all connected—a part of the bigger story, one she had been brushing up against for months. And now, more than ever, she felt she was close to breaking it open

She'd have to figure out how to spin being banned from the State Department to her uncle. His ability to pull strings was the reason she'd gotten into the room, and he would not take the news well. More than unhappy, he'd be angry. After all, he had been the one to suggest the arrangement, and he had been the one who wanted specific questions asked. And it was one of those very questions that got her banned.

While not quite at influencer levels, Amanda has a loyal social media following. Maybe she could use that to her advantage.

* * *

Jerry watched the young woman being dragged out of the room and saw the shocked faces of the other reporters as they realized that, yes, Vicki was serious. He understood why Vicki was doing this, but he was worried. She was going too far, too fast. The arrival of ETs was destabilizing global power structures and economic stability. The financial markets were going crazy. But unlike the headlines that stoked fear about alien domination, what Jerry feared was human nature. There were always those who exploited human turmoil for their own benefit.

Now Vicki was taking more questions.

"Some claim that extraterrestrials will destroy religion. What's your response?"

Vicki smiled. "Years ago, the Vatican stated that the existence of extraterrestrial life was compatible with Catholic doctrine, and that ETs could be viewed as our celestial brothers since all life is part of God's creation. I'm sure if you look deeper, many religions might hold similar views."

Jerry knew Vicki was sidestepping that question. The real problem was the people who considered ETs demons—and some of them worked in the Department of Defense.

The next question changed the subject.

"Why was free energy given to the entire world? Wouldn't it make more sense to have the United States in charge of that?"

The public didn't know for certain that the free energy schematics that mysteriously appeared on thousands of websites were sent from a U.S. location. But it happened just minutes before the first interview with Melly was aired, so there were suspicions. It wasn't public knowledge that Jessica's younger brother, Brad, had an entire backpack of alien tech designs that he still needed to distribute. Vicki had told Jerry that they planned to keep it that way. That seemed like a good idea—publicizing that information would put a target on the teenager's back.

"Why were free energy schematics given to the entire world?" repeated Vicki. "Why not? ETs are here to talk with all of humanity, not just with our country, and not just with industrial countries that have technological infrastructures. As far as the Galactic Federation is concerned, we are one and the same." Vicki shrugged, seemingly unconcerned, and signaled to a middle-aged woman—someone Jerry recognized as an anchor on the nightly news—to ask the next question.

"But won't that threaten our national security?"

"Why would energy independence threaten anyone's national security? Remember, we'll still need oil and gas—our experts have told us the energy schematics that were circulated are suitable for residential use only. I don't see how not having a utility bill threatens national security. Do you?"

The audience tittered, and the woman reddened.

"But we need to consider the implications," she continued. "What happens when someone redesigns it to deliver more power? To run factories or data centers or processing centers?"

"I think your real question," said Vicki gently, "is what happens when other countries don't depend on us. What happens to U.S. leadership if they don't need us?"

The woman, her face still red, nodded sharply.

"That's when we'll decide who we really are: who we are when no one is paying attention—who we are when we don't have a specific role in the world, who we are when we no longer have a monopoly on power and control."

"But what if someone uses free energy to develop weapons systems?"

"In theory, someone could—and they still might. But why would they? If everyone has free energy, no one will need to wage war on another country to grab their natural resources. Worldwide living standards and economic opportunities will increase, so illegal immigration will fall. Our biggest problem will probably be politicians looking for ways to ensure they stay relevant."

The room gave a polite laugh in response to that last comment.

Was Vicki being deliberately naïve? While she hadn't spent her career working on financial issues like he had, Jerry knew Vicki was no stranger to the danger of vested interests. Especially since he had helped her use those same vested interests to create a diversion when she and her young friends had been fighting against the Partnership. Lots of people had died then, and that was only a relatively limited struggle with a small number of people. How many would die when the struggle went worldwide?

The press conference was winding down; it had already gone twenty minutes longer than its appointed time. Jerry stepped forward to signal the event's close.

Chapter Two

J ames walked through the back door of the flower shop and called out greetings to the other three. Their voices—and the sound of their feet as they came down the stairs—rang out in response.

It wasn't a flower shop anymore; it hadn't been since Vicki's sister died. But with the shop closed and the Martinsson siblings needing a place to live after their family's mansion was destroyed, Vicki had turned it over to them. Two small apartments occupied the top floor—well, one small apartment and a spacious sunroom that had served as a workroom when the flower shop was still in business. The main floor accommodated Jessica's media studio, an office with Brad's computers, and a common area. The siblings were the first to come down the stairwell. They were having an animated discussion about airing the final interview with Melly tonight. Kiran followed more slowly and gave James a quick smile when he saw him.

James, like the rest of the group, was still getting used to Kiran Rao. The original *Four*—Vicki, Jess, Brad, and James —had worked with Melly to bring down the Partnership. After their victory, Vicki went back to Washington to handle the political side of ET Disclosure, while the rest of the group stayed in Los Angeles. Kiran, once a Partnership employee, had chosen to join them when he found out what the Partnership was really doing. And the fact that he and Jessica were now dating didn't hurt. James figured it wouldn't be long before Kiran moved out of the sunroom and into Jessica's apartment.

So now the Four consisted of James, Brad, Kiran, and Jessica. Brad was James's best friend, so he was happy with the arrangement. It would be fun if he could move into Brad's side of the second floor once Kiran moved in with Jessica, but his parents would fight that—he and Brad were only sixteen. Besides, his parents needed his help with their tai chi studio.

Brad paused his conversation with his sister to check his watch. "It's just a few minutes until our FaceTime with Vicki."

It wasn't FaceTime, not really. They couldn't risk anyone doing some internet sleuthing and uncovering their digital footprint. While many of the Partnership's high-level employees—at least the managers and executives—had died when headquarters was destroyed, a few had survived. No one wanted to find out if they were holding a grudge. Since Brad was a computer genius—thanks to a DNA upgrade from Melly—he designed his own computer network that rivaled the NSA's in privacy protection. James wasn't sure if Brad was bragging, but no one had tracked them down yet.

Was anybody looking?

* * *

Vicki leaned forward and smiled as the image of her young friends appeared on the computer screen; they were sitting on a small sofa in Jessica's media studio. She had driven herself crazy worrying about what to do with Beth's shop after her sister died, but now it seemed like everything had fallen into place—a place it was meant to be.

"Hey! Look at you, the new DAS, holding press conferences like a boss!" Brad was as exuberant as ever.

"I'll have you know I *am* a boss—I have fifteen employees so far and will likely be hiring more." Vicki tried to maintain a dignified expression but failed, and then just grinned at them. "I miss you guys so much."

They had all agreed to a weekly check-in to keep track of all the balls they were juggling. Brad started things off with an update on the free energy downloads happening around the world.

"Australia finally switched its internet access back on, but only after authorities put a really strong firewall in place to block downloads of the schematics. Give me another day, and that won't be a problem." He snickered.

"I'm surprised the government would do such a thing," murmured Jessica. "I mean, why? They'll just fall behind the rest of the world."

"Control," said Vicki. "Also, change is scary. But I'm surprised they're reverting back to their penal colony roots so quickly. It's clear they don't trust their citizens to behave responsibly."

"African countries aren't worrying about that, especially the Nigerians," said Brad. "It's only been two weeks, and there are already several dozen free energy units up and running, mostly powering marketplaces, schools, and health clinics."

"How can you tell that?" asked James.

"I thought the plans were only good for residential use?" Vicki asked at the same time.

"I have my ways," Brad smirked, then continued. "They *are* only good for residential use, but the energy consumption in the average home in the United States is much greater than in an average African home—and even more than in the average school or clinic—so the schematics still work. India isn't far behind the Nigerians. I wouldn't if surprised if, within the next couple of months, both countries pulled ahead of all the industrialized nations in terms of free energy adoption."

"Necessity is the mother of invention," murmured Kiran quietly.

"I'll remember to tell Jerry," Vicki said. "He's been tracking all the disruptions in the financial markets, and this will be a game changer.

James went next, providing an update on his exploration of the memory crystal, which the Galactic Federation had given to Vicki on behalf of all humanity. It contained detailed records of humanity's interactions with ETs over thousands of years, so she wanted someone to review them before releasing the information to the general public. Some of the records were explosive.

Kiran raised the issue of the "Hum."

"What's that?" asked Vicki.

"Just a hum—or maybe the sound of a muffled trumpet?—with no cause. No one can figure out the source, whether it's coming from the Earth or if it's something in the atmosphere. The sound just randomly rings out every so often in different locations around the planet. The humming lasts for about five or ten minutes, then it stops. It's happened occasionally over the years, but in the last couple of months, this has increased to about every week or so."

"And why is this our problem?" Seriously, didn't she have enough to keep track of?

Now Kiran looked a bit uncomfortable. "It's something in Hindu traditions. The *Bhagavad Gita* begins with both Krishna and the Pandavas blowing their divine conch shells. In that specific case, it was to signify the start of war, but more generally, blowing the conch shell is said to resonate across realms and purify evil. It might be relevant."

"What are the Pandavas?" asked James.

"They're like the Avengers, but with more spiritual baggage."

Everyone just stared at him. Kiran shrugged.

"I thought you could ask Junia about it; if the source of the Hum is the Earth, the Suede Nation will know about it."

Vicki let out a sigh. "That's actually a good idea. Now, what's up with your DNA upgrade? I heard you received one from Melly."

Now, they were back on familiar ground. Melly had triggered the junk DNA of Vicki, Brad, Jessica, and James to help them fight against the Partnership. But once the vibrational shift occurred, the junk DNA of all humans would be activated. The Four had all received upgrades to their ability to detect chi—the life energy that flows through all living things—turning them into walking infrared thermal detectors, which made it easier to sense people who were trying to stay hidden. They also gained unique abilities that helped them take down the Partnership. Vicki shook her head; she didn't want to think about that anymore. She turned her focus back to Kiran.

"It was like a story my grandfather would tell of the yogic masters. I never thought I'd have the opportunity to experience something so amazing myself."

Jessica rested her head on Kiran's shoulder. "Once the vibrational shift happens, other humans will have experiences and gain their own abilities."

"As long as they don't decide to take the easy way and become biologic constructs," James said quietly.

"Hopefully, the only facilities capable of making the biologic constructs were destroyed in the earthquake," Jessica said.

Vicki brought the conversation back to the point. "What can Kiran do?" She hadn't been paying attention.

"Clairvoyance?" Kiran was unsure. "While that's the word that best describes it, I really can't predict the future. Instead, I can sense possibilities. If someone needs to choose between one of three options, for example, I can tell them the probable outcomes of each. At least that's what I will be able to do; right now, I'm practicing. I need a lot of practice.

"That could be useful." Very useful, actually. Vicki became lost in thought again.

Brad broke the silence, saying, "I need to share our screen with you, Vicki."

Jessica reached over to punch Brad in the shoulder. "Brad! I told you it wasn't important."

Brad didn't react. When Vicki nodded, he typed something on his keyboard and launched a video. "This was a story on this morning's news."

Vicki felt sick; she should have anticipated this. The attractive woman holding the microphone was the same one she had thrown out of the press conference the day before.

"We're all asking ourselves what the truth is behind 'Jessica and the Bug,' but when we asked the hard questions in yesterday's press briefing, this reporter was rudely thrown out by armed security, and both my news agency and I were permanently banned from State Department grounds. What don't they want us to know? Thankfully, the State Department isn't the only source of information, even though they pretend to be."

The camera tracked the reporter as she stepped a few feet to one side, revealing a small group of young people.

"No one knows who the extraterrestrial bug is, but these people know Jessica—and they have a lot to say."

"The 'Heirs'," said Vicki, in dismay. These were Brad and Jessica's former peers. Their father had worked for the Partnership and pushed his kids to befriend his coworkers' children to help him move up the corporate ladder. Brad had an easygoing personality and got along with everyone. But his sister... Jessica had made the difficult decision to play the fool as a way to deflect curiosity and avoid questions. She had spent years pretending to be less than she was, and during all that time, she had been an easy target for bullies.

And most of them had been bullies. They were *still* bullies—entitled bullies.

"We don't like to say anything negative about Jessica," one young woman was saying delicately. *"Everyone knew how she struggled. It's not her fault; she's simple, you know."*

The reporter interrupted, *"But we've all seen her on the videos with the bug. She's asking questions—important questions. She's gone viral in every country in the world. Is this how you remember her?"*

A young woman with tan skin and ebony black hair stepped forward. Was bratty little Aija really a part of this? Vicki cast a quick glance at Kiran, who had gone rigid. Okay, he hadn't known about his sister.

"*This is not the Jessica we know, and I think it's very suspicious that she's doing this,*" said Aija. "*She's not capable of it. She's not capable of going on camera and interviewing aliens without having a nervous breakdown. She's neurotic, not normal.*"

A serious-looking young man stepped up. "*As her friends, we're concerned. This isn't normal for Jessica. It makes us wonder if she's being controlled in some way. Maybe it's the aliens.*"

* * *

Brad was *furious*. This was a smear campaign. His sister had been through so much, and now she had to face this. He kept his expression neutral as the video ended, and the others began debating how to address these accusations—and whether they should address them at all. After a few minutes, swayed by Jessica's arguments, everyone agreed they should wait to see the fallout before reacting.

But Brad didn't agree. He was a genius computer hacker. Brad wanted revenge.

Chapter Three

James pretended not to notice the sucked-in breaths and the silence that fell when he walked into the advanced class at the Cloud Hands Tai Chi Studio. The reaction had nothing to do with him. This was the first time Jessica and Brad had been to class since they fought the Partnership, and it was also Kiran's first time ever attending. His parents, Calvin and Mona—they were also the studio owners and the main instructors for the advanced class—stood at the front of the classroom. When his dad gave him a slight nod, James walked up to stand beside them and began to speak.

"This feels awkward, but we need your help; the entire world needs your help, even if they don't realize it."

The faces were skeptical, but James pressed on. "You've seen Jessica's videos with Council Representative Melly from the Galactic Federation; you might have downloaded the free energy schematics. You've heard the arguments claiming it's all deep fake. We're here to tell you it's all true—and if you're willing, you can be a part of it too."

There was silence. Then Mei, the high school-aged daughter of Chinese immigrants, stepped forward. Another student, Mei's older cousin Tian, tried to hold her back, but she shook off his hand. "Aren't you asking for help a little late? It looks like everything has been done."

By this time, Jessica had reached the front to stand beside James. "It's only just started. What you've seen on the news is the beginning."

"But we've watched your interviews with that alien and the official press conferences. If everything is true, the Partnership was the problem. But the Partnership's been destroyed. We actually saw that on the news, too. You didn't need us for any of that, so why do you need us now?"

James realized with surprise that Mei's aggressive questions were a cover for her resentment. The Four had left out the rest of the class, and she was unhappy about that. "We couldn't risk putting anyone else in danger."

"Danger!" Mei scoffed, her eyes flashing.

"My uncle Larry died, so yes, it was dangerous." James crossed his arms.

He would not cry, at least not here.

At this, Mei lowered her eyes and finally let her cousin pull her back. Larry had been a well-liked member of the advanced class. While the students didn't know the details, they were aware that he had been killed in an accident somehow related to the Partnership. They didn't know that he had deliberately sacrificed himself so that James and the others could escape.

James was grateful that Jessica came forward to finish the talk.

"Since you've watched the interviews, you know about the upcoming vibrational shift."

"When is that supposed to happen?" one of the other students asked.

"We're not sure. But we know the more prepared humans are, the more successful it will be." She explained how the shift would activate humans' junk DNA and give them abilities now deemed pseudo-scientific—ESP, clairvoyance, the ability to heal others, and intuition, for example. However, it wasn't going to be easy. On a physical level, there would be a massive disruption in the rhythms of everyday life. Many people would be unhappy about that. Others might look forward to the shift in vibration, only to discover that they weren't energetically prepared. They would be left behind when their neighbors gained these new "magical" abilities.

"That's why we need your help," concluded Jessica. "We need to start teaching people how to reach higher vibrational levels now so that when the shift comes, their DNA will be ready for it. Everyone here in this class is beginning to reach those higher vibrational levels while meditating and doing tai chi. If you could help us make a series of videos showing how to do this, we could broadcast them and reach more people."

"Are you sure you're up to it? Won't the pressure give you a nervous breakdown?" The mocking voice came from the back of the room.

From his vantage point, James could see Brad's head whip around, locate the person who had spoken, and take a step forward.

James had thought it was odd that Brad hadn't argued more the day before, when the group chose to not react to the negative media story. He had seemed unusually agreeable. But now, seeing the hard expression on his friend's face, James realized he'd been wrong—Brad was determined to protect his sister.

But Jessica didn't need protecting.

"When people can't argue with the facts, they go after the person sharing them. Advanced tech, the arrival of ETs, and the revelation that some corporations tried to control humanity—those are facts. So instead, they attack my reputation. The truth is, it's easier to judge people than to face new ideas. That's okay—we get it. But I need to warn you: working with us comes with risks. Please take a moment to think it over. If you're not comfortable, you're free to leave. No judgement."

Jessica waited for half a minute, but there were no further comments, and no one left the room. James was relieved to see Brad relax and step back. Jessica turned toward Mona and Calvin, and the three began discussing with the class how they would make the videos.

* * *

Mei followed James out the door when class ended. She was upset. She *knew* that James's uncle had been killed, but she hadn't been thinking of that when she spoke her angry words in the classroom. It was just that it was so frustrating to be left out when exciting things were happening, to be told she wasn't old enough to take risks, and warned she would only ruin things if she got involved. Her family did this to her all the time. Mei wasn't a kid anymore; she was fifteen, and her grandmother had already been married by that age. But that didn't excuse her outburst in class. James was a nice guy; she needed to apologize to him.

Mei was about to head down the hallway James had just taken when someone suddenly grabbed her shoulder and pulled her back. She turned around to find Tian glaring down at her. "Don't you think you've done enough?" he hissed. "You're embarrassing yourself. You're embarrassing our family. We need to leave."

Mei took a breath to protest, then thought better of it. She meekly followed Tian out of the studio.

* * *

It wasn't late when Jessica left the studio, but she was tired. Kiran and Brad had stayed behind with James to review the memory crystal data. Maybe she should have stayed with them, but knowing the boys, they'd be at it for hours. She'd given Kiran her keys so he could drive himself and Brad back to the flower shop once their conversation with James was finished.

Jessica could have called a ride-share, but a quick look at the app showed her the wait for the car would be longer than for the bus. A metro stop was at the other end of the block. She turned left out of the studio parking lot and headed down the street. It was a beautiful neighborhood; the sidewalk was lined with leafy trees and other greenery.

Honestly, they should consider getting a second vehicle. Brad would have his license soon, so that would mean three drivers but only one car. Which wasn't enough.

Jessica didn't know how she felt about Kiran. Correction: she did know—she liked him a lot. Was it normal to have such strong feelings after only knowing someone for a couple of months? Jessica was painfully aware that this was her first relationship. How does that happen to a 22-year-old?

But she already knew the answer. Her mother had died of cancer, even though the Partnership had a simple outpatient treatment that could have cured it—a treatment based on advanced tech they had secretly reverse-engineered from ET sources. But her mom refused it, saying it wasn't right to use something that wasn't available to everyone. The Partnership only offered it to their own: investors, employees, and their families. Her asshole of a father immediately divorced their mother, fearing it would make him look bad if his own wife rejected one of the Partnership's benefits. She and Brad spent three years watching their mother die.

Jessica was glad her father was no longer alive.

So, yes, she had been depressed, at least for a few months. But then Melly reached out to James, and eventually to her and Brad. Once Jessica realized what was at stake, she chose to continue acting the same way—depressed, anxious, and emotionally fragile—because it now served a purpose. It helped hide the truth and kept people from asking too many questions.

Jessica shook her head to clear her thoughts. She had stuff to plan. The Federation Council had agreed to allow Melly to create more videos with her, so she had to figure out themes for each episode and the questions she'd ask Melly.

She looked up. Another thirty feet to the end of the block, then another left turn, and she'd be at the bus stop.

Jessica almost stumbled when she first sensed them. Chi from two individuals, about twenty feet behind her. She glanced back—two shadowy figures were walking in her direction. How long had they been following her? They were so quiet.

Don't panic, don't panic, don't panic. She was almost at the bus stop. Just a few more steps before she would reach the corner and a busy street. Besides, maybe she was just being paranoid—she didn't know whether they were actually coming after her. It was probably silly, but she took out her phone and dialed a number.

Then she yelped in surprise when a powerfully-built man stepped out in front of her. Where had he been hiding? Why hadn't she sensed his chi? She should have sensed it. Then the realization hit—*this man was a biologic construct.*

Jessica opened her mouth to scream, but the man stepped forward and covered it with a cloth that emitted an overwhelmingly sweet, chemical smell. Her fingers clawed at the fabric, but she grew weak. She struggled for several more seconds, becoming dizzy as her vision blurred. Then her limbs became heavy, and she collapsed into unconsciousness.

The man grabbed the phone before she could drop it.

* * *

Kiran's phone rang once, then fell silent. He glanced at it, then looked again. "Hmm, it looks like Jessica was calling, but decided against it."

"She probably butt-dialed you." James gave him a look.

Kiran reddened. He felt nervous about how Brad would react to James' innuendo, but Brad started hooting with laughter.

"You like her, you like her!" Brad convulsed in laughter.

Kiran liked Brad. They had worked together at the Partnership when he was an employee and Brad was an intern, but sometimes the eight-year age difference really showed. This was one of those times. He couldn't wait until Brad started dating someone so he could pay him back in kind.

The three boys turned back to the memory crystal. Vicki had given it to James as his special project because he was a history nut. Kiran didn't begrudge him that, but he really wanted to explore India's past to find out whether the Vimanas—the flying ships described in 6,000-year-old Hindu texts—were of ET origin. That, however, wasn't their priority. They needed to figure out how to tell humanity that extraterrestrials had nearly caused the extinction of the human race without provoking mass riots.

Kiran glanced at the time and sighed; it would be past midnight by the time he and Brad returned to the flower shop. He wondered what Jessica had wanted to tell him. He'd need to ask her that in the morning when they all woke up.

Chapter Four

Vicki sighed as she scanned the conference room she had just entered. Although the table seated twenty, and an additional twenty-five chairs lined the walls, they had already reached standing room capacity. They were the hosts of the meeting, but she and her staff had not yet had a chance to sit down. Mary had warned her this would happen. She hadn't believed her.

She hadn't *wanted* to believe her.

She pushed and excused her way into the room and motioned her staff to follow. Besides Jerry, there was Mary, her office administrator, and Graham, her science advisor. Graham was a former Partnership employee who had passed along a backpack full of alien reverse-engineered designs to Larry and Vicki before the Partnership's headquarters was destroyed. She was glad that Graham and his partner Kyle had survived. When she told them this, they admitted that Larry had warned them to stay away from headquarters that night. They had lived; Larry hadn't.

Vicki made her way to the head of the table and looked at the people already seated there. They looked up. "It's our meeting, and there are four of us," she said, pointedly. Sheepishly, four individuals stood up and allowed Vicki and her colleagues to sit down. Then, Vicki shuffled her papers and looked up to address the table.

"Thank you for coming to meet with us. You all have the agenda, but first, I'd like to go around the room and have everyone introduce themselves. Please give your name, your organization, and why you're here in this room."

Mary had advised Vicki that there would be an issue with the attendees—specifically, with the *number* of attendees. Vicki had requested three representatives from each relevant government agency, stating they should be decision-makers regarding UFO and extraterrestrial policies for their respective organizations. If those agencies had complied with her request, there would have been no more than 25 people in the room. A rough headcount indicated there were more than sixty.

Vicki paid polite attention as people introduced themselves, nodding at each individual as they spoke. Mary was busy writing down names and taking notes. By the time introductions were completed, over half an hour had passed. As Mary slid her notes over to her, Vicki could see that she had actually made a quick sketch of the table with annotations of who was sitting where. As she suspected, more than half the attendees were not government employees—they were government contractors or representatives from aerospace corporations. She cleared her throat.

Thank you all for coming, but there has been a misunderstanding. I invited only government agency representatives. The rest of you need to leave.

There was immediate protest from all sides.

"We need these people here; they're the ones who do all the work!"

"You don't know what they do?" Vicki cocked her head to one side, her expression seemingly curious. "So, there is no one at all in your agency who can verify their work? Why are *you* here, then?"

Yeah, the guy had walked right into that one.

From the corner of her eye, Vicki saw Mary struggle to keep a smile off her face. Graham wasn't so polite; he let out a loud guffaw.

The man who had protested reddened. Who was he? Consulting Mary's notes, Vicki saw that he was one of the representatives from DARPA—the Defense Advanced Research Projects Agency. That made sense, as Graham had told her that DARPA was the government agency that had the responsibility of sending crashed alien spaceships to aerospace firms for reverse-engineering. Vicki took pity on him.

"Don't worry, today we'll be discussing policies, not advanced technologies—your contractor won't be necessary. If, by chance, a technology-related question comes up in the conversation, my science advisor can handle it. The contractor meeting will take place another day."

The other people in the room eyed Graham with curiosity. They clearly didn't know who he was. Graham pretended to be interested in one of the pictures hanging on the wall.

Jerry got up and opened the door, and the non-government people began filing out. Vicki could hear him telling everyone to give their contact info to the young woman waiting with the two Diplomatic Security officers who would be escorting them out. Mary would reach out to them when the meeting for contractors was scheduled.

After the door closed and Jerry was back in his seat, there were only 30 people left in the room.

"Was that really necessary?" asked a man in an Air Force uniform.

"I'm pretty sure it was," said Vicki. "Don't you remember what happened just two weeks ago? Have you already forgotten that a corporate conglomerate was on the brink of taking global control?"

"But their plan was destroyed," objected someone from one of the wall chairs. "We don't need to worry about that anymore. The people we work with and who you just kicked out of the room weren't involved."

"Are you sure?" Vicki let that question hang in the air; the silence thickened uncomfortably. Then, she continued. "I don't believe we can be sure. Private firms—the corporations and the government contractors—are the shadows of the UFO world. Rules don't bind them. They operate where the government can't. I know that the Partnership was a rogue corporate conglomerate and that most of the top people died when the headquarters was destroyed, but they weren't operating in a vacuum; I'm sure they have allies in companies all over the world."

"So, we should be preparing to continue the fight against them?" the Air Force official asked.

"I hope not. While I wouldn't be surprised if governments find they need to mop up a few people here and there, our focus today is on Disclosure. The Galactic Federation is considering whether to invite Earth to become a member. We need to figure out the best way to more forward to this. Remember, this would be an invitation to Earth for all humanity, not just the United States. Therefore, we'll need to coordinate with other countries. Maybe we could work through the United Nations?

* * *

Jerry kept his head down and his face neutral as people stood up and began shouting. Yes, this was another thing they knew would happen. He glanced over at his coworkers. Vicki appeared calm but was clearly frustrated as she checked the time. She had warned him they would need to allow the other government agencies time to vent, but she just as clearly wanted to move forward with the agenda. Poor Graham; this was his first interagency meeting—possibly his first government meeting ever. For all his impressively stocky build and weathered features, his eyes were wide like a deer's, clearly shocked. Graham would need to toughen up.

Mary was as unflustered as ever. Seriously unflustered. Jerry had heard people say she had ice water in her veins. Maybe, but he couldn't imagine anyone else handling what had been thrown at her these past weeks: commandeering office space, often over the objections of the current occupants (several dozen State Department employees suddenly found themselves without offices); onboarding new employees; requisitioning new computer equipment that would meet the security concerns of Graham (no lowest-bidder government junk for them); and coordinating clearances. Now she showed Jerry—and everyone else—just why Vicki had been so keen to have her on her staff.

"Anyone who doesn't sit down and be quiet within the next ten seconds will be escorted out of the building." Mary didn't speak loudly or even stand, but she had the presence of someone who expected to be obeyed. Jerry almost laughed when he saw the military officers responding to her almost immediately; her voice had a tone of authority that they recognized.

"This is what's going to happen," she continued her no-nonsense delivery. "We will go around the table, and each of you will have the opportunity to speak. You may ask questions, make comments, or suggest actions. DAS Heywood will either decide the issue on the spot or take it under consideration for later, but no one will have more than five minutes. Keep that in mind while you organize your thoughts."

"Bitch."

Jerry heard the soft, nearly inaudible comment, but didn't react. Neither did Mary, although she must have heard it as well. Not so Vicki, who was speaking quietly to Graham.

Vicki could have done this, Jerry realized. She was fully capable of doing what Mary was doing now—she had done so in the press briefing. But it was one thing to speak to the media in this way and something entirely different to do so with the government's military and intelligence representatives. It was a much better strategy for her office administrator to appear cold and uncompromising than for Vicki herself. She still had to work with these people. Hopefully, they would end up cooperating.

Thanks to Mary—and her threats—the next two hours unfolded in an orderly fashion. It was too bad they weren't able to come to agreement.

To a man (and they were mostly men, with only half a dozen female representatives from the government agencies), they objected to using the United Nations as a focal point for the Galactic Federation. The UN was bloated, corrupt, and plagued by mission overlap and a lack of accountability. There was little chance that a global—an interstellar—project led by the UN would succeed.

"You could be right," said Vicki. "I'd like each agency to provide a paper with any alternative suggestions you might have. Either how to set up a new department within the UN that bypasses known UN shortcomings, or a new organization entirely. We need to have this system up and running within a month—two months at the latest. Please provide your suggestions—in writing—within 24 hours to my office administrator.

It looked like a couple of people were going to protest the short timeline, but seeing the look on Mary's face, they decided not to.

"It's not just the United Nations that's the problem," said the next person. He was an older man with thinning blond hair and numerous medals on his Department of Defense uniform. Jerry recognized him as a high-ranking staff member in the office of the Secretary of Defense.

The man continued, "Another issue is that we're holding this meeting here in the Department of State. DOD has the expertise and should be the lead agency for this."

Vicki had anticipated this. Jerry observed her slowly release her breath before starting to speak.

"The military and intelligence agencies had the lead on the extraterrestrial issue for nearly a century. What were the results? A world where much of the population lived in poverty, and widespread pollution from industries forced to use obsolete technology. And let's not forget about the rogue corporate conglomerate that tried to take control of humanity. You had your chance; it's our turn now."

"We kept the world safe!" the man spat out.

"You kept the world profitable for the chosen few," replied Vicki. "The rest of us were trapped in an economic system designed to keep us controlled. Next question."

"And why you?" continued the man, refusing to cede the floor. "There are other, more senior State Department personnel—ones with better qualifications for this role. Anyone else could have come up with something better than 'Jessica and the Bug.' That performance was pathetic."

The man's comments were deliberately goading, and Jerry saw Vicki stiffen. For a moment, he thought she was going to throw the man out of the room, but instead, she smiled at him. It was not a nice smile.

"I am currently the only person in the U.S. government who has spoken with members of the Galactic Federation, and that means I have more experience than anyone else here. I look forward to reading your agency's paper tomorrow."

* * *

Mary cornered Vicki and Jerry after the meeting had ended. "Why didn't you throw Colonel Riley out of the room? Not only was he disrespectful, he referred to Representative Melly as a bug."

"But I still need to work with him—with his office. I can't afford to anger the Secretary of Defense more than necessary."

"Did you notice how similar his questions were to those in the press conference?" Mary persisted.

"What do you mean?" Jerry asked her.

"Colonel Riley is the uncle of the reporter Vicki kicked out—Amanda Riley. She asked the same questions."

Mary had looked into it. Knowing your enemies could keep you safe.

"She's also the same reporter who did that smear story on Jessica," said Vicki. "So, Colonel Riley is behind it all."

"Is Colonel Riley behind it all, or is it the Secretary of Defense?" asked Jerry.

"It really doesn't matter. I'd rather have my enemy inside my tent pissing out than outside my tent pissing in."

Mary didn't say anything more. Still, she wondered if Colonel Riley was the kind of person who was so convinced he was right that he would proudly stand inside the tent and piss all over himself.

Chapter Five

K iran woke up to light streaming into the room; Brad's bed was empty. It had been nearly 1:00 a.m. when they arrived back last night, and Jessica's door was already closed. He didn't blame her; he wouldn't have waited up for them either.

He pushed himself out of bed and went to check on the plants. The sunroom on the second floor that Brad and Kiran had claimed as their bedroom had previously been used by Beth as a workspace for her flower business. The plants had all died before they moved in, but Vicki insisted on replacing them. While Brad was indifferent about the plants, Kiran liked them. Living plants were a grounding presence—a welcome balance to all the strange things they'd been dealing with.

Everyone was excited about the aliens and the advanced technology. And it *was* amazing. However, he was more excited about the vibrational shift and the resulting trigger of human junk DNA. When would it happen? Vicki couldn't be more specific than "soon enough." She didn't know either; the ETs had told her the shift depended on many events, many of which had not yet happened. The timing was up in the air.

It was unfortunate his grandfather had passed away a few years ago; he would have been delighted by the upcoming changes. Before his family immigrated to the U.S., Grandpa Rao taught Kiran both yoga and meditation. But it was the stories from the *Bhagavad Gita* and the *Patanjali* that Kiran liked best. His grandfather was not only a master yogi, but also a master storyteller.

The *Patanjali* served as the main source of his grandfather's stories about the Siddhis – the mystical powers individuals gained as they approached enlightenment. While Vicki and the Four had not yet reached that level, they had already received specific DNA activations to help fight the Partnership. All of them now possessed the ability to detect chi (his grandfather would have called it *prana*) in others, which Kiran assumed was a form of *samyama*. James had been the first of their group that Melly reached out to, so he received the gift of channeling. Brad had been transformed into a computer genius who could create and understand complex schematics. His sister—Kiran smiled at the thought of Jessica—hadn't received any specific activations aside from the basics; she already had the looks and personality of a media figure. Vicki had received the most transformational ability—*Vashitva*, or the ability to control the elements, including Earth energies. She had been the one responsible for bringing down the Partnership's headquarters with the combination of a localized earthquake and a 15-acre sinkhole. It had been reported as a natural disaster—no one in the news mentioned that the sinkhole's edges lined up exactly with the Partnership's property line.

Kiran had received his DNA activation just a week ago: clairvoyance—or maybe it was precognition. He wasn't entirely certain about the correct label. Melly explained that it was the ability to sense potential paths and the probable outcomes associated with each path. He wasn't very skilled at it yet; he needed to practice.

Kiran glanced at Jessica's closed door. She wasn't up yet, which didn't surprise him since Jessica was not a morning person. He headed downstairs to see what Brad was doing.

* * *

The coffee was excellent this morning. When they retrofitted the flower shop, Brad had insisted on purchasing a top-of-the-line espresso machine to replace the one they lost when the Partnership blew up their home. But the mansion hadn't meant much to them. No one was hurt, and neither he nor Jessica had ever felt at home there. Their father had only bought it to impress his coworkers at the Partnership. The irony was that the Partnership ended up burning it down themselves when their interests were at risk—and turned on their father in the process. Their father, just as quickly, had turned against his own children.

Brad took a sip of his espresso. The flower shop was the first place that felt like home since their mother had passed away.

His multiple computer screens monitored the news. Governments around the world were imposing harsh regulations on free-energy technology. Ever since he uploaded the schematics to hundreds of websites, Brad had been playing whack-a-mole with internet censorship, re-uploading the designs as soon as they were taken down. Australia had been the most brazenly repressive. After disconnecting from the internet for a week, Australia had come back online—but with a firewall blocking its citizens from accessing free energy information. Brad had broken through those protections the previous evening and was now monitoring how many people were downloading the schematics. For their sake, he hoped the Australian government was focused on restoring the firewall and wasn't tracking who was downloading. He no longer had any illusions about what people would do to others when their self-interests were threatened, even when those other people were the ones they supposedly loved the most.

Other industrialized nations were being sneakier about censorship. In the United States, the government—or maybe just a faction within it—was indeed tracking who was downloading the schematics. Good thing that he was brilliant with computers—he hadn't been bragging when he told James his network security was better than the NSA's.

He revisited the progress in developing nations. If the current trend continued, Kenya would soon emerge as a leader in free energy production. Although the schematics were primarily meant for residential use, he observed that Kenyans were linking systems together to boost energy output. Examining the map, he identified Yaba, located on the outskirts of Lagos, as the center of Kenya's free energy initiatives. Locals referred to it as "Yabacon Valley."

Good for them.

* * *

James entered the flower shop to find Brad immersed in his computers. "Anything new?"

"Not really, but Australia is back in the game," he said, eyes flicking across the screen. "It'll be another few days before they can roll out a proper patch, but in the meantime, people are downloading the schematics as fast as they can." He snorted. "Censorship isn't working; I'm sort of curious to see what they'll try next."

He leaned back, scrolling through a live feed of government responses around the globe. "The UK's using AI to flag and auto-delete any posts with schematic keywords—it's only about half-successful, by the way. Germany just hit every major file-sharing platform with takedown orders, but the stuff just keeps popping up somewhere else. Canada's taking a softer approach—they're flooding social media with fake versions of the schematics that include viruses."

At this, Brad frowned. He disapproved of governments using computers to sabotage their own people.

James changed the subject.

"What are Jessica and Kiran doing? I texted Jess that I was coming over, but didn't receive a reply. We need to talk to her about the tai chi and meditation videos. My parents can lead most of the classes, but Jessica will need to be the one on camera interviewing them about the role of chi in higher consciousness. Maybe Kiran can help out since he's been meditating so long."

James turned as Kiran came down the stairs. "Jess?" he asked.

Kiran shook his head, "She hasn't come out yet; she's probably still asleep."

Brad shifted his gaze from the screen to the others. "That's odd; it's already mid-morning. If nothing else, she'd be up and drinking coffee." He picked up his phone and dialed a number. "It's going straight to voicemail."

The three friends exchanged glances and then went up the stairs without saying a word. Brad knocked on Jessica's door and opened it when he got no response.

"She's not here; it doesn't look like she slept in her bed. She didn't get home last night." Brad's voice sounded panicky.

"Not here?" Kiran stepped forward and scanned the room with his eyes. James heard the panic in Kiran's voice, too.

"What do we do? We can't call the police," said Brad.

"We have to!" Kiran was almost yelling. "We can't just sit here doing nothing—if she didn't get home, she's in danger!"

James stepped up and placed his hand on Kiran's shoulder. "Yes, she's in danger—we all are. But there *is* something we can do. Have you already forgotten about our DNA upgrades?"

Kiran turned toward James, his eyes wild, "Do any of you have some sort of location ability? I know I don't."

"Yeah, what are you talking about?" asked Brad.

"Number one: she's not dead." James saw the other two flinch when he said that. "We would have felt that; I know it. We would have felt her absence."

Brad stilled suddenly as he considered it, then nodded, "You're right."

"Two: We can assume that Jessica has been taken by someone. She never turns off her phone. If she were in an accident, the phone would still be ringing."

This time, Kiran nodded.

"Third: We have ways of communicating without using phones."

Kiran looked at James, confused, but Brad's eyes lit up in comprehension. "Of course, the pocket out-of-time."

Kiran still looked baffled, so James explained it to him.

"The pocket out-of-time is the location—the vibrational reality—where Melly triggered changes in our junk DNA. You were in that reality when you received your upgrade."

Kiran nodded.

"But we can also meet there as a group," continued James. "And when we do, Jessica can tell us what's happening to her."

"But how will she know to meet us there?"

"You are truly underestimating my sister," Brad said gruffly. "Despite the public act she put on during the last couple of years, she doesn't panic. When she's able, she'll figure it out and check for us there."

It seemed to take forever for them to calm themselves down enough to enter meditation and reach the pocket out-of-time. James made it first, then waited for the other two. If they were going to continue communicating like this, they needed to practice. A few more minutes passed, then the sparkly silhouettes of Brad and Kiran appeared.

"She's not here!" Kiran was upset.

James wasn't worried. "It was unlikely Jess would be able to come here mid-morning. Think about it—she was grabbed last night and taken somewhere. Now she's probably being questioned or something. We'll try again later."

"Who would take her?" asked Kiran.

"Someone who has something to lose if we're successful," answered Brad. "And somebody always has something to lose."

"What do they want with her?" Kiran asked, and both he and Brad looked to James for the answer.

"They probably want to stop her from doing what she's doing. Jessica is an amazing media figure. She's attractive. She's credible. She's been extremely successful in introducing humanity to aliens and making them seem appealing."

"I don't think Melly could ever look appealing," said Kiran with feeling. He was still a bit unsettled by the alien's appearance.

"Making them look like people," amended James. "I don't mean making them look like humans—they'll never be human, and we're not trying to pretend that they are. But everyone watching those videos understands that Melly is a person, not a monster."

"A scary person," said Kiran under his breath.

"Yes, she's scary, but she can communicate with us; she's intelligent and has emotions as well as a sense of humor. The videos have shown us that ETs not only developed advanced technologies but also have societies and governments with laws and accepted standards of behavior."

"Standards of behavior that seem to be higher than ours at the moment," muttered Brad.

"Exactly," said James grimly. "And over these past few months, we've discovered just how low human standards of behavior really are."

Chapter Six

V icki ended the call and put her phone back in her pocket. Times like these were why she missed having a desk phone. She wanted to slam the receiver down. She wanted to scream and throw papers. She was so angry at herself.

She should have anticipated this—Jessica had been taken!

The boys didn't know who had taken her, just that she hadn't returned to the flower shop the previous night. They did know that she was still alive; Vicki agreed that they would all have felt Jessica's absence had she been killed. And since no one had received a ransom note, she also agreed with their reasoning that Jess had likely been taken to prevent any more pro-ET videos from being made—she was the public face of Disclosure, after all. For now, at least, Jessica was probably safe.

She should have thought of this!

The plan to go to the pocket-out-of-time this evening was solid. Since all signs indicated that Jessica no longer had her phone, she would try to reach them in other ways. Calling the police—or any other authority—was out of the question.

The Four should have had the security talk at the very beginning, but everyone believed that Brad's network protection was enough. Since most of the Partnership's leadership died with the destruction of the headquarters, they had assumed they were safe from physical threats. Bad conclusion. Vicki had forgotten that individuals not connected to the Partnership might also be against Disclosure. She had forgotten about the vested interests.

She reflected on her brief conversation with the boys. Based on the timing of Jessica's interrupted call to Kiran, they believed Jessica had been taken shortly after leaving the tai chi studio. This was both good and bad. Good, because it suggested that the flower shop was probably still a safe place for them. Bad, because those who took Jessica were aware of the tai chi studio. Could they continue with their plans to film tai chi and meditation videos there? And right now, Brad was leaving the advanced technology backpack at the flower shop whenever he went somewhere. What would happen if someone searched the place? James, on the other hand, kept the memory crystal with him at all times. But if Jessica could be taken, he could too.

They would have to wait until they could get in touch with Jess; whatever she told them would guide their future actions. And how could they help her escape? Vicki sat down at her desk and put her head in her hands. Could this day get any worse?

And then, Jerry walked in.

* * *

Vicki looked like crap. It's not like she ever cared much about dressing up, but now she looked like someone had run her over with a truck. Too bad he wasn't going to make things better.

"Problems?" he asked.

"Jessica has been kidnapped," she said flatly. "I should have realized the danger. Because of her videos with Melly, everyone connects her with Disclosure—even more so than me. Anyone unhappy with the idea of aliens and revolutionary technologies will be gunning for her. We already saw it with that smear story on the news. Kidnapping Jess was the logical next step."

Jerry didn't argue with her. She was right; she should have anticipated this. He had warned her that she was moving too fast.

"Are you calling the police?" he asked.

"No, that would risk exposing everything else—Beth's flower shop, the filming that will be taking place at the tai chi studio, possibly even the advanced technologies we haven't released yet. I trust the police to look for Jessica, but I can't assume that one of them won't pass on some bit of information they uncover to the anti-Disclosure faction—something that might harm us."

"So, what are you doing about Jessica?"

"The boys will try to contact her tonight. They have ways of communicating."

Jerry didn't ask any more questions about it. Truthfully, he didn't want to know. Vicki had told him about what she and her young friends had done to defeat the Partnership, and he still felt a bit freaked out by it. Even though that extraterrestrial had activated some of their junk DNA to give them special abilities, they had almost lost—they had nearly fallen to a power-hungry organization with alien technologies that wanted to control the world. It was unsettling to learn that the remaining parts of that organization—or its backers—might still be operational. No, it was better to focus on what he could control.

"If this is a bad time, I can come back later, but I need to update you on the military."

Vicki ran her fingers through her hair and motioned for Jerry to sit down. "No, go ahead. Leaving problems for later won't make them disappear. Tell me what I need to know."

"Sam Berger called me this morning—Captain Samuel Berger. He's not our official liaison with the Pentagon, but he and I became friends when we both worked at the U.S. Embassy in Warsaw. We've kept in touch since then."

Vicki nodded her head to show she was listening.

"Sam's latest assignment is working as a military advisor in the Office of the Secretary of Defense."

"Oh," said Vicki with understanding, "the same office as Colonel Riley, the one who believes the military should be the lead for anything to do with aliens."

"Not exactly the same office—the OSD staff numbers over 2,500 people—but Sam's department works on related issues, and he was assigned to take notes for his supervisor during a recent meeting."

Jerry had heard the disbelief in Sam's voice. While military personnel often took opposing stands on issues—and argued fiercely for their own points of view—they would ultimately back down and support the decisions made by the Secretary of Defense. Strict obedience to the chain of command remained a core military value.

"Apparently, it was mayhem," said Jerry. "No actual punches were thrown, but it was close."

"There are factions," said Vicki with understanding.

Jerry nodded. "Your friend, Colonel Riley, is one of the most outspoken on the need to seize control of the UFO issue from the State Department. Sam took a quick count; he estimates that about half the room is on board with moving forward as we are now, and a quarter are extremely unhappy."

"And the remaining quarter?"

"They're holding back until they can see who's going to win, then they'll join that side."

"What does our official Pentagon liaison have to say about this?"

He hasn't contacted us; I assume he's in the group waiting to see who wins.

Vicki stood up. "I think this deserves some coffee. Mary keeps a pot going in the staff room. Are you coming?"

"There's more," said Jerry. Vicki sat back down. "Afterwards, Sam's supervisor talked to him about what happened. And what happened at the meeting is only the half of it. Sam's boss knows one of Colonel Riley's colleagues, who told him the opposition is so fanatical because they believe extraterrestrials are... demons."

"You have *got* to be kidding me. In this day and age?"

"In this day and age," agreed Jerry. "Apparently, Riley's group has talked about going against the direct orders of the Secretary of

Defense to 'protect humanity' if necessary. Sam told me that there isn't anything concrete planned at this time, but he warned me that if it comes down to it, there will be weapons and violence. Probably fatalities."

* * *

Lewis wasn't happy. It wasn't right, taking the young woman like that. He didn't mind fighting, or even killing if he had to, but he had been raised to leave women and children alone.

When did life become so complicated? It had been simple for a while. It had been simple while he was working for the Partnership. He liked excitement, and he liked being in space. Sometimes they had to fight other people, but he liked fighting too.

Lewis also liked being strong. Because of the Partnership, he was one of the strongest men in the world. Not everyone was comfortable with that; sometimes, other people in the Partnership would avoid him, pretend not to see him. And then they would talk behind his back. They shouldn't have done that; biologic constructs also have augmented hearing.

Super-soldier was a better word to use than biologic construct; it told people what he was—one of the best fighters in the world. Some of the others, however, preferred to be called biologic constructs. They said being called super-soldiers made everyone assume they didn't have brains. Which was laughable, because the Partnership had downloaded the entire internet into each one of them when their consciousness was transferred from their flesh bodies to their construct bodies.

Larry had been one of those who preferred to be called a biologic construct. He said it was to remind himself that he was no longer human. Lewis didn't understand that—he felt just the same as when he had been flesh. Except that he was stronger, faster, and more clever.

The cleverness part was because of the internet download. He hadn't done too well in school.

But now the Partnership was gone, and most of the super-soldiers were dead. Lewis wasn't happy about either of those things. He hadn't been there the night headquarters was destroyed, but most of the others like him had. Only a few were still alive.

Larry was dead too. He had died while fighting against three of the remaining super-soldiers.

Lewis didn't understand Larry. The man had sacrificed himself to destroy one of the Partnership's reverse-engineered spaceships and the three super-soldiers on board. Lewis would never have gone against the Partnership—he owed it so much. The super-soldiers were meant to be a team; they were supposed to work together to accomplish their mission, not fight against each other.

It was probably because of the women. The spaceship Larry destroyed was trying to hurt some people who had taken something from the Partnership. No one could be allowed to steal from the Partnership, so Lewis approved of going after those people. But he wouldn't have agreed to hurting them. One of the people in the group was Larry's nephew, and you were supposed to protect family. Two of the people were women. One of them was Larry's special friend. The other was the young woman he helped snatch yesterday.

With the Partnership gone, Lewis didn't have a job anymore. He had been worried about that, but the client at the job site where he was working offered to bring him on as permanent security. He could live and work on the premises, which suited Lewis fine.

But he wasn't happy; women should be left alone. And this young woman locked up in the basement had somehow been connected to Larry, so she was almost family. He should be protecting her, not kidnapping her.

Lewis glanced at the camera monitor. The young woman—someone had said her name was Jessica—was still asleep, curled up on the bed. She hadn't woken up yet. Lewis wasn't surprised; he had used a heavy dose of chloroform last night, and she was still sleeping it off.

Lewis remembered how she looked when he stepped out in front of her last night. He had expected her to look scared. She *was* scared, but her strongest emotion seemed to be surprise. As if she had imagined that no one could hide from her. That was curious; she was clearly aware of the two men trailing after her.

He looked at the monitor again. Yes, Lewis was not happy.

Chapter Seven

J essica slowly opened her eyes, feeling disoriented. She sat up and swung her legs over the side of the bed, but stayed seated. The pounding in her head and dry mouth... Nausea rose in her throat as she frantically looked around, spotted a toilet in the corner, and heaved.

Where was she? What happened? Jessica checked her pockets, but didn't find her phone. She was so confused. She lay back down again and shut her eyes.

Then, it was later.

An hour later? Three hours? Jessica couldn't tell, but at least she could think again. Now she remembered how she had been attacked after leaving the tai chi studio. The two men had been following her, and then a third man had stepped unexpectedly in front of her and put a cloth over her mouth. That's when she lost consciousness.

Jessica frowned. The third man had caught her off guard. She'd been sensing the chi of the two men behind her, but hadn't picked up on the one in front. Jessica suddenly remembered her realization at the end—that the third man was a biologic construct.

* * *

"You're sure this will work?" Kiran's voice sounded both uncertain and hopeful; he wanted someone to reassure him. Unfortunately for him, neither Brad nor James was the reassuring type. If Jessica had been there, she would have reassured him, but Jess was gone.

Brad's voice was tense, almost angry; so much was riding on this. "My sister will do her part; we need to know you can do yours."

James watched the two of them talk. "Enough, already. Can you guys stop it? We've got to start."

James had been the one to suggest Kiran use his clairvoyant ability to find the best possible path to go down tonight. While it was a good idea, Kiran had received his DNA upgrade only a week ago, so it was still unreliable. James and Brad had spent the entire afternoon trying to help Kiran improve. Emotions were running high, and they were kicking themselves. Why had they put off making sure the newest member of the Four had control of his new ability? When Vicki had received her DNA activation, they had all but drilled her to ensure she learned to use her gifts.

"We got lazy," said James, to no one in particular. But Brad and Kiran both looked up; there was understanding in their eyes.

Yes, they had gotten lazy. They had made the assumption—a wrong assumption, it turned out—that they would no longer be targets. And now Jessica was in danger.

Still, they had a plan. The best part was that Kiran could predict they would successfully contact Jessica that night using the pocket out-of-time. Once that was established, James had Kiran explore several scenarios—some more unlikely than others—to determine the potential outcomes of specific actions.

Having Jessica wait for rescue wasn't an option. Kiran had glimpsed several days into that potential future. Not only was there no rescue, but there was also an event that Kiran refused to discuss with the other two—one that left him looking grim. There were several future possibilities in which Jessica successfully befriended her captors—especially a powerfully built man—but those timelines took months; they couldn't wait that long. In the end, only one set of actions gave Jessica a chance to escape.

"I'm not sure how that works," Kiran was saying.

"You don't need to," growled Brad. "You just need to look at it and see what's going to happen."

"The first time Vicki ever saw our advanced tai chi class," interrupted James, "we were all in a super-deep meditation. We were in a different vibration than the pocket out-of-time level that you already know. It's a much deeper level, affecting our existence on this plane. Our physical bodies became mist."

"Mist?"

"Not exactly mist, but pretty much invisible. Vicki couldn't see us, so she thought the room was empty."

That wasn't exactly true. His uncle Larry was a biologic construct and had never been able to reach that deep meditative state. Reaching it depended on activating specific segments of junk DNA—and the Partnership had excluded anything they deemed unnecessary when designing the bodies of the biologic construct. So, while Vicki wasn't able to see the rest of the advanced class, she could see his uncle. But there was no reason to tell Kiran about that now.

"Oh, I think I understand," said Kiran.

"Finally," muttered Brad.

"We need you to look at the possible outcomes if Jessica goes into that meditative state, and becomes invisible to the people who grabbed her. What happens? What can she do to escape, or at least figure out where she is so we can rescue her?"

It went more quickly after that. Using "invisible"meditation as the starting point, Kiran mapped out several possible outcomes connected to the various actions Jessica could take. Some ended in disaster, others in recapture.

There was one, however, that ended in success.

* * *

Once Jessica's mind cleared completely of the drug they had used to overpower her, she examined the small room. It contained a small bed, a sink, a toilet, concrete walls, and a concrete floor, with no windows. The prefab metal door had a latch, but it was locked from the outside.

Should she make some noise? Jessica frowned as she scanned the room. A camera was mounted near the ceiling in one corner. The red light signaled that it was on—she was being monitored. Jessica returned to sit on the bed. Whoever had taken her would reveal themselves when they chose to.

She missed her phone. What time was it? Judging by her stiffness, several hours had passed since her kidnapping. The boys must be frantic.

Well, there was one thing she could do.

Great minds think alike. When she emerged in the pocket-out-of-time, the three boys were already there. And for once, Kiran didn't hold back; he hugged her just as tightly as the other two.

After general expressions of relief and assurances that everyone was fine, the Four were left with a mystery. Who had kidnapped Jessica? And why? The boys' expressions turned grim when Jess told them she hadn't sensed the man who had drugged her.

"A biologic construct?" asked Brad. The only one among them who could sense the chi of a biologic construct was Vicki, and even she had to focus really hard.

Jessica shrugged. "I assume so."

"So, there are still surviving members of the Partnership who are after us."

"Not necessarily," said James slowly. The others turned to look at him. "The remaining biologic constructs are free agents now; someone else could have hired him."

"That would be a pretty big coincidence," argued Brad. "Biologic constructs already tried to kill us after the Partnership's headquarters was destroyed. I don't think it's an accident that the people who kidnapped Jessica had a biologic construct on their team."

"I don't think it's an accident either," clarified James. "The kidnappers probably knew about the Partnership—maybe they were even business associates—which is how they were able to hire one of the remaining super-soldiers. I'm just suggesting that this current group might not belong to the Partnership directly but could be a satellite group—one that would suffer financial loss if advanced alien technologies were introduced into our economy."

"The vested interests," said Kiran, with understanding.

"After all, they didn't kill Jessica or send us a ransom note. They just wanted her out of the way."

"That may be," said Jessica, impatiently, "but right now we need to focus on getting me out of here."

"We have a plan," said James, a little smugly.

Jessica flashed Kiran a smile—a sparkly one, of course, since they were in the pocket reality—as she listened to how he used his DNA upgrade to develop the plan.

Jessica had been missing for 24 hours, and it was nearly dusk. As soon as they left the pocket-out-of-time, she should go into deep "invisible" meditation. When her kidnappers checked the camera, it would appear she had escaped. They would go down to check the locked room, but they wouldn't be able to see her. When they rushed out to search the building and the neighborhood, Jessica could drop out of meditation and walk out the door because they wouldn't bother to lock the door of the "empty" room behind them.

"Shouldn't I wait until later in the evening? If it's darker, I might have a better chance," Jessica said nervously.

"I looked at all the future paths," said Kiran. "If you wait until later, more people will be coming; you wouldn't be able to get away."

Jessica followed the plan devised by the boys. Coming out of the pocket reality, she refocused and went immediately into invisible meditation. Kiran had told her she needed to stay there for 20 minutes.

"How can I tell when the 20 minutes are up? I don't have my phone, so I can't tell the time."

"Count slowly to 1,200," said James.

She had done so, and when she opened her eyes...

It had worked! The door was open. Glancing at the ceiling, Jessica saw that the camera's red light was still on. Kiran had told her not to worry about that—that no one would be monitoring it.

So Jessica Martinsson got up from the bed and walked out the door.

* * *

Lewis wondered if he was in trouble. Jessica had escaped.

But he wouldn't be the only one in trouble. There were four guards on the security team—two men, a woman, and one super-soldier (the super-soldier was him). No one had seen how Jessica had left the room. They had patrolled and monitored the entire day. No one had entered the property. None of them had gone down to the room where the young woman had been locked up. The camera footage would prove that.

It was the camera that showed them that Jessica had escaped. The client had arrived just before dusk; he wanted to make sure everything was prepared for the meeting that evening—more men were coming to discuss the 'current issue.' That's how the client referred to it, but Lewis knew it meant those men were unhappy about the advanced technologies being released.

Lewis snorted. They were so ignorant. Had *they* ever flown in a ship that seamlessly went from water to air to space? Had *they* ever sailed among the stars? It was so beautiful. Maybe they would think differently about it if they did.

When the client arrived that evening, he immediately went to look at the camera monitor. His scream was just like a little girl's, and all the security team had come running. The client couldn't speak; he just kept yelping and screaming and pointing at the monitor. That's when they noticed that the room was empty. They all pounded down the stairs to search.

Bridget—the female security team member—had to run back up the stairs to get the key because the room was still locked. When they finally opened the door, they found the room exactly as the camera had shown it—empty of its prisoner. With the client still screaming, they rushed back up the stairs and began their search: two inside the house, and two outside. Lewis liked how the rest of the security team looked to him for guidance. This situation spelled trouble for all of them. The team understood what he was and recognized that he was the strongest. And, as if by instinct, they knew that as long as they were with him, he would protect them.

It was good to be part of a team again.

Lewis was scouting around the neighborhood. Dusk had fallen, and it was full dark. He liked the night, but the sky he could see from planetside couldn't compare with the view from inside a spaceship.

He passed by the entrance to an alley, then quickly stepped back into the shadows. The low light didn't interfere with his vision, not when all biologic constructs had augmented eyesight. His night vision sharpened the world into crisp monochrome, and he could clearly see the young woman walking down the narrow alleyway in the other direction. Lewis watched as she paused for a moment. He wondered why, then saw a figure walk past the other end of the alley. Once the other person was well past, Jessica resumed walking.

How did she do that? The other person wasn't making any noise—he would have known because of his augmented hearing. But Jessica seemed to sense where people were.

Except for him.

Lewis watched as Jessica exited the alleyway and turned onto the street. He didn't like this; he didn't like this one bit. Women should be left out of it.

Lewis turned around and walked back towards the house.

Chapter Eight

K iran's phone lit up with a call from an unfamiliar number. He
lunged for it.

"Kiran? I'm out. Can you guys pick me up?"

The address she gave them was in Santa Monica. He didn't
know where it was, but Brad did. He gave Kiran directions to a
building on Pacific Palisades Beach Road, then directed him to pull
into the parking lot of what looked like an ivy-covered mansion.

An unsmiling security guard stopped them. When Kiran rolled
down the window, Brad leaned over to wave at the guard. "It's Brad
Martinsson; we're just here to pick up my sister."

The guard's expression cleared. "I didn't recognize the vehicle.
Where's the Bentley?"

The Bentley had been torched when the Partnership burned
down their mansion. Vicki had given them Beth's ten-year-old Toy-
ota to drive.

"In the shop." The guard nodded and motioned them
through.

"What was that about?" asked Kiran.

"We're driving a cheap old car," piped up James from the back,
"and we're at the Jonathan Beach Club—the most expensive club
in the city. Membership is by invitation only. It costs a *lot* of money—the initiation fee is just under $50,000."

Kiran glanced at Brad, who shrugged. "Our dad wanted to make sure we were mixing with the right crowd. To him, people who had the most money and the most power were automatically the right crowd."

Brad turned to stare out the window, and Kiran didn't ask any more questions. Jess and Brad's dad was dead, killed by Larry when he helped the Partnership track down his children. He'd tried to help someone *murder* his own kids. Enough said.

Kiran maneuvered the car through the parking lot. From this side, facing the Pacific Ocean, the club no longer resembled an ancient, ivy-covered building; instead, it exuded the vibe and appearance of a modern, very exclusive residence.

"There she is!" James pointed across the lot, and Kiran turned to pull up outside the entrance of what appeared to be a restaurant. And suddenly, Jessica was there, and they were all laughing and crying and hugging each other.

* * *

Back at the flower shop, everyone prepared drinks before settling down to talk. James made his usual hot chocolate, while Brad and Jessica both had lattés. Kiran sometimes had coffee, and sometimes chai. Tonight, he was drinking a latté in solidarity with Jess.

"You didn't recognize any of them?" Brad asked.

"No," said Jessica. The two men trailing behind me were too far away to see clearly. If I ever saw the man who chloroformed me—the biologic construct—I would recognize him, but I don't think I've ever seen him before."

"We need to figure out who they are," said James. He was focused, but despite having Jessica back safe, he felt stressed. They had to figure this out. "Are they a remaining faction of the Partnership, or are they someone else entirely? They didn't reach out to contact anyone or send a ransom note, so it's unlikely money was the issue. We think it might be connected with Disclosure and your high profile."

But Jessica had already figured it out for herself. "I'm the person everyone sees on the videos with Melly. The people who grabbed me are probably hoping that if I'm locked away, no one else will be able to do the same thing."

"Which is ridiculous," said Kiran, gently rubbing Jessica's arm. James hoped the two of them would move in together soon so he could start rooming with Brad. He was confident he'd be able to somehow talk his parents around.

"But they didn't kill you." Brad stared into his mug. "And since they didn't kill you, what was their purpose? Why did they want to keep you alive? They didn't send us—or Vicki—a ransom note, or even a threat like, 'Stop doing what you're doing or the girl dies.' So, what was the point?"

"Who profits?" asked James, quoting one of his favorite Roman statesmen, now long-dead. "While they might not have wanted to go as far as murder—which suggests that these people aren't from the Partnership—who would have profited if Jessica had been kept out of the public eye for a while? What was she doing by making the videos—and by being one of the co-stars?"

"She was making people excited; she was showing people there's another way to live," Kiran said quickly. "And Jessica is a good-looking young woman. She appears in videos talking to and being friendly with an ET who is so alien-looking that people might have expected it to play a role in a horror film. It might be embarrassing for people—men, especially—to admit that they're scared."

Jessica looked down and blushed slightly hearing Kiran describe her as good-looking.

James groaned internally; he hadn't seen it, and it was not good news.

"They're planning something," he said. The others looked at him curiously.

"What do you mean?" asked Jessica.

"They wanted you out of the way so you couldn't tell the true story. The men who kidnapped you don't want the world to think aliens are civilized. They don't want the world to see the aliens as people—as good people, no matter how scary they might look. They don't want the world to start thinking critically about why we're living in a reality filled with obsolete technology and outdated medical treatments. They want us all to believe something else."

"What?" asked Brad, staring at James steadily.

"They want the world to believe that aliens are evil, violent, lying monsters."

"But what would be the point?" Kiran asked. "They wouldn't be keeping Jessica locked up forever, would they?"

James was feeling sick; this was exactly the point. "They only needed to keep her out of the way until they made their move. Without Jessica to tell the world what aliens are really like, what do you think everyone would believe if they saw a spaceship attacking us?"

"So, you think some of the Partnership's reverse-engineered craft survived? And maybe a photonitron also?" Kiran had worked in the Partnership's technology development section. He had helped develop the photonitron, a device capable of creating moving 3D holographic images, including radar signatures. Before the Partnership's headquarters was destroyed, Kiran had smuggled out a photonitron to help the Four in their fight against the conglomerate. But he knew that several more existed.

"We were hoping that most of the reverse-engineered tech had been destroyed when headquarters was destroyed, but we know that some of it survived. The Partnership had three reverse-engineered spacecraft that weren't warehoused at headquarters. Larry destroyed one of them." There was a catch in James's voice when he mentioned his uncle, and then he continued. "What would the world think if the news programs broadcast videos of a spaceship violently attacking a city? Vicki could tell them they were human-origin, but she's a U.S. Government employee. To most people, Jessica would be more trustworthy."

Kiran's brows furrowed. "And if they also have a photonitron, the video might show a whole fleet of spaceships attacking; the holos can't be distinguished from physical objects, at least with the level of technology the world has today. The whole world would think it's an invasion."

"We don't even have a place to start," said James, with feeling. "We don't even know who your kidnappers were."

"About that," said Jessica. The three boys looked at her. She smiled smugly as she took a crumpled envelope from her back pocket. "I picked this up as I was leaving the place where they had me prisoner.

The envelope was an unopened utility bill.

Kiran was upset. "You were supposed to just follow the instructions we gave you; it was risky to do anything else!"

Brad glared at him. "You keep on underestimating my sister," he said coldly. "That would be a mistake. She is a full team member, not someone we need to protect."

This, of course, overlooked Brad's own protective instincts, but he would never voice them—at least not in public. He was fully capable of protecting Jessica in private.

James spoke up. "Uncle Larry used to talk about how we had to practice seeing each other as colleagues rather than family and friends. He told us it would be almost impossible to ask me—his young nephew—to do something dangerous, but he would send a colleague on that same mission if the future of humanity depended on it."

Brad nodded. That had been a tough lesson.

Jessica was annoyed. "I'm not an idiot. It's not like I was nosing around. There was a pile of unopened mail on a hall table by the front door—the front door I was in the process of going out of. There was no risk."

Kiran dipped his head in apology, but James was already over this spat; now they needed to move forward.

None of them recognized the name of the LLC listed on the utility bill. The address—the house where Jessica had been locked up—was also unfamiliar; none of them had ever visited that residence. They FaceTimed with Vicki to update her on Jessica's escape, and sent her a snapshot of the bill. They also discussed the possibility that the men who had kidnapped Jessica were planning some sort of false flag event—a human-led attack that would be portrayed as an alien invasion. Vicki promised them she'd have someone at the Department of State track down the owners of the house and investigate them—the Four were too vulnerable to being spotted and identified.

* * *

After the call with Vicki ended, the young people went about their business. Jessica was still drafting a framework for future videos with Melly. Although the tall mantis being was slowly winding down her duties on Earth, she would still continue to appear in interviews with Jessica. Kiran went with James to examine the memory crystal in more detail. James had agreed to let Kiran look more closely at India's history with extraterrestrials.

No one else noticed when Brad took the utility bill to his computer. He was irritated; there was no reason for the Department of State to investigate anything when he was a computer genius and a world-class hacker. The others were stuck in a rut, expecting to use their DNA upgrades the same way they always had. They had no imagination.

Brad had told Kiran that his sister didn't need protecting, and that was true, at least to a certain extent. Jessica didn't need to be protected any more than the rest of them. However, that didn't mean that Brad would just stand idly by while she was kidnapped or smeared by the press. He had stood aside for years while Jessica had been bullied by the Heirs—the children of their father's Partnership colleagues. He understood why that had been necessary—both his sister's pretense of being emotionally unstable and his own inaction—but that didn't mean he had to accept it anymore.

Yes, the others were stuck in a rut. They had grown accustomed to seeing Brad's computer skills as a form of protection. And they weren't wrong. No one had been able to trace them back to the flower shop, and, despite all the media coverage, no one had figured out who hacked the networks to broadcast the initial interviews between Jessica and Melly on every channel. Nor had anyone figured out how it had been technically possible. Meanwhile, Brad was still monitoring thousands of websites worldwide to ensure that the free energy schematics were accessible to anyone who wanted them.

But his skills weren't just defensive in nature. He imagined their faces when they realized he was going on the offensive.

Brad smiled.

CHAPTER NINE

This was Vicki's second press conference. Was it too soon, or not soon enough? Jerry didn't know. Truthfully, they were all flying by the seat of their collective pants.

It didn't help that Vicki was angry. Although Jessica had managed to escape safely, Vicki was rattled that the young people had been in danger—that they were probably still in danger. It made her angry that she hadn't realized this might happen. Jerry had cautioned Vicki to be more conciliatory, at least in public, but it didn't look like she was taking his advice to heart.

A balding gentleman was asking a question. "Is something being hidden from us? Why are we only being shown one alien species? Are they all bugs?"

Jerry was pleasantly surprised that Vicki didn't yell at the guy even though he deserved it. The media had all been warned. Vicki simply nodded at the Diplomatic Security guards, who stepped up and escorted the man out without a fuss. Vicki turned back to the remaining press representatives and offered a thin smile.

"To date, Representative Melly is the only extraterrestrial that has been introduced to humanity because the Galactic Federation decided to allow Earth's inhabitants an adjustment period before they invite us to join—or not. This is not the first time the Federation has introduced a species to the reality that they are *not* alone in the universe, that we have neighbors. It's an identity-shattering concept, and we need time to adapt. The Federation's permanent representatives to Earth will be arriving in a month, and they do not look like Melly; they are from a blue-skinned humanoid species that closely resembles us."

Vicki had told Jerry about her meeting with Galactic Federation representatives after she was rescued from an attack by the Partnership. Her description of the ETs in that meeting was incredible. He wished he could have been there.

Or maybe not. He was still a little unsure about how he would've reacted.

A female media representative was now asking a question. "Why did the Federation send Melly as humanity's first contact? Wouldn't it have been easier for us to meet someone who didn't look so... different?"

"First of all, Melly is a very high-ranking council member of the Galactic Federation. It's an honor to Earth that she was chosen for this task. Second, maybe the Federation selected someone from an insectoid species on purpose. After all, it flushed out a lot of xenophobic jerks, none of whom will be allowed a role in upcoming developments."

Vicki was now in bitch mode. Jerry was glad to see that the assembled press representatives recognized it, as well. The next question went off in an entirely different direction.

"In your last press conference, you spoke briefly about the upcoming vibrational shift and how portions of our junk DNA will be activated. This was covered in more depth by Representative Melly in one of the *Melly Speaks* interviews with Jessica. When the vibrational shift occurs, how much will we change? How much will our personalities change if we have ESP—if we can know what other people are thinking, or if we can communicate without words? Will we still be human?"

Jerry saw Vicki give her first genuine smile of the day.

"To answer your question, we need to understand who we are. We often overlook this—historically, we've viewed ourselves as the smartest, strongest, most powerful, and most creative life form in existence. But who are we if that's not entirely true? Who will we be if we aren't the smartest, the strongest, the most powerful, or the most creative? We're still us, and who we are has value. After the vibrational shift, we will probably have a stronger sense of empathy—it would be pretty hard not to if you can sense what the person next to you is feeling. I believe we will all have a better sense of humor because we'll be better able to see the absurdities in daily life... and appreciate them. We'll still be storytellers, and I think we'll find there will be better stories to tell. And while we might not be the most intelligent or the most creative species in the galaxy, we are at a high enough level to be candidates for membership in the Galactic Federation."

Jerry relaxed as he observed the press representatives taking notes. Another person stood up.

"What impact will the alien technology have?"

"Unlike what the Partnership had planned for us—I spoke of this at the last press conference—the alien technology will not replace our humanness with artificial machines. The Federation's initial goal in contacting us was to prevent that from happening. Ultimately, we are in charge of our own evolution. The Federation will, however, introduce advanced technologies that we can choose to adopt or not. Everyone is already familiar with the free energy schematics appearing on websites worldwide. We'll also be presented with breakthrough medical technologies that will reduce global suffering and add years to our lives. Industrial processes that don't pollute are also being considered. When Earth's permanent representatives arrive next month, they'll be able to discuss this in greater detail."

In the back of the room, someone stood up and waved their hand wildly. When Vicki nodded at him, he began to speak.

"There are many honorable, professional military personnel who claim the ETs are trying to trick us—that they're really trying to get our guard down so they can attack. They're the guardians of our national security. What do you say to that?"

It was a legitimate question, but the man's tone was aggressive. Jerry was relieved that Vicki managed to keep her voice calm.

"I would suggest that people consider who profits. The military and the Partnership have enjoyed access to these advanced technologies for nearly 70 years. For me, I often think about who profited from my sister dying of cancer when a simple outpatient treatment from the Partnership could have cured her."

Jerry was shocked. He knew about Beth, but Vicki had never publicly mentioned her death before. She went on talking.

"Also, who profits from people believing life is so scary and dangerous that someone needs to defend them? We all need to remember that the U.S. government has downed dozens of alien spacecraft over the last 40 years, but never once has there been any retaliation. Our military and intelligence believe that ET spacecraft are a threat to our national security because they don't control them."

There were more questions, but Jerry was deep in thought. Who profits? He was a finance guy; maybe that was an issue he needed to look into.

* * *

Kiran had just moved out of his family's home a week ago, but he was being welcomed back as if they hadn't seen him in months.

"*Raja!*"—my little king—his mother called out as he walked through the door. She stepped out of the kitchen, holding a large spoon in her hand. Kiran could smell the spices.

"Amma, I'm so glad to see you." He bent down and kissed his mother on the cheek. "Where's Papa?"

His mother didn't need to answer because his father came up behind her and embraced him. Kiran loved his parents; this was going to be a difficult conversation.

His mother had prepared a celebratory meal. His family wasn't vegetarian, so chicken biryani was the main dish. It was paired with slow-cooked black lentils, a mixed vegetable curry, and the little crispy balls made from yogurt and gram flour that he loved so much. His mother kept urging him to eat more. His father kept up a conversation about his new job, which he was thoroughly enjoying. Although his parents had become suddenly unemployed when the Partnership was brought down, their skills were in high demand. Thankfully, their finances remained healthy.

His 17-year-old sister, Aija, was, as always, sullen.

"But Kiran, enough about us. How are you doing?"

"You know I've moved in with Brad and Jessica Martinsson."

"That was so sad—their mother died only three years ago, and now their father is dead too. The poor children are orphans." His mother was incredibly compassionate.

Aija scoffed. Kiran shot her a glare before turning back to his parents.

"Since their house burned down, they're living in a building owned by a friend. I'm sharing a room with Brad."

"But what are you doing? Did you get another job yet?"

"I'm working with Brad and Jessica. Have you seen the *Melly Speaks* videos?"

Both his parents looked at him in shock.

"You've met that alien?" his father asked cautiously.

"Yes, I have been honored to meet with her; Representative Melly is an important and distinguished individual."

"Melly is a bug," muttered Aija quietly, but Kiran heard.

"Melly is *not* a bug," he snapped. "She is a high-ranking member of an ancient mantis species. She is more intelligent and more educated than we can ever hope to be."

"But we saw the videos," objected his father. "This alien is talking about all the changes that are coming. I'm not sure we're entirely comfortable with that."

Kiran looked steadily into his father's eyes. "Do you know who *would* be comfortable with that? Do you know who would be absolutely delighted that a family member is involved with extraterrestrials coming to Earth? Grandfather would be. All the changes Melly describes—the change in vibration and the new abilities—are the *Siddhis* that grandfather taught me. What is going to happen has already been written in ancient Hindu texts."

Kiran's father appeared startled. However, he had never studied yoga and meditation with his father like Kiran had, so this was not surprising.

"I'm sure that Jessica isn't in the ancient Hindu texts," said Aija spitefully. "She's such a loser. I wonder if the whole 'Jessica and the Bug' thing is a scam. Jess is too pathetic to do it on her own."

"Shut it, Aija!" said Kiran angrily. "Jessica is my girlfriend!"

Complete silence. *This* was the conversation he knew would be difficult.

"You're dating this young woman?" asked his mother.

Kiran nodded, not trusting himself to speak.

"But Jessica Martinsson is not a Hindu; she's not even Indian," protested his mother.

"I think we need to ask whether she's even human," Aija interjected maliciously.

"Aija! If you can't hold your tongue, please go to your room," Kiran's father ordered.

Aija pushed herself away from the table and flounced out.

Kiran's father turned back to him. "Do you love this girl? Are you treating her honorably?"

"Yes, to both questions," said Kiran.

Kiran's father looked at his wife. "We both knew that moving from India would mean our children might choose a different life than the one we would want for them. We've discussed this. We have raised our child well. Now Kiran is a man; we must trust him in this."

* * *

Aija was seething. Jessica—that dweeb—was famous and on TV; everyone was talking about her, admiring her. And now Kiran was not only standing up for Jessica, he was dating her! Since her parents always took Kiran's side, she couldn't expect any support from them. It wasn't fair.

Aija stood in front of the mirror. She was pretty; better yet, her friends told her she was exotic-looking—she drew people's eyes. She would shine in front of the camera. More so than Jessica. And she deserved to be more famous than that poser.

Now, that reporter Amanda had been nice—she had recognized that Aija had something important to say. Maybe she could work with Amanda to get the credit she deserved.

Chapter Ten

V icki was meditating. Her physical body remained in her office at the Department of State, but her vibrational essence wandered through the interior of the planet. She didn't understand how it worked. When she looked down at her meditation form, she appeared to have the same body as in physical reality—same clothes, same body shape, with arms and legs. When she raised her hands to her face, she could feel her eyes, nose, mouth, and hair. Yet here she was, walking inside the planet.

And, sooner or later, she would run into Junia—she always did.

How did Junia do that? How did she sense when Vicki was in that higher vibrational state—the one that allowed her to see Junia and her people? This same higher vibrational state also allowed Vicki to travel freely through solid matter like earth, rock, and clay—materials that would be solid barriers in everyday life on the surface.

Her ability to move freely around the planet came from Melly activating parts of her junk DNA, which strengthened her link to Earth's natural energies. In addition to traveling through solid rock, Vicki could also, when at this vibrational frequency, create sinkholes, trigger earthquakes, and manipulate underground water sources. She did all three that night when she destroyed the Partnership's headquarters. Just thinking about it made her queasy—even though the people who had been killed were Partnership employees, they had been innocent.

Vicki made her way to the granite-walled grotto in the cave system where she had first met Junia and found her seated on a stone ledge with her legs swinging.

How did she *do* that?

"You're getting faster," Junia beamed, bouncing to her feet.

"You're getting taller," Vicki replied, smiling. "Or am I shrinking?"

Junia laughed. "You're not shrinking. I just keep stretching up."

Junia was a member of the Suede Nation, an Earth-native species that lived in small communities in the planet's interior. (Vicki didn't know what shocked her more: that people lived inside the Earth, or that they *weren't* extraterrestrials.) Junia was young—about fifteen years old—and was wearing a light-colored smock. Her coppery dark hair fell in ropes just past her shoulders, and her eyes, a beautiful topaz color, were shaped like a cat's.

Yet, it was her skin that left the biggest impression on Vicki. A deep brownish-red, it resembled the softest, most stunning suede she had ever seen. That's why she had dubbed them the "Suede Nation," a nickname that delighted them so much they adopted it as their own. Vicki never discovered what name they had used for themselves before that.

"Come on," Junia said, holding out her hand. "Uncle Alun's waiting, and the elders want to talk. I hope they won't act grumpy—they've been grumpy all week."

Vicki took Junia's outstretched hand, following her as she stepped through the granite wall of the cavern, pulling Vicki after her.

Vicki didn't know if she'd ever get used to it. The first time she traveled with Junia, she had felt a resistance, as if the stone itself were deciding whether to let her pass. Now, it felt like moving through dense air, like pushing through heavy, dark clouds, but with less condensation.

They soon arrived at a Suede Nation settlement. It reminded Vicki of the pictures she had seen in history books of English medieval villages, but cleaner, better built, and made of stone. Gardens filled the spaces between houses.

And there was light. How did that happen? There was no sun, moon, or other visible light source that Vicki could see. It seemed as though everything was subtly glowing. She had discussed it with the Four after her first visit to the Suede Nation, and they had all agreed it must be some sort of natural luminescence.

Junia led them to a large building in the center of the town. "It's the Community Hall," she said to Vicki in a tone that indicated it was a place of importance.

Inside, Alun stood next to a quartz spire that stretched from floor to ceiling. Several elders sat in quiet conversation near its base.

"Vicki," Alun greeted her, bowing his head slightly. He wasn't as exuberant as his niece—his presence carried a certain gravity, But one that was tempered by kindness. "We are honored."

"The honor's mine," Vicki said, bowing in return. "Thank you for seeing me."

"We're past the point of hiding," Alun said. "The Earth has decided that for all of us."

Alun was referring to the upcoming shift in vibration. It wouldn't only be the humans and other beings that would experience it; the entire planet would shift. When that happened, the Suede Nation would become fully visible. The humans needed to be prepared so they wouldn't act... rashly.

Vicki inclined her head. "I understand there are some concerns?"

One of the elders stood up and spoke first—her voice was strained. "Humans forget. You label us as 'myth' and laugh us away. Then, when we return, you hunt. We do not forget what has been done."

Another elder, a broad-shouldered man, added, "But we also remember those who left us offerings—those who built the stone circles, and who heard us in the caves and the hills."

Alun placed a hand on the quartz spire. "We've been gathering records—stories passed down, embedded in song and stone. Humans know us as dwarves, elves, the daoine sídhe. Your own myths will help you remember. That may be our best path forward."

It felt like they were discussing real stories passed down through generations. Vicki made a note to look into fairy tales.

"It's brilliant," she said. "We can use that. People are more willing to accept new truths if it resembles something they've already heard about in stories."

"But stories won't be enough," Alun said. "They'll want proof." His voice carried a question, but he was right.

"Yes," Vicki said. "If possible, I'd like to record a video. A respectful one that includes interviews. It would be an introduction to the Suede Nation, not an exposé."

Alun paused. "We've prepared a doorway. In the Appalachians. Humans will be able to enter, briefly, without needing to shift their vibration."

"That's perfect." Vicki made a quick note in her head. "I'd like to bring a small team. This needs to be a worldwide event, not just something that's happening in the U.S. In addition to the camera and video people, I'd like to invite a few representatives from countries that have stories of little people."

Some of the elders nodded. One or two looked away.

Alun said, "Please choose wisely. Bring those who remember."

Then Vicki remembered the question that Kiran had asked.

"There's a Hum," Vicki said. "People are hearing it all over. A low, resonant sound, like muted trumpets. Does it mean anything?"

The elders fell silent. Then Alun spoke, his voice low.

"It is the Earth's song. Her preparation. The Hum means the shift is underway. You must prepare as well. Or be broken by the resulting distortion."

Vicki took a deep breath, recalling the tai chi classes and videos that the Four were organizing. "We'll try. We have to."

Alun's eyes remained steady. "Try harder. The Earth waits for no species."

* * *

Junia sat very still, her hands pressed against her knees, her whole body vibrating with effort. She wanted to burst. There was going to be a video! Seen by humans! On screens! Her cousin, Bowen, would pretend to be cool about it, but she knew he was just as excited.

She snuck a glance at him—he was standing off to the side, trying to appear mature. His eyes darted toward her, and she grinned. He didn't smile back, but his ears twitched. Ha. Definitely excited.

Uncle Alun stood with Vicki at the quartz spire, speaking in low, serious tones. Logistics. Entry tunnels. Delegates. Boring, boring, boring. She already knew about the tunnel—she and Bowen had helped smooth the passage walls with touch-singing, shaping the flows of the granitoid walls to resonate with human frequencies.

Junia tapped her fingers against her leg, then forced them to be still. The elders would definitely notice fidgeting.

"Junia and Bowen should be in the video," Uncle Alun said suddenly, his voice ringing out.

She blinked. Now she *had* to sit still.

"They are of the new generation," Alun continued. "Bridgers. The ones who will walk between worlds. Let the humans see them—see the future."

Junia kept her face calm and her mouth shut. But inside, she was spinning in delight. She felt her smile creeping up despite herself and didn't fight it. This was *huge*.

Bowen finally allowed himself a small smile, too; they were in.

Vicki turned to them with warm eyes. "I would love that. Thank you, both."

Junia gave a nod. Not too fast. Just enough to convey, *Yes, absolutely, I'm going to be the best ever at this and not scream like a surface-teen at a band concert.*

Vicki and Alun turned back to logistics.

"The tunnel begins in the Appalachian Mountains," Alun said. "The entrance is near the place you humans refer to as Pilot Knob. It opens every solstice when the veil is weak so that those who wish to visit each others' worlds can do so easily."

"Do we need to wait for the solstice to bring the other humans down?" Vicki asked.

"No," Alun said. "We've already completed the preparation. The frequencies are active now."

Junia tried to pay attention, but her thoughts were racing. She was going to be *seen*. She imagined her face on human screens, imagined them saying, *There—see? They're real.* All the drawings in human books, the carvings in old temples—they'd look again and know.

Then Vicki asked about the Hum again.

Junia's excitement dimmed a little. The Hum always made her stomach turn. She liked the sound—but what it meant? That was different.

Alun spoke again: "The Earth is adjusting her tone. It's like tuning an instrument. But some strings are tangled. If humans don't shift, they will snap."

Junia fought the urge to groan. She knew this was important, but she wanted to talk about *her part in the video*. What would she say? What should she wear? Maybe she'd ask Alun about that.

She imagined standing before a camera, speaking to the humans. "We've been here all along. Watching. Waiting. Caring for the Earth you walk on."

No. That was too dramatic. Maybe she'd let Bowen go first.

The meeting continued as Vicki took notes. The elders discussed ceremony protocols, foods (could humans eat Suede foods?), the connectivity issues when recording beneath countless layers of rock.

Junia leaned her head toward her cousin, who stood beside her.

She whispered toward Bowen, "Afterward, let's practice what we'll say in the video."

He nodded without looking at her.

This was going to be *amazing*.

* * *

Bowen watched as Junia led Vicki back to the grotto where the two usually met. Vicki didn't need an escort, not anymore, but Junia was so enthusiastic that Vicki always smiled and took his younger cousin's hand to lead the way. It was hard to say no to Junia.

Everyone liked Junia; he did too. She was so curious and bright and happy. It was surprising to many of them—him included—that Junia still welcomed contact with humans after what happened to her parents. After that, his father—Alun—had taken her into the family. Junia and Bowen had been raised as siblings.

Junia often accused Bowen of being overprotective, but he would just shrug. He *was* overprotective. He was two years older, and Junia, frankly, needed protection. Deserved it.

Junia would make an excellent representative for the Suede Nation. He wasn't so sure about himself. He glanced back at his father; Alun was still in conversation with the elders. Bowen would need to ask him later whether he had been nominated for the video just to keep an eye on Junia—to keep her safe.

Bowen's eyes followed Junia and Vicki as, chattering happily to each other, they disappeared through a stone wall.

He wasn't sure whether any of this was a good idea.

Chapter Eleven

Vicki surfaced slowly from her meditation. She took a breath to ground herself, shaking off the lingering vibrational frequency of the Suede Nation. It was still morning, and soft light streamed through her office window. She'd barely centered herself when the door burst open.

"Vicki." Jerry's voice cracked. His face, typically ruddy from too much coffee and not enough sleep, was now chalk-white. "It's Lagos."

Her mind snapped into gear. "What happened?"

He closed the door behind him and grabbed the remote from her desk. "An attack. Just—watch."

She turned to the screen as he powered it on. A shaky news feed flickered to life. A large disc-shaped craft hovered above buildings, with the Lagos skyline in the background. The captions informed them this was Yabacon Valley—and it was ablaze. The camera zoomed in as a blinding beam of light burst from the underside of the craft, obliterating an entire neighborhood in seconds.

Her stomach turned to ice.

The feed cut to chaos: people running, sirens howling, news anchors shouting over each other.

Vicki's heart thudded. "This *has* to be one of the Partnership's surviving reverse-engineered craft. Someone got hold of it, and now they're carrying out the false flag event the Partnership had planned for before we destroyed it. What are people saying?"

Jerry stood rigidly by her side. "They're calling it an alien attack."

Vicki gritted her teeth. "But there's like a 99% likelihood it's a reverse-engineered craft with humans at the wheel."

He nodded. "Probably is. But optics matter. And the optics are bad."

She stared at the video again, her heart pounding. Lagos had been the leader of Africa's free energy revolution—a hub of innovation. It was one of the few places on Earth where free energy technology could flourish without Western interference. Ironically, this was because the Nigerian government had been too corrupt to manage it, leaving its private sector unfettered and bold.

"Who benefits?" she said aloud.

Jerry ran a hand through his hair. "Who always benefits when progress is burned to the ground?"

"Oil cartels. Energy companies. Anyone who has something to lose."

But another thought took shape in her mind. "What if we're thinking too small? What if the attack isn't just about energy? What if the goal is to convince the world that extraterrestrials are a security threat—and that the military should be the ones in control?"

Jerry's eyes widened slightly. "You think it's Colonel Riley and his supporters?"

"I don't know if it's Colonel Riley or other like-minded individuals. I just know that there are factions in the military and intelligence agencies who are livid that Disclosure is happening and that they aren't in control. What better way to demonstrate they should be in charge than by staging a false flag attack? A war clearly falls within the military's domain, not the State Department's."

Jerry looked sick. "And they're willing to kill all those people to get their way. So probably the destruction of Lagos is only a warning shot—and an example of how far they're willing to go. We can assume there will be more attacks if we don't give in."

Vicki switched off the screen, blood pounding in her ears. "We need a press statement. Now."

Jerry straightened up and gave a brisk nod. "Already called the comms team. You go on in twenty. But what are you going to say?"

She grabbed her blazer from the back of her chair and checked her reflection in the mirror. She looked pale, but her eyes were determined.

"We tell the truth. Carefully. But this isn't just about aliens anymore. It never was."

*　*　*

James stood up and turned off the flat screen. The image of Vicki delivering her press conference lingered, her bearing calm and deliberate, her language meticulously chosen.

"I repeat: This was NOT the action of our extraterrestrial partners. All signs point to a false flag operation, likely involving rogue Earth-based factions using reverse-engineered technology. Evidence points to the Partnership's human-developed craft. We urge global unity, calm, and critical thinking."

Bullseye, James thought. But it wouldn't be enough.

They were in the common area of the flower shop. Kiran and Jessica were sitting side by side of the sofa. Their relationship had progressed to the point that Kiran felt comfortable draping his arm across Jessica's shoulders. Brad sat cross-legged in an armchair, working on one of his several laptops.

"She did the best she could," Jessica said, her tone tentative.

"And now it's up to us," James said. "Vicki has to hold the line politically. But we—we have to hold the line energetically."

Brad leaned forward, elbows on knees. "More tai chi classes?"

"That's the beginning," he replied. "But we need to scale. Mass classes. Parks. Beaches. Cities. Anyone who can move energy needs to be teaching. And every person we teach lifts the field for everyone."

Jessica's eyes lit up. "Group coherence. It multiplies."

Brad scratched his head. "What about the media? I can hack all the networks, but this is such a major story, they might be willing to broadcast it if we just ask. They might even be willing to do a lot of the work themselves—things like livestream events, and community broadcasts."

"Do it," James said. "Try to get other studios involved. We need to push this globally. If we wait for the governments to act, we'll lose the people."

Jessica tapped her phone. "I can get us an app for guided practices and notifications. We can geo-tag group meditations to create energetic nodes."

James felt a rare surge of hope. "Perfect."

"We also need to teach meditation," Kiran said. "Not just quieting the mind—actual techniques to make contact."

"Like Dr. Greer's CE-5 protocols?" Jessica asked.

Dr. Steven Greer's CE-5—Close Encounters of the Fifth Kind—protocols were a set of meditation-based techniques designed at establishing peaceful, human-led contact with ETs. The objective was for ordinary people to meditate and reach out to ETs, bypassing government middlemen and their fear-driven narratives about aliens.

"Exactly. It's time for average people to take the reins. Vicki's got diplomacy, but real transformation starts on the ground. We need to raise our collective vibration before the Earth goes through its own vibrational shift. If not, a lot of people might not make it. Humanity also needs to connect with all its neighbors. Vicki told us she'll be introducing the Suede Nation soon. I'm not sure about the Alpha Centaurians..."

Brad leaned forward. "Speaking of the ACs, what about the memory crystal?"

James's fingers twitched. He could still feel its heat, the pulse that surged when it first touched his palm. As the Four's historian, Vicki had assigned him the task of managing the historical records embedded in the memory crystal. A gift from the Galactic Federation, it contained a complete archive of all interactions between humans and ETs over thousands of years. Unfortunately, some of those interactions with the ACs resulted in countless of human deaths.

James grew serious. "Not yet. The crystal's truth is too much. If we make all the crystal's information public now, it'll backfire. People aren't ready to learn what happened in the past. Not until they trust the present."

Jessica looked down. "All the deaths. The destruction of entire civilizations. The ACs here now didn't do that—it was the fault of their ancestors thousands of years ago."

"No," agreed James. "It wasn't their fault. But humans like things in black and white."

Kiran looked over at him. "Especially when they're being manipulated."

James turned toward him. "What do you mean by that?"

* * *

Kiran didn't like sharing his internal experiences. And they'd been odd lately—almost slippery. But these were the people he trusted most.

"I've been hearing things during meditation," he said finally. "Not words. Not thoughts. I've been getting impressions—disruptions. Like someone else is in there with me. I've been hearing things when I've been practicing clairvoyance also."

Jessica tilted her head. "Like other entities?"

"No. Not like we communicate with Melly. This feels... technical. Artificial. It doesn't flow—it pulses. It's pretty crude. Like someone trying to break in."

James frowned. "Psychotronic interference?"

At the same time, Brad asked, "You're saying someone's built a machine that does psychic interference?"

Kiran nodded. "Yes, to both of your questions. It's weak right now. Like they're testing what it can do. But it's real. And if they ramp it up, they could sway public opinion before people even realize this is happening."

He paused, then added, "A few days ago, I was meditating in the gardens behind the tai chi studio. There was no wind, no EMF spikes—everything was stable. But about fifteen minutes in, I felt a jolt, like a low-frequency pulse just behind my eyes. It shattered the stillness. I started seeing this red spiral—it felt artificial, synthetic. I could tell it wasn't anything from me. It was like a projection that was injected into my mind. I couldn't stop it. It hijacked the session."

Jessica's expression grew more serious. "And during clairvoyance?"

"Worse," Kiran said. "When I tried to focus on finding the path forward for releasing the information on the memory crystal, the image blurred every time I concentrated. But not in the usual way—not like natural psychic static. It felt like a signal jam. Like the moment I locked on a potential path, it was like I was bounced back. One time I even got audio—snippets of numbers, coordinates, and then a harsh buzzing. The tone followed me out of trance. It lasted for a few minutes before it faded."

Jessica whispered, "Someone is tracing psychic activity?"

Kiran nodded. "Or scrambling it. Then yesterday, while I was walking to the coffee shop, I felt a pressure in my head. Then this hollow thought—not mine—slid in. Just five words: *You are not safe here.* But it wasn't a thought. It was more like... programming."

"Mind control," Jessica said softly.

"It's more subtle than that," Kiran replied. "More like shaping a dream. It's nudging ideas, fears, emotions—just enough to shift a perception. And when you multiply that across a population..."

Brad looked grim. "So, we're not just battling lies in the media. We're battling psychic warfare."

James's jaw tensed. "Then, no wonder the response to Vicki's speech was so divided. Half the networks were calling for war. The other half were silent."

"They want chaos," Kiran said. "And they're seeding it mentally as well as physically."

Jessica looked down, took a breath, then looked up again. "Then we need to teach shielding, too—stuff like psychic defense, grounding, and anchoring. All the old metaphysical woo-woo stuff."

"And track the source," Brad added. "This kind of tech should a trace, shouldn't it? If we can find the signal, we can block it."

James nodded. "Let's get ahead of it. We raise the vibration. We educate. We shield. And we shine so brightly they can't hide anymore."

Jessica nodded slowly. "You think it's connected to the Partnership?"

Kiran gave a tight smile. "Anything that helps people evolve and take control of their lives scares whoever's left of Partnership—and anyone else who wants to stay in control. And they're especially afraid of this vibrational shift."

Outside, there was a soft rumbling in the distance. Thunder? Or perhaps, Kiran thought, it was something deeper.

The Hum was sounding again.

Chapter Twelve

The soft click as he closed his front door was the best sound Jerry had heard in hours. It was late—already dark—but he was finally home.

He toed off his shoes, and dropped his work bag by the door. From the living room came the gentle murmur of soft jazz—maybe Dave Koz, but he wasn't sure. The house smelled of roast chicken and warm milk.

Anne appeared in the doorway, with her hair in a loose bun, a burp cloth over her shoulder, and their five-month-old son dozing peacefully against her chest. Her eyes met his, scanning his face. "You're late," she said softly.

He didn't bother making excuses. "Long day."

She nodded. "I saved our dinners. Josh is already in bed. Adam just fell asleep a few minutes ago."

Jerry approached, leaned in, and kissed his son's fuzzy head, then Anne's temple. "You're a sight for sore eyes," he said.

"Tell me something I don't know," she joked and handed him the baby to put down for the night.

By the time he returned to the kitchen, Anne had plated the food and poured two glasses of wine. A baby monitor sat on the counter, but Adam had been sleeping through the night since he was a month old. Josh, on the other hand, would be up by 5 a.m. sharp.

They ate in silence for a while—Jerry devouring his chicken and rice as if he were starving, while Anne picked at hers. He could feel her watching him, waiting.

"You've been quiet for days," she said finally.

"I've had things on my mind."

Anne raised an eyebrow. "Jerry, the capital of Nigeria was attacked today. I have pillows that know more than I do. Talk."

He wiped his mouth, set down his fork, and took a long sip of wine. "So... Lagos."

Anne looked at him, but didn't say anything.

"It wasn't the aliens. Nor was it a terrorist attack or a hostile nation. It was us."

She froze. "What do you mean 'us'?"

"Humans, not ETs. We're not entirely certain about the make-up of the group—it could have been military, a faction of contractors involved in black budget projects, or even private-sector firms that stand to lose profits. Or maybe a combination of all three. The so-called alien spacecraft that attacked Lagos was actually reverse-engineered by government contractors. So, this was a false flag event to justify hostility towards aliens and seize more control."

Anne's voice was low. "How can you even know this?"

"I didn't—none of us did—when it first made the news this morning, but we suspected. Especially since ETs have never retaliated in the past, even in cases when our military attacked and downed their craft. But by early afternoon, we were receiving reports, eyewitness accounts, and data signatures. It all points to a human-built spacecraft."

He hesitated. "And one more thing."

She waited.

He ran a hand through his hair. "Jessica was kidnapped, briefly, during the fallout. She's safe now, but... it's likely there's going to be more violence."

Anne's eyes grew wide. She hadn't met any of the Four, but Jerry had told her how instrumental the young people had been in bringing down the Partnership.

"And at least one of the Partnership's super-soldiers survived. Biologic constructs—not robots, but not quite human either—are weapons. We thought they had all been killed when the Partnership's headquarters was destroyed, but at least one of them was involved in Jessica's kidnapping. So it's working with those who are fighting to bury the truth and maintain control. The Four are being targeted."

Jerry leaned back in his chair. Now that he had started expressing his worries, he couldn't stop.

"It's not just the military or the rogue contractors anymore. The SEC's trying to push through new regulations regarding undeclared profits from reverse-engineered technology, but now corporate resistance is starting to organize. Lagos may have given them the leverage they needed."

Anne finally spoke. "And Vicki? Where is she in all of this?"

He paused again. "Vicki was the one who destroyed the Partnership's headquarters, Anne."

She stared. "She what? What do you mean by that?"

Taking a sip of wine, Jerry said, "She literally destroyed it. You watched all the entire *Melly Speaks* series and the press conferences."

Anne nodded.

"So you know about the vibrational shift and how humans will gain certain abilities because their junk DNA will be triggered."

Anne nodded again.

"Melly activated Earth energies in Vicki. As a result, Vicki was the one who triggered the earthquake and caused the sinkhole that destroyed the Partnership's compound last month."

"I thought the new abilities would be things like telepathy and ESP," said Anne, shocked. "What would happen if everyone could cause earthquakes?"

"I'm afraid," confessed Jerry, avoiding Anne's eyes. "Vicki won't slow down. She thinks the public has a right to know, that we need to unify across species to survive whatever is coming next."

"Do you disagree with her?" Anne asked, softly.

"No, I don't, but I'm afraid. I'm afraid for you and the children. A powerful elite and at least one super-soldier are fighting against this, and they've shown themselves willing to kill to get what they want. I'm afraid that continuing to work on this will put us all in danger."

Anne sipped her wine and looked at him over the rim of her glass. "Do you want to quit?"

Jerry finally lifted his eyes to look at Anne, his expression agonized. "I don't know. Vicki needs me—someone she's known for years and can count on to have her back. But it's getting dangerous. Vicki is being reckless; I think she underestimates how far the elite will go to maintain control."

"Do you trust her?"

"Of course I trust her," he answered immediately, almost belligerently. "This is *Vicki* we're talking about."

Then he sat for a moment and added more quietly, "But this fight might destroy us all before it saves anyone."

Anne reached across the table and took his hand. "I can tell you want to stay."

"I don't know if I should." He squeezed her fingers. "It's getting too close. Our names are on more files than I like. You, the kids... I'm starting to think staying loyal to her might put all of us in danger."

Anne didn't answer right away. She tilted her head, eyes narrowed in thought. "Don't decide tonight. You're exhausted. Wait a week or two and see what happens."

He looked at her. "What if what happens isn't good?"

"Then we leave. Quietly. Somewhere safe. You've done enough."

He reached for her hand again, this time not to make a point, but to hold on.

"Okay," he said. "We'll wait one more week."

* * *

The sound of the wine glasses settling in the sink seemed louder than it should have. The house was quiet; the air conditioning humming, the music playing softly from the living room, and the rhythmic creak of the floorboards as Jerry walked down the hall toward the bedroom.

Anne turned on the faucet, rinsing bits of food from the plates, her motions slow and deliberate. She didn't want to rush. She didn't want to think too quickly, either.

Not yet.

The steam rose from the water, and her hands moved automatically: rinse, then stack in the dishwasher. Her fingers brushed against a fork and lingered there, her mind drifting back to the call from earlier that afternoon.

James had called the house.

She knew it meant that events were becoming serious. From what Jerry had shared with her, James wasn't needlessly anxious. If he had circumvented protocol to call their house directly, it meant he was concerned about Vicki.

"The Four are worried," James had said. *"Vicki's taking on too much. The destruction of the Partnership, Lagos, the media clampdowns, the corporate retaliation—she's on every radar that matters. We think she's becoming too central. Too exposed."*

Anne had listened carefully. She'd asked questions. She'd offered no promises.

Then he'd said the name: *Greer.*

Anne turned off the faucet, letting the water drip into the basin.

Dr. Steven Greer. The controversial medical doctor turned UFO researcher. Publicly dismissed. Privately... another matter.

The Four wanted to establish a new line of contact—one that didn't run through Vicki. Not to undermine her, but as a way to take off some of the burden. And the CE-5 protocols—whatever those truly entailed—might be the best opportunity for average people to create decentralized, civilian-level engagement with the aliens. The real aliens.

Dr. Greer wasn't a stranger. Anne had already reached out to him weeks prior, quietly seeking the names of corporations that were illegally profiting from alien technology. She had been surprised by how generous he had been with his time, and even more impressed with his archives. She hadn't expected to ever contact him again.

But now James was asking, Jerry was too stressed, and Vicki couldn't afford to face another front. The Four were right: if too much of the responsibility was given on a single person, it was only a matter of time before that person cracked—or was taken off the board entirely.

Anne dried her hands on a dish towel and glanced toward the hallway where Jerry had disappeared. A lamp glowed softly near the baby's door. Just enough light to see; not enough to disturb.

She wouldn't tell Jerry. Although she hadn't said it, she was more frightened about what might happen if the elites won than about any current threats. The Partnership had intended to take control of humanity, and even though the organization had been destroyed, others were taking up the cause.

Anne had felt genuine shock when Jerry told her that Vicki had destroyed the Partnership's facility—the raw power it must have taken was unimaginable. However, she also understood why Vicki had done it: the future of everyone was at stake.

She would do this herself. She walked over to her laptop on the counter and typed a message to Dr. Greer outlining what was need-ed. Hovering over the keyboard, her fingers flexed before she tapped *Send*, not giving herself a chance to second-guess her decision.

Anne paused for a moment, letting the significance of it sink in. Jerry couldn't know. Not now. Not with the look he'd had tonight—the unspoken panic in his eyes. She saw it clearly, no matter how he tried to hide it.

He was unraveling by degrees. She couldn't allow this to add to his burdens.

Better for him to see her as the support system—the anchor at home. Which was funny considering Anne's position at the law firm meant she out-earned him. No matter; she had another month of maternity leave to enjoy, so until then, she could play home defense, letting him carry the front-facing risk. She would handle the rest—behind the curtain—in the gaps between sleep cycles and diaper changes.

Anne turned off the kitchen light and padded down the hallway barefoot. The silence was heavy now, the kind of silence filled with unspoken truths.

Tomorrow, she'd check for a reply from Dr. Greer.

But tonight, she would lie beside her husband and pretend the world wasn't falling apart just beyond their bedroom door.

Chapter Thirteen

The water was still cold, just as it had been when they were children. Vicki was back in her dreamscape again.

The stream wound through the woods, bubbling over the stones and roots, murmuring secrets to the grassy banks. The trees hadn't aged a day. The sky was locked in that impossible late-afternoon glow, where time stalled and shadows stretched long.

Vicki sat on the smooth rock they used to call "the throne," knees drawn to her chest, her bare toes flirting with the water's edge. The air smelled of wet pine.

"I thought I'd find you sulking."

Vicki didn't turn. "I'm not sulking."

"Then brooding, maybe."

She smiled, despite herself. The voice behind her was warm, amused, and carried a hint of mischief. It was exactly as she remembered. Vicki looked back and saw Beth stepping through the dappled light in jean shorts and a loose flannel shirt. Her hair was pulled up in a messy ponytail. Such beautiful hair—Beth had lost it all from the chemo before she died.

"You come when I least expect you," Vicki said softly.

"Are you entirely sure you didn't call me?" Beth dropped down beside her on the rock, tucking her legs underneath herself.

Vicki exhaled. "Maybe—maybe not."

"I thought so." Beth bumped her shoulder. "So? Are you just going to sit here and pout at the stream? You used to catch frogs and throw them in."

Vicki didn't answer. She stared down at the water, watching her own faint reflection shimmering just below the surface.

"I just wanted a place that didn't hurt," she murmured.

"And this is it?" Beth asked. "A dream of a stream that hasn't existed since it was paved over for that development over a decade ago?"

"It's my dream," Vicki protested. "I can pretend."

Beth tilted her head, watching her. "You never used to want to pretend. You were the one who insisted on the truth. On answers. On *more*."

"I got more—more than I asked for," Vicki said, her voice flat. "In fact, I got all of it... and then some."

Beth said nothing. The stream did the talking for a while.

Finally, Vicki spoke again. "The world isn't ready."

"Ready for what?"

"Any of it." She rubbed her eyes with closed fists. "Disclosure. The spaceships. Aliens. The Galactic Federation. The fact that humans aren't the top of the food chain anymore. I knew there'd be resistance. I planned for bureaucratic turf wars, religious backlash, maybe even riots. But this..." She swallowed. "It's getting personal. Someone tried to take out the Four. Jessica was kidnapped. All of them are walking around, expecting to see assassins jump out from behind every tree. And now Jerry—Jerry's falling apart. Anne too. And they were *never* supposed to be part of this."

"But they are," Beth said gently. "Because they chose to be. You didn't force their hands."

"Maybe I didn't have to."

Beth looked at her carefully. "I don't think I understand what you're saying."

"Maybe I'm dangerous," Vicki replied, her voice low. "Not in the way they use it in news stories about criminals, but in the gravitational sense. Like I pull people into my plans, and they get caught in the crossfire."

Beth leaned back on her elbows. "You're talking like the entire story is already written."

"Isn't it?" Vicki asked. "Melly warned me. She said the Earth was volatile. The Galactic Federation has protocols, and if we can't stabilize ourselves, humanity won't get a seat in the room."

"She also said you were the most promising part of the equation," Beth countered.

Vicki's breath caught. "She said that? When? You've talked to Melly?"

Beth gave her a half-smile. "Vicki. You're acting like physical reality on Earth is the only reality there is. Of all people, you should know that's not true."

That stopped Vicki cold.

"You haven't reached out to her," Beth added. "Why not?"

"I... I don't know." Vicki felt guilty.

"Yes, you do."

Vicki sighed. "Because I'm afraid Melly will tell me it's too late—that we somehow missed the window. I'm afraid she'll say that Lagos, the Partnership, the retaliation... it all proves the point. That humans aren't ready to be anything but scared little apex predators with fragile egos and billionaires acting as warlords."

"But that's not what you believe."

Vicki turned, finally meeting her sister's eyes. "Isn't it? Some days I'm not sure anymore."

Beth's gaze softened. "Then maybe it's time to ask. Time to check in."

Vicki looked back at the water. A frog jumped from a stone and vanished into the stream. Ripples expanded, broke, and faded.

"I wanted to be someone who could do something," she said. "Someone who stood on the edge of something different and reached out. But now... I feel like I'm bleeding to pieces just trying to hold the line."

Beth's voice was quiet. "Then stop holding. Start *sharing*. Delegate. Trust. You don't have to carry all this alone."

"No," Vicki said. "But everything seems to hinge on me."

"Huh. Everyone needs grounding, everyone needs sounding boards," Beth said. "Talk with Melly. Ask her for the Federation's timeline. Ask what's expected of Earth. Ask what's next. And *stop pretending you're alone in this.*"

Vicki nodded, just once.

Beth leaned in and kissed her on the temple. "You're doing better than you think."

"I miss you," Vicki said. She did—with a pain that was so constricting she had a hard time breathing.

"I'm always here."

The dream shifted. The water dimmed.

Vicki woke up, her face wet with tears.

* * *

She stayed in bed for several minutes, staring at the ceiling. Beth had died. Did anything else really matter? She grabbed the remote to turn on the television, then rolled onto her side and pulled the covers tighter, her eyes fixed on the ticker scrolling beneath a suited anchor's solemn tone:

"*—rising tensions as the German Bundestag becomes the fifth European legislature this week to pass strict control laws on decentralized energy grids, citing national security and economic stability—*"

She sighed and turned the volume up.

"*Germany's new policy, titled the Energiestabilitätsgesetz, mandates that all free-energy units—whether home-based or community-shared—must be registered and remotely monitored by federal regulators. Private ownership remains legal, but commercial distribution will now require a federal license, and foreign ownership of energy tech companies is under immediate review. This follows similar actions by Canada, Japan, and the United Arab Emirates, all citing concerns about rogue states, economic volatility, and the potential for catastrophic grid destabilization.*"

"Catastrophic," Vicki muttered, rubbing her temples. "Right. And we all know what economic volatility means."

The anchor didn't pause.

"In the U.S., Senator Rusk has introduced legislation proposing a 70% federal tax on profits generated by post-contact technologies, including zero-point energy converters, anti-gravity transit, and advanced medical devices not based on pre-2025 patents. The bill has already drawn protest from citizen groups and independent researchers, many of whom accuse Congress of colluding with multinational energy conglomerates."

Vicki got up and pulled on her robe. Coffee. She needed coffee before she started screaming into her pillows.

She shuffled barefoot into the kitchen, switching on the television in the corner before opening the cupboard to take out the coffee beans.

ESTONIA DECLARES FULL ENERGY SOVEREIGNTY flashed across the screen in bold lettering. Vicki paused.

A young, sharply dressed reporter stood in front of an impressively designed building with a pink stucco façade. The ticker identified it as Estonia's parliament house.

"With a population just under 1.5 million, Estonia has become the first nation to formally disengage from Europe's Energy Charter Treaty, declaring itself 'energy sovereign' and officially withdrawing from the North Seas Energy Cooperation initiative. The announcement followed the successful integration of decentralized zero-point generators into all major municipal systems."

A clip played—Estonian President Peep Veedla, standing at a podium, flanked by businessmen, scientists, and engineers.

"From this day forward," Veedla said with quiet pride, *"no Estonian will be held hostage by oil cartels, private energy brokers, or foreign influence. We power ourselves, together."*

Vicki smiled, just a little, as she added the ground beans to her coffeemaker and pressed the button. While Estonia's success couldn't be duplicated by most other countries—its small, scattered population meant that the "major municipal systems" probably numbered fewer than a dozen—it made her happy to see someone benefit from this.

Then the feed cut again. A new line of text slid across the screen, and her chest tightened:

BREAKING: CHILEAN PRESIDENT ASSASSINATED IN SANTIAGO

Her smile vanished.

The image was grainy at first, handheld—chaos unfolded on the steps of the Palacio de La Moneda. There were screams and smoke. One clip showed security agents dragging a limp body toward an armored vehicle. Then came a still frame of President Tomás Silva—he who had been vibrant and fierce in every interview Vicki had ever seen—lying bloodied, one arm twisted beneath his body.

The anchor returned.

"Silva had been a vocal advocate for full transparency regarding extraterrestrial contact and advanced technologies, even pushing to open Chile's airspace for direct peaceful engagement with aliens. Sources within the Chilean Ministry of Defense indicate that the suspect is believed to be a Brazilian national with ties to a shadowy paramilitary group known as Falcão Negro, possibly acting on behalf of petroleum interests threatened by Silva's aggressive push to eliminate dependence on fossil fuel imports."

Vicki reached for her mug, her hands trembling slightly, and poured herself a cup of coffee.

One hundred twenty-five billion dollars a year in oil revenue, she thought. *Of course, someone pulled the trigger.*

The next story barely gave her a moment to process.

A split-screen: the Pope, in full regalia, giving a benediction outside St. Peter's Basilica—juxtaposed with an American televangelist shouting into a mic in a stadium.

"We welcome our brothers from the stars as fellow creations of the divine," said the Pope. *"Let no heart be closed in fear when grace opens the sky."*

Then:

"These things are not angels!" bellowed the televangelist, veins bulging. *"They are false prophets, and our leaders are cooperating with demons!"*

Vicki closed her eyes. A wave of exhaustion washed over her. This wasn't just disinformation anymore—it was hysteria. And hysteria could be weaponized.

She set the mug down and began getting dressed for the day, toggling the display to cycle through global headlines as she prepared:

- "Colonel Riley Met With Black budget Group in Denver, Source Claims"

- "Pentagon Insiders Call for Classified Oversight Council on Alien Tech"

- "Brazilian President Denies Ties to Falcão Negro, Warns of 'Retaliation for Meddling'"

- "Global Probe of the Partnership Expands—New Evidence Points to Decades-Long Tech Embargo"

The Partnership. Vicki paused at that headline.

There was still so much the world didn't know: how deep it went, what it cost to dismantle, and how many conspirators remained embedded in the organizations and corporations upon which they all depended.

She sat briefly at the edge of her bed, brushing her hair back, thinking of Jerry and Anne. Thinking of James, Brad, Kiran, and Jessica—hunted and still stubbornly standing. Thinking of all the tai chi students.

And thinking of Colonel Riley, an old hammer inside the Pentagon—still pounding, still trying to force the future into the mold of the past.

She checked the time. It was early, but not too early.

Chapter Fourteen

T he elevator chimed, and the brushed steel doors slid open, revealing the muted lighting and marble floors of the State Department's sixth floor. Jerry stepped out, coffee in one hand, and phone in the other, scanning the updates from overnight. He barely had time to process the headline about the coordinated corporate pushback in Southeast Asia when he heard the soft click of heels on tile.

Vicki. It was only 7:00 a.m.; most of the State Department wouldn't arrive for another hour and a half. For his purposes, Vicki was right on time.

Jerry fell in step beside her.

"The Pentagon's going public," he said without preamble. "Their press conference will take place in four days."

Vicki didn't break stride. "What's their angle?"

"My sources say it's going to be negative. They're painting the ET situation as a threat. They'll be questioning OMR's legitimacy and agenda." He paused. "They'll be asking pointed questions about you and attacking your character."

Vicki entered the code for the door, unlocking the office as she stepped inside. She draped her coat over the back of a chair and turned to face him, the morning light from the tall windows highlighting the faint shadows beneath her eyes. "When did this get scheduled?"

"Just now. Slipped out on the internal press calendar an hour ago. They've been sitting on it, waiting for us to blink first."

Vicki's lips twitched—not a smile, exactly. "We won't."

Jerry set his phone on the edge of her desk. "So what's the plan? We respond before they speak? Counter-program with a fact sheet? A panel of scientists?"

"No," Vicki said. "We don't do anything."

Jerry stared at her, incredulous. "You want to ignore it?"

"We'll livestream the visit to the Suede Nation the same day they hold their press conference. Think about it—this will be our first physical visitation. Humanity's first sanctioned contact, televised in real time." Her voice was calm, but it carried that firm tone he knew so well. "Do you think anyone is going to care what the Pentagon says after that?"

"They might care *more*," Jerry said. "The military's going to spin this like they're the last line of defense against an invasion. You saw what happened in Lagos. People are scared. They're looking for certainty."

"And the military won't give them that," Vicki said. "They'll just give them paranoia dressed in medals."

"So, what'll happen—you'll have Brad do his hacker magic and block the networks from airing the Pentagon's press briefing?"

Vicki shook her head. "Brad's ready and willing, but no. I'm not going to prevent the military from having its press conference. Let them have their say. The Four have already pissed off enough people in the defense and intelligence communities. If we start censoring military broadcasts, it'll turn suspicion into open war. We don't need more martyrs."

Jerry exhaled, rubbing the bridge of his nose. "I just think you're underestimating the influence this will have. You're betting everything on a livestream."

"I'm betting everything on the truth," Vicki said. "And the truth is that people are tired of fear. They're tired of secrets. They want something to believe in—and the debut of a friendly, non-human civilization? That'll be hard to ignore." She smiled. "Besides, I doubt anyone can hold out against Junia's charms."

"And if they spin the Suedes as puppets or infiltrators? If they bring up the Partnership, or Lagos?"

"We don't change our message," she said. "We keep telling the story that matters—the truth."

Jerry looked at her, really looked. She hadn't slept much—he could see it in the shadows and in the tension just beneath her sharp tone. But there was no doubt in her eyes.

He wasn't sure if that scared him more than the Pentagon.

"You're not bulletproof, Vicki," he said finally.

"No," she agreed. "But I'm visible. That's more important right now."

Silence stretched between them for a few heartbeats. Then Vicki sat down at her desk and powered on her computer.

"Start preparing our press liaison. We'll need to manage questions if the media becomes combative. I'll reach out to the Suede Nation to finalize details for the livestream—and to have a statement ready in case things go sideways."

Jerry gave a curt nod and turned to leave, but paused at the door. "I hope you're right."

"I have to be," she said, without looking up. "We don't have any other options."

* * *

The transition always felt like falling in reverse.

One moment, James was cross-legged on the sofa in the common area of the flower shop. The next, he opened his eyes to the sparkling reality of the pocket-out-of-time—a place that didn't exist in space as humans understood it. It shimmered like frozen light, a soft twilight stretching in every direction, the "ground" beneath his feet rippling faintly with every shift.

Their bodies appeared whole here, solid-seeming but cloaked in sparkly, effervescent light. Each of the Four—Jessica, Kiran, Brad, and himself—glowed with a subtle pulse unique to their frequency. Jessica's silhouette radiated with a sharp, high-frequency shimmer. Kiran's vibrated with a deep resonance. Brad's aura flickered like code—sharp and restless. And James, always alert and attuned, pulsed with a grounding energy. Vicki, who had arrived in the pocket before the Four, emanated a sparkling, earth-aligned vibration.

Then Melly arrived.

She didn't walk into the pocket reality—she *unfolded* into it, eight feet of radiant, terrifying, mantis enormity. She had the head and forelegs of a praying mantis and the body of a beetle standing upright. A long cape, four short hind legs, and bulging eyes on either side of her triangular head. Yet, despite all that, it was Melly's *eyes* that drew attention—their iridescent colors swirled in no fixed pattern.

James had been the first person that Melly had contacted those several years ago, and now he was the first to step forward to greet her.

"Melly, it's good to see you," he said with a smile while steepling his hands over the first bend of Melly's forelegs. The others followed his lead. Kiran came last—having only met Melly a few weeks earlier, he still felt nervous.

"You come with heavy burdens," said Melly, addressing them all. The sound of her voice, though stilted, was clear. Underneath, however, there was the *feeling* of gongs, Tibetan singing bowls, and bells.

"But your timing is aligned," Melly continued with approval. "The moment asks you to choose higher frequencies, not smaller fears."

Vicki nodded slowly. She stood slightly apart from the others, her glow brighter than the last time they had met here. She hadn't slept much—James could feel that through her frequency signature—but she was focused. Steeled, as if for a challenging conversation.

"We're getting pushback from the power structures," Vicki said. "Corporations, old alliances, the Pentagon... It's stronger than we expected. And more violent."

Jessica glanced sideways at James, concern flickering in her eyes. Kiran stayed quiet, hands clasped loosely behind his back.

"That was anticipated," Melly replied. "Anticipated, but transient. Think of resistance as a final contraction before a birth. Painful, yes. But not fatal unless you panic."

Brad snorted under his breath.

Vicki rubbed the back of her neck. "I didn't come here with the Four just to unload my fears," she said.

"Kick-Ass Quartet," corrected Brad quietly.

Vicki continued. "I need advice. You're a member of the Council of the Galactic Federation. Are we still on the timeline? Are we still eligible to join? Or have we already failed?"

For a long, cold moment, silence spread in the pocket reality, heavy and dense, like the pressure under deep water. Even the singing bowls in James's mind went quiet.

Melly tilted her head, eyes spinning like twin vortexes. "Do you believe your species has already failed?"

"I'm afraid you're going to tell me we have," Vicki admitted, her voice tense.

Melly leaned forward. "If Earth had already failed, we would not be speaking. An invitation is still possible—your window is still open. But be aware that windows also close."

All of them nodded. They knew the risks.

Melly continued, "And membership is not safety—it is responsibility. You will be held to Galactic Federation law. You will answer for your use of shared technology."

That sent a ripple through the group. Vicki, Kiran, and Jessica looked somber. But Brad, unusually silent, stared into the non-existent horizon like he wasn't really listening.

James didn't miss it.

Vicki exhaled. "That's fair. But what can we do? They're trying to regulate free-energy technology by restricting it to elites. They're telling the public it's unstable or foreign—"

"Which it is," Melly said calmly. "It is foreign. But not unstable. The instability lies within your collective consciousness."

Brad finally looked up. "That's why we were talking about launching tai chi videos and the CE-5 protocols. We've been testing a set of simple breath-based and other frequency-raising exercises. Think mass meditation disguised as gentle exercise. If enough people shift—even just a little bit—it might create a stabilizing resonance."

Jessica added, "We'd accompany it with video content from the tai chi classes—videos of people they might see in everyday life."

James felt proud of his friends; they were all doing what they could.

"Yes," said Melly. "Your physical bodies are not incidental. They are tuning forks. Your consciousness responds to motion, breath, and sound. You are correct to pursue this path."

James watched Vicki nod, taking it all in—but he wasn't fully present anymore.

He kept thinking about that morning.

He'd arrived at the flower shop early, a box of tai chi flyers tucked under his arm. Jessica had been prepping in her studio for filming. On Brad's desk next to his computer, he'd seen the utility bill—folded and dog-eared. This was the envelope Jessica had taken when she escaped from the house where her kidnappers had held her.

When Jessica went to make coffee, he'd asked Brad—casually—what he'd found out about the owners of the house.

Brad had frozen. Just for a second. Then he'd smiled. Too easily.

It was a dead end. The State Department located the owner; he and his family have been on vacation in Italy for the past month. No one was authorized to be in the place. The police were treating it as a case of squatters.

James hadn't pressed, but he wasn't going to forget either. There was no way that Brad hadn't been able to track anything down.

Now, standing in a timeless void with the future of Earth at stake, James couldn't shake the feeling that Brad was hiding something—something big. And if he was lying about one thing, what else?

Melly's voice drew him back. "You ask if this is the right time. There is no perfect moment. There is only resonance, readiness, and courage. Delay favors fear. Movement favors transformation."

James glanced at Brad again, narrowing his eyes slightly. Was Brad moving... or was he delaying?

"If all goes well, Earth will be offered observation-tier membership first," Melly said. "You will not vote. You will listen, learn, and participate without interference. If you weaponize this opportunity, you will lose it. And others will not intervene to save you."

Vicki replied for all of them, hope and despair playing across her face. "We understand."

Chapter Fifteen

Vicki sat near the front of the shuttle bus, her phone in her hand, but her eyes fixed on the window. Trees blurred past, giving way to a vast stretch of rising stone and pine as they approached Pilot Knob. Her mind whirled with a dozen urgent thoughts. Her last conversation with Colonel Riley hadn't gone well. The colonel's characterization of ETs as "demonic," while not an official Pentagon position, was gaining traction in some military circles. It would be disastrous if this spread to the public.

This visit to the Suede Nation needed to go right.

Vicki glanced around at her companions. Mary had done an exceptional job of pulling this together. With only forty-eight hours' notice, her office administrator coordinated delegates, flights, clearances, and transportation from D.C. to the remote regional airport, then arranged shuttle rentals and drivers on this bumpy backroad leading to an unmarked trailhead in the Appalachians. The second shuttle bus, carrying the video and camera crew, followed behind.

Vicki smiled to herself. She'd have to give Mary some time off. Or a raise. Or both.

Seated directly behind her was Jonathan Vann, the Cherokee tribal member the Suede Nation had informed her should be part of this delegation. He was to serve as their guide to the cave where the Suede delegation would be waiting. Vicki was surprised. Who would have guessed that the Cherokee had been in contact with the Suede Nation for hundreds of years?

The other five people in the shuttle were here because she had contacted embassies from nations with mythologies involving little people. It was no surprise that the Irish Embassy sent one of their officials. According to Mary, the embassy had begged for extra seats, arguing they deserved more due to their longstanding history with fairies. Vicki smiled to herself, recalling how Mary had threatened the Irish Embassy with no seats at all if they didn't stop bothering her. She must have been convincing, because they quickly backed down. Other representatives came from the Chinese, Russian, Filipino, and Bolivian embassies, respectively.

Vicki had never publicly admitted that the Suede Nation was native to Earth, rather than extraterrestrial. Did it matter? She'd find out shortly. Vicki wasn't sure anyone cared much about the difference between non-human Earth-natives and aliens. Not with all the changes going on. Ultimately, the vibrational shift was the driving force that would change everything in their lives and their reality.

Vicki glanced back at her fellow passengers—a diplomatic rainbow of human folklore. If this didn't go viral, nothing would.

Jonathan reached forward and tapped the driver's shoulder as they approached a dirt path that veered off the paved road. "This is it. Let's stop here."

The driver nodded. "The GPS cuts out here anyway."

The shuttle slowed and pulled off to into a clearing. The second shuttle rolled up behind them and stopped. The passengers disembarked, stretching their legs, and squinting at the bright midday sun. Jonathan led the group toward a narrow trail that dipped between two trees. As they walked, he raised a hand and signaled for silence.

"We are entering sacred ground," he said, his voice low. "Long before highways and satellites, my people knew this mountain. The guardians we knew as the Rocks lived here. They were guardians of the earth. They were fierce warriors. They did not show themselves often, but when they did, it was important to listen."

The others nodded.

They followed Jonathan for ten more minutes before arriving at a small cave entrance, concealed by a cluster of boulders and a curtain of ivy. A cool wind flowed from it, carrying the scent of stone and moss. Jonathan glanced over at Vicki.

"This is the place?" she asked.

When he nodded, Vicki signaled to the film crew, who began unpacking their equipment: cameras, recording gear, and mobile lighting rigs. Vicki watched them, silently praying that everything would go smoothly. The livestream would begin in five minutes. Her earpiece buzzed. "Signal's good. We're ready to go live."

They stepped through the cave entrance.

* * *

Alun stood just inside, with Junia and Bowen on either side of him, their eyes wide and curious. The humans' eyes were equally wide and curious. The stone glowed faintly, soft blue veins pulsing along the walls.

Jonathan was the first to step forward. He gave a slow nod. "I am honored to meet you again, Alun of the Rocks."

Alun returned the nod. "Jonathan Vann. Your people have long kept the stories. We are grateful."

Junia practically bounced with excitement, though she tried to keep herself composed. Her eyes darted to the various humans, fascinated. Bowen stood firm, arms folded behind his back, clearly modeling himself after his father.

Vicki made the introductions, and Alun invited the human delegation to board a long, low vehicle—something between a wagon and a train car, but with no visible engine—that was waiting at the entrance of a tunnel.

"It will take us to the village," he said.

Once everyone had boarded the vehicle, it began to move—smoothly and silently, with a forward gliding motion. There was no jolt, no engine hum, just the faint rhythmic breathing of the tunnel.

Vicki sat near Alun. "How does it work?" she asked.

"Intention and balance," Alun said simply. "The tunnel has been here for thousands of years. We harmonize with it."

Vicki sat quietly for the rest of the ride. She had been thinking of the Suede Nation as being at the level of a human medieval civilization. This was wrong; they clearly had some very advanced technology. She had made the mistake because she assumed technology was all of one kind.

She wondered what other mistakes she was making.

* * *

Junia stood near the town center, watching the humans disembark slowly from the energy wagon. She wanted to laugh at how surprised they all looked—how stunned—as they gazed around at the Suede village.

After all the excitement and anticipation, she wasn't sure how she felt about the humans. Vicki, yes, she liked Vicki. Vicki had a calm pulse, not unlike that of Suede elders. She spoke with care and actually *listened*—a rare trait, as Junia was quickly learning. But the others, the humans who had come to film them and who represented their nations? They were so... oblivious.

Junia bit the inside of her cheek, trying to keep her expression neutral as one of the embassy representatives gasped—*gasped*—at the sight of the stone dwellings that spiraled gently upward from the soft, glowing moss of the square. The homes radiated a soft light, infusing warmth and harmony into the space. Yet the humans blinked like wide-eyed children, mouths parted as if they had never imagined that beauty could exist beneath their feet.

How could they not know? Junia thought. *Stories and legends exist in every corner of the surface world. Yet they still pretend it's all myth. Are they blind, or just stupid?*

She crossed her arms tightly over her chest. She liked her new dress; she thought it made her look elegant—more like the people she saw on the internet. The entire village had been clothed in new smocks and pants in anticipation of the humans' visit. She hoped that she would eventually be able to get clothes in brighter colors. Today, everyone was dressed in garments of a light yellowish-green color.

Boring.

Beside her, Bowen stood straight and formal, as always, his face unreadable. They both watched as Alun and Vicki mounted the wide central platform.

"Welcome," Alun said. "You walk among the Suede Nation now. We are caretakers, watchers, and friends of the Earth. We do not seek to rule or to hide. We have simply done our duty, as we always have."

Vicki stepped up beside him, her hands folded gently in front of her. Junia watched the camera turn to follow her.

"Good people of Earth," she said. "Today, we offer you a glimpse of our hidden family—one that has lived alongside us, beneath our feet, since before recorded time. This is the Suede Nation. They are not aliens. They are not invaders. They are Earthlings, guardians, and friends."

Alun stepped forward. "We greet you with open hands and memory. Many of your stories are our stories. You called us dwarves, fairies, or gnomes. But we were always here. We only waited until you were ready to see us."

A murmur ran through the gathered humans, and Junia fought the urge to roll her eyes. *Now they believe,* she thought. *Now that it's on video. Now that someone official says it's real.*

The camera panned across the Suede village, zooming in on the the buildings, the gardens, and the children peeking from behind the archways.

"This is not a hoax," Vicki continued. "And it is not a threat. The vibrational shift approaching Earth is not a catastrophe. It's a call—to awaken, to remember, and to reconnect."

Bowen gently elbowed Junia, interrupting her wandering thoughts. She shot him a sharp glance, but his expression remained unchanged. He simply whispered, "Smile. You're on camera."

Junia forced her lips into a smile, but it didn't quite reach her eyes. Still, she did her best as the camera panned their way. She had to admit it *was* fun to be on video.

She looked at Vicki again, who stood slightly behind Alun now, allowing him to talk about Suede history, their connection to the Earth crystal, and their role as stewards. She nodded along, calm and reliable.

And the humans *were* listening.

They weren't interrupting. They weren't arguing. They weren't even asking dumb questions. They were just watching and nodding.

Junia felt something relax in her chest. Maybe she would give them another chance.

She took a step closer to Bowen and whispered, "When do we get to do our part?"

He shot her a sidelong glance. "You mean when do we get to be *stars*?"

She elbowed him, grinning now. "You know you're excited too."

"I'm terrified," he said with a dramatic sigh. "What if I say something stupid?"

Junia laughed, a warm, clear sound. "Then at least you'll be remembered."

One of the crew turned toward them, beckoning them over. Junia felt a jolt of nervous excitement surge in her stomach.

Their turn.

She stepped forward, brushing her ropey hair out of her face. The lights from the camera reflected in her topaz eyes, and she tilted her head, ready to be captured, ready to *speak*.

Maybe this *could* work. Maybe this could be the beginning of something better. Something new.

She smiled again—real this time—as the camera blinked red.

"Hi," she said. "I'm Junia of the Suede Nation. Welcome to our home."

She threw up her arms and twirled.

* * *

Jerry wasn't the only one in conference room. It was standing room only.

He leaned over the edge of the table, his eyes glued to the wall-sized display at the front of the room. The livestream from Pilot Knob was in full swing, showcasing a sweeping panorama of the Suede Nation. Around him, staff members—analysts, aides, cultural liaisons, comms team, even the janitor—had gathered in stunned silence.

No one had expected *this*.

The camera panned over the stone dwellings, the vibrant moss paths, and the softly glowing rock walls of the cavern. Junia's smiling face filled the screen, her introduction beaming out across thousands—maybe millions—of devices around the world.

"I'm Junia of the Suede Nation. Welcome to our home."

A wave of quiet awe moved through the room.

"She's a kid," someone murmured behind Jerry. "And she sounds more composed than half the diplomats I've met."

The social media comments were streaming in almost too fast to read:

"Incredible. I can't believe we never knew." "She looks like something out of a dream." "#SuedeNation is trending." "I'm crying. This changes everything." "Why did they keep this hidden for so long?" "How can I visit?"

A woman from the comms section had her laptop open, tracking engagement stats in real time. Her fingers flew across the glass as she looked up, her eyes wide.

"Jerry, we're at eleven million concurrent viewers," she said. "Eleven. Million. And that's just through the official channels. I haven't even factored in the media rebroadcasts."

Jerry exhaled slowly. "I hope Vicki knows what she just started."

Jerry turned back to the screen. Alun was now explaining the history of the Suede, their stewardship of the Earth crystal, and their reluctance to interfere with surface affairs unless absolutely necessary. He spoke with clarity, as if he had waited centuries for this moment.

"The Earth is alive," Alun said. "We are part of her, and so are you. This world does not belong to humans alone."

"He just rewrote every civics class on the planet," said someone behind him.

Jerry agreed. Yet, despite the groundbreaking video playing out before the world, he couldn't shake the tight feeling in his gut.

Colonel Riley.

The Pentagon was scheduled to hold its press briefing in less than three hours. Jerry had seen the talking points. He had seen the footage they were prepared to release—edited, filtered, and wrapped in just enough fear to nudge the global narrative into something alarming and controllable.

He knew they would portray the Suede—and all the ETs—as dangerous and evil threats. He wasn't the only one worried about it.

"What are we going to do about Riley?" asked Mary.

"Vicki says we wait," Jerry replied. "Let this video speak. Let the world see a future worth believing in. And when Riley starts ranting about 'hostile extraterrestrials,' he'll sound like the paranoid old man he is."

The camera was back on Junia—laughing now, talking about their village, their schools, and their songs. The human representatives appeared spellbound.

This was what they needed. Not just an announcement.

Connection.

Jerry let out a long breath, his heart thudding. Maybe Vicki had done it. Maybe, just maybe, this was the answer to centuries of fear. He returned his gaze to the screen.

Junia was dancing now. Twirling barefoot across the square.

"Let's show the world what hope looks like," he said.

And for the first time in weeks, he felt like maybe that wasn't just wishful thinking.

Chapter Sixteen

J ames sat on a bench in the garden behind the tai chi studio. A filtered beam of sunlight slanted through the trees, illuminating the object resting in his open hands.

The memory crystal.

It wasn't large—about the size of a pack of playing cards—but it radiated a cool, pulsing light that shifted in color as he held it. At that moment, it glowed a pale green, as if trying to reassure him that everything would be okay.

It didn't work.

When Vicki first handed it to him, she did so with the seriousness of someone bestowing a holy relic. "You'll know what to do with it," she'd said. "Eventually."

He hadn't believed her at the time.

Now, weeks later, as yesterday's livestream of the Suede Nation's introduction swept across the world, it seemed humanity was caught between wonder and chaos. The weight of that crystal felt heavier than any responsibility he had ever carried.

James exhaled slowly, focusing his thoughts. The crystal responded, flaring briefly before projecting a soft, translucent field around him—images began to flicker, suspended in air and memory.

There was no sound at first. Just scenes:

A record from impossibly ancient history: images of slender beings with silver-gray skin and luminous eyes touching the heads of proto-humanoids. Next, the modern descendants of these same humanoids building megaliths, guided by stars and symbols.

And then the impressions began—not voices, but feelings. Echoes of decisions, fears, and hopes.

The scenes changed.

Now, a vision tens of thousands of years old, from when the expedition from Alpha Centauri—staffed mainly by researchers and scientists—had gone wrong. Their primary vessel was destroyed, along with effective communication with their home planet. The ACs found themselves stranded on Earth, and several generations passed before rescue arrived. By that time, many of the survivors had assimilated into life on Earth—fairly easy to do since they closely resembled humans and were, to some extent, biologically compatible. This had a major effect on human development—culturally, technically, and genetically—all in violation of Galactic Federation rules.

The rescue operation had not gone as planned. Many of the AC survivors wanted to stay on Earth and they put up a fight. The Federation had also underestimated how much the ACs had influenced humanity. By erasing evidence of advanced technology and civilizations, a near-extinction-level event in human prehistory was triggered—a Dark Age that predated even myth. Ultimately, the Galactic Federation permitted some of the ACs to stay, as long as they remained hidden underground and didn't interfere further in human society.

James swallowed hard, letting the vision fade.

He closed the crystal's field with a soft command, and the glowing sphere dimmed in his hands. What was he supposed to do with this? Release all of it? Let humanity see the extent of their manipulation at the hands of ETs? All the suffering and secrecy?

No. Not yet.

If he revealed this knowledge now, after the Suede livestream, it would shatter everything. People were still adjusting to the idea of neighbors beneath their feet and others in the stars. Reality was changing—too rapidly for some. Introducing a species of extraterrestrials that had nearly caused humanity's extinction would provide them a scapegoat, especially for people like Colonel Riley.

The surviving ACs felt *remorseful*. Vicki had met them. They were aliens, yes, but they were not evil, and they had adhered to their agreement with the Federation, living hidden below the surface for thousands of years. Their underground civilization was almost impossible to detect because they vibrated at a slightly higher frequency than humans. But once Earth went through its vibrational shift, the ACs and their cities would become visible. Many of them had concluded that this would be the moment to end their exile and emerge to coexist with humans.

But how to tell *that* story? How could he reveal a catastrophic event that nearly ended humanity in a way that wouldn't turn the world against all extraterrestrials? And how could he suggest that humans should welcome these same aliens as neighbors?

James rubbed his temple. What he wanted—what he *needed*—was to craft a story that human minds could grasp without breaking. Maybe he could shape this information into a narrative. Still the truth, but released in a gradual trickle while slowly unpacking it. Not a dump of cosmic horror, but a layered understanding.

The challenge was time. With the Pentagon preparing to spin narratives of extraterrestrial evil, there wasn't much of it.

He returned to the crystal, holding it gently. "I need your help," he said.

The crystal pulsed once—blue now. Attentive.

"Show me the stories that give people hope. The ones that help us understand without blaming anyone. Help me see what connects us as humans in this big galactic story."

The light shimmered again, and scenes merged: a young human woman in an Ice Age cave with an AC kneeling beside her, healing her shattered leg; a group of beings standing alongside Egyptian priests as they discussed the alignment of the stars; a Mayan astronomer recording the sky under AC tutelage; and an AC scientist watching a child laugh for the first time.

James's throat tightened. These were not villains. These were... participants. Mistaken, yes. Arrogant, at times. But not beyond redemption.

Just like us.

He sat again, the crystal before him. *I'll start with these,* he thought to himself. *The good stories. The helpers. The flawed allies. We'll ease into the darker truths later. Let people feel the connection first. Let them see the hope before the pain.*

If humanity was going to learn its buried past, it should do so standing upright—not crawling in shame or rage. And when the time came to reveal the mistake—the ACs' refusal to leave, the cascade of unintended consequences—he would do it with context and compassion.

They could handle this. They *had* to. There was no turning back.

* * *

Junia sat cross-legged with her hands folded in her lap, her back against the wall of the Community Hall. Nervous energy fluttered in her stomach.

The Suede Nation elders sat in their customary circle, whispering as they shifted slightly, exchanging glances and occasional sighs. The air was heavy—not with hostility, but with worry. Ancient worry.

"The livestream was well-received," Junia offered tentatively, trying to break the silence that had followed Alun's introductory words. "The humans were respectful. Curious, but polite."

Morcan, one of the matriarchs, gave her a sharp glance. "Respectful, perhaps—for now. But their kind has a short memory and an even shorter attention span."

Another elder, old Tarran, added, "They have betrayed covenants before. They drill into the Earth like it is dead, not living. They poison the water veins and rupture sacred hollows. Fracking, they call it. A word as violent as the act."

A murmur of agreement spread around the circle. Junia stayed quiet, even though she really wanted to stand up for the few humans she knew. But she knew this wasn't the right time.

Alun slowly rose from his place in the circle. His presence always commanded respect, not just because he was her uncle, but because he was the Crystal's caretaker—and one of the few who could attune fully to its song.

"Yes," he said, his tone even and resonant. "Humans have made mistakes. Deep ones. But we too have hidden and hoarded our wisdom. We have watched their struggles and offered little. Balance was not served by our silence."

"They would exploit us!" Morcan snapped. "They will come with their drills and their laws, and their media frenzy. They will dig up our homes, put our children on magazine covers, and pick apart our culture like a lab specimen!"

"The vibrational shift is already unfolding," Alun said, raising his hand calmly. "Soon we will be visible to all—regardless of what we wish. The era of hiding is ending, whether we choose it or not."

"But the shift could bring madness," someone protested. "We are not ready."

"Then we *get ready*," Alun replied, his tone curt. Junia could tell her uncle was finally losing his patience. "The Alpha Centaurians are already preparing to share advanced technologies—clean energy, material sciences, and waste disposal that doesn't pollute. When those technologies are shared, humanity's hunger for resource extraction will fall away. They will have no reason to interfere in our territory."

"Unless they fear us," Tarran murmured. "Fear is an even greater fuel than greed."

Junia's heart pounded. She looked down at her lap, her fingers trembling slightly with the effort of keeping her face still, but then looked up.

"I... I've been asked to help," she said softly. "Vicki asked if I could work with Jessica. She wants me to be in some videos. To help tell humans who we are, what's important to us, and why we stayed hidden until now."

There was a pause. Some elders looked skeptical, others simply curious. Morcan's expression tightened, but she didn't interrupt.

"They think I have a good way of explaining things," Junia added quickly, more confident now that the words were out. "That I can help humans understand without fear. Maybe... maybe even with joy."

Alun gave her a small, proud nod. "Junia has seen their hearts more clearly than most of us have. She walks between both ways of being."

"Videos," Tarran muttered under his breath, as if the word tasted sour. "Such a human thing."

Junia's cheeks flushed with the effort to be polite. The elders were so frustrating—so *old-timey*.

"They watch videos more than they listen to their elders. If that's how they learn, then that's how we should teach them."

There was silence again, but this time it held consideration, not condemnation.

"Let the girl try," Alun said. "We cannot demand trust and give none. Let her voice be a light into their world."

Junia exhaled slowly, feeling grateful. She didn't smile—at least not yet—but inside, a flicker of excitement danced. Yes. She would talk. And maybe, just maybe, they would listen.

* * *

Kiran sat alone on his bed. Brad and Jessica were at the tai chi studio with James filming videos. He wanted to use this brief time alone to meditate, but his mind was anything but quiet.

It was happening again.

He pressed his palms against his temples and closed his eyes, focusing on the rhythm of his breath, trying to ground himself with his heartbeat. But the voices—if you could even call them that—kept returning. Not loud. Not distinct. But persistent.

Humans are weak.

You are alone.

Aliens are dangerous."

They were thoughts that arrived like fog in the morning—uninvited, unnoticed at first, and then suddenly everywhere. But they didn't feel like *his* thoughts. They weren't rooted in anything he felt. They had no *warmth,* no emotional imprint. They echoed only in his mind, leaving his gut and heart untouched.

He opened his eyes and let out a slow breath. "This isn't mine," Kiran said aloud. "This doesn't belong to me."

His voice sounded hollow, but saying it out loud helped.

He reached over to his nightstand and pulled out a worn notebook filled with notes, diagrams, and questions scribbled during countless nights. He flipped through the pages until he found the most recent entry:

Psychotronic-based Interference

Suspected: Artificially induced thoughts

Medium: Likely quantum-level resonance. Psionic tech.

Key distinction: NO emotion.

Real thoughts = resonance in heart/gut

Implants? Broadcast field? Need shielding or counter-vibration?

Kiran tapped the page with his pen, again underlining the phrase: *Real thoughts = resonance in heart/gut.*

That was the key. It had taken time to figure it out, but once he had, it became glaringly obvious. Authentic thoughts—the ones that were his alone—were a feeling in his chest, in his gut. They were joy, fear, anger, and hope. Even weak emotions had a vibration, a signature that hummed through his body. But these... these implanted ideas? They were ghost thoughts—disconnected and empty.

Which means they can be resisted.

He closed his eyes and slowed his breathing. Into the silence, he invited both sets of thoughts—the real and the false. A planted whisper came first.

"They're lying to you."

He did nothing. He just observed it. It felt cold and purely mental. There was no gut twist, no heartache—just static.

Then he summoned a memory.

Jessica's laughter, light and easy, as they teased each other over dinner (while Brad and James both rolled their eyes). The thought surfaced, and *with it* came the warm buzz in his heart. The faint flush in his cheeks. The low hum in his core.

Real—the difference was night and day.

He opened his eyes and stood, resolved now. If this was a broadcast, it should be possible to create some sort of shield. Maybe not a tin-foil hat, but something that worked with vibration and coherence. A harmonic field? A wearable device that amplified genuine thoughts and dampened external interference?

He'd need to speak with Vicki and the rest of the Four. Perhaps they could contact the Suede Nation or the AC engineers—they would have more knowledge about vibration than anyone living on the surface.

He couldn't do this alone anymore. Luckily for him, he didn't have to.

Chapter
Seventeen

J erry hadn't slept for more than three hours in the past two days. His office looked like a war room—screens lit up with livestreams, comment threads, emergency broadcasts, and encrypted message feeds from trusted contacts. Coffee cups were stacked up on one side. His laptop vibrated every few minutes with another news alert ping.

The livestream from Pilot Knob had broken records.

The global audience had surpassed four hundred million viewers within the first six hours. Translation overlays were being provided in multiple languages, and the video had been clipped, remixed, and redistributed across every conceivable social platform. Even those who didn't *want* to know about the Suede Nation now couldn't escape it.

And, stunningly, the Pentagon had pulled back.

Jerry stared at the memo Sam had forwarded to him—a resounding defeat presented as a "technical delay." The official press briefing, where Colonel Riley was supposed to issue a hardline warning about alien threats, had been postponed indefinitely. The livestream reaction data had proven too overwhelming, too favorable to the Suedes. The optics for the military would have been disastrous.

He should have felt relieved, but relief was not what twisted in his stomach now. He felt uneasy. While the public's awakening to the truth had come, it was messy and uncontrolled.

The protests first began in Buenos Aires and Istanbul, later spreading to Seoul, Paris, Melbourne, and Chicago. Some were celebrations—people in the streets with painted faces, singing songs about Earth spirits and sky beings, declaring the Suedes and others like them to be long-lost family. Others, however, were less joyful.

In Brussels, a crowd marched on NATO headquarters, shouting that Earth must not be ruled by "cosmic elites." In Scotland, a fringe minister declared the Suedes and their allies to be "the final deception," prophesying an alien Antichrist. Banks faced runs, stock markets reeled, and currency values lurched.

Then came a quiet call from Sam, who had broken security protocol to provide extra information to Jerry. Information beyond the "technical delay" notice—something that changed the entire narrative.

"It wasn't tech sharing; it was a trade," Sam had said quietly. "The Tall Whites—the ones who helped the Partnership reverse-engineer the advanced alien tech—they brokered a deal with government officials in the early '50s. That was how it all started. They promised advances in propulsion, data transfer, and medical breakthroughs—but in exchange, they wanted unrestricted biological access. They wanted DNA."

Jerry had gone cold. "You're saying the Tall Whites were experimenting—with permission?"

"The Tall Whites were experimenting with the *collusion* of government officials," Sam had replied. "Officials from the highest levels in the Pentagon signed it; those specific officers are either retired or deceased now, but it's still an active program. The Tall Whites kept their hands clean—they had a subordinate species they called the Grays carry out the physical work—but it was a trade agreement between them and us. All those stories of alien abduction you've heard about? They were true. But officials claimed those people were crazy or on drugs because they couldn't risk anyone finding out that they were the ones who authorized it."

"And no one said a damn word."

"Because they *benefited*," Sam said. "Now that the public is learning about aliens, the ones who are still overseeing that deal—they're terrified. If it comes out, they'll burn. And they'd rather kill our future than let that happen."

Now Jerry stared at the glowing screen in front of him. He replayed the footage of the Suede community on mute, watching Junia's face, bright and alive as she welcomed the world to her home. A child of a hidden nation, now stepping into the light of human civilization. Her joy reminded him of what this moment *could* be.

But there were too many people who wanted it silenced.

Recent messages from some of his media contacts hinted that they were facing subtle but growing pressure. News anchors were being told to "contextualize" the Suede story with fear-messaging. Lobbyists were quietly feeding stories to tabloids about "alien cults" and "underground threats." A slow, coordinated smear campaign was beginning. Not against the Suedes directly—but against Disclosure itself

The status quo was bleeding, and its gatekeepers were sharpening their knives.

Jerry stood and walked to the coffeepot to refill his mug. All the media outlets were covering the protests—the noise of the crowd: chanting, cheering, and arguing. It wasn't just about the Suede Nation anymore. People were waking up to the realization that *everything* could be different; that humanity had been living under a ceiling it hadn't even known existed.

And now they wanted to tear that ceiling down.

He turned back to his desk and opened a secure file containing the data Sam had slipped him—scans of the agreement, eyewitness testimonies, photos of the early exchanges, and maps of the research sites. It was explosive. If he released it now, it would blow everything wide open.

But it might also destroy the fragile hope that Vicki and the Four had worked so hard to cultivate. It might turn public curiosity into widespread panic. It could label *all* non-human beings as violators and manipulators.

He pressed his fingers to his eyes and whispered to the room, "How much truth is too much truth?"

The door opened behind him with a soft knock. He was surprised to see Vicki step in.

"You saw the latest protests?" she asked.

"Yeah. I saw."

"And the Pentagon?"

"Stalling—for now. But they're regrouping. And we've got something they'd kill to keep buried." He pushed the file with Sam's evidence toward her, and waited while she scanned it. Her face paled. Finally, she nodded.

"We need to be smart about this, not just reveal everything at once. If the public learns too much too fast, they'll turn to fear. We need to shape the story—guide it."

He shook his head. "We do, but I don't know how. But I do know one thing: this won't be stopped—and we shouldn't try. The old world's already breaking."

Vicki left, and Jerry sat down again to open a new file. Title: *The Secret Accord.* Not for publication. Not yet. But someday soon.

Because the future was coming.

And he'd be damned if he let the past bury it.

* * *

Brad's workroom, located on the main floor of the old flower shop, was usually a tranquil place. The soft hum of his computers always helped him think. In this space, time felt slower, and he could focus without pressure. But now, the quiet felt heavy. The air seemed thick, and the silence felt too sharp. The room was the same—but he wasn't. The calm had faded, replaced by a constant tension he couldn't shake.

He'd spent weeks tracking the online footprints of the so-called "Heirs"—those self-satisfied, bored children of the Partnership's elite; the ones his father had insisted he and Jessica befriend to boost the family's social connections. Some of the Heirs had inherited money, others clout, and a few both. All had inherited arrogance. They treated his sister Jessica like she was sub-human. Even after the success of her *Melly Talks* series—praised across the world for its ground-breaking revelations—they jumped at the chance to collaborate with Colonel Riley's niece, Amanda, on a smear piece, claiming Jessica was stupid. They claimed that someone must have ghostwritten the scripts and managed the camera.

Brad clicked through the profiles he had gathered, one by one. Investment portfolios. Real estate purchases. An invitation-only party on a private island off the coast of Bali. He had even found a private group chat that he had dubbed the "HeirNet." Trusts and foundations concealed their digital footprints, but it was easy enough to track if you were a computer genius.

Brad had found all of it.

One folder on his desktop glowed faintly: *Heirs – Revenge Plan.* He'd debated the name. It wasn't subtle, but then again, he was done being subtle.

He was uploading pieces already. He had planted whispers in social media forums and online communities; he had dropped hints on content-sharing networks. He would leave anonymous tips for local regulators to review later. A slow smear—just enough to peel off that shiny façade from their lives and show the world the rot underneath. One of them had already deleted his profile. Another had panicked and started scrubbing his digital history.

Good. Let them sweat for once.

Brad was so focused that he startled when someone stepped up beside him. "Kiran,"he muttered, eyes narrowing. "What are you doing here?"

Kiran just looked at him, noticing the strain on Brad's face. He didn't speak; he just looked at the computer screen.

"You're going after them," Kiran said quietly. "The Heirs."

Brad didn't deny it. "They called Jess dumb; they insinuated she's an idiot. They tried to erase her from her own work. After everything she's been through—"

"We all saw," Kiran said, "We saw the news story and read the articles. And I saw what you found about the kidnapping team, too."

Brad's eyes gleamed. "Then you understand why I'm doing this. I'm not just going to hurt their reputations—I'm going to make sure no one ever trusts them again. And the ones who took her? I traced the LLC on the utility bill to three real people. I know where they shop. I know where one of them sleeps."

Kiran leaned on the counter. "Go ahead with the Heirs. I won't stop you. They earned what's coming."

Brad blinked. That wasn't what he expected, although he should have; Kiran and Jessica were dating. "Really?"

"They crossed a line," Kiran said. "And the world deserves to know who they really are."

"But?" Brad asked, already hearing it in his tone.

"But the ones behind the kidnapping?" Kiran's jaw tightened. "That's for Vicki—and the Department of State—to deal with. There's more at play than Jessica's kidnapping. It's about Disclosure. They're part of the group that was working with the Partnership. There's military and intelligence involvement, financial elites, alien contracts, and even cover operations. If you strike first, we might lose our one shot at all of them."

Brad looked down at his screen. His finger hovered over the file marked *Kidnapping Team – Phase One.*

"I'm not afraid of consequences," he said.

"No," Kiran said. "You're not afraid of the personal consequences to you. But what about the consequences to the world? To all of humanity? What about the future? We can't screw this up."

Brad was quiet for a moment. Then he nodded once. "I'll burn the Heirs. But not the kidnappers—I'll leave them for later when the State Department has the bigger picture. And then we'll help them fix *that* problem."

Then Brad continued, "I'm leaving Aija out of it."

Kiran sat down heavily in a chair, rubbing his temples. "She might be my sister, but she shouldn't get a free pass. I'll be the first to admit she was one of Jessica's worst tormenters. I ate dinner with my parents last week, and Aija was gleeful when she talked about her role in that news story that Amanda Riley did. She showed no remorse whatsoever."

"I know," Brad said. "But she's your sister. Your relationship with your family is already strained; we don't need to add to it."

Kiran looked down at the floor. "Truthfully, I'm not sure if protecting her is the right thing to do. She needs to learn."

Brad grinned at him. "I said I'm leaving Aija out of it—I didn't say that I didn't follow her digital trail. I have a lot of information collected on her; we can make it public if we ever decide she needs to learn a lesson."

Kiran stood up and gave him a faint smile. "Fair enough."

He was almost out the door when Brad called after him, "I'll wait on dealing with the kidnappers, but not forever. If the State Department doesn't act soon, I *will*. You don't get to put Jess in a hole and walk away."

"Not acting soon is not an option," agreed Kiran as he walked out.

Brad clicked a key. The *Kidnapping Team* folder blinked closed, hidden again for now.

People always underestimated Jessica. What they didn't understand was that they were also underestimating him. Jess had spent years cultivating an image of a socially awkward, emotionally fragile young woman. Just as carefully, Brad had cultivated the image of a happy-go-lucky teenager who shrugged off insults and was liked by everyone.

Even Kiran had failed to see it. Brad turned back to the keyboard, a war of restraint and rage burning behind his eyes.

He'd promised to wait, to let things play out. For now. But the clock was ticking, and he wouldn't wait forever.

Chapter Eighteen

The sudden screams stopped her in her tracks.

Junia was returning from the moss fields when the echoing shouts tore through the tunnel—raw, sharp, and filled with fear and anger. She dropped everything without thinking, the moss scattering along the path. Her feet pounded the ground, heart racing as she bolted toward the entry cavern.

Another scream followed, then the sound of energy weapons—loud, mechanical, and alien to the natural harmony of the Suede Nation.

She rounded a corner and skidded to a halt.

The entryway to the Pilot Knob cave was chaos. Cracks fractured the smooth walls where explosives had been detonated. Smoke curled in dark plumes. The air vibrated with wrongness. And in the middle of it all—her people desperately defending themselves against attackers in tactical gear, faces smeared with mud and greed. They carried crude tech—gold-seeking gear. One had a metal detector strapped across his back.

And lying near the outer archway—motionless, blood soaking into the floor—was Bowen.

Junia didn't feel her knees give out, didn't hear herself scream. One moment she was frozen, and the next, she was running.

She had no thought; fury spilled out of her.

As she charged into battle, her body responded to the call of blood. With a sharp snap of sinew, her fingers elongated, hardened, and sprouted claws as long as knives, glimmering like polished obsidian. Other Suede defenders transformed alongside her. Topaz eyes glowing and claws bared, they met the attackers without a word.

Junia landed on the first man like a hawk. His weapon fired once—then never again.

She tore through metal and flesh with no pity.

"BOWEN!" she howled, her voice echoing off the walls of the cavern.

Two more fell—one from a blow to the throat, another from a slash across the helmet that shattered the visor and the skull beneath it. The attackers tried to retreat, but their equipment slowed them down, and the Suedes pressed the attack.

Junia started as her uncle grabbed her by the shoulders, his face ashen. "Enough, Junia! Come! Now!"

"No!" she snarled. "They killed Bowen—they killed—"

"They will answer. But we do not destroy ourselves in rage," he said, pulling her backward. "Come. We will shift the tunnel. Let the stone itself judge them."

Reluctantly—outwardly silent, but still howling inside—she followed him. Other elders joined them, forming a circle deeper in the tunnel, just beyond the fray. They held hands, claws retracted now, and began an ancient chant—low and rhythmic, synchronized with the pulse of the Earth crystal itself.

The tunnel shimmered.

Junia could feel the dimensional veil starting to thin. The air became denser. The attackers, still in a lower vibrational state, stumbled, oblivious to what was happening just beyond their perception.

And then, with a shudder, the transition occurred. Where there had been open space, there was now solid stone.

The gold-seekers—too slow, too lost in greed—never saw it coming. They were encased in less than a moment. Not crushed—but sealed, as if they had never existed, their molecules displaced into the Earth.

Junia sank to her knees, her breath ragged. Her chest heaved, grief washing over her in waves too large to voice. She felt Alun's hand on her back, warm and grounding.

"We warned them," he said quietly. "This place is not theirs to take. The Earth protects her own."

Junia stared at the spot where her cousin had fallen, now surrounded by stone. The Suedes would recover the bodies of their fallen later.

"I will remember them," she said, voice hard and trembling. "Every one of them."

"You must also remember this," Alun said, his voice stern yet kind. "Vengeance must give way to vision. Or we lose more than just our people—we lose who we are."

She nodded slowly, though the fury still curled inside her.

The story of Suede-Human relations had barely begun—and today the first chapter had been written in blood.

* * *

It was morning at the tai chi studio, and the only sound was the quiet breath and shifting feet of the small group practicing the final movements of the standing meditation set.

James moved with the rhythm, the familiar flow grounding him. His parents mirrored his movements a few feet away. The chi felt thick in the air today. Perhaps it was the full room. Perhaps it was because Jessica was filming them again.

The soft clack of a camera tripod being adjusted drew James's attention for a brief moment. Jessica stood at the edge of the room with her usual focus, capturing the session with graceful invisibility. James admired her restraint—never interrupting, never distracting—just letting things unfold naturally.

As the session concluded, students bowed to Calvin and Mona, murmuring thanks. One or two lingered to ask quiet questions, but most left smiling, with their mats tucked under arms.

Then he saw Mei.

She didn't smile. She didn't bow. She marched directly toward him, all intention and energy.

James suppressed a sigh. He knew this look.

"Hi, James," she said brightly, though there was a sharp edge to her voice. "Got a second?"

"Sure," he said, stepping away from the mat. His parents had wandered toward Jessica to chat about frame angles. He was alone.

Mei folded her arms. "You didn't tell me you were going to be filming *our* classes."

"I didn't know until this morning," James said. "Jessica wanted to expand the meditation video series she's creating. She said people were asking for more grounding content after the... you know, the livestream."

Mei's eyebrows shot up. "*That's* exactly what I mean. That livestream. You, Vicki, and the Suede Nation and all that underground city stuff. You've been part of it the whole time, haven't you?"

James stiffened. "I wasn't part of the livestream, and it's not really something I—"

"You know I could help," Mei cut in. "You *know* I could."

James looked at her—really looked. She was flushed, her voice louder than it should have been for the space. Her dark hair was pinned back too tightly, her jaw set with frustration. He remembered her practicing form sets with an almost brutal energy, frustration burning through every movement as others moved on to advanced routines, and she was told to repeat the basics again.

"Mei," he said softly, "I know this is exciting. I get it. But this whole thing—it's delicate. It's not about jumping in. It's about trust. Balance."

"I *have* balance," she snapped. "Just because I'm not in the inner circle doesn't mean I'm unstable. I've been doing tai chi since I was ten. I read listservs about vibration and resonance. I—" She paused, teeth clenched. "You think I'm just some dumb girl with a crush."

James blinked in confusion; that had come out of nowhere. "I didn't say that."

"You didn't have to."

Her voice dropped, and she crossed her arms tightly again. "You know what my cousin Tian says? That I'm an embarrassment. That I talk too much and make our family look weird. That I'll never be married off because I act like I belong in a comic book store instead of the temple."

James winced. He didn't like Tian very much. Too smug—far too smug for someone whose main contribution to the tai chi class was making snide remarks during warm-up exercises.

Mei's eyes were watery now, but her voice was firm. "I want to do something real. Something that makes a difference. Not just take classes. Not just float around with incense and pretend that's who I am. You guys are doing Disclosure. You're changing the world. Let me help—I'm not a kid."

James looked at her for a long moment. He saw the tightly coiled tension of someone who'd never been taken seriously by the people she wanted to impress the most. He remembered how that felt. How badly he'd wanted to be trusted when he was younger—when his own parents thought tai chi was just a way to calm their son's racing thoughts after too many books and too little sleep.

"You're not a kid," he said finally. "And you're not dumb."

Mei blinked, thrown off.

"But this is bigger than me. Or you. Or even Jessica's videos. People are scared. They're seeing their world turn inside out. It's not a game—you can't just jump in without preparation. You *train* for it."

Mei's shoulders sank, just a bit. "So train me."

"I didn't say no," James said with a small smile. "I said—start where you are. Keep showing up. That matters more than you think."

They stood there for a few seconds. Jessica caught James's eye across the room and gave him a small nod. He returned it.

"Listen," he added. "We're filming a series on energy awareness and subtle resonance. A lot of people are going to need help making sense of what they're feeling. Jessica's already filming with my parents, but we could use someone who understands the younger crowd. Someone who can translate things."

"Translate?" Mei asked cautiously.

"Not languages—*feelings*. Experience. Frustration. Hope. The way energy shifts when someone's been lied to their whole life. What it feels like inside."

Mei's eyes widened. "You're serious."

"I'm serious," agreed James. "Talk to Jessica. She might have something for you. But start by being useful. Not loud. Maybe, at least in the beginning, you can help position the equipment or something."

Mei gave a short, reluctant nod. But her cheeks were pink again—and this time, it wasn't from frustration.

As she turned to walk toward Jessica, James let out a long breath.

Disclosure was bringing people out of hiding—sometimes from underground civilizations, and other times from the overlooked corners of their own communities.

He could only hope he was making the right choices about who to bring into the light.

* * *

The meeting chamber smelled of fear.

Not fresh or frantic fear, but the old kind—deep and heavy, like the smell of wet ashes. Junia stood along the outer edge of the circle, behind the raised seats carved from petrified roots. Her arms were at her sides, nails digging into the soft pads of her palms. Her breath came in slow, furious pulls through her nose. She tried to look calm, and respectful. But inside, she was breaking apart. Into little pieces.

Bowen's death had changed her.

All around her, the elders murmured, their eyes clouded with grief. Her uncle Alun sat still and silent, his hands clasped tightly in his lap. He had gone silent after they recovered Bowen's body and brought it back through the tunnel earlier. The elders had been in session since then, their voices blending together in waves of sorrow and rage and confusion.

"I say we close all the entrances," Elder Rinn said, her voice papery but clear. "Seal the tunnels again. We withdraw, as we always have when the surface burns."

A rumble of agreement passed through the circle.

"And what of the shift?" asked someone else. "When the veils rise, we will not be able to hide. Shall we simply wait to be discovered by force?"

"Better that than welcoming death with open arms," muttered another.

"Better that than sending our children to die for pointless dreams."

Junia's heart pounded. The ache in her chest cracked wide open. *No. Not this. Not now.*

She forced herself to step forward calmly. "That's enough."

The murmurs stopped. Heads turned toward her, eyes glittering with fatigue and unspoken judgment.

"You are not part of this meeting," said Elder Rinn, her brows arching. "You are here as a courtesy."

Junia ignored the warning in her voice. "Being polite doesn't matter now. Bowen is dead. So are two others. And you want to pretend this didn't happen? Walk away like you always do?"

"Watch your tone, child—"

"I'm not a child anymore," Junia snapped—louder than she meant to—but the elders were lucky she wasn't screaming at them.

"I *was* a child. Yesterday. Before I saw people die. Before I killed humans. Before I saw what fear and greed did to our home."

The silence that followed was total.

Alun finally looked up. Not at her, through her. But he was listening.

"I loved Bowen; he was my cousin," she whispered brokenly, unconsciously fingering the long cut that ran down her left arm; she didn't remember getting it. "But hiding won't bring him back."

A few elders shifted in their seats, uncomfortable.

"You think hiding keeps us safe," Junia said, trying to keep her voice calm. "But all it does is keep *us* in the dark. And the humans too. And now we have trouble because we acted like the surface didn't matter."

"They came for gold," muttered one of the elders. "They came with machines and guns and greed."

"Yes," Junia agreed. "But how long did we watch them get greedy without telling them the truth? How long did we let the old stories turn into just fairy tales? Maybe if they really knew, they wouldn't have attacked. Maybe they would've stopped to think."

"That is foolish hope."

"It's better than dying in the dark," she said fiercely. "There won't be any magic to fix things. When the vibrational shift happens, the humans will see us—our villages, our people, everything. If we wait until then to tell them who we are, it'll be even worse than it is now. But right now, we still have a chance."

Her gaze swept the circle. "Or you can hide down here, and watch the world burn again. Just like when the ACs stayed behind. Just like before the Ice."

Her jab hit. Several elders flinched.

Junia lowered her voice, though the anger still burned in her. "I'm not saying we should trust humans. I'm saying we should *do* something. Work with the ones who want peace, and get ready for the ones who don't. But we can't just hope the surface will forget about us."

Alun stood slowly. Everyone turned to him.

He was pale, older than she'd ever seen him look. "My niece is right," he said quietly. "I did not think I would say this today. Not after what I saw. Not after I carried my dead son in my arms."

He paused and let his words hang in the air.

"But hiding will not save us. Not this time. The Earth is changing. The veils between dimensions thin. The surface world will crash into ours, whether we want it or not. We can shape the impact—or be crushed by it."

No one spoke for a long moment.

Then, Elder Rinn, her silver-lined fingers steepled in thought, nodded once. "Perhaps the child has grown."

Junia didn't smile. She didn't feel proud. Her grief coiled too tightly in her heart for that. She felt guilty that she was still alive while Bowen was dead.

But she met Elder Rinn's eyes. And she did not look away.

Chapter Nineteen

The engine kicked into high gear as they drove up the twisting mountain road. The car's tires clung to the edge of the pavement as Kiran carefully maneuvered the vehicle around hairpin turns. He stared intently as he drove; these narrow mountain roads could be tricky if you weren't used to them.

He wasn't.

In the passenger seat beside him, Jessica kept her eyes on the road signs as they passed, but her thoughts were miles ahead—inside a small cave, somewhere in the canyon, where Junia waited.

The silence in the car was unusual.

Brad sat in the back seat, his expression unreadable behind his sunglasses. Beside him, James scrolled through his phone, tracking their progress on Google Maps.

Jessica cleared her throat. "So... I probably should've told you earlier. This isn't going to go like the livestream did."

Three sets of eyes turned toward her.

Brad was first. "What do you mean?"

"In the email from Vicki, she told me to come here—to Big Tujunga Canyon—because there was a problem back on the East Coast," she said.

Kiran slowed the car to navigate a steep dip in the road. The trees grew denser now, with more pine and greater shadow.

"What problem?" James asked, frowning.

Jessica's voice was tense. "Because the Suede Nation was attacked at the Pilot Knob entrance."

The silence sharpened. James put his phone down as Brad sat up straighter.

"What do you mean 'attacked'?" Kiran asked as he pulled the car over to a shoulder just wide enough to park. They had arrived. He shut off the engine and turned to face her.

Now Jessica had to say the thing she hadn't wanted to say out loud. "Humans. A group looking for gold. They forced their way in through the Pilot Knob entrance and..." She swallowed. "There were deaths. Suede Nation defenders. Vicki said it's been sealed now. Permanently."

"God," James breathed.

"Junia's cousin was one of the ones killed," Jessica added. "Bowen."

Brad looked like he'd been punched in the chest. "That's... that's Alun's son. He's just our age."

Jessica nodded. "Yeah."

Kiran stared down. "They attacked. Even after the livestream. After everything."

"No," Jessica said quietly. "*Because* of it. Now they're realizing what's down there. What *valuable* things are probably down there. And people are greedy."

For a long moment, no one spoke. There was nothing to say.

They all got out of the car. Jessica's eyes darted around and landed on a trailhead where the gravel road narrowed into a footpath. "Junia said there's a small entrance here. Not one most humans would recognize. We're supposed to meet her inside."

"Why out here?" James asked. "The studio is safe. And we can make higher quality videos there because of all the equipment."

Jessica gave a sad smile. "She's not coming to us. Not anytime soon. She's changed. Vicki said there's something broken inside of her—that Junia won't be trusting us as easily now. It's like she grew up overnight. But she still agreed to meet. She still wants to talk."

Brad took a few steps ahead to stare out across the ravine. His fists were clenched. "She still wants to talk, after her cousin was murdered. That's huge."

"I think she wants people to know the truth," Jessica said. "On *her* terms."

Kiran scanned the slopes, the ridges, and the brush. "You think this entrance is active? Not another dead end?"

Jessica nodded. "Vicki said this one's old. Hard to find. But that Junia's people opened it for us."

James took a long breath. "It's not right, Jess. We did this to them."

"No," she said softly. "*Some* of us did. The rest of us have to be the ones who stop it."

They formed a loose half-circle, looking toward the footpath. The trail narrowed into a crease between two boulders that jutted out. Jessica felt her stomach roil.

"Vicki told her we'd bring the camera and lights," she said, patting the bag over her shoulder. "She wants to be recorded."

"She trusts us?" Brad asked, skeptical.

"I think she's trying to," Jessica said. "And I think we owe it to her—to all of them—to show up."

James nodded slowly, while Kiran stayed silent. Brad followed behind.

Together, they started down the path toward the cave and the hidden entrance waiting in the mountain's center.

They didn't know what Junia would say.

But they knew they had to listen.

* * *

The room smelled like old files and stale coffee.

Sam Berger shifted in the high-backed chair, one of two dozen people around the rectangular table inside a SCIF—Sensitive Compartmented Information Facility—deep within the Pentagon.

The SCIF served as a secure area for storing, processing, and discussing sensitive classified information. Designed to prevent electronic eavesdropping and data leakage, all SCIFs were governed by strict physical and cybersecurity protocols. Access to any SCIF was tightly controlled and limited to individuals with the appropriate security clearance and need-to-know.

Everyone in the room wore uniforms—dress blues, fatigues, or civilian suits so expertly tailored they screamed three-letter agency. Even Sam. But he wasn't really supposed to be here.

Colonel Doyle had a scheduling conflict," he'd told the guards outside. It was the only information he'd been given.

But now, as the argument reached a new crescendo, Sam had a sneaking suspicion: Colonel Bradley Doyle, his direct supervisor, hadn't been double-booked. He'd *ducked* this meeting entirely as too risky.

Too damned political.

"This conversation has been a disaster," barked General Halsey, a man whose chest was heavily decorated with medals. "And I don't mean the Suede Nation livestreams. I'm talking about the sympathetic commentary, the whistleblowing, the amateur Disclosure advocates who think this is some galactic TED Talk. We're losing control of the narrative."

Across the table, a younger man in Air Force blues challenged him. "Control? We never had control. Not over this. The people out there are terrified and fascinated—and rightly so. We've lied to them for decades. They're waking up, General."

"And if we hand them the whole truth at once," snapped Halsey, "they'll riot in the streets. Our economy—our sovereignty—could collapse. You want a hundred million people thinking Earth is a galactic zoo exhibit? Or a weapons depot?"

Murmurs around the table. Some nods. Others shifted uncomfortably.

Sam kept his face neutral. Inside, his stomach roiled.

He wasn't here to talk, just to observe. Doyle had made that very clear: *Keep your mouth shut, Berger. Take notes. Report to me directly.* But sitting here now, watching grown men and women argue about what the public deserved to know—or didn't—Sam felt out of his depth.

Someone mentioned Vicki Heywood's name. Another person dismissed the *Melly Talks* videos as "glossy influencer propaganda." A tall man from Naval Intelligence mumbled something about "containment protocols" that Sam didn't quite catch.

Then it happened.

Colonel Riley—from a different section in the Office of the Secretary of Defense than Sam—leaned back in his seat with a quiet sneer. "Look, I don't care how cute the girl in the videos is. I care that she's not dead. After what she saw—what she *stole*—she should've vanished permanently, not just from a *basement*."

A few faces froze.

Sam blinked once.

His mind backtracked fast, like hitting rewind on a security tape. *Basement? Stolen?* He kept his breath even. Kept his hands still.

But inside, something cracked.

They were talking about Jessica. The girl Jerry had mentioned. The one who'd filmed the *Melly Speaks* series. The one who'd been *kidnapped*.

Sam had assumed—*hoped*—that part had been a rumor. One of the wilder online speculations. But now...

He knew. He *knew*.

And the man who had just casually dropped the truth about it wasn't even hiding it. Wasn't even hiding that he wanted her dead. Which meant either arrogance or assurance. Maybe both. It meant they were *still* playing by the old rules: silence, threat, removal.

He suddenly felt dirty just breathing the same air as them.

Across the table, someone launched into a technical mono-logue about psychological destabilization thresholds. Sam didn't hear a word. He stared blankly at the printout in front of him, watching as the ink blurred on the paper.

All this time he'd been on the fence. Not out of cowardice, but caution. The world *was* volatile, and Disclosure could be the match that set it all on fire. He didn't want war. He didn't want chaos.

But what he wanted even less was to be one of those people keeping humanity deliberately *blind*. People who'd abduct a girl to silence her. People who sat in rooms like this and decided who got to know the truth—and who disappeared.

He looked down the table at Riley, who was now chuckling at a comment General Halsey had made about "surgical containment."

You bastard.

Sam didn't speak. Didn't give himself away. He just sat there, face blank, spine straight, exactly the way he'd been trained.

But in his mind, something snapped into place.

He would not be part of this.

When the meeting adjourned—when the memos were typed and the reports submitted—he would do his job. He'd report back to Colonel Doyle about what they'd said. Maybe even play dumb about the kidnapping comment.

But his *real* report would go elsewhere.

To Jerry. And Vicki.

And when the moment came—when the curtain lifted for good—he knew which side of the line he'd stand on.

* * *

Junia crouched in the shadow of the stone overhang, the cave behind her pulsing faintly from the vibrations of their hidden world. She could feel the energy signature of the entrance—a living vibration, still raw from the sudden overload that had sealed Pilot Knob for good. Even from across the country, she could still feel it.

She shifted on her heels, her eyes fixed on the narrow trail below where dust swirled in the afternoon light. They were coming. She could sense them. Not just hear their approach; she could feel it in her bones and her blood. The Four. The ones the Suedes called the Guides—Jessica, Brad, James, and Kiran.

Her hands clenched in her lap.

Her cousin Bowen's face flashed before her eyes again—not peaceful in death, but filled with rage. It was all wrong. There had been blood. The entrance had been breached by those humans, and Bowen had paid for it with his life. And it was her fault because she convinced him to give them a chance.

And now here come the humans again, she thought bitterly. *More humans. Always more.*

Junia rose slowly, standing straight despite the stiffness in her spine. The coppery ropes of her hair fell across her face, but she didn't brush them back. Let them see her anger if they had the eyes for it. Let them choke on it.

But then, just as quickly, the anger faded. Curiosity tugged at her—a softer, quieter blade. These weren't diplomats or camera crews or treasure hunters. These were the ones the old songs spoke of. The Guides. The ones Vicki had vouched for. The ones her uncle Alun still dared to believe in.

What kind of children does the Earth send to speak for her now? she wondered.

Her gaze moved over the dusty ridge where the trail curved up sharply. Any moment now.

She needed to say something—something that could break through all the confusion and old mistakes. Something that might help people understand before the next time things turned violent.

But what could she say that was strong enough? And would they even listen?

Her fingers curled again, and her jaw tightened. She could still taste the iron bitterness of her cousin's death. See the look in his eyes in those final, brutal seconds before—

No.

She turned her face away from the trail and took a long breath. The vibration of the cave thrummed through her soles, a reminder of the world they stood on, and the world they were about to enter.

And then the realization hit her. *They don't know what they're doing either.*

She wanted to meet them—she *needed* to meet them. To look into their eyes. To know if she could trust them. To know if they could be friends.

A rustle in the brush, voices... a flash of movement.

They had arrived.

She turned back toward the trail, her expression hardening again. Grief flared suddenly, blinding and sharp, and she felt herself sway.

Bowen should be here, she thought savagely. *He would've had diplomatic words to say. Something wise. Something hopeful.*

But all she had was rage. And questions. And a single, selfish urge to spit on the world that had taken him.

Piss on them all, she thought. *Let them prove they can be better than they were before.*

She stepped forward into the open, her topaz eyes gleaming like cut glass.

"Welcome," she said, her voice flat. "You're late."

Chapter Twenty

J essica hunched over the editing console, the glow of the screen bathing her face in a sharp light as the cave scene played for the umpteenth time.

"If you come down here again, if you try to take from us—"

"We won't ask questions."

"We'll bring the rock down."

On the monitor, Junia's topaz eyes gleamed like torchlight. The jagged cut running down the side of one arm—new since Bowen's death—caught a sliver of light, adding a harsh glimmer. Her voice, once bright and laughing, now carried an iron chill. And then—there they were again—the claws.

They emerged from beneath the skin of her fingers like blades springing from a sheath. The sound—an organic rasp, not metal but bone—sent a chill down Jessica's spine even now. Knife-long, obsidian-dark, and vibrating slightly with energy.

"We were soft before. We will not be again."

Jessica paused the playback. The image froze with Junia's claws fully extended, her gaze locked on the unseen camera with an intensity that seemed to pierce the lens.

Jessica leaned back, arms crossed, heart racing. She hadn't known about the claws. No one had warned her. Probably no one had known.

The girl—no, *young woman*, Jessica reminded herself—had changed since Vicki's original livestream. Back then, she had been curious, exuberant, and peppering everyone with questions about surface life. Life had been full of fun. Junia had wanted Disclosure more than anyone. Now she looked like an omen—a living harbinger of grief and violence.

A part of Jessica wanted to cry. Another part wanted to call Vicki and scream: *This is too much.*

But mostly, she sat frozen by the cost of deciding. How much of this should she show the world? She tapped a key, skipping ahead.

Junia stood near a cave wall now, fingers spread, claws withdrawn, but her energy still tense. "Watch," she said flatly. "Watch and remember." She reached her hand toward the stone, her eyes fluttering shut.

The rock began to tremble.

Jessica leaned forward, bracing her hands on her knees. The camera shook slightly—Brad had been holding it—before righting as the stone above them groaned and shifted. With a grinding sound, a jagged slab broke away from the ceiling and slammed into the ground just inches from Junia.

"We don't need weapons. The living stone answers our call."

Jessica stopped the playback again, sat still for a long moment, and then buried her face in her hands.

She knew how the public would react. A week ago, they had swooned over Junia's laughter, and had drawn fan art of the cat-eyed girl who danced and twirled. They were ready to *love* the Suede Nation. But she could already see the hashtags that would follow this:

#SuedeThreat, #CaveMonster, #ClawsLikeKnives

Jessica lowered her hands. "God, Junia, what did we do to you?"

But she knew. Humans had killed Bowen. Humans had invaded their home. Humans had come with greed in their eyes and weapons in their hands.

Jessica's gut twisted. She had to stop thinking of this as some sort of PR disaster—this was the truth. Junia hadn't been performing. She'd been *honest,* for goodness sake. Grief had sharpened her, and then rage had made her fearless.

Jessica remembered how it had felt to be kidnapped by those who opposed Disclosure. How her voice had trembled for days afterward. Junia had lost more than her confidence—she had lost belief.

There was a soft knock at the door. Jessica startled.

Brad poked his head in. "Coffee?" He held up two mismatched mugs.

"Sure."

He caught a glimpse of the paused screen and whistled low. "That shot's going to blow people's minds."

"Or blow up the whole process," Jessica muttered.

Brad came in, set one mug down beside her, and leaned on the edge of the desk. "You going to show it?"

She paused. "I don't really have a choice. If I cut it... it's like I'm saying the truth is too much for people to handle. Or that what happened—the attack—wasn't really that serious."

He nodded. "But if you leave it in, you're giving fuel to everyone who says the Suede Nation is a threat."

"I shouldn't hide what Junia and the other Suedes feel," she said quietly. "And I shouldn't hide the the violent behavior of humans. We've had too many people lying to us. This isn't a lie. It would be a lie to hide it."

The two of them sat in silence for a long moment. Jessica turned back to the console and hit play again. Junia's voice echoed in the chamber.

"We were here long before your governments knew the shape of the sky. We are older than your fear. If you want peace—earn it. If you want war—we will end it before you even see us."

Brad exhaled. "Powerful."

"Terrifying," Jessica said. Then, with conviction: "Perfect."

She adjusted the timestamp, pulled the full sequence into the working draft timeline, and began typing her introduction voiceover.

"This is Junia. She trusted humans once. We broke that trust by attacking her home and killing her people. Now she's showing us who she is. And who the Suede Nation has always been."

She looked at Brad. "I'll add subtitles. Nothing else. No commentary. No edits."

He nodded slowly. "You sure?"

"No," she said. "But truth doesn't wait for perfect timing." She hit *Render*.

The fans on the machine started to spin, their noise gradually rising in volume as the files were processed. Somewhere beneath her, beneath all of them, the Earth watched and listened.

And waited.

* * *

Brad sat hunched in his darkened office, staring at his computer. The hum of the commercial refrigerator in the common area was the only reminder that this place had once sold roses and lilacs, not served as a nerve center for planetary upheaval. He hadn't moved in nearly an hour—not since he'd finished watching Junia's video for the third time.

Her face—older now, raw with grief and rage—still lingered in his mind.

Claws.

That part hadn't been scripted. Jessica had handled it like a pro, but Brad nearly dropped the camera when Junia extended her fingers and turned them into weapons.

And her warning was blunt, not dressed up in diplomacy.

"We were curious. We were hopeful. You killed my cousin. Try again, and we will bring down the ceiling over your heads."

She had demonstrated it too. In the footage, the ceiling slab had dropped like... well, like a rock. It was vibrational manipulation, both beautiful and terrifying.

Had it been the right decision to include it in the final cut? The truth had teeth now. It would scare people, but that was the whole idea. And if they didn't tell the truth, all of it, they wouldn't be much different from the Partnership—the conglomerate that hoarded alien tech, lied to the public, and sold humanity's future for short-term gain.

No. Jessica was right, they shouldn't hide this.

With his internal dilemma resolved, Brad clicked away from the video and pulled up a tracking dashboard he'd coded weeks earlier. Rows of green blips illuminated a world map, scattered like confetti across Africa, South Asia, and parts of South America. Free energy prototypes, both large and small, built from the schematics he'd released anonymously. The plans had spread like wildfire on message boards and back-channel servers, and now the open-source tech was thriving and evolving across continents.

He'd expected someone to try and shut it all down. Many had.

He opened a second window—one of his ghost accounts pulling obscure defense contractor feeds and encrypted communications. He found the Lagos attack—it was now buried in financial analyses and energy reports, dismissed in the West as a "tragic incident during early-stage adoption of alien tech." They had already forgotten about it. No one cared that the "alien" attack had been a false flag event engineered by Partnership holdouts—an attempt to scare people away from anything to do with extraterrestrials. In fact, the financial sector wouldn't have cared even if it *had* been an alien attack.

Too late—the world had smelled profit.

Brad scrolled deeper into a flagged thread: unmarked helicopters outside Singapore, a facility in Bangalore burned to the ground. Nothing in mainstream channels. But buried in the chatter between worried engineers and anonymous posters were consistent hints:

"We saw the patch—corporate, not military."
"Why target wind and solar and this?"

"That new facility outside Warsaw went dark. No survivors."

He leaned back in his chair, the muscles in his neck aching. Some of the old conglomerates—governments included—were sending mercenaries. The fossil fuel empire wasn't going down quietly.

Brad copied the links into a clean file, encrypted the data, and began composing an email to Jerry and Vicki. Both of them needed to see it. Vicki, because she had the leverage. Jerry, because he was the finance guy. Together, they could do something to to make these bastards sweat.

Before he hit send, he paused. His reflection in the monitor looked tired—older than just a few months ago. Jessica was out there taking the heat. James was translating a millennia of secrets. Kiran was holding his family together by a thread.

And Brad? He was behind the screen, tearing down empires one line of code at a time.

Good.

Let them come. Let them underestimate him.

He smiled and clicked *Send*.

* * *

The air still hummed with the residue of vibration shifts. Junia sat on the ledge above the chamber floor, her legs curled beneath her. She hadn't spoken since the Guides left.

Not to Alun. Not to the elders.

Certainly not to herself, although her thoughts had been anything but silent.

Her claws had come out so fast.

She hadn't planned that part. Jessica hadn't flinched—and Junia *respected* her for that—but the others had gone very still. Except for Brad, who usually had the look of someone hiding mischief behind his eyes. Brad had staggered and nearly fallen over—she almost laughed thinking about it.

Then she remembered the moment her claws extended—flesh stretching, bones shifting, those long, shining blades catching the dim cave light. And the fear in the eyes of the young humans. It made her feel a little guilty.

But wasn't that the point? To make them feel afraid? To make humans think twice before bringing violence to the Suedes?

Junia exhaled sharply. Her claws stayed retracted, but the pounding in her chest hadn't subsided. She thought of the tunnel—crushing down like a wave of thunder—and the blood in it.

Bowen.

He wouldn't have wanted this. Or... maybe he would have. He had always been more suspicious of humans, more cautious about opening up. It was all her fault because she was the one who had laughingly urged him to come and try new things—things like meeting the humans. Bowen had not only been her cousin but also her best friend.

Bridgewalkers. That's what Uncle Alun had called them.

"You and Bowen," he'd said once, resting a hand on her shoulder, "you are the bridge and the crossing both. Not of tunnels, but of trust."

And what had she done? Junia had faced the Guides—their open eyes, their strange humanness—and instead of building, she'd threatened.

But that was for her people's defense. Because humans brought death into their home. Because if she had shown softness, it would have been seen as an invitation, not a boundary.

She stood up and walked slowly in a circle around the stone chamber. Its energy always calmed her, but now it pulsed with her regrets.

She should have asked Jessica more questions. Brad, too—he carried something sharp behind his grin. James had watched her like he knew sorrow. Kiran... Kiran had the stillness of a deep river.

They were not what she had expected. Not soldiers. Not politicians.

Not her enemies.

But the moment had been too raw, too painful. And so instead of serving as a bridge, she had become the gate—closed and guarded.

She pressed her palm against the warm stone, feeling its vibration shift gently to meet hers. This chamber recognized her. It didn't judge.

The Guides had left hours earlier, and she could still smell their presence—sandalwood, dust, wind, and something like citrus. She closed her eyes and whispered, just for herself: "I wish I'd had more time."

She wasn't sure if she meant with them, or with Bowen.

Maybe both.

Chapter Twenty-One

The blinds were partially closed while the overhead lights remained on. Vicki sat at her desk, her jaw tight. Jerry stood nearby with his arms crossed, watching her handle another call on speakerphone.

"Of course we're aware of the video, Governor," Vicki said, carefully modulating her voice. "No, the claws weren't CGI. She is a member of the Suede Nation, not a Hollywood actress."

A pause. On the other end, the governor's voice rose into a tirade. Something about containment, public panic, and escalation. Vicki's nostrils flared.

"She was responding to a *lethal incursion* into her people's territory. They didn't start the violence." Her tone sharpened. "If you invaded any sovereign nation and murdered their children, would you expect a welcome basket?"

She tapped the screen to end the call. She was so tired. The drama was insane.

"Sixth call like that in the last hour," she muttered. "But none of them can hold a single thought for long. Terror now. Denial tomorrow."

Jerry shifted on his feet. "You knew the video would have an impact."

"I did. But I expected better than this hand-wringing melt-down. They don't know what's going on and it shows."

The door opened without a knock. Mary stepped in, clutching a folder and wearing a tight-lipped expression.

"Senator Long called again," Mary said. "He's worried that Junia's claws might incite 'global cultural trauma.' His exact words. Also, some Congressional staffer tried to push a memo claiming we staged the entire thing using deep fakes."

Vicki looked at her blankly. "Aren't we all supposed to be adults?"

Mary raised an eyebrow. "At the moment? They're acting like preschoolers."

Jerry offered a weak chuckle, then turned serious. "Do we know who leaked the entrance location?"

The question hung in the air.

Vicki leaned back. "No. But it's easy to narrow down the list. Only one team—ours—had access to the Pilot Knob cave location before the attack."

Mary closed the folder. "Do you want me to quietly review the background checks of everyone who had clearance?"

Vicki nodded.

Jerry lowered his voice. "If someone gave coordinates to ex-tremists, that wasn't just carelessness. It was on purpose."

"I know," Vicki said. "And that makes it treason."

Mary's voice was flat. "Do you want it handled off-record?"

"No," Vicki said. "We're not going to brush it under the rug. But I do want it fast. We're at the edge of a critical turning point, and the last thing we need is someone inside dragging humanity backward."

Mary gave a crisp nod and left the room.

Jerry walked to the window, pulled the blinds all the way up, and looked out over the city.

"You think Junia regrets doing the video?" he asked.

"She didn't look like she regretted it."

"No," Jerry said. "But she looked... changed. Even the Four remarked on it."

Vicki picked up the tablet again. The paused frame of Junia mid-sentence stared back at her—eyes flinty, hands set, claws extended.

"She's mourning," Vicki said. "And she's making sure it doesn't happen again."

More calls lit up the screen. She ignored them.

"She's not the one who should be explaining herself," Vicki said. "We are."

* * *

Kiran stood at the front of the tai chi class, watching the group as they settled into place. Jessica adjusted the camera while James helped Brad check the sound levels. Calvin—James's dad—moved between the students, answering questions here and there. These were the most advanced students at the Cloud Hands Tai Chi studio, and they were skilled in chi, posture, and breath. Most had been with the studio for years, and their movements were controlled and focused. Today, however, they were there for more than just movement.

Kiran cleared his throat, and the room grew quiet. He looked at the faces in front of him. They were attentive—open—but he could also feel the tension beneath their calm. The interference was everywhere now—background noise in the mind that didn't belong.

"I want to talk about something you've probably already noticed. You're meditating and practicing breathwork, but you're feeling sudden irritation or intrusive thoughts for no clear reason. You've probably asked yourself: Is this just stress? Am I doing something wrong?"

Heads nodded. A few students looked toward him more sharply now.

"This is mechanical interference," Kiran said, his voice calm. "Rogue advanced technology that is being used against us. It sends thoughts into our minds through ways most people don't even know are possible: smart devices, subliminal suggestions, cellular signals, and Wi-Fi. The signals are so well hidden that people don't notice them, but they're powerful enough to change how we think, how we focus, and how we feel. This isn't our imagination. This isn't anxiety. It's engineered."

He scanned the room. He had their attention. A few faces showed relief—they had experienced it already, even if they hadn't known what it was.

"You're not alone if you've been feeling tired in a way that sleep doesn't fix. If you're distracted for no reason or overly emotional in moments that don't justify it. And you're not wrong if you've begun to suspect that your thoughts aren't entirely your own."

Kiran walked slowly between the rows of students.

We don't know who is doing it, but we know why. They want humanity stuck. They want your attention drained, your confidence shaken, and your thinking clouded. They want you to question yourself so deeply and so often that you stop trying. They want humanity to remain manageable—controllable."

He returned to the front of the class.

"Everyone in this room has already made a choice. You've seen the first signs of what's possible—through movement, through breath, and through consciousness itself. You've recognized that your mind isn't just a processor of tasks or an information storehouse. It's also a source of direction, a source of freedom. And it belongs to you. Just by being here, you're already saying you don't agree with a world that tells us what to feel, what to be afraid of, or who to be.

He gestured toward the recording equipment—the tripods, cameras, lights, and microphones—and the unblinking red light indicating that the recording was live.

"This class isn't just for you. It's for everyone else. Everyone who hasn't made it here yet. Everyone who's still wondering if they're going crazy. Everyone who feels something is wrong but doesn't know how to describe it. Everyone who's reaching for peace and being handed more noise."

He drew a breath. The students held it with him.

"This is how we start to fight back. This class. This video. Just by you being here. The techniques we're about to share aren't complicated. They're not elite. They're not reserved for the few. They're for everyone. This is how change begins—by helping people remember who they are."

He allowed the silence to settle.

"Now we begin."

No one interrupted. Jessica moved quietly behind the camera, capturing his words.

"You don't need to be able to detect subtle energy to manage it. You just need tools. So I'm going to share five simple techniques that anyone can do. They work even if you're surrounded by chaos, even if you're tired, and even if you've never meditated in your life."

Kiran stepped forward and spoke in a measured tone.

"First: Pause—take a moment. Don't rush to engage with the thought. Don't argue with it. Don't assume it's you. Just pause."

"Second: Ask—ask yourself a question. Does this thought have a feeling? Not a story or logic—a feeling. What emotional imprint does it leave?"

He waited a moment. Several students nodded.

"Third: Locate—Where is this thought? Can you feel it in your body? In your chest or gut? That's usually where emotions are anchored."

Kiran moved his hand to the center of his chest.

"Fourth: If there's no feeling—ignore it. If it feels empty and lacks connection to anywhere in your body, let it go. It's not yours."

A few students took quiet breaths, as if trying the techniques out right then.

"And fifth: If you're unsure, refocus on your breath. Don't get stuck trying to solve it. Just go back to your breath and be patient."

He scanned the group, sensing the shift. Their awareness was already turning inward. The static didn't disappear, but it calmed.

"This won't protect you from everything," he said, "but it gives you a solid foundation—a tool to help you see things more clearly. Not everyone can meditate for hours or track subtle frequencies. But everyone can stop and ask themselves: Is this mine?"

Kiran stepped back, joining the students, now simply another member of the class. Calvin began guiding them in what he referred to as "moving meditation." His voice was low.

"Slowly shift your weight from side to side, keeping your attention light. As Kiran said, let the thoughts come. Apply the steps. Feel your breath. Notice when you begin to respond rather than react. There's a difference between the two—find it."

The class began swaying—knees soft, arms relaxed, and their breath deepening. Calvin walked slowly among them, adjusting a posture here and softening a wrist there. Some had closed their eyes, while others kept their gaze forward but unfocused.

Kiran felt it again—a subtle edge of interference, faint yet persistent. A ripple across the mind. It wasn't his imagination or emotion. It was... synthetic. Trying to stay hidden.

Kiran grounded himself with his breath. *They're trying to reach into our minds,* he thought. *But we're not helpless.* The class continued to breathe, to move, to anchor.

And the static receded.

* * *

James glanced over his shoulder and spotted Mei standing just outside the camera setup's frame. She wasn't trying to be noticed, but her focus was intense. Her hands were clasped in front of her, knuckles slightly white, eyes tracking every movement Jessica and Brad made with the equipment. The lights, the markers on the floor, the instructions being passed from Jessica to Brad as they finished up the filming of the advanced class. Ever since James had suggested that Mei could help, Jessica had let her assist with the setup—but it was clear that wasn't enough for her.

James motioned to her. "Mei."

She waited a beat before crossing the floor to him, her steps quick, silent, eager.

"You still want to help?" he asked.

"Yes," she said, without pause. Her eyes didn't waver. "Whatever I can do. I want to help."

James nodded once and turned toward where Jessica was speaking with her brother. He tapped her on the arm and waited until she turned. "Jess. Can I grab you for a second?"

Jessica stepped back, brushing her hair away from her face. "What's up?"

"I think you should film Mei."

Jessica looked over at her. Mei's face had flushed slightly, but she stood her ground.

Jessica raised an eyebrow. "Why?"

"She's not an expert," James said. "She's not a teacher or even a member of the advanced class. She's still figuring things out. That's why. She's younger, and she's working through the same confusion and questions that most people out there are dealing with. That makes her valuable. People watching these videos—they're going to trust someone who's going through it with them."

Jessica considered that for a moment, then nodded. "Alright. Let's set her up after the movement segment."

Mei let out a breath and gave a quick, grateful bow to them both.

As Jessica turned to make the arrangements with the camera crew, James stepped aside, letting Mei gather her thoughts.

Then he heard it.

A voice, quiet, just to the left behind the divider.

"Great," came the mutter. "Mei's going to explain higher consciousness now. This should be a disaster. The family is going to be so upset about it."

James turned his head and saw Tian, Mei's cousin, leaning against the wall, phone in hand, his mouth twisted in contempt.

"Tian," James said, his voice even but loud enough to catch the young man's attention.

Tian looked up. "What?"

"Stop it."

Tian gave a lazy shrug. "Just saying what everyone's thinking. Mei always messes things up."

"No," James said. "You're saying what you think will keep her small enough that you don't have to deal with the fact she's outgrowing you—both you and your family. You've probably been doing that her whole life. You should stop trying to tear everything down and build something instead."

Tian scoffed, but he didn't reply.

James didn't wait for one. He turned back toward the set, where Mei was now standing near Jessica, quietly receiving directions. Her shoulders were straight. Her expression was focused. She didn't waver.

The cameras began to roll again.

Chapter Twenty-Two

Aija sat on the edge of her bed, arms crossed, her phone resting facedown beside her. The late afternoon shone on the walls in a dappled pattern, but she didn't notice. Her thoughts were crowded—too loud to let her see anything clearly.

Her parents hadn't even tried to pretend they were neutral. After their initial protest about Jessica not being Hindu, they had capitulated. And then when Kiran brought Jessica around—soft-voiced, space-obsessed Jessica with her half-lost expressions and all that vibrational nonsense—it was as if nothing else mattered. Her mother had called Jessica "charming." Her father had said she was "interesting." As if that erased the fact that she was the embodiment of everything ridiculous about Disclosure.

And Kiran? He could do no wrong. He was meditating, aligning, and teaching strangers how to breathe. Suddenly, he was some kind of guru. He hadn't even gone to college, and now he had government clearances and people filming him like he was some Vedic sage out of ancient history.

Aija clenched her jaw. When she had tried to explain to her parents how unfair it was, they had told her to let go of jealousy.

Jealousy? As if she were some petty child. They didn't see it. They never had. Kiran had always received their approval. The benefit of the doubt. She was the one who was told to "wait," to "grow up," to "be more respectful."

She swiped her phone open again and looked at Amanda Riley's last message. The reporter was already hinting that there could be a story—maybe even a segment—if Aija had more to say. And Aija did. She had plenty. So what if a few details weren't exactly confirmed? She'd seen that video of Junia. The claws, the rock shifting. That was real. Who was to say there wasn't more they were hiding?

If people believed the Suede Nation could collapse tunnels from beneath cities—and if she presented it right, framing it as something already in motion—then maybe they'd stop treating all this Disclosure stuff like some utopian fantasy. Maybe they'd stop treating Jessica like a saint. Maybe they'd finally start listening to her.

Aija stood up and paced. The idea that she was just making things up made her a bit uneasy. But it wasn't like it was entirely false, either. If those creatures could do what Junia did in the video, then wasn't it logical to wonder if they had plans? And if those plans were dangerous? She wasn't fabricating—she was extrapolating.

She tapped out a quick voice memo to Amanda, tightening her phrasing, adding emotion, making her tone sound urgent but measured. She described how the Suedes had been seen near surface infrastructure, how they'd been spotted observing tunnels and power plants. None of that had been confirmed—or even hinted at by anyone—but it hadn't been disproven either. It *could* be true, so that was enough.

She felt her heart start beating faster as she hit send.

This was how it would begin. No more being ignored at dinner while her parents talked about Kiran. No more teachers comparing her to her "enlightened" older brother. This time, she was making waves.

Let them ignore her now.

Let them try.

* * *

Jerry rubbed the side of his jaw, feeling the prickle of stubble and tension beneath his skin. The office lights hummed above him, and the air had grown stale from too many hours without a break. His monitor displayed the access logs for the last thirty days: encrypted messaging timestamps, badge-ins, document pulls—everything Mary had flagged from the Communications Office.

It wasn't enough.

Mary had already sifted through the usual layers: social media posts, side devices, browser histories, and financial records. Nothing had jumped out. No last-minute trips to West Virginia. No sudden increases in bank balances. No encrypted messages to burner accounts or foreign proxies. Whoever leaked the coordinates to Pilot's Knob knew how to remain invisible—or understood the internal processes better than they should.

He leaned back in his chair and stared at the list. Thirty-eight employees. That had been narrowed down to six after Mary excluded those who were on medical leave, out of the country, or had airtight alibis. Now, he was stuck.

Six people—all cleared, all polished, and all working in the Communications Office where the damn livestream prep files had passed through in secured, digital file packages. Some of them had handled those files several times, while others had done so only once. Was someone testing the system? Was the leak part of something much bigger?

The memory of the Junia video flared in his mind again. The way she'd looked—grief behind her eyes, rage in her voice. And then the claws, and the rock crashing down in a single roar. The message had been clear: the Suede Nation would not lie down and wait to be crushed. They had power, and they would use it.

Now the cavern entrance was a war zone, with satellite imagery showing signs of forced excavation and radiation traces that shouldn't have been there. Had the attackers been using a reverse-engineered energy weapon, maybe supplied by a surviving

Partnership employees? The attack had failed—but it had left blood. And Bowen's name now sat like an accusation in the reports.

Jerry clicked through each of the six files: photos, security logs, and communication histories. He paused at Layla Hendrickson's profile. She was good—sharp, trusted, and had ten years of inter-agency liaison work under her belt. She'd worked at the U.N. liaison desk during the early Disclosure days. There was nothing obvious on her record. However, she had accessed the pre-brief documents twice in one day—once from her desktop and once from her phone. That wasn't standard procedure.

He made a note.

Then there was Oscar Finch. Quiet, efficient, and a recent hire. A bit too clean. His background indicated that he came from a defense contractor that Vicki had blacklisted for hiding records about ET artifact research. How had he managed to get through?

He toggled over to Mary's internal memo again. She had written a single line beneath the Communications Office heading:

"Either we're dealing with a mole, or the whole system is compromised."

Jerry sat still for a moment, thinking about it.

If it was one person, then it was a calculated betrayal. If it was more than one, then something deeper was eating away at OMR. Someone—some *group*—might have seen the broadcast footage, and decided that protecting the old power structures mattered more than humanity making contact with aliens.

He stood and walked to the whiteboard across the room. At the top, he wrote: "Motives." Underneath, he drew three bullet points.

- Loyalty to the traditional world order

- Financial leverage from collapsing industries

- Fear of non-human contact driven by ideology

He stared at them, then added a fourth.

- Fear of change

Then he wrote:

OMR Compromised?

6 candidates.

1 leak.

1 attack.

Global response: spiraling.

He heard Mary's voice through the door before she entered, low and clipped, as she finished a call. She held up her phone while closing the door.

"They're coming down hard from the Hill," she said. "Three separate offices just called Vicki's line demanding a formal hearing about the Suede Nation's 'threat potential.' I don't suppose you've got a miracle ready?"

Jerry shook his head and pointed at the board. "No miracle. But maybe a fracture line."

She followed his gesture to the name Oscar Finch.

"Defense contractor, right?" she said. "From ValorSys?"

"Yeah. One of the companies that hid the Partnership's reverse-engineered technology. We flagged them two months ago. Somehow, he still got cleared and hired."

She pulled out her tablet. "I'll start cross-checking all internal comms from his desk. If he's in this, there's more than just him. If he's not—well, then we're looking at something a hell of a lot harder to root out."

Jerry exhaled. "I want to know why. Not just who. What was worth giving away the location of the entrance? Was it to provoke the Suedes? To sabotage Disclosure? Or was it just greed?"

Mary's eyes narrowed. "Could be all three."

She left without waiting for a response.

Jerry settled back into his seat, dragging his hand across his face. The screen flickered back to the logs. He clicked on Oscar Finch's name again and began to dig deeper.

Someone had broken faith. And if they didn't stop it now, they might not get another chance.

* * *

Aija adjusted the collar of her jacket as she stepped into a quiet corner of the upscale café, her eyes scanning for the woman she was meeting. Amanda Riley was already seated, immaculate and poised, her hair perfectly arranged, a phone in one hand and a tablet in the other. She didn't look up until Aija sat down across from her.

"You're Aija Rao," Amanda said, setting the tablet aside. "Thanks for meeting me."

Aija leaned forward. "I figured you'd want to hear from someone who's actually seen what's going on. The others are keeping quiet, but I'm not going to lie for them."

Amanda gave a practiced nod, encouraging but neutral. "Tell me what you know."

"They're dangerous," Aija said, her voice low but firm. "That thing in the video, Junia—that wasn't just a warning. It was a threat. You think claws were all she had? She said their people could bring down entire cities. They can shift rock. Collapse whole mountains. And she isn't even the strongest one."

Amanda's expression barely moved, but she pressed record on the small device beside her coffee. "Go on."

"They're planning something," Aija continued. "The elders down there, the ones in the Suede Nation—they're furious. Everyone's acting like the Suedes' response to those gold hunters was just a one-time thing, but there's way more going on. People are saying they've been scouting the surface for years. Quietly. Deciding where to strike first if they have to."

Amanda raised her eyebrows slightly. "Strike?"

Aija nodded. "Junia didn't say it directly, but her message was clear. If the Suedes feel threatened, they won't just defend themselves; they'll act first. And honestly? Some of the people working with them are too dumb to notice."

Yeah, everyone knew that Jessica was simple-minded. While she hadn't come out and named Jessica directly, Aija knew Amanda was smart enough to get the hint. Hopefully, the reporter would also do something to bring *that* to the public's attention.

Aija smiled.

"You're saying a preemptive attack," Amanda said, voice carefully flat.

"I'm saying you should ask whether it's already in motion. If I were you, I'd start looking around the entrances—see who's going in and out. And find out who's protecting them. Someone in the government is helping them hide."

Amanda leaned back slightly, assessing. "And why are you sharing this?"

Aija smiled again. "Because people deserve the truth. And because you're the only one not kissing up to those freaks. You're showing what no one else will."

Amanda studied her for a second longer, then asked, "And what do you want?"

She had already thought about this. "Put me on camera. I know how to talk. I know how to get people's attention. Everyone else in this Disclosure circus is just trying to act humble or mystical or whatever. I'm not going to pretend. People want someone who tells it straight."

Amanda tilted her head. "You want to be famous."

"I want to be heard," Aija said. "And if that makes me famous, good. I'm not going to waste time chanting in a cave like Jessica and her friends. I actually live in the real world."

Amanda smiled with just the corners of her mouth. "Let's stay in touch. I think you could be useful."

Aija nodded, satisfaction settling in her chest. This was the beginning of something bigger. Finally, someone was paying attention to her.

Chapter Twenty-Three

The glow of the screen filled the room. Brad leaned forward in his chair, arms crossed, eyes fixed on the footage Jessica had flagged earlier. The cursor blinked for a moment before he pressed play, letting the clip run again.

Mei was in the frame, sitting on a plain mat, her hands fidgeting in her lap. Her eyes didn't focus on the camera the way trained speakers did. She glanced off-screen once and then looked down as she spoke, her voice a little unsteady, tension in her posture.

"I didn't think I could meditate, and at first it felt like I was failing," she said in the recording, eyes flicking off-screen again. "I thought it was for people with special brains or something. But when I tried what Kiran said—stopping, checking if the thought had a feeling—I could do that. And I started noticing stuff. I hadn't ever realized before that so many of my thoughts didn't feel like anything. They were just noise. I went back to my breath, and it got quiet."

She paused. The camera picked up her uncertainty, her nerves, and her decision to keep going. Brad didn't move. He kept his eyes on the timeline, watching the way she took a breath after finishing her sentence. She wasn't trying to impress anybody. and that's what made it work.

"I'm not really good at meditation. I'm not someone who sees colors or energy or whatever. But I could do this. It made me feel like I had control again."

Brad rewound the video and replayed that section again. He had wondered if James was making a mistake by putting Mei on camera, but now he could see she was perfect. Mei was awkward, young, and a little overeager. But she didn't pretend to know more than she did. She just spoke. Her voice cracked once, and her hands fidgeted. She didn't smile very much. But all of this was the reason people would believe her. She didn't sound like someone trying to sell anything. People would trust her because they wouldn't feel pressured. And she didn't sound like she had a script. Mei had the kind of credibility that polish could never manufacture—because she *was* unpolished. She sounded like someone who had been stuck and found something that helped her pull herself out.

Jessica had done well capturing it. The audio was clear, the background was neutral, and the lighting didn't wash out Mei's skin or eyes. Brad would trim a few seconds, but otherwise it was perfect for the outreach campaign. Real people explaining how to protect their inner landscape from outside manipulation—that's what people needed now.

He clicked *Save As* and added a tag to the file: *Uplift Series – Real Voices*. Then he sat back in his chair and stretched out his fingers before opening a second folder: *Heirs – Revenge Plan*.

The files were clean—nothing obvious or personal. Brad knew how to cloak his actions. It wasn't illegal—not technically. He wasn't hacking accounts or accessing private systems. While he had done that before to get the information he needed, now he was using open-source footage, social media posts, and public livestreams. All he was doing was repackaging them.

Brad looked at the names in his file. Although many of the young people he and Jessica knew during the Partnership era had

mistreated his sister, he was now focusing on those who had uploaded videos mocking Jessica after the *Melly Talks* series aired.
They'd laughed at her, called her fake, and claimed she was acting—that she was part of an elaborate con to promote an anti-capi-
talist narrative. Some had posted cruel parodies. Another had edited
her voice to stammer like a malfunctioning robot. The most recent
clip had paired Junia's warning with circus music and a caption that
read: "*When cosplay meets crisis.*" That post had gone viral. All of
them had been eager to be interviewed by that reporter, Amanda
Riley, who Vicki told them was the niece of Colonel Riley at the
Pentagon.

Brad didn't believe in forgiveness when people took potshots
at those who were risking everything. He hadn't responded—not
publicly. But privately, he had been developing his counterattack for
weeks.

He opened a subfolder.

His first project was already in the queue: a deepfake of one of
the lead mockers, Cassidy Henson. Brad had used public video from
her livestreams to create digitally altered footage. In his version, she
sat poolside, explaining how her father had secretly profited from
recovered alien tech, and that she thought "it was hilarious how easy
it was to distract people with makeup and lifestyle videos."

The lipsync was perfect. The lighting matched an influencer
panel she had been on in Tokyo. Brad had even added a few expressions she had shown elsewhere—eye rolls, a bored shrug—to make
it feel more natural.

He added the tagline: #SatireLeaks. That was the trick. Never
publish as truth—publish as parody. Let people question what was
real.

Then he added a banner to the bottom of the video: *"Cassidy
Henson: Influencer or Informant?"* and posted it to a satire account
with 70,000 followers that he managed under a pseudonym.

Brad paused. Cassidy was one of Aija's closest friends, and in
many ways, her behavior was less extreme than Aija's. But Aija was

Kiran's sister, so he was leaving her out of it. Kiran hadn't asked him to, but Brad realized his sister's boyfriend was fighting enough battles without having to take on his own little sister.

Next, he opened a meme batch labeled *"The Parrots."* These featured three other kids—Mike, Omar, and Lyla—each auto-edited to repeat their original critiques of Jessica, but twisted into gibberish. The algorithm had rendered their voices slightly higher with each loop. Brad had inserted a subtitle overlay: **When you've memorized the script but forgot to read the updates.**

Brad closed the file and opened the next: Devon Rhys.

Devon had once joked that Jessica probably "meditated herself into Stockholm Syndrome." Brad's video showed him being "interviewed" by a mock late-night host, admitting that he had signed a nondisclosure agreement with a tech firm that had tested emotion-dampening chips on student populations. The questions were real, lifted from another interview. The answers were taken from soundbites Devon had given during a young leaders business panel, and Brad then pieced them together to form a new meaning. Again, it was clearly satire. However, the effect was immediate: people would laugh, then wonder.

But this wasn't random cruelty; Brad had his own rules and adhered to them strictly.

He never faked a crime. Never used anything personal. Never involved family or children. No threats. No private medical information. Just ridicule—targeted, strategic, and public.

They had humiliated his sister. They had treated her like an easy punchline while she tried to help the world adapt to a new reality. They had done it with smirks and cameras, believing that no one would ever put a halt to their cruelty. Now they would learn that public figures could be held accountable for their words, even if no law was broken.

Brad set the videos to upload automatically, each one routed through anonymous accounts on platforms known for speculation and satire. He had created several usernames weeks earlier, gradually

gathering followers and mimicking accounts that specialized in political comedy and viral remix content. The captions were short and
sharp.

"When the influencers get too comfortable."
"Critics are not even pretending to be fair anymore."
"Disclosure, but make it fashionably corrupt."

He leaned back and folded his arms.

It was time.

He pressed *"Start Queue."*

The videos would go live one by one over the next twen-
ty-four hours. None of them would be taken seriously by mainstream media—at least not immediately—but they would circulate.
They would provoke conversation and make the Heirs look like
hypocrites, opportunists, and spoiled relics of a world being rewrit-
ten.

And most importantly, they would make Jessica untouchable.

Brad sat in the silence that followed. The files were gone now,
lost in the noise. He had other things to focus on tomorrow. No
more distractions—he had work to do that could help humanity
move forward.

But tonight—tonight had been for his sister.

* * *

Amanda entered the secured meeting room with her press
badge tucked away. She had dreamed of moments like this—not just
being in the room, but being *seen* in the room. Fame was always the
goal, but today's meeting demanded assurance, not ambition. Her
uncle had called her here in person—rare, considering he usually
kept his distance, doling out offhanded advice over holiday dinners
like he was doing her a favor. But this time was different. She wasn't
just the niece with potential. Now she was a key player.

And he finally realized it.

Colonel David Riley stood at the head of the small briefing
table, reviewing a file. He didn't look up until she took a seat. His

eyes, cold and unreadable, settled on her with a flicker of recognition that bordered on approval.

"You're late," he said, without emotion.

"I wasn't scheduled," Amanda replied. "You asked for an update. I came with one."

He nodded, conceding the point, sitting down and setting his files aside.

"I assume this has to do with the girl you've been meeting?" he asked.

"Aija Rao," Amanda said. "Kiran Rao's sister. Connected to Jessica Martinsson through the Partnership, the *Melly Speaks* series, and the Junia videos."

Colonel Riley folded his arms, waiting.

Amanda continued. "She brought me a story—one that fits the narrative we've been preparing. She exaggerated, probably invented some of it, but it tracks with known Suede capabilities. She claims the Suede Nation is preparing to move against surface infrastructure. She describes clawed warriors, tunnel collapse threats, and plans for expansion."

He remained silent, processing.

"She wants publicity," Amanda added. "She's desperate to be on camera. And she's willing to say anything if she thinks it gets her a platform."

The colonel's expression didn't change, but his voice dropped slightly in volume.

"She sounds useful," he said. "You'll use her again?"

"I'll keep her in the loop," Amanda replied. "But she won't get control over the story."

"You've confirmed that the footage of the Suede girl with claws is real?"

"It matches the livestream footage, and there were no signs of manipulation. While the threat was implied rather than stated, the effect is the same."

He stared at his files without seeing them.

"This is what I've been waiting for," he said. "A visible threat. Emotional enough to activate the public, and specific enough to justify action."

Amanda nodded. "The exposé will run next week. I'll be providing edited segments, interviews, and a special piece on the threat of underground incursions. The visuals are clean. It's going to move fast."

Colonel Riley's lips pressed into a flat line. "It needs to."

Amanda waited. She could feel there was more coming.

He continued. "Once the public begins to accept the possibility of surface attacks from subterranean non-humans, I'll have the go-ahead to propose a physical response. Targeted and controlled—entirely defensive, of course."

"You'll have support?" Amanda asked.

"Enough," he said. "There are units that have already been briefed. The language of the resolution will focus on containment, resource protection, and infrastructure security."

"And if OMR objects?"

"They won't be in a position to stop it. They'll be responding to the media storm. Vicki Heywood will have her hands full. Let her scramble. We'll move while they're still drafting talking points."

Amanda leaned back, smiling, and shifted the subject a bit. "You thought I wasn't capable."

He looked at her directly. "You were wasting time chasing trends and soft interviews. But this—this is useful."

"I've always known how to influence a story," Amanda said. "You just never asked."

"I didn't think you'd want to be involved."

"I didn't want to be irrelevant," she corrected him.

Colonel Riley gave the smallest nod of approval.

"You'll be sent a classified memo with the talking points we'll want emphasized. Follow the script where necessary, but keep the tone sharp. A story about threats from beneath our feet will get everyone's attention."

Amanda gave a nod of understanding. As she turned to leave, her uncle spoke once more.

"This is the first move. Not the last."

She didn't reply. She didn't have to. Her role was already unfolding, perfectly timed. The story would break, the panic would spread, and the old world's machinery would roar awake, packaged and sold as protection.

And when it did, her name would be on everyone's lips—not just as a witness, but as the one who lit the spark.

CHAPTER
TWENTY-FOUR

Vicki's breathing slowed as she sank into meditation. The physical world faded until the glare from fluorescent lights and the smell of recycled office air fell away. Her body remained seated on her mat in her office at OMR—Mary had strict instructions that she not be interrupted—but her awareness moved inward, deeper than thought, deeper than sensation.

The pocket out-of-time unfolded around her—not a place, but a dimension between dimensions. The air had no temperature. Light did not come from any direction; everything was an illuminated mist. While her usual senses dimmed, her consciousness remained sharp. Looking down, Vicki saw her body was once again a misty, sparkling replica of her body in physical reality. For some reason, that gave her comfort.

Then Melly appeared, resolving into form beside her, without sound or motion. Her iridescent, polychromatic eyes were whirling as she radiated calm.

Vicki didn't wait for pleasantries.

"I'm losing control."

Melly inclined her head, inviting her to continue.

"There was an attack on the Suede Nation with three dead, including Junia's cousin. Now, Junia's on video showing her claws and demonstrating that she can collapse tunnels with a thought, and the humans are terrified. I get it. They saw something they don't understand and assume it's a threat. We're getting calls every hour—diplomatic cables, security memos, reports of economic shockwaves."

She paced back and forth in the space, though there was no ground beneath her feet.

"And Jessica's still being dragged through the mud. That smear campaign—it's ugly. They're calling her delusional, unstable, and brainwashed. And they're doing it in front of millions of people. The Four are doing everything they can to keep the public grounded, but the pressure is mounting."

She took a breath. "And now we have a leak—from our office. Someone inside OMR leaked the location of the Pilot Knob cavern and gave it to the people who attacked the Suede Nation's entrance. We know it came from the Communications Office, but Mary's sweep didn't catch anything conclusive. I don't know who to trust."

Melly remained quiet, absorbing every word. When she finally spoke, her voice—layered with the resonance of Tibetan singing bowls—was direct.

"Why haven't you used the ability you were given?"

Vicki blinked. "What?"

The feeling of small bells—Melly was clearly amused. "Your DNA was upgraded. You can sense truth. You can feel when someone is deceiving you. Why haven't you done so?"

Vicki stood frozen. She had no answer. Her truth-telling gut had been one of the abilities Melly had unlocked in her junk DNA. It didn't require effort; it was simply there, accessible.

"I forgot," she said aloud. "I've been pulled in every direction. Every crisis has been immediate. I haven't had a moment to stop and think about what I *have*, just about what I don't."

Melly's gaze was unblinking. Not judgmental, but clear. Now there was a serious *feeling* of gongs. "You cannot lead if you do not trust your own perception. The tools you were given were not decorative. They are functional. Use them."

Vicki nodded, grounding herself in that certainty. "Of course. I will."

There was a pause between them.

"Now there's something else I need to ask," Vicki said. "The two Pleiadians—the Galactic Federation's emissaries. They've contacted me to say they're coming to Earth and would like to make a statement to the United Nations. They say it's time."

"It is time for humans to see them," Melly responded, nodding. "But not for every truth to be shared."

"You're talking about the Alpha Centaurians," Vicki said, her voice tight. She had been struggling with how to introduce the ACs to humanity without triggering a frenzy of hysteria.

"Yes. Their ancestors refused to leave Earth when they were told to do so. Their decision, while born of desperation, caused enormous ripple effects. Human suffering increased because of it. You know this. The memory crystal James holds confirms it."

"I also know the ones alive now aren't responsible for what happened,"Vicki said.

"Correct. But human history is not known for subtle distinctions." Melly's eyes whirled. "If they are introduced too soon, they will be rejected. Worse—blamed. It could fracture what you are trying to build."

Vicki ran a hand through her hair, the burden of that choice sinking in.

"So, we wait. For now."

"Until humans develop greater awareness. Until they have seen that cooperation with other beings is possible. The Suede Nation has been introduced. If they are not protected—if trust cannot be established with those who are native to this planet—how can others be accepted?"

"You're right," Vicki said quietly.

"Let the Pleiadians speak. They carry light, and their presence will help ease the tension. But wait on the Alpha Centaurians. They have lived within your planet for thousands of years—a few months will make no difference."

Vicki nodded. "Has someone from the Federation informed them of that?" she asked hopefully. She didn't want to be the one to break the news that their move to the surface would have to wait.

The feeling of small bells and laughing. "Yes, the Council itself has already spoken with them."

"But there's something more—and, if possible, it's worse. It might destroy everything we've been trying to do." Vicki's shoulders hunched. This had been eating at her ever since Jerry had told her about it. "Decades ago, the military made an agreement with the extraterrestrials we call the Tall Whites. It was a trade deal—access to and assistance with alien technology in exchange for human DNA sampling."

Melly nodded her head. "Yes, we know about this agreement."

"But the general population did not—only a few officials in the military and the top leadership at the Partnership did. The people who were abducted and had their DNA sampled did not consent. They were kidnapped—taken against their will—and subjected to terrifying medical procedures. Many feel they were violated. Then the military—who was aware of what was truly happening since they were the ones who had authorized it—deliberately ridiculed and humiliated the victims. Many of them had their lives ruined. Almost all of them experienced varying levels of trauma for the rest of their lives."

Melly didn't say anything.

"How are we going to make this public? These people were victimized and betrayed by their own government. And the officials at the Pentagon who are still administering the program—they're worried enough about the public outcry and backlash that they'll do anything to keep it quiet. Anything at all."

The sound of muted singing bowls. "This is another truth that need not be shared at this time."

"But we can't keep this secret!" Vicki said with feeling. These victims deserved to know what happened to them, deserved to know the truth. And the world deserved to know what those in leadership had done.

Melly's eyes whirled. "I did not say this would be kept secret, just that you don't need to share it at this time. There is already a process in place that will release the information at the right time. This is an issue the Council is overseeing. Everything is not your responsibility."

Vicki let out a breath she hadn't realized she was holding. The tension in her body began to unravel, not because the problems were solved, but because she remembered she wasn't alone—everything wasn't all up to her. Beth had told her the same thing. Why did she keep forgetting this?

"I'll start with what is mine to deal with—the mole," she said. "I'll speak to each person in the Communications Office directly. As you reminded me, I'll know who is telling the truth and who is not."

"Yes," Melly said. "And when you do—move quickly. Waiting would cause problems."

The words took hold in Vicki's mind as she closed her eyes and let the reality of the pocket out-of-time dissolve.

When she opened them, she was back in her office. The light hadn't changed. The clock had barely moved. But everything inside her was different.

No more playing defense—it was time to take control.

* * *

Sam shifted in his chair for the third time in five minutes. The high-back government-issue chair wasn't the problem—it was the growing pressure behind his temples and the realization that he was once again in a room where he didn't belong, filling in for a superior who always seemed to develop "conflicts" when the agenda turned radioactive. He stared at the mission board screen at the front of the room as Colonel Riley paced slowly and deliberately, hands clasped behind his back.

"Once my niece's story runs next week," Riley said, voice clipped and certain, "we'll have the public momentum. The optics are in our favor—non-human threats from within the planet, betrayal by the State Department's Office of Multispecies Relations, and a lack of readiness at the diplomatic level. We'll move immediately."

The map on the screen changed: red-marked zones across the continental U.S., overlaying possible Suede Nation access points. Sam's breath hitched as he realized how accurate the military's data already was. Although he knew there were various entrances to the Suede Nation, those locations were classified even within OMR. Did Jerry know he probably had a mole?

Riley continued. "A resolution is in the process of being drafted— a friendly Senator has agreed to introduce it in Congress within twelve hours of the exposé. We'll frame it as a necessary defense measure that will include containment of subterranean threats, protection of national resources, and strategic safeguarding of infrastructure corridors—especially in urban zones."

There were nods around the table. Sam kept his expression neutral, but he felt a cold bead of sweat trickle down his spine.

A uniformed general to Riley's left cleared his throat. "And once it's passed?"

Riley had a plan. "Military authority will be exercised over all non-human contact and subterranean zones. We will have full operational command and intelligence integration under existing defense protocols. State and civilian diplomatic agencies will be cut out."

"OMR?" someone across the table asked.

"Dissolved in practice if not on paper," Riley said. "They can keep their briefings and their talking points. We'll take the operations. They can write press releases from the outside. And that's where they should be—the Department of State should never have had a role in this. The military has had point on the extraterrestrial issue for over seventy years."

Sam felt the blood draining from his face. He looked down at his notebook to avoid making eye contact. His pen hovered over a blank page, but he wasn't even pretending to take notes.

"Wait a second," said a mid-level intelligence advisor at the far end. "This exposé that your niece is about to broadcast—how much of it is actually true?"

The room went still for half a second.

Colonel Riley turned to face him completely. "What's true is that the public believes what they see. And what matters is that the military is prepared to act, not flinch. We're not here to debate mythology. We're here to control a rapidly destabilizing situation."

For a moment, no one replied.

Then a younger intelligence officer across from Sam leaned forward, his shoulders tense. He glanced at the others, measuring the silence, then spoke with deliberate control.

"Sir, with all due respect, we've seen better coordination and intelligence flow coming through the State Department's OMR office than through our own interagency process. We know what they're working on, and we know where our assets align."

He paused, his voice low but insistent. "At least under OMR's lead, the United States is at the center of the developments. We've been the primary contact point for interspecies diplomacy, which gives us leverage globally. If we sideline them and move unilaterally under a full military directive, we risk breaking the coordination we've built with our allies. Worse—if other nations see us taking a hard security posture, they'll do the same."

The officer took a breath and pressed on. "What happens when Russia or China announce their own contact protocols with non-human entities? What happens if they establish their own partnerships and use them to bypass global negotiation channels? We'll lose the diplomatic edge, and there's no guarantee we'll maintain operational control."

He looked directly at Colonel Riley. "Strategically, sir, pulling OMR out of the picture doesn't just isolate them. It may isolate us."

Sam was shocked—the man had balls.

Riley's face darkened. "That's a coward's answer."

The officer stiffened.

Riley's voice rose, cutting through the air with a definitiveness that silenced the room.

"This is not about international approval," he said, his eyes locking onto the younger officer who had spoken. "It's about control—ours. We are not going to hand over national security to a committee of pencil-pushing bureaucrats hiding behind diplomatic protocols. These people"—he gestured toward the air, broadly referencing OMR, the Department of State, and anyone else not wearing a uniform—"have had their chance. They've held press conferences. They've coddled non-human entities. And what have we seen in return? Claws and collapsed tunnels, market chaos, and civilian panic."

He stepped forward, gripping the edge of the table.

"We are not going to stand down while foreign powers maneuver behind closed doors, preparing their own arrangements, building alliances that exclude us. We are not going to let Russia or China—or anyone else—dictate how this new world unfolds."

He leaned in, his voice harder now.

"We don't need to beg for consensus. We don't need to pause for approval. We assert command. We set the terms. Everyone else adjusts to us. That's how we win."

He straightened, scanning the room for any sign of resistance. No one spoke.

Sam's heart raced. He recognized that look on Riley's face—the clenched jaw, the icy glare, the lack of nuance. The mood in the room had shifted. No one would dare to challenge him again in here.

His hand moved slowly, quietly pulling his phone under the edge of the conference folder. He checked for signal. Blocked, of course, he knew that—no outgoing calls.

He would have to wait. As soon as this meeting ended, he'd return to his office and call Jerry directly. They needed to know what was coming. Once Amanda's exposé went live, there'd be no room to maneuver. The military would exploit the fear to establish dominance, and OMR would be swept aside as an afterthought.

Sam looked up again. The map was still glowing red.

He swallowed hard and waited for the meeting to end, every second bringing disaster closer.

Chapter Twenty-Five

Jerry sat across from Vicki's desk, watching her carefully. The blinds were half-drawn, the overhead lights set low. Her shoulders were straight, but her eyes held a look of exhaustion. She was holding herself together—he'd seen her do it before. But he knew her burden—the mole, the Pentagon... It was all weighing her down.

Two hours earlier, he'd watched two Diplomatic Security agents escort Oscar Finch out of OMR's office suite without ceremony. The man hadn't protested. He hadn't looked confused. He'd looked like someone who knew the game was up.

Jerry ran a hand through his hair, still trying to fully grasp what she'd uncovered.

"You got him," he said quietly. "You didn't just catch the leak. You found out *how* he got in."

Vicki nodded, not looking up from the report she was skimming. "Finch was exactly what we thought—embedded, feeding everything he could to Colonel Riley's office. He had a backchannel open for weeks."

"And Human Resources?"

Vicki finally looked at him, her voice calm but tight. "Someone high-up in HR bypassed the block we have on candidates from all collaborators with the Partnership, including ValorSys. That restriction should've flagged him, but it didn't. He was pushed through. Which means we're looking at a second deliberate breach—one that's internal and well-placed."

Jerry exhaled slowly. "We're not just being watched. We're being dismantled from the inside."

Vicki set the report down.

"He didn't resist interrogation," she said. "Didn't even try to lie. Once I pressed, once I let myself *feel* what he was holding back—I knew. He didn't care if he got caught. He already believed Riley was going to win."

"And what did you feel?" Jerry asked, cautiously.

He kept his tone even, but a note of hesitation slipped into his voice. He still wasn't fully comfortable asking about the abilities—the *changes*. The DNA upgrades that Vicki and the Four had received from Melly were no longer theoretical, and that unsettled him.

He wasn't afraid of *her*. But he was afraid of what it all meant.

While he understood, at least on an intellectual level, that the vibrational shift would eventually touch everyone—and Melly had explained that humanity's so-called "junk DNA" would begin expressing new potential in stages—it didn't feel reassuring. It felt abstract and remote. And now, with the pace accelerating, with military factions moving to seize control, and with non-human beings stepping into full view, it felt like something important was slipping away—normalcy, perhaps. Or predictability.

He thought about Anne and their two sons. What would it look like as their DNA began to shift? Would it be gradual? Would it hurt? Would they still be the same people and have the same personalities? Or would something deeper twist inside of them, until they no longer responded to the world the way they used to?

So much of the world was now driven by forces outside his grasp, and the ground beneath them—both figuratively and literally—was starting to feel unfamiliar.

He didn't want power.

He just wanted to know that his family would still recognize themselves by the time this was over.

"I felt emptiness," Vicki said, unaware of his internal monologue. "Not fear or guilt—just certainty. Finch believes this whole office is temporary—that OMR is a placeholder until the military takes over."

Jerry leaned back in his chair. "They're already planning it."

She looked at him. "What do you mean?"

He glanced around—which was unnecessary because they were alone in Vicki's office—then leaned forward. "I just came from a secure phone call with Sam—he's standing in for his boss on this issue. He gave me a summary of a high-level Pentagon strategy session. Some people might think Riley's harmless, but he's not even hiding what he's planning anymore."

"Go on."

"They're going to use Amanda Riley's next exposé as a catalyst. As soon as it airs, their allies in Congress will introduce an emergency resolution. They'll frame it as a matter of national defense. With its focus on containment, protection of infrastructure, and the control of potential 'subsurface threats,' the measure will transfer authority for extraterrestrial affairs and Disclosure from civilian and diplomatic oversight to the military. Again."

Vicki didn't speak. Her expression didn't change. But her jaw tightened.

"They're using public fear as a lever," Jerry continued. "Just like before. Only this time, it won't be reversed by a clever livestream or public charm. We got lucky once with Junia and the Suede Nation video. But we won't be that lucky again."

"We don't need to be lucky," Vicki said, her voice quiet. "We've got something else."

Jerry raised an eyebrow.

"The Pleiadians have made a formal request to address the United Nations," she said. "The Council has appointed them as its representatives to Earth, so they want to speak in Geneva. In person. Their message will focus on humanity's path forward as a participant in the Galactic Federation—specifically during this period of vibrational shift."

Jerry sat up straighter. "You're sure?"

"I received confirmation during meditation. Melly communicated it to me directly. They'll appear fully—no disguises, no holograms. They look human, but their skin is light blue. Close enough to be relatable. Different enough to remind everyone that the universe is bigger than they ever imagined."

Jerry's mouth was open slightly. "And how will this help the Suedes?"

"They're going to be part of the message," Vicki said. "The Pleiadians plan to refer to them as long-standing neighbors—peaceful and connected to the Earth. They'll say the Suede Nation has only shown aggression when threatened. It'll counter Amanda's smear piece directly—without confrontation or defensiveness. Just the truth."

Jerry nodded slowly. "That could cut through the panic and give people a positive story to hold onto. But other people will be upset that the Pleiadians won't be landing on the White House lawn—they'll claim we'll be giving up American authority to a multinational organization."

"Not our problem," Vicki said. "But we need to inform State's Bureau of International Organizations—they're the ones that deal with the United Nations. That said, we've never vetted them. For all we know, Riley's got ears in there too."

"Should we keep it quiet?"

"No. We need to bring more people into the loop —carefully." She opened a drawer and pulled out a folder. "We'll bring in the Principal DAS. Just him. We meet with him in person, and I'll vet him. My gut can tell me if he's reporting to Riley, or even hiding something else. If he's clear, we go forward and brief him. If not..." At this point, Vicki gave a sigh. "If not, we'll figure out something else."

"You're going to vet him yourself?"

"I have to—there's no one else. We can't afford another Finch. Not when the whole world is about to watch."

Jerry stood. "I'll get him scheduled. Quietly."

Vicki gave a small nod. "He's higher ranking than me, so by rights we should be meeting in his office. So give him my apologize and tell him we need to meet in our offices—our security is better. We can't lose this. We don't surrender to people who think control is the same thing as leadership."

As Jerry left the office, he didn't look back. He didn't need to. For the first time in days, the knot in his chest had loosened. They weren't just reacting anymore.

They were making the next move.

* * *

The house was finally quiet.

Anne sat at the kitchen table, finishing a glass of wine. She had unloaded the dishwasher an hour ago, but she still hadn't gone to bed. The clock above the stove read 11:25. The hum of the refrigerator was the only sound, aside from the soft, rhythmic snoring coming from the bedroom down the hall. Jerry had gone to bed just after ten. The boys had fallen asleep even earlier; Josh was worn out from his day at pre-school, and Adam, despite just turning five months old, was a certified sleepyhead.

Anne took a slow breath. She hadn't even turned off the lights yet—just left them dim, casting a pale glow throughout the room.

Jerry had already shared everything with her earlier that evening: Colonel Riley's involvement, the Pentagon's plan, and the exposé Amanda Riley was preparing to release—an article filled with distorted claims about the Suede Nation. Colonel Riley and his allies intended to use that initial wave of public panic to seize control over Disclosure—cutting OMR and Vicki out of the picture entirely.

But somehow, once again, Vicki had found a way forward. The blue-skinned Pleiadians had somehow been in contact with her—Jerry didn't know the details. They were set to address the United Nations in Geneva, not only to affirm the Suede Nation's peaceful role on Earth but also to present a broader vision of Earth joining the Galactic Federation.

Anne admired Vicki not only for her ability to stay composed amid chaos but also for her consistency. She kept finding the next step, moving forward while people like Riley only pushed back.

Anne still hadn't told Jerry what she was doing.

He had enough on his plate. His voice had cracked a little earlier when he'd talked about the pressure, and how close they'd come to losing control of the narrative. How hard it had been to root out the mole. He was scared about how vulnerable everything still was. She could see it in his face, even when he didn't say it directly. He wanted to protect her and the kids. He wanted something solid to hold on to.

So she hadn't told him.

She hadn't told him that over the past three weeks, she'd been working with Dr. Steven Greer and his team—that she'd pored over files to help collect material—firsthand accounts from CE-5 practitioners across the country— to be edited into a series of videos meant for distribution by the Four—Jessica, Brad, Kiran, and James—as part of their Disclosure campaign.

She also hadn't told Jerry that she'd offered to help organize a small CE-5 training circle in the backyard—just a few women from the neighborhood who were open-minded, curious, and tired of being relegated to the sidelines of their own futures.

It wasn't that she didn't trust him. She did. With everything.

But she knew Jerry. Knew the way his shoulders had tightened every time aliens were mentioned on news programs. Knew how he kept go-bags in the hallway closet "just in case" something changed overnight. He didn't say it, but she could feel it: he wanted their family to stay safe. He was watching the wave of Disclosure roll in and trying to build a wall against it high enough to protect their home.

But Anne knew better. No wall would hold.

The world was already different. The Hum in the air, the people asking questions, the children drawing pictures of mantis alien visitors and tunnels beneath the earth—they were all part of the shift already. No one was sitting this out. Not anymore.

She sighed and switched off the light. The kitchen darkened, and the silence grew deeper.

She wanted the same thing Jerry did. She wanted their boys to grow up with choices. With a future that wasn't dictated by secrecy and fear. But to do that, people had to see more than what the military allowed. More than what fear mongers put on screens. They needed the other side of the story. They needed contact—direct, human, quiet, and real.

She stepped into the hallway and paused at the boys' door. Adam was curled under a blanket in his crib. Josh sprawled out in his bed, a foot hanging off the mattress. Peaceful. For now.

Anne watched them a moment longer, then turned toward her bedroom. Jerry's snoring had softened into the familiar rhythm she'd known for years. Steady. Reassuring.

She lay down beside him a few minutes later, careful not to wake him.

She didn't know how much longer she could keep her involvement quiet. But she wasn't going to stop.

Jerry was trying to keep their world from falling apart.

Anne was working to help build the one that would come next.

Chapter
Twenty-Six

T he communications center was packed.

Rows of monitors displayed the same feed. The overhead lights had been dimmed, and every chair in the room was filled. Staff leaned against walls, perched on the edges of tables, and stood clustered near the doors. The silence was absolute—sharp, focused, and reverent.

Vicki stood near the back of the room next to Jerry. Her arms were crossed, not out of defiance but to keep her emotions contained. The air carried a rare mix of tension and hope—a feeling she'd become used to in the weeks since Disclosure began.

On every screen, the United Nations emblem slowly faded, and then they appeared.

Two of them—one male and one female.

The Pleiadians stood together at the podium in the Geneva chamber, their appearance striking: tall, blue-skinned, with even features and calm, attentive expressions. Their clothing was simple—clean lines in light-colored fabrics that shimmered subtly under the lights.

Gasps flowed through the room like a wave, followed by a stunned silence.

They looked human. Familiar enough to connect with, but strange enough to remind everyone these were real aliens.

Vicki let out a breath she hadn't realized she'd been holding. The moment was here.

She reflected back to the meeting with Principal DAS Robert Thomas from State's UN Liaison Office. It had only been two days ago, though it felt longer.

She had insisted on seeing him privately in her office—no aides or other intermediaries. That set the initial tone. She was asking for his trust while not returning it.

At first, Thomas had bristled, clearly expecting her—as the lower-ranking official—to come to his office. He had also assumed he would be receiving a briefing, not facing a cross-examination. But she had explained —perhaps more directly than was diplomatic—that she needed to verify his intentions. With everything at stake, she couldn't risk a leak, not even from a well-placed, long-trusted diplomat. If disclosed prematurely, the damage could be irreversible.

He hadn't taken offense. To her relief, he nodded once and said, "Ask."

She had used the ability that Melly's upgrade had given her—a sort of gut-level resonance. When people lied, her stomach churned with the disconnection between their words and their internal state. When they told the truth, the alignment was unmistakable.

Thomas had passed her test with flying colors.

Then, when she told him that the Pleiadians were planning to address the United Nations within two days, his reaction had startled her. Not skepticism or disbelief, but joy—pure, unguarded delight.

"Finally, he had said."Finally—something we can share that isn't fear."

Vicki thought that would be the end of it, but then some-thing unexpected happened. Deputy Assistant Secretary Thomas had leaned forward, voice low, and asked her if she'd consider visiting his office to screen the rest of his team. Not because he suspected anyone, he quickly added, but because he knew how fast loyalties could shift—and how easily opportunists could slip into places no one was watching. He understood that even with good intentions, it was easy to get caught up in chasing influence, safety, and access.

He didn't want to lose control of his own shop.

Now, standing here as the Pleiadians began to speak, Vicki was thankful she had followed her instincts. She had given Thomas an exclusive—advance notice of one of the greatest events in human history-and he had reciprocated with unshakeable support. It felt good to have an ally in the building.

The male Pleiadian envoy stepped slightly forward. His voice was smooth and carried no accent. It had been modulated for clarity across languages, but still sounded completely natural.

"People of Earth. Members of this assembly. We greet you as representatives of the Galactic Federation and as neighbors in your local star sector. We appear today as allies, not intruders. As stewards of cooperation, rather than architects of control."

All around the room, OMR staff leaned in, hanging on every word.

"Humanity is not alone. You have never been alone. And you are not the only intelligent species native to this world. The Suede Nation, known by many names across your folklore, has lived peace-fully within your planet for millennia. They have shown restraint. They have shown patience. And they have only shown their strength when forced."

The second envoy stepped forward now. Her voice was clear.

"We are aware of recent acts of violence committed against Suede communities by misguided human actors. We view these acts with grave concern. We call for restraint, understanding, and accountability. The Suede Nation has been a good neighbor to your kind. We sincerely hope there will be no more attacks by fanatics who put their narrow self-interests above the good of the world."

A wave of low murmurs spread across the room. Heads turned to stare at Vicki. Some OMR staff smiled faintly,but no one spoke above a whisper.

Jerry shifted slightly at Vicki's side. She leaned toward him.

"You talked to Sam?" she asked quietly.

He nodded. "Just before we came in. Riley's still moving forward. He pulled out of his press conference after the Suede Nation livestream, but he won't this time—he said he's not making that mistake again."

"So he's going to try to force the resolution?"

"Yup," Jerry said, his voice clipped. "Amanda's exposé drops in two days. Riley's plan is to ride the backlash and use it as a hammer. He'll frame the Pleiadian speech as too abstract and idealistic. He'll say it doesn't address the threat directly and that we're still exposed—still vulnerable. And he'll tell them that *only* the military can provide a real defense."

Vicki didn't respond right away. On-screen, the first Pleiadian began to speak, first in flawless French, then Spanish, Russian, Arabic, Hindi, and finally Mandarin. Each language conveyed the same message: unity, cooperation, a path forward, and full acknowledgment of Earth's multiple intelligent species.

It was a diplomatic masterstroke.

The broadcast would play well across the globe. The tone, the appearance, the careful word choice—it was all calibrated to lower fear, not raise it.

Vicki took a long breath and let herself feel what the moment meant.

There was pride in that moment. It marked the result of months of constant effort, of holding firm under pressure and trusting her instincts. But there was fear, too.

Because now it was officially public and there was no turning back. No hiding behind speculation or classified briefings. Humanity wasn't walking toward the future anymore. They were being pushed into it, ready or not.

She glanced at the people around her. They weren't whispering anymore; they were nodding. One woman was quietly crying, while another had pulled out her phone to take a photo of the screen—in violation of security rules.

Vicki didn't stop her. They needed moments like this—evidence that not everything had to be hidden in the shadows.

She glanced back at the monitor.

The Pleiadian envoys stood resolute and composed, like the calm center in the eye of a storm. Nothing would be the same again.

* * *

The air in the Community Hall was still. The only sound was the distant chatter of a surface-world broadcast, coming from the crystal panels that now showed the United Nations chamber. The Pleiadians stood tall on the screen, their presence both otherworldly and familiar, their voices resonating out.

Junia sat in the last row of seats, hidden in the shadowy curve of the chamber wall. The elders sat in silence at the front, their long robes neatly folded around their legs, eyes fixed on the projected image. Her uncle Alun sat among them, his face unreadable and his spine straight.

Junia's fingers were locked together in her lap. She gripped them tightly, as if that might settle the turmoil inside her. Her legs trembled beneath her, though she forced her posture to remain still.

She knew she should feel proud. The Pleiadians, in formal, careful voices, were naming the Suede Nation—*her* people—as friends. As good neighbors. As peaceful. People from the Galactic Federation were speaking about the Suede Nation with respect—and the whole world was watching. After centuries of myths, lies, and being ignored, the truth was finally being heard on the surface. But Junia didn't feel anything at all.

Her throat was tight. Her eyes burned. Her chest felt as though it might crack open from the grief.

She kept her eyes down, focusing not on the speakers but on the faint glow of the floor beneath her feet. Her mind was stuck in the same loop. Over and over and over the words repeated themselves.

The humans don't deserve this. Not yet. Not after what they did.

It had only been two weeks since the attack at Pilot Knob. Two weeks since Bowen had died, struck down by enemy fire as he fell defending the outer tunnel. The humans who had come—greedy, hostile, and armed—had not come to talk. They had come to take.

And they had taken everything from her.

The sadness was heavy in her chest, but beneath it surged something hotter—fury. She knew the history of her people. How many times had the Suedes offered friendship, only to be met with fear and violence? The humans didn't deserve their guidance. Their history was soaked in blood—always taking, always destroying what they didn't understand. Greedy, short-sighted, and dangerous. Bowen hadn't really trusted them, but he had trusted *her* that this was the right path. He had died for that trust. And Junia could not forgive it.

She could not forgive herself.

She clenched her hands tighter, nails digging into the skin of her palms. No one turned to look at her, and she felt grateful. No one needed to see her like this. Not now.

One of the Pleiadians was speaking again—measured, articulate, and full of phrases like *cooperation*, *non-aggression*, and *mutual learning*.

Junia wanted to scream.

Did the humans even realize what it cost her to be called peaceful? Did they know how hard it was to keep from lashing out every day?

Because *she* hadn't forgotten Bowen's face. His laughter. His certainty that she would lead one day—that they both would, side by side.

She blinked hard, and for a moment, her vision blurred. The room wavered. How could she be expected to sit with the humans now? How could she be expected to greet them, to smile at them, and welcome them?

But the path was already there in front of her. She knew her people were depending on her to follow it.

Alun had spoken to her about it just yesterday. His voice hadn't carried a tone of instruction or even encouragement. It was resignation—like truth and grief too heavy to bear.

"The world knows your face, Junia," he'd said, after the session with the elders had ended and the chamber emptied. "They've seen you. The humans have seen your fire, and they've seen your restraint. You can stand between us and them. The elders feel it. I feel it."

She hadn't responded. She'd known it already.

Since the broadcast—the one where she'd spoken through tears and grief, where she had shown her claws and warned the world—she had felt the shift in the way the others treated her. The glances from the young Suedes, the nods from the elders, the way Alun now paused before speaking to her, not only to correct, but to truly listen.

She was no longer just a child with curiosity and a restless mind. She was becoming the one they would look to. Even though she was only fifteen years old.

Yes, it would have to be her.

She pressed her lips together, holding in the shaking breath. She couldn't fall apart here. Not where the elders could see her.

She looked up at the screen again. One of the envoys was saying her people's name now—"the Suede Nation"—and describing them as *guardians of the Earth's deep structures*. He said it with respect.

Junia felt nothing but a yawning emptiness inside her. Respect was not justice. Recognition was not grief's end.

When the speech ended, a low ripple of approval spread among the elders. A few exchanged glances. They were pleased. They believed this would turn the tide.

Junia stayed still.

She would do what they asked. She would sit across from humans. She would speak into their cameras. She would walk on the surface if it came to that.

But she didn't know if she would ever forgive them.

Not for the attack.

Not for the lies.

Not for Bowen.

She didn't know if she would ever forgive herself.

I will do this. But I will not forget.

CHAPTER TWENTY-SEVEN

The aroma of coffee permeated the air, drifting through the space where flowers once filled glass vases. The common area on the main floor had long since been transformed. Part living room and part command center—the walls were lined with whiteboards covered in notes, and a tangle of camera equipment stood in one corner. While there was a communal kitchen upstairs in what was now Jessica's small apartment, the general consensus was that a single flight of stairs was too far to walk when caffeine was needed. An espresso machine, still hissing faintly, had been installed on a former potting counter.

James was the only one not drinking coffee; his drink of choice was hot chocolate. Jessica and Kiran sat side by side on the sofa, sipping from their mugs. Brad stood nearby, pacing near the counter, with a single shot cooling in his cup, untouched.

"That Pleiadian speech," James said. "They didn't pull any punches."

Kiran nodded, voice calm. "No. They were direct. Maybe more than anyone expected."

"Especially the part about the UN being used for personal agendas," said Jessica.

"Yeah," Brad said, pausing in his pacing. "I'm sure that part hit close to home for a lot of the delegates."

"They didn't name names," James added, "but I'm sure the guilty parties felt like the Pleiadians were looking straight at them."

Jessica glanced at him. "They said they *know*. That there are... methods. That certain patterns of energy leave a kind of signature. So they don't need surveillance to know when someone's manipulating power for selfish gain. Imagine being one of those corrupt officials sitting in the audience listening to all this—they'd have been panicking, wondering what was going to happen to them."

"'This cannot continue,'" Kiran quoted. "That was what the Pleiadians said."

"It's not something that anyone would expect to hear when aliens first talk to humans. Did you notice their voices didn't change much until that moment?" Jessica said. "Then it was like a switch flipped."

Brad gave a small huff. "Steely, but calculated. Almost like they've had this conversation before. On other worlds."

"They probably have," Kiran murmured. "Again and again and again—same story, different planets."

James nodded. "They spelled out they're here to help guide us through a *species-level* transition—not country-by-country. And that's why Galactic Federation membership isn't for nations. It's for all of us—for humanity as a whole."

"Which won't sit well with most governments." Brad finally picked up his cup and took a sip.

"Or power blocs," Jessica said. "But it's the only way forward."

Brad finally stopped pacing and took a seat.

"Well," he said, exhaling slowly, "if the Pleiadians are willing to go public like that, then I think it's time we move to the next step too."

Jessica looked over and raised an eyebrow.

"You mean—?"

"Yeah," Brad said, nodding. "I got in touch with Graham and Kyle a couple of nights ago. They've been bouncing between field assignments and lab reviews at OMR, and checking out the free energy sites I've been tracking. Since the free energy schematics dropped, implementation has gone faster than any of us expected—pop-up test sites, independent installations, private retrofits. And, unsurprisingly, there have been attempts to sabotage many of them. Not to mention the attack and destruction in Lagos. But still... It's happening. The move from fossil fuels is well underway."

He reached for the laptop beside him, tapped a few keys, and turned it toward the others. Two schematic previews appeared side by side.

"Now we've got to figure out which tech is next. And how to do it responsibly."

James leaned forward. "What are we looking at?"

Brad pointed at the left screen. "This is a zero-point medical regeneration chamber. It works on vibrational field alignment, repairing cellular damage—even early-stage organ failure. It's small and light, so it's portable, at least if you have a pick-up truck. Of course, it's not magic; it doesn't bring people back from the dead. But it'll make hospitals obsolete for a lot of things."

Jessica's breath caught, thinking of their mother. "That would... revolutionize everything."

"And this," Brad said, pointing to the right screen, "is a consciousness link interface. It's a wearable device—not a chip or anything invasive. It acts as a translator between neural impulses and non-verbal contact frequencies. It'll enable people—with training—to communicate telepathically. Like what James is doing with Melly. But the device would make it possible for the average person to do it without having to wait for their junk DNA to be upgraded."

Kiran's brow furrowed. "That's too big—people aren't ready."

"That's what I thought," Brad replied. "Graham and Kyle agree. But the designs are clean, and we're past the point of secrecy. The question is—should we go physical first or mental?"

Silence fell around the table again.

Jessica stared at the schematics. "If we release the medical tech, we help everyone—instantly. It would de-escalate a lot of tension. Fear of suffering and death? We all have that—it's instinctual."

James rubbed the back of his neck. "But the consciousness tech? That sounds to me like something the Partnership would develop. Then weaponize. And then keep secret from anyone except its own people while using it against everyone else."

"That's *exactly* what this is," Brad reminded him pointedly. "The advanced tech designs we have are ones given to us by Graham and Kyle—they copied them from the Partnership labs and passed them to us before the facility was destroyed."

Kiran said nothing for a while, then spoke quietly. "I think we need to remember what Larry said about being a biologic construct."

Everyone went quiet, thinking about James's uncle, who had sacrificed himself so that the rest of them could escape.

Kiran continued, "His artificial body gave him lots of advantages, but he was no longer able to evolve—he couldn't reach the higher levels of consciousness that the rest of the advanced tai chi class could. He told us that when the vibrational shift happened, he would be left behind. I wonder if people who rely on machines like the consciousness link interface might miss the chance to develop psychic abilities when the vibrational shift occurs."

Jessica met Brad's eyes. "What do you think?"

Brad looked at them, then down at the schematics.

"I think humans are on the edge of something big. We can't push them off the cliff, but we can influence how they land. I don't want to repeat the mistake of following what the Partnership did—they developed tools that provided people with short-term gains, but in the long run, it kept them under the Partnership's control."

James nodded. "Medical tech now. We can revisit the consciousness interface later on if we feel the need."

Jessica sipped her coffee. "And stay visible the whole time. No more working in the shadows. No more secrets."

Brad reached across the table and closed the laptop.

"Okay," he said. "Let's do it right this time."

* * *

The lights in Vicki's office were dimmed. On her monitor, a global resonance map pulsed in shifting hues—bands of luminous data drifting over topographical outlines. Thin golden threads traced ley lines across continents, looping and intersecting like some sort of ancient architecture, while deep red markers signaled where she had sensed anomalies.

Vicki sat in front of it, a mug of coffee warming her hands. The Hum was changing. It had begun as a subtle background frequency—one that only the highly sensitive could hear occasionally. But now, even the most unaware were reporting it—in cities, on mountaintops, at sea, and in deserts.

She tapped a point on the map near the Horn of Africa, where two lines converged above a cluster of resonance markers she had logged herself. When she had first visited the area—descending into the interior through meditation—the earth energies were gentle as they curved beneath the tectonic boundaries. But the last time she passed through there, she felt pressure. Movement. Something was getting ready.

The Suedes had told her the Hum was the Earth preparing to shift.

Vicki found it ironic that she was technically in charge of the transition—at least in the U.S.—yet she still didn't fully understand what the vibrational shift actually was.

Would it happen suddenly, like a snap, with all frequencies realigning in a single moment? Or would it roll forward slowly, like a tide moving across the surface of the planet?

She pressed two fingers to her temple, trying to focus. The DNA upgrade that Melly had given her enabled her to work with Earth energies; she could feel and manipulate stone, ley lines, gravity wells, underground water, and magma. To her, the interior of the planet wasn't just stone and void. It was alive. And now, it was humming.

Was the Hum a countdown? Or a warning?

She turned back to her desk, glancing at her notes. She had recorded every moment she spent inside the Earth—each meditation-travel marked with coordinates, date/time stamps, and resonance descriptions. Some sections of the planet remained quiet, while others were restless.

Would the infrastructure buckle under the strain? Would bridges give out? Subways? Power grids? Or worse—would human bodies, unready for the shift, go into shock?

What if someone's nervous system couldn't adjust?

She exhaled. No one had answers yet. Not even Melly. The Galactic Council had said the shift was natural—inevitable—and that most people would adjust. But *most* didn't mean *all*. And Vicki couldn't stop picturing the ones who wouldn't. Those who'd feel the change tremble inside them and not know why.

A soft knock pulled her from her thoughts.

Mary stepped inside without waiting for a reply. "Don't mean to interrupt your underground spelunking," she said dryly, "but I figured you'd want to hear this."

Vicki raised an eyebrow. "What now?"

Mary held up her phone, already scrolling. "Reactions to the Pleiadian speech are coming in—and it's a landslide. Social sentiment is trending positive in forty-two out of the top fifty media markets. Even the usual skeptics are quiet. They're still reeling from the fact that the Pleiadians looked... well, *human*."

Vicki allowed herself a thin smile. "The blue skin didn't throw them?"

"Apparently, most people welcomed it. Clearly alien, but not terrifying like Melly. Also, someone started a viral hashtag—#GoodGalacticNeighbors—after the part where the Pleiadians talked about the Suedes. There are already over one hundred memes of Junia looking fierce, claws out, with a flower crown photoshopped onto her head."

Vicki blinked. "Seriously?"

Mary nodded, deadpan. "There's one with the caption '*Mess with the Earth, get the claws.*' Kids seem to love her. Adults are mostly confused."

Vicki leaned back slightly against her desk. "And Riley?"

Mary shrugged. "He still hasn't given a public statement, which means he's probably stewing. But his niece's exposé is scheduled to run on news programs tomorrow morning."

"Good. Let the Pleiadians soak into the narrative first."

Mary crossed her arms. "You did the right thing, making sure they spoke first."

Vicki didn't answer immediately. Her eyes drifted back toward the map.

Mary followed her gaze. "Still trying to figure out the Hum?"

"It's shifting," Vicki said quietly. "And I don't know how fast. Or what it'll do to people. Or to the planet's systems."

"Well, whatever it is," Mary said, "you'll handle it."

Vicki turned to her. "You're not worried?"

"I'm always worried. But I'm also realistic. People are watching the skies now. They're paying attention. And you're not alone in this."

With that, Mary turned and walked back out, leaving Vicki in silence once more.

Vicki moved toward the map again and tapped another node—deep under the Andes, near an ancient convergence point. The resonance there had shifted just two days ago. Brighter. Louder.

The Earth was vibrating. It was waking up.
But exactly how would that happen?

* * *

OMR OBSERVATION MEMO
Classified Briefing - Internal Use Only

Subject: Global Behavioral and Sensory Anomalies – Ongoing Indicators of Vibrational Disruption

- **[The Oregon Herald]**
  "Children in Local Preschool Exhibit Unexpected Telepathy During Game"
  Teachers left stunned as toddlers 'guess' unseen images with startling accuracy.

- **[@TreeHearted – EcoTalk Forum Thread Title]**
  "Can Trees Talk? I Think Mine Just Did"

- **[The London Chronicle]**
  "'I Saw a Color That Doesn't Exist,' Claims British Graphic Designer"
  Reports of 'new colors' emerging during deep states of consciousness.

- **[Reddit – r/Paranormal]**
  "My Dog Packed Up and Left. And So Did Four Others in the Neighborhood."

- **[The New York Standard]**
  "Psychic Episodes on the Rise: Are We Changing as a Species?"
  Experts weigh in on wave of subtle sensory anomalies worldwide.

- **[TikTok – @deepend_trish]"My Cat Told Me to Quit My Job"**
Over a million views and rising. #TelepathicPets trending.

- **[El Diario de La Paz]**
"Bolivian Farmers Hear Singing in the Rocks"
Unexplained harmonics linked to underground resonance.

- **[The Sydney Observer]**
"Children Claim They Can 'See Thoughts' of Others"
Local schools requesting guidance as reports increase.

- **[The Kyiv Times]**
"Mass Dreams Share Identical Symbols—No Connection Between Dreamers"
All reported same glowing shape in sky, described as 'comforting.'

- **[The Independent Wire]**
"Wave of Resignations Linked to Sudden Shifts in 'Life Purpose'"
Doctors call it a social contagion. Others claim "Young people just don't want to work anymore."

Analyst Note:

Events suggest nonlinear acceleration in cross-species telepathy, location-based resonance, and shared perceptual anomalies. Recommend immediate correlation with HUM field intensity logs and Suede Nation predictive models.

END OF BRIEF

Chapter Twenty-Eight

Mei stared at the untouched rice in her bowl as her aunt's voice cut sharply through the buzz of lunchtime conversation. The chopsticks in her hand felt slick and awkward. Her stomach churned.

"I'm telling you, they're not even hiding anymore," Aunt Liena said. "That girl, what's-her-name—Jessica—just letting those underground creatures threaten us on camera like we're supposed to thank them for it. And now, look, it's happening just like the news said it would. You saw what that reporter showed."

The television was off now, but the image still lingered in Mei's head. Amanda Riley's exposé had aired that morning—loud, dramatized, and slickly edited. Mei had watched it alone from the couch, curled under a blanket, the glow of the screen filling her with unease. There was spliced footage, twisted narration, and bold on-screen text warning viewers of "underground threats" and "claws aimed on the surface."

And then came the "eyewitness": Aija Rao—earnest-looking, dramatic, and animated with concern. And she had spouted absolute lies.

Mei had gripped her knees and thought, *That's not what happened. None of that is true.*

And now, around her grandparents' long, rectangular table, surrounded by a dozen relatives from her extended family, the lies were being treated as fact.

"You think we're supposed to be friends with monsters who live in caves?" Uncle Wen snapped, shoving another spoonful of food into his mouth. "They've had their chance. If they wanted peace, they'd stay hidden."

"They're not monsters," Mei said quietly.

No one heard her.

Across the table, Tian—her older cousin, smug and ever-critical—spoke with the confidence of someone who'd never questioned his place in the world. "Jessica is a fake," he said, waving a chopstick. "That video series? It was staged. You can see she's coached. And now her little 'helpers' are all over the internet acting like they're the chosen ones."

Mei's hands trembled, but she set her chopsticks down and looked up. "Jessica isn't fake."

Several heads turned.

"I know her. And James. And Brad and Kiran too," she said. "You do, too, Tian, so you shouldn't be talking like that. They're the ones making the real videos—not the fake ones that say the Suedes are dangerous. I've been helping them at the tai chi studio."

Her uncle scoffed. "Helping them how? Getting their tea?"

"No," Mei said, trying to keep her voice from wavering. "I'm in their videos, too."

That earned outright laughter from everyone. Her mother actually choked a bit on her food.

"I tried to tell them what a disaster you'd be," said Tian, snickering. "I warned them, but they still went ahead and put you in videos?"

Mei nodded. "Yes."

"Doing what, standing in the background? Holding signs?"

"I talk," she said. "About meditation. About what it feels like when something interferes with your mind. I help explain things."

"Come on," Tian said. "That's not a job, Mei. That's the kind of thing people pretend to care about when they've already failed at everything else."

"Enough," her grandmother said sharply, but no one paid any attention.

Her mother pushed her bowl away. "You're embarrassing the family, Mei. You're repeating government propaganda and being a tool for those lunatics."

"I saw the real video—the raw footage," Mei said. Her voice was louder now. "Jessica and James showed me. Junia wasn't threatening anyone. She was angry and sad. Her cousin was killed by humans who came looking for gold. *That's* why she showed her claws. And the part in Amanda Riley's piece where she says Junia called for war? —That *never happened!*"

The table went quiet for a moment. Then:

"Don't raise your voice," her mother snapped.

"You need to stop embarrassing your parents," Tian added. "This has always been your problem, Mei. You fall for anything. Anyone gives you a scrap of kindness, and suddenly you think you're special. That you're part of something important."

Mei felt her hands curl into fists under the table.

"You've always chased after things that were never meant for you," Tian continued, voice louder now, feeding off the silence in the room. "The dance team that you tried out for but couldn't get on. The science fair project you entered, but didn't even place. And now this? Aliens? Meditation? Like any of it makes you special?"

He shook his head slowly, as if he pitied her.

"We've accepted you'll never amount to anything. It's time for you to accept it too."

Her chest burned, but no one spoke up. Not her mother. Not her aunt. Not even her grandmother, who just stared into her tea as if none of this was happening.

They had all heard him. And none of them disagreed.

Mei stood up.

"I'm not falling for anything," she said. "I made a choice. She looked directly at Tian, then at her mother, and then let her gaze sweep around the table. "You can call me a screw-up. A disappointment. Say it to my face if it makes you feel better. It's not like I haven't heard it before. Say what you want. But I've seen things that are real. I've *felt* them. And none of you were there. You don't *know*."

Her grandmother shifted, lips parting as if to speak—but she hesitated, her brow furrowing. Then slowly, she closed her mouth and said nothing.

"I'm not going to sit here and act like I didn't see it with my own eyes," Mei said. "And I'm not going to let any of you shame me into silence just because you're afraid. I'm not going to be quiet just because it's easier for you to criticize something than to understand it."

She stood up, pushing her chair back with a soft scrape against the tile. "I know the truth. And I'm not going to pretend that I don't just to make you feel more comfortable."

She picked up her phone, jacket, and bag without another word; the silence around the table was now absolute.

She walked into the hallway, stepped through the entrance, and closed the door behind her.

* * *

Aija sat cross-legged on her bed, her phone in her hand, the screen still glowing from the paused video clip. The exposé had aired just a few hours earlier. She had watched it twice already—first with smug satisfaction, then with growing unease.

She looked good on screen. Her hair was perfect, and her words were clear and confident. She had hit every rehearsed beat—concerned citizen, insider insight, a warning the public needed to hear.

She should've felt triumphant.

Instead, her stomach twisted.

The group chat with the Heirs had gone strangely quiet. Earlier in the day, Devon had texted in a panic—his main social media account was suspended for "suspicious activity," even though he swore he hadn't posted anything. Cassidy's credit cards had stopped working—she claimed it was just a technical glitch, but Aija no longer believed that. Two others had been locked out of their cloud storage accounts, and personal files were either corrupted or erased. Rumors were flying in private messages. No one knew what was going on, but everyone felt attacked.

Everyone except for her.

Nothing had touched her.

Not her socials. Not her phone. Not her bank info. No glitches. No consequences.

And that—more than anything—made her stomach churn.

It had to be connected to Jessica. It was the only thing that made sense. Her other friends had gone after her publicly, gleefully. Aija had too—probably more so, if she was honest with herself. But when Amanda filmed her, Aija had been careful about the words she'd used. The camera had captured her sharing "what she'd heard"—she'd never claimed to have actually witnessed anything herself. Still, she had been front and center, spreading stories about both Jessica and the Suede Nation.

So why was she untouched?

Her eyes shifted toward the window. Bright early-afternoon sunlight poured in, but somehow her room felt dark.

She heard footsteps in the hallway, slow and deliberate. A firm knock at her door.

She sat up straighter. "Yeah?"

The door opened, and her parents stepped inside together—her mother's arms folded tightly, her father's expression unreadable.

Aija's throat went dry. "What's going on? Is everything all right?"

They didn't sit. They didn't smile.

"We saw the interview," her mother said.

Aija forced a smile. "Did you think it went okay? I thought—"

"You dishonored our family," her father said flatly.

Her breath caught. "What?"

"You spoke about things that were not yours to speak about," he continued. "You involved yourself in something dangerous, in a situation larger than you understand."

"I was just—everyone said someone needed to push back," she said quickly. "Everyone thinks the Suede Nation is—"

"Enough," her mother said sharply. "Not only did you go on camera and gossip about world events that you had no knowledge of, but you insulted Kiran's girlfriend."

Aija blinked.

"We're sending you to stay with your auntie," her father said, "in Mathura."

Aija stared at them. "What?"

"We called her as soon as we saw the news story," her mother said. "You'll leave tomorrow."

"You can't be serious."

They had to be joking. Her aunt's household, located in an isolated rural area in India, might have money—there were large, echoing rooms with polished floors, custom-made wooden furniture, numerous verandas, and beautiful gardens maintained by full-time groundskeepers—but it was steeped in tradition. Yes, there were plenty of servants, but it would be unbearable—there was no WiFi or any signal at all.

That meant there was no streaming, no social media, and no calls unless she could find the one working landline hidden away in a hallway cabinet. Her aunt didn't believe in "screens," saying the electronics got in the way of living an honest life. So there would be no texting after dark, and certainly no catching up on global events or alien news while sipping chai on the veranda.

Aija could already imagine it: the endless family expectations, the pointed remarks about her behavior, the not-so-subtle comparisons to her more obedient female cousins. Her time there would consist of long days following orders, wearing clothes in fashions she disliked, and being surrounded by relatives who viewed discipline and blind obedience as virtues.

Between the rigid expectations and a complete disconnect from modern life, every minute there would feel like torture.

Her father's expression didn't shift. "You need time to reflect. Time away from the internet, from your friends, from this behavior. You need to understand that being seen does not mean being respected. You need to learn how to behave."

Aija's ears rang.

"But I—why now? I'm not the only one—"

"You are our daughter," her mother said, voice clipped. "What others do is not our concern. You should start packing your suitcases."

They stood there a moment longer, as if waiting for her to protest more. She didn't. Her voice had dried up.

Without another word, they turned and walked out.

Aija sat frozen, her phone still resting on the blanket beside her. The image on the screen had gone dark.

She had wanted to be seen—now, she was. And yet someone, somewhere, had decided she was not worth attacking.

That was what frightened her most of all.

Chapter
Twenty-Nine

T he koi pond reflected the late afternoon light, small ripples on the water suggesting the lazy movement of fish beneath the surface. The stone benches where they sat were warm from the sun, bordered by trimmed bamboo and overhanging citrus trees.

Jessica sat at the edge of one bench, her phone balanced in her hand, the brightness of the screen dimmed. The familiar voice of Amanda Riley sounded from the tiny speaker: polished, firm, smug.

"...multiple credible sources have confirmed that members of the so-called Suede Nation have displayed aggressive postures and are capable of collapsing entire underground structures using unknown technology or biologically-enhanced traits. One young witness—Aija Rao—warned that there may be an internal divide among alien factions, and that these creatures, while appearing peaceful, have the potential to threaten human sovereignty."

Now Aija's face filled the screen, confident and composed, her voice clear: *"There are things people aren't being told. Monsters that hide in the Earth, with weapons made of rock and vibration. And yes, I believe they pose a risk—because no one is making them follow rules. Jessica Martinsson tries hard, but the poor thing just isn't up to it."*

Jessica didn't blink or look away from the screen. She'd seen it already—twice—but it still stung. It wasn't just the words; she felt obliged to study every frame, every shift in tone, and every misleading pause between words. This wasn't merely manipulation. It was a slow poisoning of public trust, designed to seed doubt and let fear grow in the cracks.

Sitting on the bench opposite her, James had his eyes closed. Kiran sat next to her in silence, staring at the water. Brad was the only one fidgeting, occasionally adjusting his sunglasses or pulling at a thread on his cuff.

The three boys weren't watching the screen. But all of them could hear it.

Amanda was speaking now, "*So we have to ask—who is really in control here? Is it the Department of State? Or is it these beings, whose powers we do not yet understand? Does anyone in the U.S. government really understand what's going on?*"

Jessica locked her phone and let the screen go dark. The words still hung in the air.

Kiran finally spoke, his voice almost savage. "Aija made it sound like she was in the room when Junia said those things."

"She wasn't," Jessica said.

"I know," he replied. "We know. But most people don't."

"She makes it sound like the Suedes are plotting war."

"Her inflection was deliberate," James added without opening his eyes. "She posed everything as a question to avoid liability, but the insinuations were clear."

Kiran's gaze was fixed on the pond. "My parents called. Just before I came out here."

Jessica glanced at him. "What did they say?"

"They've decided to send Aija to India. To stay with one of our more traditional aunties so she can 'learn humility and how to behave.' Their words."

Brad let out a low whistle and leaned back on the bench. "Not surprised. She stepped in it big time."

Jessica sighed. "I want to be relieved, but I'm not."

"You're allowed to be both," James said. "She tried to hurt you. She hurt all of us."

"She hurt the Suede Nation and humanity's relations with extraterrestrials," Jessica said quietly. "That part matters more."

Kiran exhaled slowly. "I'm sorry."

"You didn't do it," Brad said.

"No," Kiran agreed. "But she's my sister, so I feel responsible—and embarrassed. Not just for what she said, but because she *wanted* to say it. She wanted attention so badly she'd sell out people she's never even met."

There was a pause.

"Colonel Riley's Pentagon briefing is scheduled for tomorrow," Brad said.

Jessica's gaze shifted to him. "Don't you think he'll wait to see what traction the exposé gets?"

"Probably not. He'll use whatever momentum it gives him to frame the Suede Nation as a threat and claim that OMR didn't act fast enough. Amanda's exposé is instilling just enough paranoia so that when he holds the press briefing and suggests the military take control, it will feel like common sense instead of a power grab."

Jessica nodded slowly. "He'll use the fear the exposé generated to make people believe the Suedes are hiding weapons and plan to attack."

"Which is why," Brad said, with no small amount of satisfaction, "I've already taken care of it."

Jessica gave him a wary look—it was a look shaped by the experience of living with her brother. "Taken care of it how?"

"I've launched a preemptive campaign," Brad said, holding up his phone. "Social media saturation. Preemptive counter-narratives and embedded short clips from Junia's full interview—put in context, but without any edits. I've cleaned up some old Partnership clips, as well as included memes, commentary, and testimonials. I've seeded it across influencer channels, forums, and alternative-news aggregators. Later today I'll add shorter clips of Junia's interview with side-by-side video of the exposé showing how Amanda and Aija distorted the truth."

Brad smiled to himself, "It's already trending in five countries."

Jessica leaned forward. "You did that today?"

He grinned. "Last night. I figured one of us needed to play offense."

"The media campaign sounds good," said Jessica, thinking. "But it's not enough. We need a central place to host everything. Somewhere public but secure. A site people can access that can't be traced back here. Riley's going to push for control of the narrative. We need to create our own platform—our own website."

James nodded. "A central place people can go for information."

Jessica looked energized now. "A hub where we post videos, news summaries, and our own content rather than depending on other websites for exposure. We already have the tai chi and meditation videos, and I just received the CE-5 footage from Jerry's wife. She's been working with Dr. Greer. It's really good stuff."

"We can post those too," Brad said, already making notes in his phone. "And both the Suede livestream and the Pleiadian UN speech. It'll be a feed of reliable sources. We'll update it daily."

"I can do weekly commentary videos—" Jessica offered. "—short and focused, to answer questions we're seeing. And when Melly and I finally manage to coordinate our schedules, we'll be doing another *Melly Talks* series."

James glanced at Brad. "You can keep the site untraceable?"

Brad didn't even look up. "Already halfway there. I'll put it on a secure private network that hides where it's really coming from, keeps the addresses changing, and scrambles the usual tracking methods. I'll also mix in extra fake data to throw off anyone trying to spy on it. No one's tracing this back. I'll make it searchable by keywords, so it gets picked up by aggregators."

Kiran looked over. "You're still going to release the advanced med tech schematics separately?"

Brad's fingers didn't pause as he nodded. "I'll have the basic site setup for our new website done by midnight, but we won't depend on just that one source. In addition to posting them on the website, I'll be uploading thousands of copies to thousands of locations using auto-replicating drops and peer-to-peer chains. Even if they shut ten thousand down, ten thousand more will pop up. The information's out there. No more gatekeeping."

Kiran exhaled again. "It won't stop Riley. But it'll slow him down."

"It might do more than that," James said. "It might remind people who's really telling the truth."

Jessica turned toward the koi pond. One of the larger fish surfaced, its scales briefly catching the sunlight before it disappeared again into the murky green water below.

The studio door opened behind them.

"Ten minutes," Mona called from the doorway. "The class is finishing warm-ups. We'll be ready for you soon."

Jessica nodded without turning.

They would film more today—tai chi forms, breathing exercises, and meditations to help people reach higher states of consciousness. It would help to serve as a counterbalance to the carefully curated news cycle. But she knew that after the class, the real work would still be waiting.

Truth didn't spread by accident. You had to give it legs.

* * *

The lights were low in the studio's office, with only the glow of the desk lamp illuminating the paperwork his dad had left scattered across the surface. James sat in the old wooden chair near the filing cabinet. The studio beyond was quiet and dark, the busyness of the day already gone.

The filming had gone well, with the advanced students moving through the forms with practiced ease, their breath syncing with the space around them. Jessica captured it all—she was getting faster and more confident about directing. Brad barely looked up from his laptop but still managed to handle audio and duplicate recording.

Then they had filmed Kiran doing a short intro at the koi pond. His presence on camera was calm and reassuring. James could see that Kiran's early training with his grandfather was paying off.

Afterward, Kiran and the Martinssons had left together, heading back to the old flower shop. Jessica would be editing late into the night. Brad would probably disappear into his workspace, filled with monitors, cables, and electronic equipment, to fine-tune the new website until sunrise. Kiran would make sure they both drank water and eventually got some sleep.

James had stayed behind to help his parents close the studio. But they had both disappeared into the back garden and hadn't yet returned.

He leaned back in the chair and exhaled, watching the clock tick over to 10:35. Nearly twenty minutes had passed.

The door creaked open.

His mother entered first, her mouth set in a tight line. His father followed, closing the door behind them quietly. Both still wore their teaching *gi*—loose-fitting pants and cross-tied jackets—but their posture wasn't as relaxed as it usually was after class.

James sat up. "What's going on?"

Mona came around the desk and sat on the edge. Calvin stayed standing, arms crossed, his expression unreadable.

Mona looked at her son and took a breath.

"There's something we need to tell you," she said. "Some things are changing."

James suddenly felt uneasy. "Okay..."

His mother exchanged a glance with his father. "It's about Mei."

James stiffened.

Mona continued. "She left her house—walked out around midday. It wasn't safe for her to stay. She hasn't told us everything, but she made it clear—she can't go back."

James stared at them, trying to make sense of this new information. "What do you mean, not safe?"

"Emotionally," Calvin said. "Not physically. But there's a lot of emotional abuse going on, and she's been the punching bag. It was enough."

James blinked. "And...?"

Mona offered a small, tight smile. "We told her she could stay at our house. With us."

James's brain paused. *Wait, what?*

He didn't say it out loud.

Instead, he leaned back slightly and asked, "You've already decided this?"

His mother nodded. "Yes. She has nowhere else to go. And we believe her."

Belief. That word gave him pause. How many people believed in Mei? He had seen how Mei's cousin Tian behaved. What would it be like to go through life with your family constantly calling you a failure?

James had noticed Mei watching him during filming today. Not in a creepy way—not as if she had a crush on him. But still in a way that made him uncomfortable. It felt like she was noticing things he hadn't intended to show. Had she been wondering what it would be like to live with his family?

And, James admitted it to himself, she *was* annoying— a bit loud, a bit too eager, and clearly still carrying whatever chip on her shoulder made her practically vibrate with the need to prove herself to everyone in the room.

But he didn't say any of that. He just nodded slowly.

"Okay," he said. "So, she's... still here now? She didn't go home after class ended?"

Calvin reached for the office door and pulled it open.

There, standing just outside, was Mei.

She wore a soft hoodie two sizes too big and held a duffel bag by her side, as if she wasn't sure she was allowed to set it down. Her eyes flicked nervously between Calvin and Mona before looking at James.

She gave him a small nod.

"Hi," she said, her voice quiet. "I didn't know if I should come in."

James didn't say anything. But he felt proud of himself that he didn't glare either. He simply returned the nod.

"We've got space in the guest room," Mona said gently, stepping past James and reaching for Mei's bag. "Let's go home and get you settled."

As they walked out, Mei paused at the doorway and looked over her shoulder at James.

"I'll try not to be in the way," she said. "I promise."

James didn't answer.

They all filed out of the studio and into the parking lot. As his mother chatted softly with Mei, James scrubbed a hand over his face.

This was going to be... something.

But just what, he wasn't sure.

Chapter Thirty

The wine in his glass had gone still, so Jerry swirled it gently. Anne sat across from him on the sofa, one leg tucked under the other. She was watching him, waiting.

"The kids are finally down," she said. "So you can talk now. You've been holding something in since you got home."

Jerry nodded. "I've been trying to confirm a line of connection. And now I have."

Anne leaned in slightly to listen.

He set his glass down. "I traced the people who kidnapped Jessica. Not directly. But close enough."

Anne didn't speak, so he went on.

"They're tied to defense contractors. Not fringe players—these are established companies. Ones that used to work with the Partnership before it went down. These weren't operations running rogue. They had institutional cover. They had long-term contracts. Some of them were even tied into intelligence back channels."

Her expression tensed. "You're sure?"

I've cross-checked everything twice: subcontracts, off-book accounts, and employee travel orders. I even ran across internal memos showing projected post-Disclosure profits. They had expected all the alien tech—maybe even with patent protection—to be handed over to them once the truth became public.

He sat back, his jaw tightening. "And when the Partnership was destroyed, they didn't want to give up their chance to cash in. They just waited. They kept their structure in place and waited for someone else to get things back on track."

"Colonel Riley," Anne said quietly.

Jerry nodded again. "They're not in daily meetings with him, but they've been backing him—funding events and coordinating messaging."

Anne's grip on her wine glass tightened.

"They don't understand what this is," Jerry said. "Disclosure. It's not a procurement cycle. It's not just who gets to build the next weapons system. They thought if they made Jessica disappear, the movement would slow down. They thought this was about influence—about media exposure and public image."

"And now Brad's dumping the advanced tech everywhere," Anne said.

"Everywhere," Jerry confirmed. "And it's not just the free energy technology. There have been thousands of uploads of the schematics for the new medical device. Patent-free. No licensing. Engineers in three different countries have already prototyped working models. Governments and major corporations are playing catch-up. And these guys—the ones who backed the kidnapping—they're panicking. They were promised control. They were promised wealth. Now they're watching their grip dissolve."

Anne's breath caught, "What can OMR do?"

"I'm not sure," Jerry admitted. "I've got enough evidence against these firms to make it public and make it stick. But the country is still figuring out how to process everything else. It might be too much."

Anne leaned back slightly on the couch, her expression thoughtful. "I can call in a few favors at the firm," she said. "This isn't the first time we've done that. You remember the dividend issue a couple months ago—the one tied to companies hiding revenue streams from reverse-engineered tech? Once we flagged it, stockholders went straight to the SEC demanding transparency. The pressure worked. If we dig into this group's financial trail, we'll probably find things they don't want out in public."

Jerry shook his head slowly. "That was about money. This is different."

Anne's gaze didn't waver.

"They kidnapped someone, Anne. They tried to silence Jessica. They went after her because they thought she was just a communications strategy. They don't see people—only threats to their control."

"I know."

"And it's likely they were behind the attack in Lagos," he said, his voice a little shaky. "There are too many overlaps—timing, signals, the use of tech no one should have had access to. These aren't just executives manipulating the market; they're happy to use violence. There could be real-world consequences."

Anne was quiet for a moment, considering what he said. Then: "That doesn't mean we stay quiet. If anything, it means we should do everything we can."

"I'm not saying we should stay quiet. I'm saying we can't underestimate them."

She nodded once. "We'll be careful. I'll start with civil channels—some public pressure, shareholder inquiries, and asset exposure. No courtroom. No subpoenas. Just enough heat to make them stumble."

Jerry studied her expression. "You're serious about this."

"I'm always serious when people use power to cover up violence. Especially when they do it thinking no one will ever hold them accountable." She leaned forward, resting her elbows on her knees. "They came after Jessica. And they killed all those people in Lagos. I have a feeling we aren't going to get a second chance to do this right."

He let out a slow breath. "Just promise me we keep the kids safe."

"We will," Anne said. "I'll take every step like someone's watching. Because they probably are. But I'm not backing away. We didn't come this far just to let the old world smother the new one before it even begins."

* * *

Once again, Anne let the moment pass.

Jerry was talking, his voice tired, going over timelines and risks, strategies and fallout. She nodded when she needed to, said the right things, asked sharp questions when they were needed. But she didn't bring it up—not now. Again, not now.

She hadn't told him about her work with Dr. Greer. Not really. He knew she respected the man's ideas. He knew she supported CE-5 outreach in theory. But she hadn't shared how involved she'd actually become. How she'd stepped in to help edit and organize the CE-5 videos. How she'd sent them directly to Jessica in a careful email with no explanation.

The videos were already released. Jessica and the others had them. That phase was over. Her name wasn't on anything. As far as she was concerned, her involvement had ended there. It didn't need to be a discussion now—especially not with everything else piling up on Jerry's shoulders.

He was already stretched thin—juggling OMR and the fall-out from the exposé, tracking Riley's next move, and helping Vicki keep everything from collapsing under the pressure. He didn't need more. And he certainly didn't need to worry about his wife slipping out a few nights a week to sit in the backyard with their neighbors and stare at the sky.

She hadn't planned on forming a group; it just happened. One evening, a conversation over the fence turned into questions. One question turned into shared curiosity. Now, twice a week, four women from the neighborhood gathered in her backyard after dark, each bringing a blanket and a thermos of tea. They sat in a quiet circle, followed the CE-5 protocols, and kept logs.

It began as something simple—calm breathing and focused meditation.

But there had been moments.

Once, the air around them had subtly shifted, as if the pressure had changed without any alteration in temperature. On another occasion, a light had appeared overhead—too slow to be a plane, too fast to be a satellite—and responded when they flashed a laser pointer at it, once, then twice. And then it had made a sharp 90-degree turn and zoomed away at an impossibly high speed.

There were nights when all they did was sit, breathe, and feel foolish. But there were others that left them changed in a way none of them could fully explain.

Still, she said nothing to Jerry.

She told herself it wasn't about hiding anything. It was about timing. He was under pressure. The videos were already in good hands. No one needed to know about the backyard gatherings. Not yet.

She would tell him eventually. When things calmed down.

If they ever did.

* * *

Kiran was surprised to find James already at the flower shop when he came down for his morning coffee. Brad was still sleeping upstairs, and he assumed Jessica was still asleep too.

"You're here early." Kiran walked over to the espresso machine and flipped a switch so it could warm up.

"Well, I have a key," said James.

"You're still here early. What gives?

"I was hoping you could help me."

"Me?" Kiran poured beans into the grinder. At the growl of the burr, the aroma of coffee began filling the air.

"It's the memory crystal," sighed James. "It has entries going back thousands of years, detailing hundreds of human-alien interactions. It's not just one civilization. The records cover different cultures, languages, oral histories, and even direct encounters that were never written down. But I keep circling back to India."

Kiran poured the coffee grounds into the portafilter, tamped them down, and locked everything into place. He placed his cup under the spout and then hit *Brew*. He turned around to face James.

James continued. "So much of Indian tradition... It doesn't sound like myth. It reads like something literal."

Kiran nodded once. "That's because it *is* literal. The Vedas, the Mahabharata, the Ramayana—Western culture tends to assume these texts are symbolic. But they're not. They record historical events, and they do it without asking the reader to accept supernatural events on faith."

James leaned forward slightly. "I'm going to be releasing sections of the memory crystal that deal with the Indian experience. I was hoping you could help me put the Hindu epics into context."

Kiran answered immediately. "You'll want to start with the *vimanas*. They're the most obvious connection."

James nodded. "Flying machines."

"Yes. Sometimes described as disk-shaped, sometimes shaped like chariots. Powered by what the texts call mercury or fire, and able to fly in any direction. Some could cloak themselves. Others carried whole battalions. Pilots were trained in complex maneuvers. That's not religious language. That's engineering."

James smiled faintly, scribbling notes. "And the battles?"

Kiran exhaled. "The *Mahabharata* and *Ramayana* are filled with aerial warfare. One story tells of two commanders engaging in a dogfight high above the planet, using what are called 'celestial weapons.' The *Brahmastra* is one of the most well-known. It was said to create firestorms and destroy entire regions. The descriptions of the aftereffects are difficult to explain unless you're talking about nuclear-level technology."

James looked up. "So you believe it was real? That these stories weren't just symbolic?"

Kiran's voice didn't waver. "I believe it was exactly what it sounds like. Advanced beings—devas, rishis, sages—interacting with humans. Some with ships, some with knowledge. Sometimes they interfered. Sometimes they taught lessons, and sometimes they *were* the lessons. But yes, I believe the events were real. Am I right that the memory crystal shows they were aliens?"

James nodded. "Yes, and that's what worries me. What happens when we tell people that those beings weren't divine? That they were visitors from elsewhere. Not gods—just... more advanced?"

Kiran took his espresso and sipped it thoughtfully before answering. "In Hindu thought, gods aren't like the Western concept. We don't say they're omnipotent. They aren't immortal. We call them *devas*—celestial beings. They live long lives, they operate on higher planes, and they have supernatural powers. But they're still bound by karma. They live. They die. They reincarnate. They learn. They change. They experience the whole cycle of life and death."

"So they're already viewed as... beings, rather than perfect gods."

"Exactly," Kiran said. "If it came out tomorrow that Indra was actually a visitor from another world who had access to a vehicle that could bend space or manipulate gravity, most people in India wouldn't be scandalized. They'd probably nod and say, 'We already knew that.'"

James blinked, then laughed under his breath. "That's not how people would react in Europe or the U.S."

"No," Kiran agreed. "For many cultures, godhood is a binary. You're either divine or you're not. In India, it's a spectrum. You can be a teacher, a being of light, a warrior, a protector... and still be part of the cycle of and death. The cosmic order is flexible. And complex. Most people are used to that."

"So you don't think this would be disruptive?"

"I actually think it would be *affirming*," Kiran said. "Especially for scholars and spiritual gurus who've spent years arguing that these stories weren't just myths. Older generations might still hold on to ritual interpretations, but many young people would see it as validation. It wouldn't weaken the culture—it would strengthen it."

James looked down at his notebook, slowly flipping a few pages. "Good. That makes things easier. I think we'll release the first series next week. Four videos. I'll need your help framing the language. I don't want it to sound like we're trying to debunk religion. That's not the goal."

"I'll help," Kiran said. "But remember—this isn't just about belief systems. It's also about what happens when people realize they've been closer to the truth than they were told."

James nodded.

Kiran said, "Will they be upset with themselves for not noticing what was right in front of them, or will they blame the religious leaders who misled them?"

James nodded again. "It could go either way."

* * *

The India thing had been relatively easy to deal with—lucky for them that Kiran was now part of the Four. However, the big thing was something James hadn't mentioned to anyone.

He had intended to work with the memory crystal chronologically, starting with the earliest records and working his way up to recent events. But he couldn't resist taking a peek at what had happened when the Partnership began collaborating with the Tall Whites. What he found out scared him.

The Partnership—through the military—was cooperating with the Tall Whites under a secret agreement that traded alien tech for access to human DNA. And not just through a laboratory. Ordinary people had been abducted by aliens and subjected to medical procedures, only to be publicly ridiculed by the military in order to keep the agreement hidden. People lost their jobs, were accused of lying, and saw their marriages break down. Some were even driven insane.

James was horrified.

This was too big. Too big for him. Too big for the Four. He needed to talk with Vicki.

Chapter Thirty-One

The surface air smelled different. Dry, thin, and open. There was more motion in it, more dust, and more disorganization. Junia stood a few feet from the rock-faced hillside, a thin layer of granite hiding the newly-shaped entrance behind her. It would look solid to humans, but pose no barrier for Suedes. The elders had decided that while they needed additional passages to the surface, they wouldn't make entrances that these lower vibrational humans could use. Bowen had paid for that mistake with his life.

Alun stood silently just behind her. He was there to support her, not to speak. That role had been left to her.

Ahead, five humans waited under a canopy. Scientists. They were all dressed in lightweight field clothing, equipped with tablets and notebooks, and carrying too many assumptions. Junia could sense their expectations stretching out, trying to define who she would be before she had even spoken.

She walked forward, stopping a few feet from the canopy.

"Thank you for meeting us," said a tall woman with gray at her temples. "We've heard so much. And we're honored."

Junia gave a nod but did not echo the sentiment; she wasn't ready to go that far yet. "You're here to learn. So let's start."

She let her eyes move from one face to the next. They were of different ages and had various accents, yet they shared the same expression: anticipation mixed with doubt. She understood what they saw—a girl, perhaps a teenager, slight and barefoot, standing calmly on the dirt as if she belonged to two worlds. Which, she did.

The tall woman gestured toward a set of sample kits. "We were hoping to collect some readings—materials near the entry point, maybe energy signatures."

"You won't find anything you understand," Junia said. "Not yet."

A man beside the woman frowned. "We've brought sensitive equipment. Spectrometers, oscilloscopes, thermographic lenses. We'll at least get baseline data."

Junia let that pass. "What you measure is surface structure. What you *miss* is vibration."

One of the others—thin, sharp-nosed, and wearing glasses too narrow for his face—let out a quiet breath and quickly scribbled something in his notebook.

"I've read some of the reports," he said without looking up. "The terminology your people use—vibrational levels, frequencies of consciousness—it doesn't fit within any accepted scientific framework. Frankly, it sounds like pseudoscience."

Junia stepped closer.

"We walk through stone," she said. "We pass through walls, and cross layers of Earth that your drills can't even scratch. We shift frequency instead of breaking matter. What part of that is unclear?"

The man glanced up. "Extraordinary claims require extraordinary proof."

Junia tilted her head, and when she spoke, there was a bite to her words. "And what have you humans proven? That you can dig holes. That you can tear down forests. That you poison the air you breathe and the water you drink. You're still stuck to the surface of your planet. We've been living beneath it, inside it, part of it, for longer than your oldest temples have stood."

The group fell quiet.

Alun remained still behind her. She was glad he was there—his presence felt reassuring.

She redirected her attention back to the group. "If you want to learn about the inside of the world, you need to stop treating it like a cave system or a bunch of tunnels. Reality has layers. What you see depends on your energy level. Your bodies only know a narrow range of vibration. That's why it's hard for humans to see us unless we lower our energy to match yours. And that's why you can't go where we go unless we open the path."

The tall woman nodded slowly. "We've read some early notes from the State Department's Office of Multispecies Relations. OMR issued several reports about dimensional frequency. Admittedly, it's new to us."

Junia focused on her. "You'll need to unlearn what doesn't work. Your science has helped you a lot, but it won't get you through the shift unless you learn to change. The Earth is already changing. You've heard the Hum. That's not a mystery. That's a signal."

Another scientist, older and bearded, stepped forward. "You're saying Earth is shifting to a different... vibrational state? And we have to rise to meet it?"

"Yes," Junia said. "The people who don't change will stay stuck in a smaller version of this world. They'll still be here, but it won't be the same Earth the rest of us are in. The two groups—those with higher vibration and those with lower—will start to see different things, feel different emotions, and live in different ways. Over time, their worlds won't line up anymore. And one day, they won't be connected at all.

The thin man opened his mouth again, but Junia cut him off.

""You can ignore it," she said. "But what we told you is still true. Your tools won't catch up fast enough. Your words won't explain it. And the world won't stop and wait for you to believe it.""

He said nothing.

Junia inhaled deeply. The surface air felt a little less foreign now. Less hostile.

She went on. "You don't have to believe me right now, but the shift will be messy. Some people won't be able to handle it. That's why I agreed to talk to you. You're scientists. You ask questions. You might be the ones who can help people see what's coming... if you're ready to look past what you know now."

The tall woman stepped forward, her hand extended in a quiet gesture of respect. "We're listening. And we'll share what we learn with humility."

Junia looked at the hand. Then she shook it briefly.

"I'll meet with you again," she said. "Not far from here. There are things we're ready to show you. But don't bring more tools. Bring better questions."

She turned and walked back toward the hidden entry. Alun followed in silence.

Only once she reached the edge did she glance back.

The scientists were watching her, unsure, still sorting through what they had seen and heard.

And Junia sensed a new feeling developing in her chest. Not pride. Or even satisfaction.

It was responsibility.

For the first time, she believed she could speak for her people—and be heard.

And then *she* heard the exclamations of the scientists as she and Alun stepped straight through solid rock.

* * *

James adjusted the mic level slightly on the interface panel, watching the small green bar flicker with each breath. Jessica was across the room, seated at her desk, fine-tuning the lighting with the sliders on her computer. The makeshift studio had become more efficient since just a few weeks earlier, when they had struggled to put together a new workplace after the Martinsson mansion burned down—no more clutter, no more extension cords running across the room. Jessica had a system now. Everything had a place. Everything was labeled.

He stared at the notepad in his lap, reviewing the bullet points he'd jotted down the night before. Cave drawings. Roman records. Aboriginal contact stories. He knew this material inside and out. Humanity had known about it, at least in fragments, for decades. These were the examples people brought up in documentaries and late-night podcasts, half-dismissed, half-believed. That was exactly why he was starting here, rather than with something more exciting.

It was familiar.

While it was the truth, it wasn't the whole truth. But it was close enough to feel safe to people whose entire worldview had already been rattled.

Jessica turned to him. "We're good on audio and lighting."

James nodded, still seated. "I want to open with the cave paintings in Chauvet and Lascaux. Not the animals—the humanoid figures. The ones with elongated heads and oversized eyes."

"Do you want a still image cut in?"

"Yeah. Add the petroglyphs from Val Camonica after that. The figures holding what looks like tools or rods."

Jessica tapped a few notes into her laptop.

James continued. "Then I'll bring in the Roman texts—Livy's account of 'shields blazing in the sky.' And that one from Pliny where multiple flying discs hovered over a military encampment, stayed stationary for hours, and then vanished straight up."

Jessica looked up. "We have documentation from the crystal for those?"

"Yeah," James said. "And that's where we make the 90-degree turn, and I start adding what the crystal shows. The Romans saw what they thought were flying shields. But the crafts weren't weapons—they were observation drones from an extraterrestrial scientific expedition, programmed to map population patterns and document how humans responded to organized authority. Rome was a test case for social behavior under imperial expansion."

Jessica raised an eyebrow. "Not what they taught us in history class."

James shrugged. "No, but you have to admit it makes sense now."

He flipped the page in his notepad.

"Then I'll jump to the Aboriginal accounts. The star-beings weren't just visiting—they were in communication with the Aboriginal elders. What's interesting is that the exchange of information wasn't about technology—it was about rhythm, cycles, and consciousness. They had that in common—both cultures maintained a deep connection to the land and non-linear time. The star-beings used those points of alignment to maintain long-term resonance. The Aboriginals had their Dreamtime and songlines. It wasn't random contact—the star-beings sought out the Aboriginals on purpose."

Jessica was still listening, but he could tell her mind was already framing the edit. She would match each spoken section with visual overlays, subtitles, and context slides. It was becoming routine, but she never felt bored by it.

James looked back at his notes.

"Same pattern with some of the Native American legends. Sky beings descending, giving warnings. Symbolic language that, when I cross-reference it with the memory crystal, matches incidents of planetary visitations by ETs. These weren't mythological stories—they were logbooks."

He let out a slow breath. "But I'll keep it low-key. I'll walk them up to it slowly instead of dropping them in it."

Jessica nodded. "Western audiences will recognize the stories."

James continued. "Exactly. But to be honest, these are some of the most boring stories in the memory crystal. I'm starting with them so that Western audiences have an entry point that doesn't scare them. People are already struggling. The U.S., the UK, parts of Europe—supply chains are strained, currencies are unstable, and energy markets are crumbling now that the free-energy prototypes are being built without restriction. They've found out that beings are living in the inner Earth, and have seen aliens addressing the United Nations. People need a break. I'm going to ease them into it."

"Hmm, that's strategic," Jessica said.

"That's the line I'm trying to walk. In the next session, I'll move to the India material. The stuff Kiran helped me with. Vimana schematics. Translations from the Vedas that read more like flight manuals than religious texts. The crystal's records of what the extraterrestrials were doing in India are amazing." James paused. "I'll save the Alpha Centaurians and how they almost caused the extinction of the human race for the end—the end of the entire series."

Jessica grimaced, then turned her attention to something on her screen.

James looked down at the desk for a second. For a moment, his mind drifted to the morning's breakfast.

Mei had been sitting at the table.

It was strange seeing her there with her tea and quiet voice, offering to toast bread or refill his dad's mug. She wasn't acting loud or defensive anymore. She looked like someone trying to prove she could be useful.

His mom had said they'd start letting her help with the beginner's tai chi sessions. She was already folding towels, greeting people at the door, and managing class sign-in sheets. No one asked her to. She just did it. It was hard to square that with the kid who used to blurt out awkward comments every time there was silence.

He wasn't sure what he thought about it yet.

James blinked, focused back on the present, and glanced at the setup again.

"Are you ready?" Jessica asked.

"Yeah." James sat up straighter and adjusted the mic stand. "Let's do the segment on ancient contact."

Jessica gave him a three-count, and the camera light turned red.

James looked straight ahead.

"We've been told that ancient stories were myths," he said. "But across continents and cultures, they point to the same thing—visitors from above. And now we know, from their own records, why they came."

He paused just long enough to breathe.

"They were watching. They were listening. Not to guide us, but to understand what we were becoming."

Chapter Thirty-Two

The secure room had no windows. The overhead lighting was intentionally dim—flat, functional, and lacking variation. The heavy door had been locked behind them. Electronic devices—phones, tablets, and watches—had been collected and stored in lockers just outside the entrance.

It was a SCIF, a Sensitive Compartmented Information Facility. Access was strictly limited. No signals came in or out. It was the kind of room used when the topic couldn't risk exposure to foreign intelligence—or to the public.

The full Senate Select Committee on Intelligence was seated around the long conference table, arranged by seniority. Staffers lined the perimeter. A few individuals at the far end were not introduced. Vicki didn't ask who they were. From the way they held their silence and watched without blinking, she could guess they were from the intelligence community.

She stood at one end of the table. Jerry was to her left, a thick binder of supporting documents in front of him. The air in the room was unmoving, almost stagnant. No one had spoken yet.

Finally, the committee chair, Senator North, folded his hands and addressed her.

"Please take a seat, Deputy Assistant Secretary Heywood," he said. "We appreciate you coming in ahead of the Pentagon's press conference. I trust you know why you're here."

Vicki nodded as she and Jerry sat down. "Yes, Senator."

"You've been briefed, I assume, on the remarks Colonel Riley is expected to deliver later today."

"I've seen the outline distributed to your office, yes."

Of course she had. Everyone in OMR had read that paper—it was filled with offensive innuendo and lies. Riley was being so outrageous that she might have laughed, except she knew many people would believe him.

Senator North gave a short nod and leaned slightly forward. "There are concerns. Serious ones. Let's begin with this: Why is the United States not the lead liaison to the Galactic Federation? This nation, through your office—through the Department of State's Office of Multispecies Relations—initiated Disclosure. Why are we not in control of this process? Why are those Galactic Federation representatives in Geneva instead of here in Washington?"

Vicki glanced down the length of the table, looking at each senator in turn before releasing her breath. *Stay calm.*

"Because this is not a national matter," she said flatly. "Membership in the Galactic Federation is not bestowed to countries. It's extended to entire planets. Their framework doesn't recognize national borders. It recognizes sentient species."

A few senators exchanged glances.

Vicki continued. "If this committee believes that the United States should be the sole representative because we were first to act, then I would suggest that such thinking disqualifies us from leadership. The Federation is watching. They are evaluating how we treat one another. If our first reaction is to keep all the power and ignore others, we've already failed to meet their most basic expectations."

A younger senator from the Midwest leaned forward. "You understand, of course, that U.S. interests must be protected."

Vicki looked down, struggling to keep a neutral expression. *Ugh*—this was their main concern: money and control. When she was sure she had her feelings in check, she looked up and addressed the senator's question.

"I understand that self-interest is exactly what led to the near collapse of global trust in this country's institutions," she said. "Just because we spoke first doesn't mean we deserve to be in charge. If anything, we have a greater responsibility to behave with maturity and restraint."

There was a beat of silence. Then Senator Holloway, a senior member who often voted along defense industry lines, interjected.

"Has OMR been too soft?" he asked. "You've deferred to these alien groups. You've allowed the Suede Nation to be introduced without clear vetting. You've made no move to secure any defensive guarantees. Meanwhile, Colonel Riley will argue this afternoon that the Suedes and other nonhuman entities represent a potential threat to global safety."

Vicki didn't look away—this was a question she welcomed and had prepared for. This kind of thinking was how organizations like the Partnership had amassed as much power as they had. She smiled as she answered.

It wasn't a nice smile.

"They're only a threat," she said, "to the idea that a small, unaccountable group should control what the rest of humanity is allowed to access, how it is allowed to live, and what it is allowed to do."

Holloway raised his eyebrows. "That sounds like you're accusing this body of something."

Vicki's voice sharpened. "I'm reminding you that you were all briefed on the Partnership's activities. That organization reverse-engineered alien technology in secret. They planned to use it for control—not to benefit citizens, but to maintain a power structure that not only excluded the public, but also the majority of the U.S. Government itself. And if we're being honest—which I think we should be, since we're in a SCIF; and if we can't tell the truth here, then where can we?—the Partnership planned to control all of humanity. We're talking modern-day slavery. Every person in this room knows it."

Under the table, Jerry's foot nudged hers in warning. Vicki didn't stop. She was on a roll.

"The talking points Colonel Riley intends to use? They could have come straight out of a Partnership strategy memo. Keep the population afraid. Withhold information. Accuse reformers of betrayal. All while claiming it's for national security."

Senator Holloway shifted but didn't speak. He was starting to look uncomfortable. Vicki continued.

"I'm asking you directly: Are you prepared to act like the Partnership? Are you ready to block life-saving technologies? To prevent clean energy from reaching people who need it? To force them to breathe polluted air because a handful of corporations don't want their market share disrupted?"

The room was quiet again.

Senator North leaned back slightly, then glanced at his notes.

"One of the colonel's claims—perhaps his most controversial—is that the aliens and the Suedes are not just a security risk. He's going to suggest they are... demonic. That their existence challenges human sovereignty, or perhaps even divine order."

Vicki didn't flinch.

"The ones who killed Bowen—the ones who tried to blast their way into the Suede Nation territory, searching for gold and God knows what else—those were humans. They came prepared for violence: they were armed, organized, and they killed. And they did it because they couldn't stand the idea of an Earth-native species existing in peace beneath their feet without their permission."

She looked directly at Senator North.

"If you want to talk about demons, start there."

No one spoke for several seconds.

Jerry closed the binder in front of him but didn't say anything. The point had been made.

Vicki kept silent just long enough for it to sink in. Then she added, calmly:

"We have a choice. We can lead by being open, working together, and including others. Or we can try to keep it all to ourselves and turn it into another global power struggle. But if we choose the latter, the Galactic Federation will simply move forward without us. The United States will be left behind."

She reached over and pushed the binder across the table to Senator North.

"Everything you need to verify what I've said is documented. Every nation on Earth has the opportunity to participate. The Galactic Federation will not engage with any country trying to dominate the rest."

Senator North stared at her for a long moment. Then he reached for the binder. "Thank you for your candor," he said.

Senator North's hand was already on the binder, poised to take it, when a voice interrupted from midway down the table.

"Before we adjourn," said Senator Wilson, a third-term legislator from a swing state with several military installations. "There's one thing I think we're not addressing clearly."

North hesitated, then gestured for him to go on.

Wilson leaned forward slightly, both hands flat on the table.

"Whether or not Colonel Riley's views are extreme—and I agree, some of his language is over the line—the reality is that his influence in the Pentagon is significant. He has friends. People who believe he's saying what they can't say out loud."

No one around the table contradicted him.

"And while most of us sitting here may not fully agree with him," Wilson continued, "we're still left with the problem of public perception. The public sees inaction as weakness. So do our allies. For that matter, so do our adversaries. Congress needs to demonstrate strength. We need to show we're in control of what's happening."

Vicki's jaw tightened, but she didn't speak. She suspected she knew what he was going to say next.

Wilson continued. "So I'm asking—can OMR do something that signals that? A gesture of some sort. Could the Pleiadians be invited to Washington for an official visit? Or could we negotiate some kind of treaty with the Suede Nation—a formal agreement, signed by both sides, where the Suedes commit not to take any hostile action? That would reassure the public. It would show we're managing this transition."

Vicki straightened before he'd finished speaking. Her response couldn't wait.

"No," she said, her voice sharper than before.

Wilson blinked. "No to which part?"

"No to all of it," she said. "Because everything you just listed is for show. It's not leadership. It's performance. You want photo ops. You want language to appease a narrative that Riley has already warped beyond recognition."

Wilson opened his mouth, but Vicki didn't give him the space.

"You don't need a treaty with the Suede Nation. They have never attacked anyone. They exist in a vibrational state none of us even knew about until six weeks ago. The only reason they were forced into visibility is because humans invaded their space—armed, aggressive, and looking to steal resources they didn't want to earn."

"Still," Wilson began.

"No," she said again, louder this time. "Because this entire line of thinking accepts that Riley has set the terms of the conversation. That his paranoia is now the baseline we must all respond to. That is not leadership. That is surrender."

The room went quiet.

"If Congress wants to lead," she said, her voice level now, "then Congress needs to stop chasing headlines and start making decisions that will hold up ten years from now. You want strength? Strength is restraint when others are panicking. Strength is cooperation when the easy choice is isolation. If the United States wants to show it belongs in the room with the rest of the Galactic Federation, then it needs to start acting like it."

She paused long enough to make sure her point was understood.

"I will not ask the Suede Nation to sign a treaty to promise not to retaliate against another invasion. I will not ask the Pleiadians to pose for a press conference so you can call it leadership. If you want to be part of what's coming, you need to rise to meet it. Not drag it back down to politics as usual."

Wilson didn't respond. The rest of the room remained silent.

This time, when Senator North reached for the binder, no one interrupted.

* * *

INTERAGENCY FIELD INTEL BULLETIN
Classified Briefing - Internal Use Only

Subject: Anomalous Geographic & Behavioral Reports Post-Suede Disclosure/ Pre-Shift Manisfestations

- [TerraWatch Global]
  "Geographers Say Entire Ridge in Northern Wales Is 'No Longer Where It Was'"
  Instruments unchanged, but coordinates return different results each time.

- [NRP Morning Edition]
  "Students in Pennsylvania High School Organize 'Silent Noon': Hundreds Meditate Instead of Attending Class."
  Principal baffled by lack of protest when detentions are handed out.

- **[TikTok – @ChantHackers]**
  "Humming Open Gates in Abandoned Spaces"
  Participants receiving 'messages' or 'emotional downloads' during toning rituals. #HumChallenge

- **[Pathline Observer]**
  "Trailhead in Eastern Oregon No Longer Connects to Its Own Map"
  Updated GIS data shows inconsistencies measured in meters.

- **[School Insight Weekly]**
  "Teachers Report Students 'Toning' During Recess"
  Children hum in unison for 20+ minutes, say it helps them 'stay here.'

- **[The Daily Mail]**
  "Neighbors Say Longtime Residents 'Just Aren't There' Anymore"
  The lights are on. The cars are parked. We can see them—but it feels empty.

- **[Reddit – r/Glitch_in_the_Matrix]**
  "My Street Just Skips a Number Now. #Missing-House"
  I know there used to be 11 houses. Now there are 10. No one else seems to care.

- **[Vero Creek Tribune]**
  "Locals in Vero Creek Claim Grocery Store Moved One Block East—Overnight"
  City planning board has no records of relocation.

- **[Facebook Post – 'EarthShift Stories' Group]**
  "My Garden Wall Wasn't There—I Walked Through

It by Accident"
My dog did it too. Just kept walking like nothing was there.

Addendum: Analyst's Note

Reports continue to escalate in number and frequency. Anomalies are spatial, perceptual, and behavioral. Alignment with previously described pre-shift patterns by Suede Nation elders and multiple Galactic Federation contacts appears increasingly likely. Recommend broader cross-check with ley line resonance shifts and Hum intensification sites.

END OF BRIEF

Chapter Thirty-Three

The screen lit up, and for a moment, Junia wasn't sure what to expect. A wall of faces greeted her—teenagers from a high school in a place Jessica had called "Los Angeles." Their images were framed by a classroom, a neutral room with posters on the wall and colorful folders stacked near a whiteboard.

Their expressions varied: nervous, excited, skeptical, and curious.

If she was going to decide how to treat humans going forward, she needed more than filtered stories and diplomatic reassurances. The memory of Bowen's body still tugged at her thoughts—sometimes sharp and cold, other times hot with anger. The humans who had stormed the tunnel had not asked questions. They had not listened. They came to take and destroy.

And Bowen had trusted her when she urged him to give humans a chance.

Junia didn't trust humans. Not anymore. She trusted Vicki... mostly. But one person wasn't enough. She needed to see others, especially the younger ones—the ones not yet fully shaped by adults. Were they like the intruders, ready to destroy anything unfamiliar?

Or were they different? Could they change the path humans were on?

Now they were here. Their faces filled the screen, eyes blinking back at her from a classroom above ground. They didn't know it yet, but they were her test. How this hour unfolded would shape everything she decided to do next.

Junia knew that Jessica was somewhere in the room on the other side of the camera, but an unknown teacher introduced the session and then stepped back. The students leaned forward, and the screen flickered slightly. Someone spoke first.

"Hi, Junia. I'm Carter. Um, can I ask you something kind of random?"

She nodded.

"Your eyes—they have those vertical slits, like a cat's. Why?"

In the background, Junia could see the teacher grimacing. Apparently, this was not on the list of approved questions. In a way, this made her feel better. These young people were not blindly obedient.

Junia moved her head so the students could get a better view of her face—and her eyes. "Because I don't live where you do. In the interior of the Earth, we don't have sunlight. We have other light sources—crystalline, bioluminescent, and vibrational. My eyes adjust to a wider range of light frequencies. The shape helps with that."

"Oh. That's... actually really cool."

"It's practical," she said. "Where I live, round pupils wouldn't be very useful."

"And pink teeth," said someone. "Your teeth are light pink."

Junia gave a wide smile so everyone could see her teeth. There were exclamations of surprise. Seriously? Did these young humans only care about appearances? But then the conversation changed.

"Um, what kind of music do you guys listen to down there?" This question came from a girl in front.

Junia blinked. The question was unexpected. "Music?"

A ripple of laughter passed through the group. But it wasn't mocking.

"Yes," Junia said more clearly. "We have music. Of course."

There was a murmur from the students. Someone else asked, "Do you use instruments?"

"Some. But most of our music comes from vibration through crystal. Sometimes percussion—stone, water, and shell." She smiled slightly. "Not so much stringed instruments like you use."

"Wanna hear one of ours?" the girl asked, already reaching for her phone.

Junia nodded.

A moment later, sound poured into the room—a pulsing rhythm with layered vocals and something metallic beneath it. The beat was simple and insistent. Junia listened without speaking. To her ears, it felt... compressed. Flattened, almost. But there was a sense of heart in it.

"Thank you," she said after a few seconds. "You play it loud. That's a lot of energy in a short pattern. We... stretch things longer. Let the tones unfold."

They looked intrigued.

"Can we hear some of your music?" another student asked.

Junia turned to one of the off-camera Suedes assisting her and nodded once. Music began to play, producing a deep, resonant hum layered with shimmering tones that shifted slightly depending on how one listened. There was no melody in the human sense, but it filled the room with a sensation more than a sound.

The students were still as it played.

"That feels... different," someone said. "Like it's happening inside me."

Junia allowed herself a small smile. "Music is not only for the ears. It's for connecting—connecting people, and connecting the Earth with those who depend on it for their lives. It's not just expression; it's alignment."

She saw nods. Some thoughtful, some confused.

Then a hand went up, tentatively. A girl's voice followed. "Can I ask... what really happened? During the attack? At the place where you live?"

In the background, the teacher grimaced again.

The air changed, and Junia exhaled. "Yes. You can ask."

She told them.

About the screaming of stone when the tunnel was breached. The flash of weapons fired in greed. The confusion as vibrations collapsed in on themselves when humans, who didn't understand what they were doing, pushed too far into a world they could barely see.

She detailed the moment the defense response began—the noise, the fury, the desperation, and the fear. She didn't hold back on the details. Blood. Collapsing walls. The final instant when she witnessed Bowen's death. About her grief. Her anger. Her guilt.

For a long moment after, no one spoke.

"I'm sorry," the girl said softly.

"I am, too," Junia answered. "The Suede Nation didn't want this. We don't want war, but we are not helpless. That was a hard truth to learn. And a harder one to show. My cousin didn't even want to give humans a chance—I'm the one who convinced him."

"It wasn't your fault," the girl said. "You didn't cause those men to attack. And it's not our fault either. It's not wrong to want something different."

Junia froze, feeling an emotion in her chest she couldn't identify. The girl was more perceptive than she thought humans could be.

Another student leaned in closer to their camera and changed the subject. "We saw the video. With your claws."

Some gasps and giggles followed.

"Yeah," someone said. "That was kind of awesome."

Junia looked at them carefully, then held up one hand.

Her fingers flexed.

With a thought, the bone-shards extended—long, sharp, curved, obsidian-black.

Several students squealed and jumped back. One clapped. Someone else whispered, "That's so cool."

Junia pulled them back in again. "They're not for display. They're for survival. They come when needed."

"Do they hurt?"

"No." She paused. "But what happened that day did."

The room was quiet again, but not cold. Not scared.

These faces were real to her now. Curious. Imperfect. Young. She didn't feel as separate from them as she had feared—at least not in this moment.

A boy in the back asked, "Are you going to come visit a school someday? Like, in person?"

"Maybe," Junia said. "Maybe when the Earth shifts enough for you to see more clearly. Maybe when more of you are ready to listen."

"We are," someone said.

She nodded.

Then a girl spoke up. "So what should we do?"

Junia tilted her head slightly. "Do?"

The girl nodded. "To help. I mean... to be useful. Or a part of things, instead of just watching. My mom says we should stay out of it."

Junia stayed quiet for a moment. Not because she didn't know what to say, but because the question actually struck at the heart of the issue.

"You've already started," Junia said. "You're listening. You're asking. That's more than what your mom is doing—it's more than most adults are doing."

She let the statement hang there. No one interrupted.

"The Guides have been making videos," she said. "Meditation, awareness, vibrational adjustment. Watch those. Practice. Learn what it means to bring your own frequency into harmony. It matters more than you think."

A few students began typing quickly, likely pulling up links; Brad's website—*Truthsplosion*—had been trending on social media ever since it launched. Others were still focused on her.

"But that's not all," she said. "You need to lead."

The students exchanged glances. Some looked uncertain. One boy laughed awkwardly. "Us? We're just in high school."

Junia met his gaze through the screen. "So am I—or at least what's considered high school in the Suede Nation. I'm fifteen years old."

That got their attention again.

"I'm not seen as an adult by my people," she said. "But I stood in front of our elders. I spoke for my community. I made choices after we lost so much. Not because I wanted to—but because no one else could, or would."

A girl in a hoodie whispered, "You're brave."

""No," Junia said. "I was angry. I was sad. But I didn't want fear to decide what happens next. The elders wanted things to go back to the way they were, but I knew that couldn't happen. That's why I spoke up."

She leaned closer to the camera. The light from the human classroom flickered as someone—probably Jessica—adjusted the angle on the other end.

"You don't have to wait for someone to say you're old enough," she said. "Adults say that when they don't know what else to do—when they want to stay in charge. But the truth is, you're already part of this. You can already see what's going on. The old world—the one with rules that always made sense—is falling apart. And most of you can feel it already."

She scanned their faces on the screen, watching their expressions shift.

"The adults keep saying they want things to go back to normal. But normal didn't work for everyone. It was already breaking. They still think that if they try hard enough—if they make the right rules or stop people from talking—everything will go back to how it was."

Junia leaned in slightly, her voice low but firm.

"But it won't go back. And deep down, you already know that. That's why you're here, asking questions. That's why you're listening instead of ignoring it. You can feel that things are changing. You just haven't been told it's okay to do something about it. I'm telling you now—you don't need anyone's permission. You need to stop waiting for someone else to tell you it's your turn to be involved."

They nodded.

Junia kept talking. "If you want the world to be different from the one your parents know, you need to do something now. Learn things. Ask questions. Speak up. Don't let adults say that you don't understand. They're the ones who are lost—not you."

Several students began typing again—maybe taking notes, maybe chatting with each other. It didn't matter. She had their attention.

"You're not powerless," she finished. "You're not too young. You're exactly the right age to begin."

Silence followed for several seconds.

Then a voice—clear, youthful, confident—spoke from the group: "Okay. Then we will."

Junia didn't smile. But again she felt that same strange emotion in her chest. And now she could identify it.

It was hope.

* * *

The sunlight coming in the front windows of the tai chi studio, caught specks of dust as Mei gently swept near the entryway. She moved quietly, careful not to make noise or drag the broom too hard against the floor. The space had already been cleaned once in the morning, but she was doing it again. It gave her something to focus on. Something to keep her hands busy.

She had already wiped down the benches near the coat hooks and refolded the stack of white hand towels, even though they were neatly arranged. Everything she did here was extra, unnoticed—just the way she preferred it. If she remained useful but unobtrusive, maybe they wouldn't change their minds. Maybe the Coopers would continue letting her live with them. She wasn't entirely sure she had made the right choice by leaving her home—she just knew it was too hard to breathe there anymore. It was too hard to keep herself smaller than her spirit.

The sound of the front door opening broke her thoughts.

James stepped in, shoulders slightly hunched as if his thoughts were pressing down on him. He blinked when he saw her. For a second, Mei noticed he was surprised to see her there.

She straightened a little and tucked the broom against the wall.

James gave her a nod. "Hey. Thanks for helping."

The words were simple, but Mei felt her spirits lift anyway. She beamed at him before she could stop herself.

"Oh, it's nothing," she said quickly. "Really."

He scratched the back of his neck. "Still. My parents and I appreciate it."

Mei didn't know how to respond. A part of her wanted to fill the silence with something funny—or maybe express her gratitude?—but instead, she simply nodded and returned to folding one of the towels she had already folded twice. Her role at the studio still felt too tentative.

James didn't leave. He lingered near the doorway to the inner room, then turned back toward her.

"My parents and I will be watching the press conference tonight in the office," he said. "Colonel Riley's."

"Oh." Mei looked up. "That's the one where he's going to say the military should take over all the Disclosure stuff, right?"

James nodded. "He's going to say a lot of things. Most of them wrong. Dangerous, even. It's going to get ugly, and a lot of people will believe it."

Mei was confused. "And you're going to watch it... why?"

"Because we need to know what the fight looks like," he said. "We don't get to ignore it just because we're tired."

There was something behind his voice. Not anger. Not despair. Just a kind of heaviness. Mei noticed the way he stood—still, like someone who'd spent a lot of time on their feet recently.

"I think you should join us," he added after a moment.

Her hands stopped moving.

"Me?"

"Yeah." He gave a short nod. "You've seen what's behind it all. You've seen what it means to pick a side. You're part of this, whether you planned to be or not."

A quiet filled the space between them. Mei nodded slowly.

"Okay," she said. "I'll come."

James gave a brief smile—more in the eyes than on his face—then turned to walk back toward an inner room.

When he was gone, Mei sat down on the bench she'd just cleaned. Her hands rested in her lap, the towel forgotten.

He wanted her there. He saw her.

It wasn't much, but it was enough to breathe easier.

She wasn't a guest anymore.

Maybe she'd made the right choice after all.

Chapter
Thirty-Four

S am stood against the back wall of the meeting room, arms crossed tightly and posture straight. His badge was clipped visibly, though everyone here already knew who he was. Or rather, who he was standing in for. Again.

His supervisor, Colonel Doyle, had excused himself from attending yet another high-level meeting related to Disclosure. The excuse was the same as last time: a scheduling conflict. Sam knew better. Doyle wanted deniability. The pressure was mounting around Colonel Riley, and no one wanted to get burned if things fell apart.

Around the long oval table, several senior officers sat quietly, some flipping through printed transcripts from the press conference the night before. A few had highlighted entire paragraphs. One of the civilian advisors passed Sam a copy without comment. He took it, even though he had already seen the press conference live. Like everyone else in the room, he hadn't expected Riley to go that far.

The door closed. Rear Admiral Folsom cleared his throat.

"Let's get started."

A general near the center leaned forward, fingers steepled.

"I want to begin by acknowledging that last night's address was... more aggressive than briefed," he said flatly. "Colonel Riley's remarks exceeded the scope we were told to expect. He framed OMR as weak, claimed the Suede Nation was actively infiltrating U.S. infrastructure, and called for emergency authority to—his word, not mine—'contain the extraterrestrial contagion.'"

A few heads shook slowly.

"He used the word *contagion*?" someone asked quietly.

"It's in the transcript. Page three."

A Marine Corps colonel near the end of the table spoke up next. "There are also unconfirmed reports this morning of a failed attempt to seize access to the DoD's joint Disclosure coordination files. IT flagged anomalies in remote credential usage from Riley's side of the building around 0200 hours. If true, it suggests either he or someone under his command tried to move beyond speech to subversion."

The tension in the room thickened.

"Is anyone confirming that with Cyber Command?" Folsom asked.

"They're running trace logs," came the response. "We'll know more within the next hour."

No one said anything for a long moment.

Then another voice—Major General Estrada—spoke from the opposite side of the table.

"We all know Colonel Riley has powerful allies. But this is no longer about political influence or media framing. This is about structural risk. If he continues to escalate, we're going to find ourselves in direct conflict with the Department of State. It would be a genuine inter-agency crisis, not just noise."

There were nods. No arguments.

Sam shifted slightly but stayed silent.

"We can't go to war with State," another officer said. "OMR has done nothing provocative. They've complied with all required briefings. We've reviewed their files. Nothing in their conduct warrants the narrative Riley's pushing."

A civilian tapped his pen against the table. "The truth is, we had the lead on this file for seventy years and it brought us to the edge of disaster. The Partnership nearly succeeded in hollowing out global autonomy right from under our noses— from *within* our own command structures. If we want credibility, we can't pretend that didn't happen. The State Department has accomplished more in just a few months than we did in nearly a century."

Another officer added, "And we can't claim this is hypothetical anymore. The public has seen the footage of the Suede Nation. There are blue-skinned space aliens standing on a UN podium and talking about a Galactic Federation. This isn't an issue we can bury with classifications or sideline with containment rhetoric. The whole world is watching."

Sam finally spoke. "Then the question is—what do we do about Colonel Riley?"

Silence again.

Then Major Estrada exhaled. "He has to be shut down. Not quieted. Not reassigned. Shut down. He's compromising readiness and undermining civilian control. Threatening an entire branch of diplomacy and coordination."

There were no objections.

Folsom looked around the room. "How do we move forward?"

"We can open an internal review," someone suggested. "Bring in UCMJ oversight. We have clear grounds now: overreach, abuse of authority, and a potential security breach."

"We can also begin signaling to Congress that Riley's stance is not representative of the broader command community," another officer added. "Start peeling away his base of support."

"And the media?" asked a staffer from the communications team.

"We don't fight his words with more words," Estrada said. "We let the facts build the wall around him. He's isolated himself already. Now we finish the work."

No one contradicted the plan.

Sam remained silent. He didn't need to speak again. He would deliver the notes to Doyle who, without a doubt, would stay quiet and wait to see where the power shifted. But Sam already sensed which way the wind was blowing.

Colonel Riley had gone too far. And this time, the room wasn't going with him.

*　*　*

Mei was wiping down the counter of the front desk for the second time that hour when the door opened and the chime rang out above. She looked up, cloth in hand.

Seven teenagers stood clustered in the doorway, looking around uncertainly. They were dressed like any other students—jeans, jackets, a few backpacks slung over shoulders—but their expressions were focused. She recognized some of them; a few had asked questions during the classroom livestream with Junia.

Mei set the cloth aside. "Hi. Can I help you?"

A tall boy near the front spoke first. "We're here for the class."

They stepped forward and gathered in front of the reception area, looking at her—not as if she were just some assistant helping out at the front desk, but as someone who might be able to provide them with something they needed.

She wasn't used to that. Back home, nothing she did was ever enough. Her family measured worth in status and wealth. Even when she did everything they asked, it never felt like she was doing it right. She was always too loud, too disorganized, too slow, or too emotional. Too much or not enough—never just right.

Mei blinked. "The next intro class isn't until the weekend. Calvin and Mona are teaching the advanced class this morning."

Another girl stepped forward. "We don't mean the class on the schedule. We're here because we want to learn. About energy. About the vibrational shift. So we can help."

Mei's hand tightened slightly around the edge of the counter. "No one else is here, and I'm not really... I mean, I'm just helping out here. I'm not an instructor or anything. I'm not trained."

"That's okay," said a boy in a gray hoodie. "We don't need perfect. We just need to start."

The rest of them nodded. One of them reached into her bag and pulled out a small notebook.

Mei opened her mouth, then closed it again. Then she replied, "I can't say anything about that kind of stuff. It's not my place."

Standing here now, she heard that familiar voice in her head once more. It was a voice she had heard throughout her life. *You're not supposed to lead. You're not ready. You'll embarrass yourself. Stay out of the way. Let someone who understands it do the job—you'll only make a mess of it.*

The girl holding the notebook looked directly at her. "Junia said that young people don't need permission to lead. She said if we want a different future than the one our parents are building, we should go ahead and start making it. The old future is broken—waiting for someone else to fix it is just another way to make our future disappear."

The others stood a little straighter at the words. No one spoke for a moment.

Mei looked at them with their hopeful faces and quiet resolve. She thought about her own family—about the dinners where her voice was never heard, the warnings, the belittlements, and the quiet dismissals. She remembered Tian and the look on his face when he said she would never amount to anything.

And about how it had felt to pack her bag and walk out anyway.

She had wanted something different. She still did. But did she need to wait for someone to give it to her?

Mei had spent most of her life waiting—for approval, for praise, for someone to say, "Yes, you're ready." But no one ever had. And maybe they never would. That thought used to make her feel small. Today, however, it made her feel something else: tired, perhaps—but also clear.

If no one was going to say she could live her life the way she wanted to, then maybe that meant it was up to her to say it for herself.

Mei took a breath. The kind of breath Mona and Calvin had taught her to use—deep, slow, and present.

Then she stepped out from behind the reception desk. "Okay. Come on over. You'll have to wait for Calvin and Mona if you want the real instruction, but I can show you what I know. The basics. Enough to get you started."

One of the students grinned. "That's all we need."

They filed over, setting down their bags, pulling their hair back, and shaking out their shoulders.

Mei walked toward the center of the reception area. Her voice, when she began to speak, did not shake.

"You're going to start with the breath," she said. "Because that's where everything begins."

* * *

Vicki woke up with a start. She had been dreaming about Beth again. Her sister had put her arms around her and told her it would be all right. *It's not all your responsibility. Other people are doing their part.* In the dream, Vicki had been crying.

She looked at the clock: 3:00 a.m. With a sigh, she turned over and pulled the covers up to her chin. She had two more hours before she had to get ready for the day.

* * *

INTERNAL MEDIA BRIEFING
Internal Use Only – Not For Distribution

Subject: Youth Behavioral Patterns Since the Suede Nation Livestream& Global Hum Phenomena

- **[The Sierra Beacon]**
  "Teens Skipping Test Prep to Meditate in Local Park"
  One mother called the police. The kids didn't resist—just smiled, then returned to silence.

- **[Reddit – r/TeenUprising]**
  "My Daughter Walked Out of Her SAT Class to Sit Under a Tree"
  She didn't argue. She said, "I already know what I need to know." Then she walked away.

- **[TikTok – @GroundedYouthCollective]**
  "We Don't Need Extra Credit to Be Awake"
  Video shows dozens of teens humming in formation across school fields. Caption: *We're done waiting for permission.*

- **[The Chronicle of Suburbia]**
  "Students Ignore Counselors, Refuse College Prep Meetings"
  "They look at me like I'm giving directions to a place they're not going," one advisor said.

- **[Facebook Post – Parent Watch SoCal]**
  "Why Are They All So Calm?"
  Our daughter missed tutoring again. When we scolded her, she nodded and said, "You'll understand soon." That was it.

- **[Podcast – Beyond Behavior, Ep. 92]**
  "The Kids Aren't Acting Out—They're Opting Out"
  Educators say punishments don't work anymore. The stu-

dents aren't angry. They just don't care about the rules we made.

- **[Twitter/X – @OldTownCoach]**
  "They Skipped Practice. All of Them."
  I yelled. No one reacted. One of them said, "You don't see it yet, that's okay." Then they walked away. Now, how are we going to win football games?

- **[The Garden Hill Ledger]**
  "High School Seniors Refuse to Apply to College, Choose Forest Retreat Instead"
  They said they were "preparing for the shift." One parent asked, "What shift?" The teens just smiled.

- **[Instagram – @ThePauseGeneration]**
  "We're Not Being Rebellious. We're Being Real."
  Captioned under a reel of teens toning on a hillside at dawn, ignoring texts from their parents.

- **[YouTube – Channel: EarthListening]**
  "Detention Room Filled With Silent Meditators"
  A teacher left crying. "They weren't angry. They just sat there with their eyes closed. I've never felt more irrelevant."

Internal Note:
Pattern emergence consistent with low-frequency attunement clusters and non-reactive group states. Social defiance absent; substitution with collective non-engagement. Recommend cross-analysis with Suede Nation vibration indicators and CE-5 proximity reports.

CHAPTER
THIRTY-FIVE

This was the first time Anne had set foot on the premises of Bennett & Roth Legal Group—the law firm where she was employed—since going on maternity leave when Adam was born five months earlier. She had another month of leave remaining, but it looked like she'd be returning early. Jerry stood beside her in a plain dark suit—not as her husband, but as the official representative from the State Department's Office of Multispecies Relations. Anne carried a thick folder filled with statements, timelines, and legal summaries.

She followed one of the firm's junior partners into the large corporate conference room her firm reserved for high-stakes meetings. Stopping just inside the doorway, she scanned the table. Eighteen chairs, all but two occupied. The board members from Alton Synergy and ValorSys Group had arrived together, flanked by legal advisors and shareholder representatives. At the far end, Cryder's executives sat clustered, speaking in low tones. Anne didn't acknowledge any of them just yet.

She walked to the end of the table and placed her folder in the exact center. No one reached for it. Good. That likely meant they still unsure how they were going to play this.

Jerry moved to the chair on her left, sat down, and placed his tablet on the table in front of him. Anne didn't sit.

The room was cool—not cold or uncomfortable—but just enough that anyone already on edge would feel their body react. Anne had made sure of that earlier. The firm's building manager had confirmed the lower temperature settings himself.

When the last name was called during introductions, Anne took a step forward. She didn't walk around. She didn't wait to be invited. She simply began.

"As counsel for several shareholder groups and public accountability clients," she said, "we are here today to present new findings regarding the financial, legal, and ethical exposure your companies now face."

One of the board members from Alton Synergy leaned forward. "We were informed this meeting was about dividend irregularities."

"It was," Anne replied. "Until we began to follow the revenue streams. What we found extended far beyond withheld assets. This now involves deliberate collusion with a criminal organization, violations of international law, and corporate involvement in lethal operations."

The room shifted. Some people turned toward their aides. A few narrowed their eyes at her.

She pointed to the folder sitting at the center of the table. "In that binder is a detailed report outlining actions taken by your companies after the collapse of the Partnership—actions that were coordinated, covert, and in several cases, directly criminal. But today I'd like to focus on actions that go beyond dividends and asset concealment."

A representative from Cryder asked. "What actions, exactly?"

Jerry stepped in. "Let's start with the kidnapping of Jessica Martinsson."

The silence was sudden. Anne continued.

"Jessica Martinsson is a civilian who was targeted and kidnapped on U.S. soil by salaried employees of Cryder Advanced Systems. "This was not a subcontracted security action. There is not plausible deniability through third-party channels. You made the mistake of relying on your own infrastructure. Your own resources. Your own people."

Anne smiled at the rest of the table. "And before we all start pointing fingers at Cryder, we have the communication trail—both email and voice records—confirming coordination of this event between all three corporations."

One of the shareholders stood. "This is ridiculous."

A board member interjected, "This can't be linked to us directly."

Anne continued talking as if she hadn't heard them.

"The reason for the abduction was strategic. Ms. Martinsson was playing a visible role in the public Disclosure process. Your internal communications show that you considered her visibility a threat to your expected post-Disclosure profits. You believed that, by removing her from the public eye, you could stall or disrupt technological access by the public. That belief drove your employees to commit federal crimes, including unlawful detention, coercion, and obstruction of an interagency initiative."

"Your companies not only undertook a criminal operation that endangered an American citizen," she continued. "You also promoted fabricated claims against the Suede Nation—branding them as demonic, violent, and a threat to human civilization."

"The Suede Nation—" one executive began, but Anne cut in.

"—is a publicly known, sentient species. Your attempts to frame them as hostile entities created tangible threats to their safety and triggered the violent incursion at Pilot Knob, resulting in multiple deaths. Those *murders* make you liable—not just ethically, but criminally."

"This occurred at the time the U.S. Department of State was in formal discussions with the Suede Nation. There are many within the Department who are describing your interference as treason," commented Jerry affably.

The room fell silent. Two men blanched.

Anne continued. "The three of you also cooperated in the launch of a false flag attack on a free energy facility in Nigeria. You knew the Lagos facility was a leader in the adaptation and deployment of this technology. You understood it would threaten your long-term profits. So you destroyed it. A dozen people died during that attack. And that's murder."

Anne paused, then said, "Again."

"The evidence—" one of them started.

"—is conclusive," Anne said. "We have contractor logs. Drone telemetry. Electronic communications. Witnesses. Documented interactions. There is no room for ambiguity."

Several shareholders now turned toward one another, speaking in hushed tones. An older man at the end of the table stood up slowly and faced his own board.

"Is this true?"

No one answered him.

Anne placed another document on the table. "If your concern is exposure, you're already too late. Bennet & Roth released a public statement the moment we began this meeting. We didn't want to violate legal ethics rules, so our public statement says nothing beyond, "*We have expressed our concerns to the appropriate parties.* That said, every one of your shareholders is a party to all legal proceedings. Because parties have the legal right to all relevant documentation, all your shareholders were sent a complete copy of the information in this folder."

Anne smiled again. She had been smiling a lot during this meeting.

She added: "Bennett and Roth does not have the authority to forbid these shareholders from going to the media."

Exclamations erupted from the table. Anne waited for the noise to subside before she continued. "We are not here to negotiate silence. We are here to inform you that legal proceedings are beginning, and that shareholder collectives are preparing class actions. There will be criminal referrals to international courts."

Jerry added, "The Departments of both State and Justice will be involved."

An unraveling began in the room. Phones were picked up. Some executives got up and moved to the corners, already calling legal counsel. Another muttered something under his breath and walked out entirely.

Anne remained standing. "You can't build the future on suppression and violence. You tried. It failed. The only question now is whether you intend to take responsibility for what comes next."

A board member in front, daggers in his eyes, spoke up for the first time. "Do you realize what you've triggered?"

Anne replied calmly. "This isn't the trigger. This is the result."

* * *

Brad sat at his corner workstation, with two monitors running. One displayed a pulsing, color-coded map of global ley line activity, Hum resonance, and energy interference reports. The other showed a list of open data sources—geological, atmospheric, and low-frequency sensor feeds compiled from independent research stations. The files had been collecting for weeks, but only recently had they begun to form clear, repeating patterns.

Jessica walked in first, carrying a cup of of coffee. Judging by the expression on her face, she was still in editing mode. She paused beside his desk and glanced at the screen.

"That's new," she said. "What am I looking at?"

"Something I've been tracking since last week," Brad said. Then, calling out, "James, Kiran—you might want to see this too."

The other two came in without asking questions. James pulled a chair close, while Kiran walked up behind him. Brad opened a new window and overlaid the latest Hum resonance data onto the existing map.

"Certain locations are showing identical disruptions," Brad explained. "Mapping anomalies. Terrain drift. Instrument confusion. And before you ask, this isn't just weird GPS errors or corrupted logs. The instruments recalibrate on-site, but still can't fix the readings."

He clicked to zoom in on the Pacific Northwest. An area just northeast of Mount Shasta was outlined in faint blue, its data signature marked by non-responsive geolocation pings and inconsistent altitude readings.

"Here, and here," Brad pointed to similar areas in Argentina, Mongolia, parts of Norway, and the interior of Australia. "These zones aren't just 'hard to scan.' They've become quiet. Nothing transmits properly in or out. And it's not because of signal interference. The data doesn't bounce. It just... doesn't register."

Jessica leaned closer. "You mean it's being blocked?"

"No. There's nothing to block. It's more like..." He caught himself before drifting into analogy. "It's not there in the way we expect it to be. But we know the locations exist. Hikers report them. People live near them, sometimes inside them. But the moment tech tries to pin them down—anything electromagnetic, sonic, even photographic—the output degrades."

James nodded slowly. "Are they expanding?"

Brad brought up a time-lapse series. Each area had begun small. Over the past month, however, they had expanded. Not rapidly, but deliberately and evenly.

"It's not random," Brad said. "And it's not harmful because I'm not reading anything destructive. But it is spreading."

Kiran stepped forward and pointed to one region in northern India. "This is near an old pilgrimage route. There are stories of locations disappearing for days at a time. And then reappearing."

"Same in Bolivia," James added, pointing to a region in South America. "That's near the singing rocks phenomenon I've seen reported on the internet."

"I've been calling them 'quiet zones,'" Brad said. "Because th ey're... quiet. Not empty. Just beyond the reach of normal observation—our tools can't measure them."

Jessica frowned. "So are they still physically there? Like—could we walk into them?"

"Yes, apparently that's not a problem. But more and more people are reporting irregularities when they try to film. Issues like blurs and blank spaces. The sensors have difficulty recording the interior of the zones. There's signal at the edge, then it's... different. Never an error message. No drops. Sometimes static, sometimes just a null."

James was staring at the map. "And people live near these?"

"Some, yes. They largely started out in deep wilderness. But now there are some small communities that are either partially or entirely located within a zone. I cross-checked the news logs, social feeds, everything I could find. You know what's weirdest? No one's panicking. It's like the people near them are adapting."

"They would have to be," Kiran said quietly. "They're living near areas where physical assumptions break down."

Jessica finally asked the question all of them wanted to ask out loud. "Do you think this is related to the vibrational shift?"

Brad nodded once, relieved to get it out in the open. "I'm not guessing. I'm certain. These zones are forming along predicted ley line intersections. They aren't merely signs. They're the outcome."

"What happens if they keep spreading?" James asked.

"*If* they keep spreading?" asked Brad incredulously. "Have you listened to anything I've said? Large areas of Earth are beginning to operate on a completely different baseline frequency. This is it—this is the vibrational shift. Ready or not."

Kiran looked thoughtful. "But there's nothing to say that the transition from one vibrational state to another is an instantaneous event—it could be a process that takes years. After all, moving from one astrological sign to another is said to take centuries."

"Are we ready to bet on that?" asked James. "From things Melly, Junia and the Galactic Federation reps have said, we can expect things to move pretty fast—probably within a period of several months. And if people can't adjust their own energy to match, it's going to feel... off. But not harmful—at least not at first."

Kiran looked thoughtful. "This is why we're training people. Meditation, energy awareness, chi flow—it's not optional anymore."

"I know," Brad said. "And we're already behind."

Chapter Thirty-Six

Vicki sat at her desk, sorting through a backlog of field reports from OMR's diplomatic coordination teams. Most of it was routine—summaries from State's U.S. Mission in Geneva, updates from the Suede Nation contact liaisons, and brief reports from the CE-5 response team regarding new public sightings and coordinated contact meditations. The map of global ley line resonance remained active on the second screen to her right, steadily updating with reports from Brad's dynamic overlay system. That morning, she had already seen two new quiet zones register.

Mary walked in without knocking. She held a red folder under her arm and dropped it onto the desk without ceremony.

"It's a batch of official complaints. Mostly from senators and governors."

Vicki raised her eyebrows. "How many?"

Mary checked her notes. "Eleven letters. Eight senators, three governors. Some co-signed. It looks like they've coordinated talking points. They want responses."

Vicki opened the folder and leafed through the first few pages. The language varied slightly, but the structure of the arguments was nearly identical.

"We are concerned that the United States government seems to have relinquished its authority over matters related to extraterrestrial affairs to non-governmental organizations and unelected entities..."

"Our constituents are demanding to know why American taxpayers are not directly benefiting from alien medical advances and energy technology."

"...The failure of the State Department to secure a binding treaty with the Galactic Federation has left American energy providers and healthcare companies unable to compete with the unregulated, disruptive technology now flooding the global market."

Vicki didn't finish reading. She flipped through the remaining letters and glanced at the final page. It was signed by a governor from a coastal state, whose largest hospital network had recently filed for financial protection. One line stood out: *"Our systems are being collapsed by uncoordinated, foreign intervention in domestic markets."*

She dropped the entire packet into the trash bin beside her desk.

Mary remained standing.

"No response?" she asked.

Vicki shrugged. "What would be the point?"

Mary crossed her arms. "They're demanding to know why their state agencies and private contractors are losing control."

"They already know why." Vicki tapped her desk lightly. "They're not actually asking for answers. They're performing for their donors and the media cycles."

She turned to the main screen and pulled up the latest update from the Galactic Federation's ambassadors in Geneva. A new press release was being translated for distribution to all UN member states. The Pleiadians had made the Galactic Federation's position clear: humanity would move forward together as a planet, not as a collection of corporate regions or political factions. Participation would be earned through cooperation, not extracted through leverage.

"They want Washington to be in charge," Vicki said flatly, referring to the writers of the complaint letters. "They want their state, district, or energy lobby to be the gatekeeper. And they're angry because no one is listening to them anymore."

Mary nodded slowly. "A few of the letters reference economic collapse. Energy markets, insurance losses, even pension funds. One mentioned that the grid in his state may be unsustainable within months."

"They were warned," Vicki said. "We told them when the first schematics were released. The world is changing. That includes how power is made and distributed. It includes how we understand disease and wellness. What they're experiencing isn't sabotage. It's obsolescence."

Mary opened her tablet. "Should I prepare a reply for congressional staff?"

"No." Vicki was sure about that. "They want a treaty? Let them go to Geneva and ask the Pleiadians for one. Let them sit at the table and explain why they think they should be in charge of the entire planet's future. Maybe they'll get a polite answer. Maybe they won't."

Mary's tone was even. "You're not concerned they'll try to override OMR's authority?"

Vicki stared directly at her. "OMR's authority isn't theirs to override anymore. And frankly, it's already out of my hands—they just don't understand that yet. They think it's still a game of administrative mandate. But the playing field has changed."

She turned the screen back to the map, which displayed the quiet zones. One had started pulsing near central France, and another had doubled in size in the western U.S., near the Four Corners area.

"The Earth isn't negotiating with bureaucrats. And neither are the ones watching from above. They've made contact with everyone—not just the people with offices on Capitol Hill."

Mary exhaled. "So... we just ignore them?"

"We keep working," Vicki said. "We keep moving forward. Anyone who wants to help is welcome. But no one gets to hold the process hostage because their profit margin shrank."

Mary gave a short nod. "Then I'll let the media team know. No comment on the letters."

As she turned to leave, Vicki added, "Tell them to expect more. The louder the Hum gets, the more people like this will panic. It's not about leadership. It's about control. They're losing it. And they know it."

Mary stepped outside. Vicki glanced again at the discarded folder in the trash bin. She didn't regret tossing the letters. The world they described no longer existed.

* * *

Jessica adjusted the microphone and glanced at the clock. Right on time. A knock came at the door. When she opened it, Ambassador Halbi, one of the Galactic Federation ambassadors stood waiting alone, no vehicle in sight. She didn't ask how he got there even though there had been no sound of transport, no sign of a craft, and no warning. Also, she knew for a fact that he had been in a meeting at the United Nations in Geneva just two hours ago.

They smiled at each other—having FaceTimed the night before, they'd already skipped the awkwardness of a first meeting. He followed her into the recording setup and took the offered seat. Ambassador Halbi looked human, aside from the light blue tone of his skin. His posture was straight, his hands resting easily on his knees. His gray eyes met hers with an expression of quiet goodwill. Jessica pressed the record button and introduced the session for the archives.

She moved into her first question.

"Ambassador Halbi, can you explain the Galactic Federation's current purpose in its interactions with Earth?"

The ambassador responded promptly. "We are here to advise, not interfere. Humanity is entering a transition. We assist only where asked. Observation and invitation are the limits of our current engagement."

Jessica nodded and looked at the screen to be sure the audio was coming through clearly.

"And your presence here with me—does that fall under observation or invitation?"

"Invitation," he said, smiling. "You asked. I came."

Jessica noted those responses in her notes and moved on. The session had officially begun.

"Let's talk about the UN. I know this has been said before, but a lot of people were surprised you chose it as your main point of contact. Why not a national government—or a coalition of developed nations?"

The ambassador folded his hands. "This is not a national issue. The planet is one biosphere. Your social divisions are real to you, but they are not important to us. In truth, holding onto them would be dangerous. If the Galactic Federation spoke only with the wealthiest or the loudest, we would be supporting the same systems that brought your world to the edge of ecological and social collapse."

Jessica nodded, having expected that answer. Still, she knew that many in the audience needed more. "But the UN has issues of its own—bureaucracy, inefficiency—"

"Bureaucratic red tape," the ambassador said lightly, a trace of humor in his voice. "Yes, we're learning that phrase. It slows progress, which is unfortunate, because we don't have time for delays. The vibrational shift isn't waiting for committee schedules—it's already happening. Whether your diplomats have reached consensus or not doesn't change the reality unfolding on your planet."

Jessica tried not to smile. "So why still use the UN?"

"It remains the only existing institution designed to serve all of humanity, not just one subset. We begin with what exists. We do not endorse all of its behaviors, but its purpose has potential. That is enough for now."

Jessica scrolled to her next prompt. "UN officials pushed back when all your talks and speeches were posted to websites online. They wanted to restrict access."

"We declined," Halbi said with a nod. "Our communication is for all humans, not their intermediaries. It is not classified material. If it reaches a child in the hills or a family in a remote village, it has fulfilled its purpose. We do not recognize gatekeepers."

Jessica glanced at the camera recording them. "There are also criticisms of UN operations—criticisms of malfeasance and influence-peddling."

The ambassador's tone remained even, but it sharpened. "We are aware. Several individuals within the UN have acted in ways that benefit themselves at the expense of others. They are being removed. Quietly. By the end of your week, they will be gone."

Jessica didn't ask how. She wasn't sure she wanted to know.

The ambassador continued. "We understand the discomfort this causes. But your people have suffered long enough under leaders who serve themselves first. That model is not compatible with the vibrational shift or with joining the Galactic Federation."

Jessica made a note, hesitated, and then looked up. "You said earlier you don't interfere. Some will claim this *is* interference."

"We are not taking part in your political processes. We are removing obstructions. Those who block access to shared planetary knowledge are no longer allowed to hold such positions. This is not political—it is structural." He paused. "And we are grateful for your broadcasts. They make sure that what is said cannot be distorted or misquoted. Truth must be shared freely."

Jessica's throat tightened a little. "Thank you."

The ambassador gave a slight nod. "It is your work, Jessica. We are only the speakers."

Jessica checked the next question. "I want to ask about something we're tracking," she said. "One of my colleagues has started mapping what he's calling quiet zones. Areas where instruments behave strangely, where people are experiencing unusual calm or even perceptual changes. Are these connected to the vibrational shift?"

The ambassador nodded. "They are. These zones are physical signs of subtle energy shifts happening across the planet. As the vibrational field changes, it creates spots where the old resonance starts to lose its hold. You could think of them as early markers—places where the density of the current reality begins to thin."

Jessica frowned at her notes. "So the vibrational shift is already happening?"

"Yes," the ambassador replied. "The process is underway. It will not be instant, but it will not be long. From this point, the full transition will complete within several of your months, no more than one of your solar years."

Jessica exhaled. "Not everyone will make the shift. What happens to them?"

The ambassador didn't answer immediately. His gray eyes remained steady.

"They stay in the energy they chose. That version of reality will continue for a time, but it will grow more different as the new energy gets stronger. At first, people who shift and people who don't will still talk, see each other, and share the same spaces. But over time, it will feel harder and more uncomfortable for both sides, and understanding each other will become more difficult."

Jessica's stomach tensed. "You mean...?"

"They will drift apart. Over time, their awareness will narrow to the path they are on. Those who shift will move forward, while those who do not will continue in the reality they helped shape. The timelines will split."

"Is there anything we can do to help them?" she asked.

"You already are. You are offering the truth. You are showing the path. Each must choose. No one can be forced."

Jessica nodded. "Thank you for being clear."

The ambassador inclined his head. "All of us need to be clear. This is a key time period for Earth."

Jessica turned to the camera. "That's all for this session. We'll upload the full transcript and video shortly."

The ambassador was already standing. He did not need an escort. He had come and would leave the same way—whatever way that was.

Jessica watched the front door after it closed. For a long moment, she stood there, hearing nothing at all.

Then she went back to her studio, reached for her laptop, and began uploading the footage.

Chapter Thirty-Seven

J unia stood quietly looking at the Earth crystal.

The cavern was huge—bigger than any building on the surface—but there was no echo. The air didn't move. A gentle light filled the space, though there was no visible source. Her eyes had already gotten used to it. She could see just fine, but the light didn't work the way it did above ground.

Before her was the Earth crystal. The Suedes had many names for it, but none translated easily into human language. It was as long as several city blocks and rose in a slow, uneven curve, like a mountain growing from the inside. Its surface was dark—not sharp or smooth—but covered in flowing lines and seams that gently pulsed if you stood close. It didn't feel like just stone or metal. It was easier to feel than describe.

Junia stood close, only a few paces from where the base of the crystal met the cavern floor. The air around it vibrated faintly. Not enough to be measured, just enough to be sensed.

She lowered herself to the ground, sitting on her knees. For a long while, she said nothing.

Her thoughts returned to Bowen.

He would have knelt here too, running his fingers over the lines in the stone, trying to figure out what they were. He always believed there was more hidden beneath the surface—not just the surface of the Earth, but the surface of people, too. He acted like he didn't care, like he didn't believe in anything. But that was just a bluff. Inside, he had been just as curious and excited as she was. That's why they had always been so close.

Junia exhaled. The guilt was crushing her. And the ache in her chest hadn't dulled. It had simply moved deeper.

He should have been here, watching the surface unfold and hearing the young humans speak during their livestream session. She thought about their music, their questions, and their awkward attempts at connection. He would have loved every minute of it.

She scooted closer to the Earth crystal, now only a few inches away. It loomed above her, and as she neared, the low vibration seemed to intensify slightly. She pressed her palm against the surface. Then she leaned forward and gently placed her forehead against the stone.

"I don't know what I'm doing," she whispered.

There was no sound from the crystal. No reply—at least not in the traditional sense.

"Is there a way ahead? Should I keep going?" she asked, eyes closed. "I want to believe that humans can be part of what's coming. But I can't forget how Bowen was killed. And it was my fault. I can't just pretend it didn't happen."

The crystal's vibration remained consistent, but a resonance began to form—not a voice, not words, but a sense of focus. Her thoughts sharpened. She felt her heartbeat slow and sync with the pulse of the crystal.

The sense she received wasn't emotional comfort; it was a re-calibration. The Earth crystal did not offer answers; it offered alignment.

He did not leave you alone. You are not carrying this for him; you are carrying it with him.

Junia swallowed.

The path cannot be divided into theirs or yours. The path is the one you walk together.

Her knees dug slightly into the ground. Her fingers pressed against the stone.

Others are not prepared to lead. That is why you are speaking. You speak because you remember what they have forgotten. You speak because you must.

Junia opened her eyes. Her forehead remained pressed against the surface. The vibration continued, but she no longer needed to interpret it. She understood.

The Earth crystal wouldn't tell her what to do. It wouldn't take away her choices. It just reminded her she was doing the right thing. That her grief was not a burden but a connection. And that Bowen's memory was not about absence, because he was still a part of her.

She pulled back slightly and rested her hand once more on the surface of the stone.

"I hear you," she whispered.

Then she stood.

There was no ceremony, no flash of knowledge or revelation. Yet, her steps felt different now. She understood what she had to do.

* * *

Mei stood at the front of the group in the middle of the reception area, her voice quiet but clear as she guided the high school students through the next breathing exercise. The studio was peaceful, with both Calvin and Mona leading their own students in the classrooms. The reception area was the only available space left that had room for them. The group of seven students sat on spread-out mats with their eyes closed. It was a little disorganized, but it worked. Most of them had been coming daily for a week now, arriving at the studio in pairs and small groups, asking thoughtful questions, eager to learn. Some had begun helping clean afterward without being asked.

"Inhale through your nose for four counts," Mei said. "Hold. And now exhale slowly."

The door swung open suddenly. Mei glanced up to see Tian enter the room, hands in his pockets, his expression already tinged with mockery. He surveyed the space, then fixed his gaze on her.

"Seriously? This is what you're doing now?" he said loudly. "Leading breathing classes like you're some spiritual expert or something?"

The students looked toward him, some confused, others annoyed.

Mei's breath caught in her throat. Her hands fell to her sides. She stared at Tian, unable to utter a word. Her shoulders tensed. It was just like before—the sudden interruption, the voice of someone who tore her down.

"What are you even doing here?" Tian continued, stepping forward. "Saw your little moment on that video with the alien girl. Guess a few compliments went to your head. Now you think you belong here, leading classes and handing out wisdom."

A hot wave of embarrassment crawled up Mei's neck. Her arms stiffened at her sides, unsure whether to defend herself or fold in and disappear. She wanted to run—to bolt from the room before anyone saw how much Tian's words had affected her. She wanted to yell, to shout back that he didn't understand. But more than anything, she wanted to vanish entirely, to be erased from the center of attention she never asked for.

Her mind spun with doubt. Maybe he was right.

She wasn't a teacher. She hadn't trained under any master. No one had certified her, and she didn't have years of experience. And if she admitted it, she wasn't all that good at tai chi. She had only taken the classes and watched Mona and Calvin, moving as they did. She was just... trying.

Trying to be useful. Trying to contribute. Trying not to be a burden in someone else's space.

The quiet recognition from the students, the way they listened when she spoke—had she misread it all? Had she let herself believe she was more than she was?

Maybe she had no business leading anything.

A hollow space opened in her chest. The shame sat there, heavy and dull. She lowered her gaze, wishing her body would take the hint and sink into the floor.

Then she heard a voice.

"Why are you talking to her like that?" Tara's voice cut through the room. She had gotten off her mat and now faced Tian directly, arms crossed and chin raised.

Tian turned toward her, surprised. "Excuse me?"

Another student, Kai, joined her. "You heard her. Mei belongs here. You don't. So if you've got a problem with her, maybe you should be the one to leave."

Tian scoffed. "I'm her cousin. This is family business. You don't know what you're talking about."

"We don't need to," said Jules, stepping forward beside Tara. "We've been coming here every morning. Mei doesn't talk down to us. She doesn't act like she's better than anyone. She just shows up and shares what she has."

Tian's expression hardened. "She's not a teacher. She has no idea what she's doing."

"Neither do we," Tara snapped. "That's why we're learning. She's honest about what she knows. She shares it anyway. That's more than I can say for most adults."

Jules added, "You walked in here thinking you could humiliate her, but all you did was show everyone how small *you* are."

The room had gone still. Even Mei, frozen in place behind the group, could hardly breathe.

Tian opened his mouth again, but Kai cut him off.

"No one here asked for your opinion. And we don't need your permission to learn from her."

For a moment, Tian didn't speak. His gaze darted over the students—five of them now standing between him and Mei. He seemed to realize, maybe for the first time, that his opinion didn't matter in this place.

He turned without another word and stalked out. The door closed silently behind him with an air of finality.

Silence settled over the group. Then Tara turned, giving Mei a reassuring nod.

"You good?" she asked.

Mei managed a small nod, her throat tight. But when she spoke her voice didn't waver.

"All right. Let's pick up where we left off."

* * *

James stood silently in the side hallway, his back against the wall. He had come in from the back garden, intending to look for some files in the front office. Instead, he had stopped short when he heard Tian's voice echoing from the main practice room.

What he witnessed left him unsettled.

Tian had walked in like he owned the place, hurling insults as if they were facts. Mei was in the middle of leading a breathing session for a group of high school students who had started showing up regularly—the same students who'd surprised them all the week before. She froze for a moment under Tian's barrage, but the students didn't. They'd stepped in to defend her without thinking twice.

That part—their defense of her—James hadn't expected.

He had thought of Mei as quiet and cautious, someone more likely to apologize than to assert herself. While she had always seemed too loud and awkward as a tai chi student, that changed when she had come to live with his family—she moved around the house and the studio carefully, barely making a sound unless asked a direct question. Last week, during dinner, she mentioned that some teens had arrived asking questions. Since everyone else was busy, she had offered to show them a few breathing exercises.

"I didn't mean to take over or anything," she'd said, looking at her plate. "I know it's not my place."

His mother had immediately stopped eating and looked at her directly. "You weren't taking over. It was the right thing to do—we all need to help."

His father had nodded. "And we need more people stepping up. Time's running short."

James had watched Mei absorb that praise cautiously, as if she didn't fully believe it was real.

James had been surprised then. But seeing this now, he understood.

No, she hadn't taken anything over. She had simply stepped into a space that was waiting for someone willing to fill it.

And now, standing in the shadows and watching her calmly resume her session, he realized how much she had taken those words to heart.

She gave the students a signal, and they followed her lead, inhaling and exhaling together. Her voice was even. There was no shaking in it.

James felt a wave of respect wash over him. It wasn't just that Mei had stood there and endured Tian's mockery; it was that the students had followed her, defended her, and trusted her.

He had assumed, back when his parents first offered her a room, that it was the kind thing to do. Necessary, perhaps. But he hadn't expected much. Not because he thought poorly of her, but because she seemed uncertain of herself, unsure of where she fit into all of this.

That had changed.

James turned from the doorway and returned quietly to the garden. He didn't want to interrupt the class. Not now.

Mei wasn't a visitor anymore. She wasn't just someone being helped. Now, she was someone people were listening to.

She had taken a chance. She had offered what she could.

And this time—in this place—that was enough.

CHAPTER THIRTY-EIGHT

The conference room deep in the west wing of the Pentagon was soundproofed and unmarked. There were no nameplates, no formal agenda, and no hearty greetings. Inside, six military officers sat around the long table. Sam took the last empty seat without waiting for an invitation.

He had come alone. And this time Colonel Doyle hadn't sent him. Sam had stopped expecting Doyle to take initiative weeks ago. His supervisor was always five steps behind and afraid of confrontation. Watching the decline of leadership had left Sam disillusioned. Someone needed to take action.

He looked around the table, nodding to each person in turn. Most returned the gesture. A few didn't bother. The gravity of the conversation left no room for small talk.

Rear Admiral Folsum opened the meeting. While a Navy officer would typically refrain from commenting on matters concerning an Army officer, both worked in the Office of the Secretary of Defense, and Riley was within his chain of command.

"Colonel Riley is not well. That's not a secret anymore."

No one disagreed.

"He's become erratic," he continued. "He's given unsanctioned briefings, issued threats about traitors, and is pushing for independent control over all extraterrestrial contacts and assets."

Another officer shifted uncomfortably. "That's more than paranoia. That's unilateral action."

"Riley has become a loose cannon," agreed someone from the far end of the table. "He's released at least three memos accusing other branches of treason for 'failure to comply' with his security framework. He says the Department of State—through OMR—is infiltrated, that the Suede Nation is preparing an attack, and that the Galactic Federation is attempting planetary subjugation."

"It's obstruction," Sam said, struggling to keep his voice dispassionate. "He's trying to stop the U.S. from establishing protocols with other nations. He's rejecting every diplomatic route OMR or State has proposed."

Someone to Sam's left spoke up. "The man's talking about 'cleansing' compromised elements. He says the Pentagon is riddled with them. Says loyalty can't be assumed anymore."

"He's isolating himself," said a Navy admiral quietly. "People are beginning to avoid him. His aides are requesting reassignment. His presence in meetings is disruptive. We're managing him, not working with him."

There was a pause. No one wanted to put the next step into words.

"He's still a decorated war hero," someone said. It was Major Estrada, seated next to Folsum. "Don't get me wrong—I don't support Riley. But he led joint ops in two theaters. People won't forget that. You move against someone like Riley, you better be ready for some blowback."

Sam looked directly at him.

"We all took an oath," he said. "The Army's motto isn't '*Honor the past.*' It's '*This, we defend.*' So tell me—are we defending our country if we let someone hijack its future because we're afraid of his medals?"

Silence.

Sam continued. "Riley talks about national security. But what he's doing weakens us. He poses a threat to the continuity of government. He's obstructing global cooperation. He's setting us up to fall behind while other nations adapt. That's not defense. That's sabotage."

Estrada cleared his throat. "You're proposing formal action?"

Sam didn't flinch. "Proposing formal action is above my pay grade, but I would recommend that the Pentagon launch an investigation. Under the Uniform Code of Military Justice. Article 88 and Article 133 at a minimum—contempt toward civilian authority and conduct unbecoming an officer. We need to move now. If we wait, he could do something that can't be undone."

Estrada looked at Folsum. "Would he go that far?"

Sam answered for him. "He's already way past that line. You just haven't acknowledged it yet."

Folsum sighed, "I'll authorize the recommendation. I'll notify Army General Counsel and the Inspector General."

Another officer added, "We'll need a discreet chain of custody. If Riley catches wind of this, he may retaliate."

"I'll handle that," said Estrada. "Quietly."

Sam exhaled. Not relief. Just forward movement.

Rear Admiral Folsum looked around the room. "Then we're in agreement. This begins now."

The meeting ended with no ceremony, no summary, and no smiles.

As he rose from the table. Sam thought about Doyle. Still hiding in his office. Still pretending that inaction was neutral.

It wasn't.

Walking down the wide corridors of the Pentagon, everything looked normal. But nothing was.

* * *

The room had glowing crystal walls. Junia sat at a long table crafted from some sort of natural material. Six members of the Alpha Centaurian council were seated across from her. Behind them, three younger ACs sat quietly against the wall. They did not speak. They were not introduced.

Junia didn't ask about them. She already felt uneasy about being here. The request from the Alpha Centaurians to meet with her alone had come as a surprise—she really didn't know them. Of course, she knew they were neighbors, living in the Earth's interior just like the Suede Nation did. She'd also visited their crystal city several times—always in the company of other Suedes. But she didn't *know* them.

Junia had asked her uncle for advice. Alun told her it wouldn't hurt to find out what they wanted. Yes, it was unusual for their neighbors to ask to speak to one of the Suede Nation's young people (unprecedented was more like it—this had *never* happened before in the history of Suede-AC relations), but the Alpha Centaurians had always been good neighbors.

So here she was, swinging her legs as she sat, because the ACs were tall—a little taller than even most humans—and the chair was too high.

Representative Brandori was the speaker. "Junia of the Suede Nation. Thank you for accepting our invitation."

"We are all curious," Junia replied. "My uncle, the elders, and me. The ACs don't usually invite young people to meetings—especially without anyone else present."

"This is not exactly a formal meeting," said Representative Lacino. "But it's not informal either."

Junia cocked her head. This was beginning to sound interesting. "Then what is it?"

"We wish to speak with you about the timeline," Brandori said. "The timeline for when humans will be informed of the existence of the Alpha Centaurians."

This was why they wanted to talk to her? That was foolish of them. Junia, struggling to keep from flinging her arms up in exasperation, folded her hands in her lap instead. Alun had advised her she needed to act more like an adult, as befit her new role.

"I heard there isn't a timeline."

"Exactly," said Representative Oixal. "And that is becoming a problem."

Junia looked around the table. All six council members were watching her closely. Their expressions were composed, but she could feel tension beneath the surface.

"Why are you talking to me?" she asked them. Now she spoke slowly and clearly, as if to little children who were having trouble understanding simple instructions. "This is a human thing—it has nothing to do with the Suede Nation. You know Vicki. Speak to her."

There was a long pause.

"We are reluctant," Brandori said. "There is... shame."

He didn't elaborate. Junia didn't need him to. Everyone in this chamber had known Representative Lyrith. Everyone knew that she had wanted to move to the surface and that she disagreed with the conditions Vicki had insisted upon. The councilwoman had not handled disappointment well. When she was prevented from moving immediately to the Earth's surface, Lyrith allied with the Partnership to hunt down Vicki and the Guides. And now she was dead. Everyone in this room had witnessed the aftermath of what Representative Lyrith helped unleash.

"Vicki is not vindictive," Junia said. "She would listen. She *likes* listening."

Vicki *did* like listening. Junia wondered if that was something diplomats did—using listening as a way to get other people to tell them about themselves. She noticed that she always talked a lot to Vicki, but Bowen would tell her she always talked a lot anyway.

Bowen!

A flash of pain ran through her. The familiar guilt. Then Junia shook her head to clear her thoughts and turned her attention back to the conversation.

"Yes, Vicki would listen," Brandori was saying. "But she carries the burden of the world's coordination. You are different. You speak freely. You act independently."

Junia tilted her head. "I don't act without considering what Vicki might think." She felt like she should defend her friend.

"No," said Brandori. "But you no longer wait for her permission."

That struck a nerve. Junia said nothing.

Brandori continued, "You speak with your own voice. We saw how you spoke to the humans—the scientists and the young people. We observed how you stood firm in defending the Suede Nation after the attack. You didn't yield to anyone. You showed them your pain, your strength—and how dangerous it would be to stand against you."

Junia didn't know if she liked him bringing that up. Yes, she showed the world her pain and her claws, but somehow, she still considered that *private*. And now the ACs were using it as a reason to convince her to do something? She exhaled slowly.

"So now you want me to tell Vicki she should introduce the ACs to humans so your people can move to the surface?"

"We want you to understand why it matters," Brandori said. "Our young people have seen what is happening. They have watched the broadcasts and the livestreams. They have seen the videos. They want to be a part of this shift with you and the young humans."

Junia's gaze drifted toward the three sitting against the wall. About her age, they watched her hopefully.

Brandori followed her gaze. "Those three have given us a choice. Either we speak with Vicki and take steps to be visible to the surface world—or they will go without our approval."

Junia's eyebrows rose. "They said that?"

"They did."

"They're not wrong," she said. Her face was expressionless, but inside she was grinning.

When Representative Lacino spoke, she was frowning. "We do not wish for them to act in ways that threaten our stability. Most of us do not want to live on the surface, and it would be foolish to jeopardize the well-being of the majority for the desires of the few." She glared at the young people.

"They don't wish to be left behind," Junia said. Her voice had grown sharper. She hadn't meant it to. She sat back in her chair.

Inside, her thoughts twisted in uneasy circles. She thought about the Guides—how hard they were working to push the shift forward. The Partnership had destroyed Jessica and Brad's home. They had tried to hunt them all down to kill them—James's uncle sacrificed himself to save them. They had suffered so much, yet they continued to move forward. Then she remembered how the high school students had listened to her and asked questions. She had told those kids that they didn't need permission to lead. Not from adults. Not from anyone. Because the adults didn't have answers anymore.

Now here sat three young ACs, watching her, silently asking the same questions.

And here sat their elders, asking her to help maintain a system that was already crumbling.

Junia felt conflicted. She loved Vicki. Trusted her. Vicki was one of the reasons she had stepped into this role. But even Vicki was part of the old structure—one that valued leadership, approval, and control.

That model was already disappearing.

Junia looked down at her hands, thinking of Bowen. He had never been fond of authority and would have encouraged the younger ones to step forward. He would have spoken to them directly.

She looked up.

"I'm not going to talk to Vicki," Junia said. The faces of the AC council dropped. Then she said, "But I do have a plan. And it's not going to be about waiting. If your youth are ready, they can come with me. Like everyone else, they'll find their way. Hopefully, all of us will find it together."

The three young ACs looked at her with expectation on their faces. Their eyes held hope, but also caution, as if they were afraid of being disappointed.

Brandori nodded. "Thank you, Junia."

"No," Junia said. "Don't thank me. Just listen to them."

She stood. The meeting was over.

She motioned to the young ACs as she walked out of the chamber, and she could hear their footsteps as they followed. They didn't speak. But she could feel their presence as they stepped into whatever came next.

This was going to be *fun!*

Chapter Thirty-Nine

T hey had been busy.

Jessica sat between James and Kiran at her editing station, a row of dim lights strung casting a glow over the monitors. On the main screen, paused in mid-frame, was a digital visualization of ancient Vedic symbols layered over a map of pre-Aryan India.

James leaned back and rubbed his temples. "We're going to get blowback for this."

Jessica looked at him. "For saying the Vedic gods were extraterrestrials?"

He nodded. "Yeah. I mean, there have already been claims that Disclosure is a threat to world religions."

Kiran laughed. "I've already told you we're not telling Hindus anything they don't already know."

James glanced at him—Kiran wasn't thinking about the implications.

"Yeah, but the issue is that this is the first episode we're saying anything about religions at all. Even if it's not about a person's own religion, people will be afraid that if Hindu deities are redefined as extraterrestrials, their own beliefs might be next."

"Kiran?" asked Jessica.

He nodded. "James and I have already talked about it. My grandfather used to tell me stories where the gods weren't just metaphors—they were *real*. Powerful, yes. But not infinite. Not eternal. The devas aren't omniscient creators—they're advanced beings who live long lives in other realms. That's not news to most people in India."

He paused. "Honestly, it'll be more like confirmation than contradiction."

Jessica considered that. "So... they'll be fine with it?"

Kiran nodded again. "For the most part, yes. It's the people outside of India who might panic."

James scrolled through his phone, then held it up for the other two to see the screen. "They already are. There are protesters outside the Press Club in D.C. holding up signs that say 'Earth First' and 'God Has No Aliens.'"

Jessica grimaced. "I saw that. And that church in Kentucky—what's it called?—The Covenant Road?"

Kiran answered, "The one that said alien contact is the work of the devil?"

James was the one who responded. "They posted a video last night. Called the Suede Nation "masked demons.' Said Vicki was a herald of end-times."

Kiran shook his head. "You know how I'd respond to that?"

Jessica looked at him.

"If a couple has a second child, it doesn't mean they love the first one any less."

James blinked. "Ummm, what does that have to do with anything?"

Kiran smiled. "I'm using it as an analogy. Humanity thought we were the only intelligent life in the universe. We were the firstborn and—in our minds—God's only child. Now, we learn there are others. That doesn't diminish us—it just means the family is bigger than we realized. But some people are reacting like jealous siblings, misbehaving and acting out."

Jessica nodded slowly. "So there will be an adjustment while the first kid gets used to having a brother or sister."

"Pretty much. And just like in a real family, things will eventually settle down. It won't happen overnight, but eventually people will stop screaming about their place in the universe and start listening again."

James paused the video. "Okay. That actually helps. Let's finish this segment and then switch to the Hopi material."

There was so much to cover—James didn't know how they would get through it all. Even if they tackled two or three events per episode, they'd be at it for several years. He'd have to find another way—a quicker way—to share this information with humanity.

But not right now. At this moment, they just had to finish editing this episode. James rubbed the bridge of his nose, where his glasses used to be.

Jessica opened the second folder and dragged the new files onto the timeline. The screen filled with stylized artwork and scanned cave drawings from the American Southwest. A calm narrator's voice played from the speakers:

"In Hopi tradition, the people were guided from a previous world to this one. A cloud marked the journey during the day and a moving star at night."

James tapped a key to pause. "That's what's in the memory crystal too. The cloud and the star—they weren't metaphors. Those people were describing spacecraft in the only way they knew how."

Kiran leaned forward. "It lines up. Some of the Hopi drawings show domed structures floating above the ground. Others show beams of light descending from them."

Jessica nodded. "And the Ant People?"

"They weren't mantis beings like Melly," James said. "But they were from a related species. According to the crystal, they were part of an insectoid race assigned to planetary support missions. When the Earth faced a cataclysm—volcanoes or earthquakes or whatever—they guided the Hopis underground until it passed."

Kiran gestured at one of the paused frames. "That chamber—the one with the spirals on the wall—that's where they lived?"

"According to the footage," Jessica confirmed.

"And the Hopi just... went with them?"

"The ones described as the 'righteous ones' did," said James. "They say the Ant People were kind to them—sheltered them, brought food, and taught them how to survive. Some Hopi clans still consider them sacred."

Kiran stared at the monitor. "I wonder what would happen if we played this at an archeology conference."

"They'd laugh," James said. "Then they'd panic. Imagine all the academic careers that will be destroyed when this comes out. But it's just the beginning. The memory crystal will rewrite thousands of years of history."

He leaned back slightly, eyes on the screen but his voice gaining momentum.

"Ancient Mesopotamia? It wasn't the first civilization—it was just one of the few that survived the cleanup. There were entire city systems before it, wiped out or hidden by the Galactic Federation teams that came to erase the evidence of the unauthorized Alpha Centauri contact. Egypt's pyramid technology? Not just math and manpower. The memory crystal shows gravity-field manipulation techniques introduced to a priest-engineer caste that later had their knowledge scrubbed and whitewashed as myth."

Jessica tapped her fingers on the edge of the desk, listening.

"And Gobekli Tepe," Kiran added. "Twelve thousand years ago. Architecture that shouldn't have existed yet. According to the memory crystal, it was one of the teaching sites. A location where early humans were instructed in foundational principles of geometry and energy flow. When the Federation came back to erase the evidence, they buried it. Literally. To prevent it from interfering with the timeline they'd chosen."

James nodded. "That's the part that's going to really hit people. Not just that aliens existed, but that everything we thought we knew—about timelines, innovation, and cultural development—has been manipulated. And censored."

Jessica exhaled slowly. "So textbooks have to change."

James gave a short nod. "Textbooks, museum exhibits, national myths, religious chronologies. All of it. We'll have to start over—not from scratch, but from what's true."

Kiran looked at him. "And a lot of people won't want that."

"No," James said. "They won't. But they're not going to have a choice."

* * *

In the garden behind the Cloud Hands Tai Chi Studio. Kiran stood at the edge of the koi pond as students came out from the studio. Mei had raked the gravel paths earlier, and the lines were still crisp where she had worked.

Kiran waited until the last student had taken their seat; some were on the benches, while others sat directly on the ground. Then he settled down at the edge of the pond, folding his legs underneath him.

"Close your eyes," he said quietly. "We'll begin with breath."

The air was still. Even the fish in the pond appeared motionless. As the students inhaled and exhaled, Kiran felt the Hum rise—not from one direction, but from everywhere at once. It wasn't loud in the traditional sense. It passed through his skin and muscles, brushing across his nerves like a frequency that bypassed hearing altogether.

"It's louder today," someone said.

Kiran nodded without opening his eyes. "It is."

The Hum pulsed beneath their breath. Then something shifted. The leaves overhead shimmered faintly. Not color or movement—something less visible than either. The students began to hear it: not just the Hum, but tones emerging from it—layers of sound that rose and felt like voices singing in a language without words. It wasn't music in the traditional sense. But it had a geometric structure with pattern and depth.

Kiran opened his eyes.

"Does anyone want to say anything?" he asked. "What are you experiencing?"

A boy named Daniel raised his hand, then lowered it when Kiran nodded at him.

"I don't know how to describe it," Daniel said. "It's like time is... stretching. But not in a bad way. Just slower. Like it's not in a rush anymore."

Another student nodded. "The colors looked brighter for a second. Like, around people. Around you."

Kiran nodded. "That's a sign your biophotons are being activated."

A few of the students looked at him questioningly, so he explained. "Biophotons are little particles of light in the ultraviolet and low visible light range. All people have them. Plants and animals, too—all living things. Normally, we can't see them at all. But as they become activated, you'll see new colors, new glowing lights around living things."

"The Hum is activating our biophotons?"

"No, it's more like *you* are activating your biophotons—by raising your vibration through meditation and tai chi. But it's a team effort because the Earth is beginning to raise its own vibration. So what you're experiencing is a sign your awareness is adjusting. Your senses are tuning in to the shift."

He glanced around the circle. "The Earth is moving. Not just through space, but through vibration. Our solar system is entering a region of the galaxy that resonates at a higher frequency. The Earth is made of both energy and matter, so it will start to harmonize with that frequency.

"What happens to people who can't tune into it?" asked a girl with thick braids. "People like my mom. She doesn't believe in any of this. She thinks meditation is just... me being dramatic."

"My little brother," said a boy, his voice tight with stress. "He's only five. He can't do this stuff. What's going to happen to him?"

Kiran folded his hands. "That's a real fear. I understand it. But you're already helping your family."

"How?" another asked. "My parents don't come here. They won't even listen when I try to explain."

"Vibration isn't about belief," Kiran said. "It's about resonance. When you meditate, slow your thoughts, and raise your awareness, you start to shift your frequency. And simply by being in that state, you begin to affect the space around you."

The students looked back at him silently.

"It's like sound. When you play a piano, a strong, sustained note will cause nearby strings to resonate with it. Your presence—your alignment—it contains vibrations you'll carry into your home. You don't need to preach. You don't need to explain. Just be."

A few nodded slowly.

"But what if they don't make it?" another boy asked. "What if the shift happens and my family gets left behind?"

Kiran looked down, hands resting on his knees.

"That's not how it works," he said. "This isn't a doorway you pass through once. It's not a cliff—it's a gradient. There will be phases. And it's not your responsibility to carry them across. But just being around them will make it easier for them to find their own paths."

He looked out over the students. "When the Four talk about the vibrational shift, they're talking about alignment. Like how a tuning fork vibrates in harmony with another. Earth is aligning with something larger now. As it rises, those who can meet that resonance will feel more... at home. They'll gain abilities that current science says shouldn't exist. And those who resist it? They'll feel pressure—discomfort. Their lives will remain filled with stress. But the possibility—the invitation—to raise their vibration will remain. It's not one moment. It's a process."

The Hum deepened. Kiran could now see the calm in the students' bodies. Shoulders that had started the session stiff had relaxed. Breaths had slowed. Tension had disappeared from their eyes.

"I'm scared," one girl whispered.

"So am I," Kiran said honestly. "But don't look at fear as an obstacle. It's an invitation to notice what you care about. And that, in the end, is what will guide you."

Chapter Forty

V icki stood by the window of her office, gazing out but not really seeing anything. Her mind moved through the last few days with a clarity that surprised her.

The first meeting had been with the French Ambassador. She had nearly canceled it, anticipating more complaints or questions about access to alien technology. However, when he arrived, he expressed something that surprised her: gratitude.

"Madame Heywood," he had said in accented English, his voice low but measured, "I thank you. Formally. On behalf of my government. On behalf of France."

Vicki had tilted her head. "What for?"

He replied. "For finally doing what your government should have done decades ago. The COMETA report—perhaps you've heard of it?"

She nodded. She had read it. The 1999 study had been bold, especially for its time, asserting that an extraterrestrial presence was real and likely involved with Earth. It had also taken direct aim at the U.S. government for its secrecy on the issue.

"We tried," the ambassador had said. "Our scientists and military officers—they believed the evidence was clear. But we waited. We waited for your country because..." He paused. "Because we owed you. Because of Normandy. Because of debts and old alliances.

And now—now we see how much time was lost. Maybe if we had spoken up all those years ago, things might have turned out differently."

There was regret in his voice.

There had been nothing for her to say in return. So she hadn't.

Before leaving, he added quietly, "You, Madame Heywood, are not what we expected. That is a compliment."

The next meeting came just a few hours later. The Chargé d'Affaires from the Nigerian Embassy had entered with a straight spine and steely eyes. There had been no small talk.

"We remember Lagos," she said. "We remember the lives lost. And we appreciate that you refuse to let their memory be buried."

Vicki had met her gaze. "I honor them, too."

"Most of our people," the Chargé had said, "believe we were punished for daring to take the lead. We probably were. But even with that setback, we are still leading. Nigeria will be the engine of innovation in all of Africa. Our engineers are developing the technology; our cities are adapting. The free energy tech has reached schools and clinics. And this time, the technology will not be stolen from us."

"I'm glad," Vicki had said honestly. "There are those in the U.S. still making the process as difficult as possible."

At this, the Chargé had almost smiled. "We noticed. But in Africa we are used to red tape. We cut through it."

Still at her office window, Vicki allowed her thoughts to wander to the most surprising meeting of the week: the senators.

She hadn't wanted to see them—she was tired of talking to politicians. When their request came, she told them they'd have to meet at her office rather than on Capitol Hill. This was not only a break with protocol, it was a slap in the face—senators didn't come to bureaucrats.

They came anyway. Four of them—three men and one woman, all looking weary and clearly unsure of how to begin.

She had anticipated complaints about lost revenue or demands to ease up on the spread of alien technology so their political campaign donors would have time to 'catch up' and make profits. Instead, the senior-most senator had cleared his throat and said quietly, "I wanted to thank you for whatever role you had in the release of the medical tech."

Vicki's expression must have changed because he added, "My mother had stage IV lymphoma. Her doctors told us to take her home and make her comfortable because there was nothing more they could do. Then some people opened a clinic in my state and put in three of the reverse-engineered medical devices. Of course, they couldn't say it was medical treatment—our laws don't allow for 'unapproved' medical procedures—so they had a big sign that said it was *For entertainment purposes only*." The senator let out a short, humorless laugh. "My dad pushed her in using a wheelchair, and only an hour later, she walked out on her own. *On her own!* Completely cured—her doctors say there's no cancer left. Her vitals are better than they've been in years."

Another senator had nodded in agreement. "Same with my brother—but it was spinal cord damage from a car accident, not cancer. He's not only walking again, he's back at work."

That had thrown Vicki off balance, if only briefly. But the gratitude wasn't why they had come.

It was what came next.

"We don't know what to do," the woman had said. "With the young people."

"They're changing," said one of the men. "We've all seen it. They're not rebellious in the traditional sense. They're just... ignoring us. Teachers say they meditate during recess. Parents say their kids look at them like they're confused by what they're saying."

"They don't argue," added the fourth. "They just don't respond."

"They're not fighting us," the senior senator said. "They're walking away."

He'd looked straight at Vicki. "What do we do?"

She hadn't answered right away. In truth, she didn't know what they could do. The young people weren't rebelling to get attention. They weren't asking for permission. They were just tuning out the noise.

"They've already moved forward," she said eventually. "They're not waiting for the adults to lead. We can either decide to follow or be left behind."

The senators had sat with that for a moment. No one protested. No one tried to argue.

Now, alone in her office, Vicki finally returned to her desk. The world was changing. The usual levers of power were no longer enough to steer it.

And that, she thought, might be the best possible news.

* * *

Anne kept her posture still—she sat at the far edge of the room just behind the back row. Her chair was positioned just outside the camera's view, near the entrance—somewhere her presence wouldn't be questioned, and would likely go unnoticed. She wasn't officially on the panel, and she wasn't about to give anyone grounds to accuse her of violating legal ethics by seeming to act as a spokesperson. But her clients—the shareholders—had made their position clear, and now they were stating it publicly.

At the front of the room, six shareholders sat before an array of microphones. Their statements were prepared, but each spoke with enough frustration and disbelief to make an impression.

"We invested in a company we thought was focused on advanced aerospace development," said one woman. She was in her mid-fifties, wearing a green blazer and wire-rimmed glasses. "We did not expect to be bankrolling a kidnapping operation."

There were murmurs from the journalists in the front row. The cameras shifted slightly.

Another shareholder, a man in his sixties, adjusted the paper in front of him and spoke directly into the mic. "I received quarterly updates and investor statements that omitted a major fact: that the company had not only been secretly collaborating with what the government now calls the 'Partnership,' but had diverted company funds and assets to help carry out an attack in Lagos. Twelve people were killed. That wasn't just bad business. That was criminal."

Anne's phone vibrated softly in her hand. She tapped the screen, her thumb scrolling through a growing cascade of posts on various social media platforms. Each post quoted or referenced the press conference. The hashtags were already taking hold: #ShareholderRevolt, #LagosTruth, #Profits&Crimes. She noticed several reposts of news segments that had aired only moments ago, with clips showing shareholders reading directly from their statements.

At the microphones, a younger shareholder leaned in. "You're going to hear a lot in the coming days about how this is being 'politicized.' But this isn't politics. This is accountability. These companies lied to us. They withheld critical financial information. They moved money into black operations. They orchestrated a PR campaign that painted another species—the Suede Nation—as hostile in order to justify supporting that attack. I don't care what your politics are—that's fraud and complicity in violence."

Anne checked her phone again. Another journalist had just posted a live quote from the floor: *"Shareholders say they were unwittingly funding violent criminal conspiracies disguised as classified contracts. Lawsuits are expected to total billions."*

She didn't smile openly, but the corners of her mouth twitched.

The panelists took turns answering questions. Several reporters attempted to push back, asking if the shareholders were only upset due to lost profits. The older man remained unfazed.

"Of course, we're angry about the money. We were misled. But that's not what we're here to talk about. We're here to talk about the lives that were lost. About that young woman who was kidnapped. About people in Nigeria who were murdered because our money funded something that never should have happened."

Anne caught the eyes of one of the corporate PR reps standing near the back. His arms were crossed, and his jaw clenched. She looked away—not her problem.

A younger journalist raised her voice. "Do you believe these companies should face criminal charges in addition to civil ones?"

The woman with glasses shook her head. "That's not our role to decide. We're shareholders, not prosecutors. However, we are demanding that the Department of Justice investigate every aspect of this. And if crimes were committed—as they appear to have been—then yes. Charges should follow."

That statement earned a wave of camera clicks.

Anne sat back. She didn't need to speak. Her role was in the filings, the affidavits, and the courtroom motions. This was for the public record. This was pressure. And it was working.

She tapped her screen again. A trending post from a political analyst: *"Class-action shareholders striking the tone the DOJ wouldn't dare. If corporate collaboration with Partnership is proved, these lawsuits may force more transparency than any government hearing to date."*

Anne turned off the screen and slipped her phone into her pocket. The statements were done. The message was out.

She stood up quietly and stepped out through the side door without drawing attention. The press conference wasn't over, but her part—at least for now—was complete.

* * *

INTERAGENCY FIELD INTEL BULLETIN
Distribution: Internal Use Only

Subject: Societal andInfrastructural Shifts Related to Free Tech Dissemination and Pre-ShiftBehavioral Adaptation

- **[National Education Weekly]**
  "Districts Pivot to 4-Hour School Days Amid Youth-Led Meditation Trend"
  Multiple school districts have shortened instructional hours to allow students time for personal meditation and grounding practices. Superintendents cite a notable drop in disciplinary cases and rising student-led initiatives in vibrational practices.

- **[Health Alert Wire]**
  "Reverse-Engineered Medical Tech Leads to Unexplained Recoveries"
  Reports surge from international clinics using alien-derived medical applications. Outcomes include reversal of terminal illness symptoms and restoration of neurological function. Lagos, São Paulo, and Johannesburg identified as focal implementation zones.

- **[Civic Lens Media]**
  "Mass Protests Outside Aerospace Firms Named in Disclosure Reports"
  Ongoing demonstrations target companies confirmed to have cooperated with the Partnership. Protestors demand transparency and reparations for technology suppression and misinformation campaigns. Public response remains highly coordinated and nonviolent.

- **[Planetary Frequency Observatory]**
  "Schumann Resonance Spikes to Historic Levels—Brainwave Implications Under Review"
  Field sensors across multiple regions confirm spikes above 12 Hz. Researchers investigating impacts on cognition, circadian rhythm, and cross-species empathetic response. Correlated with emergence of 'quiet zones' and dream-pat-

tern convergence.

- **[Global Financial Register]**
"Big Pharma Shares Nosedive Amid Rise of Alien Medical Applications"
Significant market destabilization tied to the public rollout of alien-based healing modalities. Pharmaceutical lobbying groups issue emergency statements urging "regulatory stabilization." OMR analysts flag growing disinterest in traditional prescription models.

END OF BRIEF

Chapter
Forty-One

J erry sat on the couch, remote in hand, barely paying attention to the television. The boys had been asleep for hours, and Anne had gone to bed just 15 minutes earlier. They had shared celebratory glasses of champagne as she told him about the shareholders' press conference. It was great news, but he was feeling tired. He ought to follow Anne's example and head to bed.

Then the news anchor's voice cut in with carefully measured urgency.

"Today's resignations mark a stunning collapse for several executives once considered untouchable in the aerospace and defense industries," the anchor reported. *"These companies were named in the preliminary filings of the class action suit alleging collusion with the Partnership, a network responsible for acts of political and humanitarian sabotage."*

Behind her, photos of the corporate boardroom members flickered one by one. Faces that had once appeared in glossy financial magazines were now labeled under a different banner: *"Resigned Amid Partnership Scandal."*

Another panelist spoke over the broadcast. *"These are not small-time players. This is top-tier leadership from three major defense contractors and two aerospace companies. What we're witnessing is the breakdown of our economic and power structure."*

A third commentator interjected, visibly disturbed. *"The big question is how this wasn't caught earlier. There were signs. There were rumors. Why didn't anyone follow up?"*

Jerry scoffed softly. "You never asked the right people. And the profits were big enough you ignored the signs. Everyone ignored the signs." He lifted his champagne glass and downed the last few drops. The sense of relief didn't come with joy; it felt more like an old burden had finally been lifted.

He turned off the TV and went to the kitchen. While pouring himself a glass of water, a ping signaled that he had a new message. It was from Sam: *You up? Got an update.*

Jerry tapped to call.

Sam answered immediately. "It's done. Riley's out."

Jerry didn't speak at first. "You're serious?"

"Yeah. It's official. Army CID wrapped up their investigation yesterday—it was bad."

Jerry returned to the living room. "How bad?"

"Worse than we thought. Documented cases of intimidation, obstruction, even tampering with classified logs. They didn't even need to dig very deep. He was so sure he was right, he didn't bother covering his tracks."

Jerry said nothing, waiting.

"They gave Riley a heads-up that an official reprimand was being prepared. I think they hoped he would step down quietly. Instead, he doubled down. He gave a speech two nights ago to a group of mid-level officers about 'institutional rot' and 'insider subversion.'"

Jerry sighed. "He really thought he could still scare people into loyalty."

"Exactly. So this afternoon, Rear Admiral Folsum delivered the order himself. He walks into Riley's suite with two MPs. Didn't even sit down—just reads the statement: relieved of command, pending court martial. Riley goes pale. Then red. Then tries to punch one of the MPs."

"He did *what*?"

"Swung at him. Missed. The second MP had the cuffs on before Riley could get off another word. He was yelling. Something about treason, betrayal, conspiracies... I didn't catch all of it."

"And his staff?"

"Shell-shocked. They were just standing there. Most of them looked embarrassed, honestly. Folsum turned to the next-highest officer and said, 'You have interim command until further notice. Carry on.' Then he walked out. That was it."

Sam continued. "Riley's record ends in disgrace. He was a decorated war hero, but his last act in uniform was trying to punch an arresting officer. That's what people will remember about him."

Jerry looked toward the muted television, where the headlines continued to scroll. The anchors were still questioning how this could have happened. Still pretending to be surprised. But they hadn't been asking the tough questions. Not when it counted.

He didn't feel vengeful. He felt clear.

The tide had turned.

* * *

Lewis sat on the edge of the cheap motel bed, the television flickering in front of him. His duffel bag lay packed in the corner, though he hadn't been asked to go anywhere in several weeks. The news anchor's voice carried evenly through the speakers, calmly reporting a story that was anything but calm.

"More fallout today from the developing Partnership investigation. A total of eight executives from various defense and aerospace firms have been arrested or have resigned amid allegations of criminal conspiracy, fraud, and complicity in kidnapping and sabotage."

Lewis's jaw tensed. Faces appeared one by one on the screen—people he knew by their first names, individuals who had issued the orders, people who had paid him.

"Among those arrested is Lionel Wexler, former Director of International Operations at Valence Systems—"

He didn't need to hear more. He knew that Wexler had been the one to greenlight the Lagos operation—the same one who insisted they "send a message" after Jessica had begun hosting the *Melly Speaks* series. It was Wexler who said it didn't matter if the target was a civilian, not when the civilian was "interfering with global power structures."

Lewis turned the TV off.

He sat for a long time, staring at the black screen. His reflection looked back. Strong. Solid. He was designed that way. Powerful muscles, reflexes faster than any normal man's. His nervous system was reinforced. Sight and hearing were augmented. His blood carried nanocells. Every organ was optimized. He was a biologic construct; he had the entire internet downloaded into his brain.

But he thought for himself. He always had.

They called it a "contract assignment," but it had been a hit: a sanctioned kidnapping. He followed orders because that's what he was made for—orders, missions, jobs.

Still, something had shifted within him. Not at the beginning, but when he saw Jessica afterward. Not scared or broken. She had been furious. It had shaken something inside him.

They were meant to target the Partnership's enemies—eliminate corrupt operatives and take down their facilities. Not grab people's kids. Not silence citizens. That wasn't the deal. That wasn't the code.

And now, those executives—those well-dressed criminals—were being taken away in handcuffs under flashing lights and cameras.

It should have felt like justice.

It did. But it also meant he was without a job.

Lewis stood and walked to the window. The motel was half empty. No one had spoken to him all day. No assignments. No clients. No encrypted messages on his burner phone.

He liked being busy. That was the whole point. Being built like this—wired for performance—without work to do was wasteful. He liked being strong. But strength without having anything to do? What was the point?

He had trained to break into facilities, hold his ground in combat, and move unseen. But no one was hiring people like him anymore. Not with the Partnership exposed. Not with the shift coming.

People were meditating now. Talking about frequency, vibrations, and new realities.

He didn't know what to make of it.

He ran a hand over his scalp. He could vanish—disappear off-grid. He knew how. But he didn't want to disappear. He wanted to be useful. He wanted to be part of a team. Not for pay necessarily—he didn't need much—but for purpose.

He opened the duffel bag and took out the photo he kept folded in a side pocket. It was old— a training unit that had long disbanded. He was the only one left. Even then, he stood slightly apart.

Maybe it was time to find the others. The ones like Jessica. The ones who were building something instead of tearing things down.

Maybe they wouldn't want him...

But maybe they would.

He folded the photo and slipped it into his jacket. He didn't know what the next move was, but he knew he was done following orders from people who thought lives were disposable.

He was made to be strong.

Now he had to decide what that strength was for.

* * *

Vicki sat at her desk, arms crossed, eyes fixed on the monitor. It was early morning, and the website was already open—one of the latest uploads. The Four's new outreach platform—*Truthsplo-sion*—had become a central hub in recent weeks, an ever-expanding digital library of Disclosure, the vibrational shift, public participation, and everyday people stepping into new roles. This video was under a new section they had quietly titled *"Personal Practices—Global Impact."*

She clicked play. The screen filled with a backyard. It was familiar. Too familiar. She had been there several times.

She reached for her desk phone and hit the internal button for Jerry. "Can you come in here a minute?"

Less than a minute later, Jerry stepped into the room, coffee still in hand. He looked tired but alert. "What's up?"

Vicki nodded to the monitor. "Come look at this."

He walked around to her side of the desk. When he noticed the video, his expression darkened. "That's... that's my backyard."

Vicki didn't say anything. She just clicked the button again to replay the video from the beginning.

The opening shot was a little shaky, with someone holding a handheld camera. Anne's voice provided a brief description: *"This is CE-5 session number four. Participants: me, Dana, Leila, and Marie."*

The camera panned to reveal Anne sitting cross-legged on a blanket with her eyes closed. She was flanked by three other women, each in a meditative posture, palms up and breathing evenly. There was no dramatic soundtrack or post-production, just the night sounds of the yard and a few blinking lights in the sky.

Jerry leaned forward slightly. "Wait—what? What is this?"

Vicki paused the video. "It's Anne. She's been leading CE-5 sessions. They recorded this one in your backyard. The Four uploaded it to show what ordinary people are doing to help."

Jerry stared at the screen. "She never said anything to me. Not one word."

"I figured you hadn't seen it, or you would've mentioned it to me," Vicki said. "So I called her. Right before I brought you in."

He turned slowly to face her. "What did she say?"

"She said it wasn't a secret. She said she would've told you, but every time she thought about bringing it up, you were buried in briefing papers or stressing about the mole, or Riley, or something else. So she let it go."

Jerry rubbed his forehead. "Yeah. But still. That's not nothing. That's... I don't know. A whole new thing."

"I get it," Vicki said, her voice low. "But Jerry, look."

She pressed play again. The camera remained focused on the backyard. Then something shifted.

Tiny orbs—blue and silver—floated across the screen. Not dust, not lens flare. They moved deliberately, rising and weaving through the trees. One drifted over Anne's shoulder and hovered. The air surrounding the women shimmered slightly, as if the edges of the yard had lost cohesion.

"Brad ran an analysis of the footage before he posted it," Vicki said. "It's real. And it's not just light distortion. That's vibrational resonance. The Four included it as proof that the shift isn't just happening during official events or in quiet zones. It's happening wherever people are tuning in."

Jerry's eyes hadn't left the screen. "She's doing something. She's really... moving things forward."

"She is," Vicki said. "And not just in the courtroom. This is what it's all about. The Four believe the shift isn't going to succeed because of what officials or government agencies do. Things are going to change because of big infrastructure programs. It's going to happen because people like Anne do this: quiet, consistent, intentional practice."

Jerry folded his arms. He wasn't angry anymore—just uneasy. "I should have seen it. I was right there."

"She didn't hide it from you, Jerry. You were just pulled in five directions. And Anne didn't want to take up space when she could just... do the work quietly."

On the screen, the orbs danced once more before fading away. Anne and the other women gradually opened their eyes. The camera cut out.

Vicki paused the video again. "That's who she is. She's not waiting for anyone to give her permission. She's already showing people what's possible."

Jerry nodded slowly. His voice was quiet. "And I missed it."

"Now you haven't," Vicki said.

They sat in silence for a moment, both looking at the frozen frame on the screen—ordinary women in an average backyard, doing something powerful without needing an audience.

Then Vicki added, "They'll be uploading more like it. People need to see themselves in this. Not just government briefings or scientists. This is what will tip the balance."

Jerry stepped back. "She's right," he murmured. "Anne's right."

Vicki didn't reply; she didn't need to. She clicked back to the homepage and showed him the title bar that was still being tested: *"The Shift Belongs to Everyone."*

Chapter Forty-Two

Kiran kept both hands on the steering wheel as the rented minibus wound its way up the narrow road toward Big Tujunga Canyon. He didn't speak much. The air inside the vehicle was quiet. Jessica and Brad were reviewing notes for the upcoming session. James leaned against the side window, watching the canyon pass by. Next to him was Mei, who hadn't said much since they left. He wondered why he had invited her to come along; Mei was still annoying. But she'd stepped up when no one asked her to, which counted for something.

Four of the high school students Mei had been teaching sat together in the back—Tara, Jules, Mateo, and Eli—all of them watching the winding landscape with curiosity.

Kiran finally broke the silence. "What's Junia going to say this time? More warnings? Another confrontation?"

"I don't know," Jessica said. "Just that we needed to come, and that we should bring recording equipment and the students. That was all."

"Think she's going to yell at us again?" James muttered.

Jessica gave him a look. "She wasn't yelling. She was standing up for her people."

"Yeah," James said. "By popping out claws and terrifying all the politicians. Not exactly a conversation starter."

"She was right to do it," Mei said quietly.

James glanced at her. "I didn't say she wasn't."

Brad joined the conversation without looking up from his laptop. "Well, we're almost there. Might as well see what happens."

No one responded.

Five minutes later, they pulled into the turnoff near the cave. Everyone got out, gathered their bags and equipment, then walked the remaining distance to the cave entrance. The opening in the rock was wide and smooth. The entrance looked like it had been recently cleared.

Which it probably had, James thought. The last time they had been there, Junia had unsheathed her claws and brought a slab of rock crashing down to the floor. Now, the ground looked as if it had been swept clean.

This time, Junia didn't meet them at the entrance. Instead, they went deep into the cave, following a gently sloping tunnel. Around a bend, the cavern opened up. Light shimmered softly from an unseen source. The ceiling was high, with the stone above curving into a broad dome.

Junia was standing in the center, but she wasn't alone.

They all stopped.

There were two more Suedes—slightly shorter and younger. Next to them stood three tall, slender figures. They looked human at first glance, but the elongated shape of their skulls set them apart. Their skin was pale, and their clothing uniform and plain.

"These are Alpha Centaurians," Junia said, without greeting them. While not hostile, her cold tone made clear that the death of her cousin was still in her thoughts.

The students stared. Even Brad stopped recording for a minute.

Junia turned to the Four. "You already know the story, but most humans don't. These are the descendants of those who stayed behind. They were here long before most of your current civilizations. But they stayed underground. Their elders, like ours, keep arguing about when—or even if—they should show themselves to humans."

Jessica stepped forward, her voice calm. "What are we doing here now?"

Junia looked directly at her. "We are done waiting. The future doesn't belong to the people making decisions in government buildings. It belongs to the people who will live in it."

She turned toward the three ACs. One nodded.

Junia faced the humans again. "It was not my decision to bring you here. It was theirs—they wanted to meet you." Then she nodded toward the high schoolers. "We've all been asking the same question—what now? What next?"

Brad checked the lens on his camera. "So this is the big reveal of the Alpha Centaurians? The official introduction?"

"No," Junia said. "It's a handoff. The elders can no longer guide this. They have too much fear. Too much caution. We will live in the new world—it's time for us to build it."

"What do you mean?" asked Kiran.

Junia looked at the students again. "Your young people see what's happening. They're learning and changing. They're stepping forward. The youth of my people and the Alpha Centaurians have also seen it and feel the same way. We're ready to be part of it."

One of the ACs glanced at the students with a shy smile before lowering her gaze to the ground.

Junia continued. "The elders—the elders of all three of our peoples—said it wasn't time. That it would frighten humanity, and that revealing the Alpha Centaurians would cause panic. But the young ACs are tired of waiting. They're ready to act. They said they'd reveal themselves on their own if we didn't."

Jessica looked at the three ACs speculatively. "They're serious?"

"They're ready to step into this world," Junia said, nodding. "Because they watched you. They watched all of you, especially the students. The ones learning to shift their energy. The ones refusing to obey rules that no longer make sense."

Mei glanced at the students, who were watching the exchange with wide eyes, then looked back at Junia. "What do you want from us?"

"We don't want anything," Junia said. "We're inviting you to talk. To plan. To build."

James stepped forward. "Without the elders?"

"Yes," Junia said. "With each other. This place, this time—it's for those who will create the next world, not those who are still trying to patch up the last one. If it's always the elders speaking, the old world will simply repeat itself."

They all looked at each other. The humans. The Suedes. The ACs

Jessica took out her notebook, and Brad and Kiran began setting up the cameras.

*　*　*

Vicki stood at the back of the comms center, arms folded, her gaze locked on the main screen. Around her, aides and analysts leaned forward, their eyes fixed. The livestream was playing from the cave, and the silence in the room was complete.

Jessica had messaged her earlier that morning: "Watch this one. You'll want to see it. Junia didn't say exactly what it would be, only that it's important."

Vicki had rearranged her schedule, called Jerry and several senior staff members, and now they were all gathered in the room. She didn't know what was coming, but she could feel anticipation building.

On the screen, Junia stood next to a group of young humans, two young Suedes, and three humanoid beings with elongated skulls. They stood motionless beside her.

Vicki's eyes narrowed.

"Alpha Centaurians," Jerry whispered to her. "That's them."

The room stayed quiet as Junia's voice rang out clearly through the feed.

"These are the Alpha Centaurians," Junia said calmly. "They are descendants of explorers who came here long ago. Some of you know parts of the story. Some of you believe myths. And some of you remember only the destruction. We've listened to the stories and we've seen the scars."

A rustle passed through the comms center. Several people whispered, but no one turned away from the screen.

Junia paused, looking at the camera.

"We've listened to what the elders have said. We've read their documents and heard their advice. While we're grateful for the guidance, we—young humans, young Suedes, and young ACs—have decided that what happened thousands of years ago is history. It's not our future. Their choices don't have to be our choices."

Vicki's stomach twisted. She had postponed this introduction for months. She had repeatedly argued that the world wasn't ready, that people would riot. Introducing another species—especially one linked to the near extinction of humanity—could provoke governments into a reactionary and retaliatory response.

And now Junia had made the announcement herself.

Junia continued. "This isn't about what the past requires. It's about what the future demands. We've decided to go forward together. You can join us. Or stay behind. But we are not waiting any longer."

There was a low murmur among the staff in the room. One woman began whispering to another, only to stop when the camera feed cut to Jessica, who gave a quiet summary. Then the stream ended.

Vicki's jaw tightened. Part of her wanted to be furious. This wasn't the plan. She had spent weeks negotiating, planning, waiting for the "right" time to roll out the AC introduction. She had stalled repeatedly out of caution—with the full agreement of the Galactic Council. Now Junia had done it. No protocol. No committee vote. Just done.

Months of stress, late nights, and hard diplomacy—all undone by a young Suede with a camera and a livestream.

Next to her, Jerry muttered, "She actually did it. Just like that."

Vicki gave a short laugh. "She did. Better than we ever could. Even the Galactic Federation thought it was wiser to wait."

Jerry blinked at her. "You're not upset?"

"I was. For about ten seconds." She turned toward him. "But both Beth and Melly were right. It wasn't all up to me. It never was. But it also wasn't up to *us*. We were never going to be the ones to carry it forward. It had to come from the the young people."

Then Vicki thought back to the other hot potato—the secret trade agreement between a few military officers and the Tall Whites: classified alien technology exchanged for access to human DNA. The enormity of it still made her stomach twist. Not just the moral breach, but the implications. When this came to light, when the public learned...

But Melly had told her that this—like the introduction of the ACs to humanity—was not her burden to carry. "It's being addressed," she'd said. Vicki hadn't asked what that meant, or by whom. She had simply let it go. But the wave of relief that washed over her in that moment had felt like a betrayal of her own integrity. She'd expected to feel ashamed. Instead, she'd nearly cried.

She heard the same relief in James's voice when he had called her—scared—after uncovering the same information in the memory crystal, and she was able to tell him that Melly had told her to ignore it. That same unspoken, guilty relief.

Now, Vicki wondered how this information would be shared with the public. Surely not through Junia and the Suede Nation—this issue had nothing to do with them. But perhaps it could be resolved with as few problems as Junia faced when introducing the ACs to humanity.

A girl could hope. Vicki laughed quietly to herself.

Then, a shift in the air stilled the room.

To one side of the comms center, a shape appeared—not walking in, not entering through a doorway—but simply... fading in. An eight-foot-tall mantis being, unmistakable in form and motion, with her multifaceted eyes blinking slowly. Someone everyone recognized from Jessica's interviews.

Melly had arrived.

The silence shattered as several people screamed, while others quickly stepped back. They might have rushed for the door, but the room was too crowded. Instead, a man on one side of the monitors collapsed in a faint.

Vicki moved forward quickly, raised her hands and steepled her fingers gently over Melly's forelegs.

"Welcome, Melly," Vicki said, intentionally loud so all could hear her. "You've seen the young people's video?"

Melly responded with a clarity that resonated through the room, her voice ringing out with an overlay of gongs. "Yes. The future has stepped forward. The young have chosen their path."

"It's a good choice," Vicki said.

Melly inclined her head, eyes whirring, the feeling of bells. "They are aligned with the shift. The path is taking shape and they will carry the frequency forward. Others will join when ready, or they will stay behind. But the path will be open to all."

Behind them, staff members watched in silence. No one moved; no one spoke. From the smell, Vicki suspected that someone had peed their pants.

"You're here now," Vicki added quietly.

Melly's voice was firm. "You have played your part well, but you've been carrying the burden for far too long. You are no longer alone."

"I know," Vicki said. "The era of secrecy and gatekeeping is over. And I'm ready."

Together, they faced the screen again, now blank but still humming faintly with the last signals of the stream that had changed everything.

Epilogue

The smell of coffee lingered in the common room of the old flower shop. The space had changed over the months—more cushions, more cables, more whiteboards with scribbles in four different handwritings. Yet James appreciated that it still felt like their space—private and protected.

He leaned back in one of the worn chairs, his eyes on Mei. She was seated at the far end of the sofa, watching the others speak but contributing little to the conversation. This was her first time here, and James could sense the careful restraint in her body. Not exactly nervousness—more like reverence. A quiet gratitude. She hadn't spoken much, but her presence was relaxed in a way it hadn't been before. She was finally inside the circle.

She smiled faintly at something Kiran said about uploading the next memory crystal video. She wasn't trying to impress anyone or seek credit. Just being here was enough.

James glanced at Jessica, who caught his eye with a nod. She saw it too.

Then came the knock.

All five of them froze. It wasn't loud, but it was sharp. Jessica's head tilted, eyes narrowing.

"We're not expecting anyone..." she started.

"We didn't sense anything," Brad said quickly, already on his feet. "We didn't sense anyone's chi."

They knew what that meant—the person at the door was a biologic construct.

Before anyone could move further, Mei was already up.

"I'll get it for you!" she said brightly.

"Wait—Mei—" James called, but she had already crossed the room and pulled the door open.

A tall man with broad shoulders and an expressionless face stood on the step. He wore simple clothes—dark slacks and a dark shirt—but his presence was overwhelming. Every movement and detail, from the stillness of his arms to the calm in his eyes, laid plain his nature. He was a weapon.

Kiran stiffened beside her. "Super-soldier."

"I remember him," Jessica said in a low, urgent voice, barely above a whisper. "He was the one. The one who took me." Her eyes were locked on the figure in the doorway, her body frozen.

They all fell silent and began to edge back from the door. Mei looked at them, confused—uncertain about what was happening.

The man didn't react to Jessica's words. His face remained expressionless, his posture neutral. Not a threat—yet. But not harmless either.

"I saw the broadcast," he said. "You will need a protector."

James stepped forward now, the absurdity overcoming his fear. "And *you're* volunteering for the job? You think we're going to trust you?" he asked angrily.

The man's eyes locked onto James. "I will protect the family of my fallen comrade."

James blinked. "What—?"

"Larry," the man said.

James froze. The others were silent.

The man kept speaking slowly, his words deliberate. "He gave his life. For you. For them. He was one of us."

Jessica stood up, her voice ragged. "You knew him?"

"I saw what he became," the man replied. "I saw his choice. He showed us we could choose something else. Most of us decided we liked what we were."

The room was silent. Mei stood at the edge of the group, her eyes darting from one face to another, uncertain of what was going on.

James cleared his throat. "And now you want to help?"

"I want to make my own choices, to decide how I live—and I can protect you," the man said again. "I don't want to be the boss. I only ask to stand guard."

James felt his throat tighten. Larry had always stepped in to shield them, always taking the hardest hits. This man—this biologic construct—was offering the same thing. Not as a soldier. Not as a weapon. But as someone changed by what Larry had done—by how Larry had lived his life.

The others—even Jessica—looked at James. Larry was his uncle—it would be his choice.

"Yes," he said slowly. "We could use a defender."

He stepped back and opened the door wider.

"And a friend."

The man nodded once and stepped inside. No one stopped him. Mei was the first to move by offering him her seat. Jessica still looked stunned, but she didn't say anything. Not yet.

Brad broke the silence. "What's your name?"

The man paused. "Lewis."

James smiled a little. "Welcome, Lewis."

About the Author

Nancy Nelson retired after 25 years as a diplomat with the U.S. Department of State, then spent a few more years launching her kids, and traveling the world. Now she lives in California and explores the possibilities of humanity's future paths.

Hum Rise is the second of the Disclosure Files Series, and is Nancy's attempt to weave a story of people facing the need to choose who they wish to be in a future with many options.